At that moment she felt the touch of his hand upon her head. Tenderly, he stroked her auburn tresses, his calloused palms rasping slightly against the fine texture. She traced the line of his scar with her lips then, as if to take away any vestiges of pain remaining on the marred skin. His fingers strayed to the bare flesh of her shoulder. Aurore gazed up at him. How wonderful it felt to have him touch her! Little ripples of shivery warmth spread from her neck down to her breasts. As she pressed herself against him in an agony of desire, Aurore was no longer afraid. She had wanted him for so long. She had been waiting for this all her life . . .

DRUMBEAT OF DESIRE

DIANA SUMMERS

PLAYBOY PAPERBACKS

Published simultaneously in the United States and Canada by PBJ Books, Inc., formerly PEI Books, Inc., 200 Madison Avenue, New York, New York 10016. Printed in the United States of America. Library of Congress Catalog Card Number: 82-82115.

ISBN: 0-867-21208-X

First printing December 1982

CHAPTER 1

Aurore was not beautiful by the African standards of Ile Celeste. Her skin was *café au lait*, a heritage from her French father and her half-white, half-Wolof mother. She was tall and lithe like the Wolof girls of the island, but her figure was full for an eighteen-year-old, and her hair was of an alien dark-red hue.

At the convent school in Thiès, where she had spent the last four years, Aurore had worn her long red curls in a ribbon-tied ponytail. Now, however, her tawny tresses flowed free, rippling in the warm afternoon wind, splashing over her bare shoulders. Her sparkling green eyes betrayed a tempest in their depths. It was her eyes, with their message of smoldering desire barely held in check, that intrigued Cherif Baye.

Aurore knew this. She had learned it when she was quite young. Indeed, it was the reason her father had decided to send her away from Ile Celeste when she was fourteen.

Not that Aurore had done anything very wicked. A few kisses, the sweet touch of Cherif's hand on her budding breast; that was all. But her father had seen the beginnings of desire and the knack Aurore had for manipulating boys, and he had thought to himself that to be a bride at fourteen—not at all an unusual age for an island girl to marry—was not a fate he wished his daughter to choose without considering the alternatives. And so Aurore and Cherif had been separated.

Now, four years later, on this June day in 1946, they were together again on Ile Celeste.

Aurore stole a glance at Cherif as they walked hand in hand up the trail from the Wolof village toward the berry patches in the hills. He was no longer the gawky youth of fourteen she had left behind. Cherif had shot up like a sapling in these past four years, and he had filled out more than most Wolof men did. Still, he had the long, rangy build of his people, complemented by broad shoulders and a powerful chest, along with the tapered jawline, thin lips, and pronounced cheekbones typical of them. He might have looked austere if not for the dimple in his cheek playing in the sunlight.

Last night at the *bara* in honor of her return, Aurore's first glimpse of Cherif had startled her. He had worn an elaborately embroidered purple *boubou* that flowed loosely from his shoulders to his ankles without concealing his long, muscular arms. His matching turbanlike headcloth displayed a single white pearl centered above his almond-shape dark eyes. The pearl was the mark of his status as the second son of the village chief. The blackness of his face had been rich and solid and deep, his expression serious. Aurore had been impressed, but she had also been concerned that her playmate of yore might be gone forever.

Today was different. Today Cherif Baye appeared as Aurore remembered him. He was bare-chested like the other young men of the village, and he wore faded work pants handed down from his older brother and cut off above the knee.

Looking at his exposed upper torso, Aurore was reminded of swimming with him four years earlier, when he had worn nothing at all. She well remembered what he had looked like naked, the sudden stiffening that had made him blush and dive into the lagoon, the surge of hotness that had gone to the core of her and made the nipples of her bare breasts tingle and harden so that she too had sought concealment under the water.

What would Cherif look like naked now that he had grown to manhood? She closed her eyes for an instant. The picture projected upon the inside of her eyelids both embarrassed and intrigued her. Aurore tripped and clutched at Cherif's sinewy arm for support.

"Your feet are tender from the shoes of Thiès," Cherif teased her.

"Traders from villages all over Senegal come to Thiès with their families. As on Ile Celeste, many don't wear shoes."

"I meant at the European school. I have been told it is a rule that the students wear shoes. I have been told it makes their feet smell like old goat meat left in the sun too long." He laughed so hard that the next thing she knew he was rolling on the ground with merriment.

Aurore found herself laughing with him. "You haven't changed at all," she said, and she meant it. She brought her own laughter under control. "Well, I'm not just going to stand here while you have a fit," she told him. And she skipped nimbly up the trail.

Admiration flashed from Cherif's dark eyes as he watched her move. Her plain cotton *boubou* was tied in a knot above her breasts and fell to her knees. It was not designed to hide the voluptuous charms of womanhood developed by Aurore during her four-year absence. It enhanced the creamy off-white roundness of her bare shoulders, revealed her shapely thighs when the material hiked up as she moved above Cherif on the trail, emphasized the rise and fall of her full breasts and the provocative undulation of her derriere beneath the green cotton. She twirled with her long red hair flying wildly in the wind and her persimmon-red lips parted to reveal strong white teeth laughing at him.

Aurore read his gaze correctly and was satisfied. She waited alongside a *cedrat* tree for him to catch up with her. There was a small clearing here, and she dropped to the grass and looked up at him flirtatiously. Cherif sat down beside her. He slipped his arms around her to kiss her.

Aurore avoided the kiss and slipped from Cherif's embrace. She leaned away from him, grasped a low branch of the *cedrat* tree, and swayed from it without rising. Her green eyes surveyed him mischievously from under long, red-gold lashes.

"You do not wish me to kiss you?" Cherif didn't wait for her to answer. "So be it." He got to his feet and made her an elaborate Muslim bow. *"Fananlen ak diame!* Good-bye!"* He turned on his heel and started back down the trail.

"Cherif!"

Her voice stopped him, but he did not turn around. "Yes?"

"I was only fooling." She stood up straight in front of the *cedrat* tree. "You may kiss me." Aurore closed her eyes and swayed slightly like an early-blooming hibiscus in the warm summer breeze.

Nothing happened. Aurore opened her eyes. Cherif was continuing down the trail away from her. "Cherif! What's the matter?"

"I am a Muslim, the son of a Wolof chief. The woman does not tell me when to kiss. I tell the woman."

"Oh, Cherif!" Aurore raced after him and flung her arms around his legs, catching him off balance so that he toppled to the ground. "Have you forgotten me so?" she asked him, kneeling on his chest with her hands on his shoulders. "Don't you know when I'm teasing?"

"You were teasing?" His voice thundered, but once again his dimple betrayed him. "Teasing me? Cherif Baye? The son of the chief?" He sprang, and Aurore found herself flung to the ground, their positions reversed.

His mouth was greedy on her sun-warmed lips. His persistent tongue sent a thrill all through her. His strong, ebony hand tightly cupped the flimsy green material over her firm white breast. The fullness of his weight atop her squeezed the breath from her body. Through his faded denims, Aurore could feel the hard, thrusting spear of his aroused young manhood.

When the kiss was over, she scrambled out from under him. Gasping, she backed away in confusion and looked at Cherif with something approaching awe. "You never kissed me like that before," she stammered.

"We were children. Now we are grown."

"Why do you smile at me like that?"

"Like what?"

"So—so—devilishly!"

"When we were younger, you used to say my smile was impish. Now it is devilish." Suddenly Cherif's face broke into a boy's grin from ear to ear. "So the imp has grown up, too, and now he is a devil."

"You *are* the devil!" Aurore found herself laughing again. Suddenly it was very good to be home. "And I don't think you've grown up at all," she added. "You're just fresher."

"But I have grown up." He was unexpectedly serious. "My father says that soon I must think about taking an *awa.*"

Aurore was surprised. All Muslims used *awa* colloquially to mean "first wife." But surely Cherif wasn't old enough to be thinking of such a prospect.

"And which of the village maidens is to be the lucky girl?" Aurore affected unconcern.

"None of them. I am a devil, remember? A devil requires a witch for a fitting mate. Preferably a white witch. What do you think of that?"

"You must go to Dakar. There are lots of French white girls there. One of them should be witchy enough for you."

"I prefer to look closer to home." He took two firm steps and stood over her. "Under my nose, for instance."

"Surely a chief's son's nose would not be satisfied with smelly feet." Taken by surprise, Aurore did not know how to respond, so she took refuge in their previous banter.

"You will bathe your feet in perfume." His tone was teasing, but his eyes were quite serious now and intent on Aurore, gauging her response.

"Is this a proposal, then?"

"A formal proposal will come later. My father will call on your family. What I would like to know now is how the idea strikes you."

Aurore was silent for a long moment. Her mind was in a turmoil. "You used the word *awa*. Do you intend to take a second wife? A third? More?"

"I am a Muslim."

"That's the problem." Aurore was serious. "I don't think I would want to share my husband with other women."

"Is this the only thing that makes you hold back?"

"I'm not sure," Aurore answered honestly. "I wasn't expecting this today. I expected only to walk with a childhood friend at siesta time. A friend," she added pointedly, "whom I haven't seen for four years—since we were children."

"We could compromise on the problem of the wives," he persisted. "I would vow not to take a second wife unless after five years of marriage you have not borne me a son."

"And if I have?"

"Then you will be my only wife for as long as we both live."

It was a great concession, Aurore knew. But was it enough? She looked at the boy-turning-man waiting for her answer. She knew that her body desired a man. But was that love? Aurore wasn't sure.

"I've just come back, Cherif." She chose her words carefully. "It's too soon. I want to think about it. Please?"

Her eyes melted his uncharacteristic formality. In a twinkling, Cherif was her mischievous childhood playmate again. "I know what is bothering you," he teased her. "You are afraid that I will take Leita Ousbane for my second wife. Then you would have to share the household with her." He laughed uninhibitedly.

"You should take Leita for your first wife. I saw her last night. She has grown into a beauty."

"That would be even more difficult than marriage with a nonbeliever like you. Leita is of the Dyola people. She follows the uncivilized bush teachings of her grandmother, Ouna the *katt*. She is a faith healer like the witch doctors in olden times. She believes in fetishes and spells and voodoo. She's a crazy old lady. And she grows worse all the time.''

"And Leita? Your bride-to-be?" Aurore baited him. "Is she demented, too?"

"We used to think so when we were children. Remember how she used to follow us around?''

"You." Aurore corrected him. "She used to follow you. She had a terrible crush on you.''

"And she was very jealous of you," Cherif remembered. "Ah, yes," he chortled boyishly. "It should be very interesting having the two of you for my wives.''

Aurore stuck her tongue out at him. "Perhaps neither of us will be foolish enough to marry a crazy boy like you.''

"We will see about that." Cherif shaded his eyes with his hand and looked up at the sun. "Siesta time is over," he realized. "I have to get back. There are fishing nets to be hauled in, and the other men of my boat will be waiting.''

"And I have berries to gather.''

They parted. Aurore watched for a moment as he loped down the trail. The muscles of his naked back rippled under his ebony skin in the leaf-speckled sunlight. From this distance, he looked like a full-grown man, the tall and imposing son of the village chief. But when Aurore was with him, Cherif seemed a boy to her, just as she still seemed a girl to herself rather than a woman.

Marriage? Was she really old enough to think of that? Yes, she was eighteen, but still—Aurore shook the nettlesome thoughts from her head and started up the hill toward the berry patches.

She had not been picking berries long when she experienced the uneasy sensation that she was being watched. She heard a rustle in the underbrush. Straining her ears, she heard it again, this time more distinctly.

Pretending to be engrossed in what she was doing, Aurore slowly backed toward the sounds. When she reached the bushes, she whirled around and parted them with both hands. The black girl hiding there tried to back out of sight, but she wasn't quick enough.

"Leita!" Aurore recognized her immediately. "Leita Ousbane! What are you doing?"

The girl didn't answer. She simply stared at Aurore with open hatred. She was breathing quickly in fury; her small, high, uptilted breasts strained against the frayed cloth of her faded *boubou;* half a dozen tiny braids rose from her skull at electrified angles; she held her arms rigid at her sides, the hands twisted like talons tensed to strike.

"How long have you been spying on me?" Aurore demanded.

A strange smile twisted Leita's lips. There was no humor in it, only hostility. Still she didn't reply.

"Were you watching Cherif and me before?"

"You were making fun of me!" the Dyola girl blurted out, spitting the words venomously.

"You were eavesdropping! It serves you right if you didn't like what you heard."

"You turn Cherif against me! He wants me, but you turn him against me. I heard you!"

"Nonsense! Cherif has a mind of his own. If he wants you, then he will tell you so."

"There are other ways a man tells a woman besides words."

"I suppose so. But you won't make Cherif want you by spying. We're not children anymore."

"I know that." Leita laughed wildly. "And so does Cherif. Only you are still a child, I think."

"I don't know what you mean. And as for you and Cherif, what you do is your own business, not mine."

"And I suppose you don't care?" Leita snorted. "You lie!" She backed further away. "You want him for yourself! To be his only wife and I should not even be his second! I heard you!" Leita retreated yet further, bent forward and hissed at Aurore. *"Bambara!"* She called her a bastard. "Milk-skinned *bambara!"*

The inference that her mixed birth was illegitimate enraged Aurore. Quickly she scooped up a handful of loose earth and flung it at the hissing, cursing girl.

Aurore was not prepared for the vehemence of Leita's response. Like an arrow catapulted from a bow, she sprang upon her. The movement was so quick and so furious that Aurore was borne to the ground.

She felt the clawlike hands ripping at her bare shoulders and neck. Sharp teeth bit into the soft white flesh of her arm. A kick sent searing pain along the length of her spine.

Aurore fought back. She punched one of Leita's small breasts with all her strength. She drove her knee into the soft flatness of the black girl's stomach. She closed her teeth over a spiral of braided hair and strained to tug it loose from the scalp.

Leita was thin and aggressive, with the strength of coiled wire. But Aurore had the weight of her voluptuousness on her side, and also a cunning that Leita's fury denied her. Finally Aurore prevailed, pinning the black girl to the ground and holding her there until her rage had seemingly subsided and she stopped struggling.

Aurore got to her feet. She looked down at Leita and shook her head sadly. What was there to say? She turned away and started over to where she had left her berry pail.

As she bent to pick it up, her eyes caught the flicker of a fast-moving shadow. Instinctively Aurore ducked. The movement saved her life. Leita had produced a small dagger from her bodice and tried to plunge it into Aurore's back.

Now, as Aurore turned to face her, the dagger struck again. This time the target was Aurore's breast, over her heart. She sprang backward. The point missed the breast but came away with a swath of the green material that had covered it.

Aurore turned and fled then, sprinting across the berry patch and into the underbrush. She could hear Leita's footsteps behind her, but she didn't look back.

Her only hope was to outrun the Dyola girl and lose her in the bush.

Fate smiled on Aurore. The storm cloud that had shielded the sun while the young women wrestled was neither a false harbinger nor alone. As Aurore ran, other rumbling clouds were turning the customarily blue skies of Cap Vert gray. Soon they were clashing with thunder and lightning, and rainwater poured over Ile Celeste. With the help of this raging torrent, Aurore had no trouble losing Leita in the woods covering the heights of the island.

When she realized she was safe, Aurore stopped a moment to get her bearings. The rain beat an icy tattoo on her shoulder. She huddled at the base of a mango tree and gazed around her. In the storm, after four years away, nothing seemed familiar.

A slash of lightning split the darkened afternoon sky. By its illumination, she saw looming over her the one unmistakable landmark on Ile Celeste: le Château de Beausoleil!

The château was an example of African architecture plagiarized and adapted by genderations of Western intruders. It was in the style of the nouveau riche French châteaux of the mid-nineteenth century, when the architectural vogue was to copy the Romans who had copied the Greeks, add imitations from Swiss chalets, include at least one decoration recognizably from the palace at Versailles, and impose all this upon the turreted, stripped-down square that was the basic structure of the Moorish castle. Only its sloping pediments, triangular and round, with their blatantly Italianate design, and the four French-style balconies with their intricate wrought iron grillwork and their full-length doors, remained true to any style at all.

A *bambara* edifice indeed was le Château de Beausoleil!

It had been built by Aurore's great-grandfather in the mid-nineteenth century. André de Beausoleil was a French colonial administrator in charge of peanut-oil exports from Dakar. The city, cluttered with the riffraff still engaged in the illicit shipping of slaves from the harbor island of Goree, was not to his taste. The stench of the slave trade, past and present, permeated Dakar.

André's people were wealthy Marseilles ship owners. Some day, he would take up his rightful position in the family business. Meanwhile, there was ample money for him to live where and how he chose. He chose Ile Celeste, less than an hour by dugout canoe from Dakar. The inhabitants were friendly and lived in a village on the seaward shore of the small island where they made their living by fishing. The hilly center was uninhabited and wildly beautiful. It was here that he built his château.

Aurore had lived in the château with her French father, her French-Wolof mother, and her half-sister from her mother's first marriage, until 1939, the year the Second World War broke out, when she was eleven years old. Then Justin de Beausoleil, André's grandson and Aurore's father, moved his little family to the Wolof village. Gloomy and foreboding as the old limestone structure looked in the storm, it nevertheless held many pleasant childhood memories for Aurore.

She did not hesitate to seek shelter in the château. Once inside, she untied the knot of her *boubou* and spread the material out to dry. She found an old hand-made quilt in a carton in one of the closets and wrapped it around herself. Feeling nostalgic, she wandered about the place.

The high polish of the solid oak floors she had slid on in her childhood had faded sadly. The sun had destroyed the brightness of the draperies. The silvering was peeling from the ornate mirrors, rodents had nibbled the cushions of the Louis XIV couches so that the stuffing showed through the frayed edges, and there was mold on the underside of the rolled-up carpets. But the château had probably been in much worse condition when Aurore's father had first set eyes on it in 1916. At that time it had stood uncared for and empty since his grandfather, André de Beausoleil, had lived in it some sixty years before.

Now, shivering under her quilt in the emptiness of the mansion, the storm raging outside, Aurore brushed the tears from her cheek as she remembered the love that had pervaded her happy childhood years here. Events had moved so quickly, so inexorably, as to turn it into a distant memory. The war had come, as Papa feared, and they were forced to leave the château and live in the village. Shortly afterward, Aurore was sent off to school. And then, just last year, Papa died.

Papa's death had been the most terrible blow of Aurore's life. Due to the lingering effects of old war wounds, Dr. de Beausoleil had always fatigued easily and emanated a certain frailty. But to Aurore, he had always been firm and dependable, possessed of a strength that transcended the physical, the counterweight to her own mercurial nature, the anchor of her security. But one night after he went to bed, his heart stopped beating and he never awakened. So sudden! So unexpected! His wife, his stepdaughter Sabine, and Aurore had not yet recovered from the shock.

Not long afterward, the Second World War ended in Europe, and Aurore had wondered fleetingly about the fate of her relatives in Marseilles. Papa's death had made them seem quite remote at that time. Now, however, in the château where she had grown up, with memories of Papa warming each chilly, damp room, Aurore could not help but be reminded of how important Papa had thought it was to maintain contact with his family, no matter how tenuous and one-sided.

"Our Marseilles family has never accepted my marriage, and they may never accept you; nevertheless, they are our family and we must always hold ourselves open to reconciliation with them," Papa had told her. "Blood is blood!"

How strongly Papa had believed this. After the rift with his family caused by his interracial marriage, he had kept informed about the family through an old friend in Marseilles. Frequently in the letters Aurore received at school from Papa there had been news of these faraway relatives she had never met.

Before Aurore left for school, her father had received a color photograph of them. It had been taken in the spring of 1939, a few months before the Second World War had broken out. It showed Maurice de Beausoleil—Papa's brother—his wife, his son, and his daughter gathered informally around a garden table.

Aurore had noted the resemblance between Papa and his brother. True, Justin was slender, while the picture showed Maurice as stocky, perhaps verging on corpulent, but both brothers had the same strong, square jaw with the de Beausoleil cleft. There was a stern look in Maurice's eye that reminded Aurore of Papa when he was enforcing some sanitary regulation he deemed necessary to the welfare of Ile Celeste. Both had the pronounced cheekbones and firmly molded noses of the French aristocracy. But while there was always a smile lurking at the corner of Papa's sensuously full lips, Maurice's mouth was set so firmly in the photo as to give him the look of a humorless martinet.

Maurice's wife, Colette Marie de Beausoleil—Aurore's *tante* Colette—was strikingly beautiful. Not quite forty when the photograph was taken, twenty years younger than her husband, *Tante* Colette looked more like a sibling to her children than their mother. Her hair was golden blond; her complexion a delicate alabaster pink-and-white; her features lively, coquettish, Parisian. Even in the subdued *haute couture* of the late 1930s, her figure appeared full-bosomed, slim-hipped, and long-legged—the sophisticated ideal of French high society of that period. Impressed, Aurore had nevertheless wondered at a certain calculating coolness in *Tante* Colette's blue eyes.

Delphine de Beausoleil, Aurore's cousin, was an unpolished replica of her mother. The picture showed her as a sixteen-year-old schoolgirl, her flaxen hair tied by a ribbon in the inevitable ponytail, her slender body girlishly awkward in loose white middy blouse, short black skirt, and knee-length stockings. Her complexion was of the same delicacy as *Tante* Colette's and her countenance lit by a similar liveliness. Her eyes were blue like her mother's, but not as cold.

The eleven-year-old Aurore had been most intrigued by the fourth figure in the photograph, her cousin Blaise Honoré de Beausoleil. He looked like neither his father nor his mother. Even seated, he was a head taller than anybody else in the family grouping. Only twenty-one when the picture was taken, he already wore a full black mustache that followed the down lines—with their hint of cruelty—at the corners of his mouth. Yet Blaise's eyes, blue like his mother's, were neither cold like hers nor fawning like Delphine's but rather clear and warm, and perhaps even idealistic. At any rate, the child Aurore liked to think she discerned a youthful idealism shining from them, although his features seemed more adaptable to irony than idealism. It was not a conventionally handsome face. The lines were too hard, the expression too much that of the buccaneer. There was arrogance and a toughness beyond Blaise's years.

Something inside Aurore resonated to that expression of independence. Or perhaps it was the way Blaise's white shirt was rolled up over his well-tanned arms to display his bulging muscles. His shoulders were so broad, his chest so deep! He wasn't thin, but there obviously wasn't a spare, unmuscled ounce of flesh on him.

Wandering the damp and chilly château, the musty quilt pulled tight around her nakedness, Aurore smiled wryly at how innocently infatuated she had been with this stranger during her puberty. And how would she feel about this phantom idol of her childhood now? He would be twenty-eight years old, ten years older than she. Would he be anything like the image she had formulated from the Marseilles letters?

They had provided rich source material for a romantic young girl. In his teens, Blaise had been the most junior member of a famous Alpine mountain-climbing expedition. Still under twenty, he had taken up auto racing and eventually captured a third place at Le Mans. The following year he had sailed an open boat from Brest to Tenerife. Somewhere among Aurore's father's papers there was a newspaper clipping describing that exploit.

However, not all the stories about Blaise were pretty. There was parental unhappiness at his gambling, at his unsavory companions, at the brawls in which he occasionally participated. One ugly incident, on the Marseilles waterfront, left Blaise with a knife scar on his chest and a reputation for agility with a baling hook more suited to a longshoreman than to the son of one of Marseilles's leading families. Even more disturbing, there was a scandal involving a debutante Blaise had compromised and then subsequently refused to marry.

Maurice had indulged his son's adolescent adventures. But with war just over the horizon, when Blaise enlisted in the French paratroops, he did so against his father's wishes. Maurice de Beausoleil, a privileged Frenchman by birth, was like many of his class sympathetic to the French Fascist movement that admired Hitler.

In 1940, France fell. Maurice de Beausoleil was instrumental in setting up the collaborationist Vichy regime in Marseilles. His shipping business operated hand in glove with Vichy, to the advantage of the Nazis.

Blaise returned home briefly. He and his father had a violent argument in which he accused Maurice of being a traitor and his father ordered him from the house. Blaise fled France and joined the Free French forces led by General DeGaulle in London. Less than a year later, Maurice de Beausoleil was murdered by the Marseilles underground.

After his death, his wife Colette and daughter Delphine maintained their upper-class Vichy status. They too were collaborators, albeit relatively harmless ones. When a dinner party was given to honor a visiting Nazi dignitary, Colette's grace and charm made her a logical choice to balance the table. And if a younger German officer lacked an escort, the budding beauty of Delphine recommended her to fill the void.

Meanwhile Blaise was among those parachuted into Dakar to organize the underground for an invasion by the Free French in September, 1940. Aurore would never forget how excited she had been when her father received that news. Her cousin Blaise in Dakar! So close!

But Blaise never came to Ile Celeste. The invasion of Dakar was repelled. He fled into the Senegalese interior, plunging into the hell of the El Djouf Desert and heading northeast toward North Africa.

It was two years before they had news of him again. He had rejoined the Free French in North Africa and participated in a daring commando raid on General Rommel's headquarters. Blaise personally captured a high-ranking German field officer. This officer had revealed Rommel's problems with overextended supply lines, information that proved to be a key factor in the *Afrika Korps's* eventual defeat. Blaise had been decorated by the British General Montgomery personally for this exploit.

Again there was a lapse in news about Blaise. It was long after D Day before they learned of his part in the invasion. He had been parachuted into Normandy prior to the landings and had set up strategic underground radio stations reporting German troop movements in France. This time he was decorated by the Free French and the Americans.

The last Aurore had heard, Blaise had returned to Marseilles. Here he had alienated himself from the French resistance movement by beating up a Maquis leader bent on shaving the heads of his mother and sister to brand them collaborators. This was the same man who ordered the hanging of the Vichy puppet who had run the De Beausoleil Shipping Company during the war.

Along with his mother and sister, Blaise now owned this lucrative business. But Marseilles was impossible for Colette and Delphine. All their former friends had either fled the city or taken their punishment as collaborators. Blaise was making arrangements to transfer the headquarters of the shipping business elsewhere. Aurore had heard nothing beyond that.

Ambling from room to room in the château, she wondered about them. Where had they gone after Marseilles? What were they doing? Their lives were so different from hers! They had been the cream of a society that no longer existed. It was all very confusing, Aurore thought. Would she ever meet them? That romantic and contradictory figure, her cousin Blaise; would she ever see him in the flesh?

The storm outside was abating. The thunder was a distant rumble, fading away. The wind had died down to a warm, muggy breeze. The rain had stopped.

Aurore put her *boubou* back on, tying it so that the breast that had been bared was now concealed and left le Château de Beausoleil. She had to return quickly to the village. Her mother, Odile, was not well. Sabine, Aurore's half-sister, had been caring for her all day. It wasn't fair to Sabine. Aurore knew she must do her share until Maman got over this indisposition. She hurried down the trail toward home.

It was dusk. The underbrush was wet, steamy, clinging. Heat lightning split the brooding, purple-gray African sky. It illuminated the surrealist specter of the baobab tree on the high knoll overlooking the village.

The baobab tree, with its mystic symbolism to the people of Ile Celeste, watched over their thatched-roof homes like some grotesque sentry. Its twining, snake-like roots sucked life from the arid soil. The short, thick, contorted trunk, with its interlaced strands of sepia bark, stood like a gnarled gnome braced against the strongest gale, and the twisted limbs stretched torturously toward the sky, the leafless branches ending in a meshwork of groping twigs.

Approaching it, Aurore heard a strange sound like the baying of some wild animal, wounded and in pain. Another flash of heat lightning revealed the figure of Ouna, the *katt*. The old crone stood with her arms stretched up to the baobab tree, her large, protruding eyes quite wild, a spine-chilling incantation spilling from her withered lips in a fury of howling.

Trembling, Aurore drew closer. Ouna's scraggly gray hair was soaked. Rivulets of rainwater glittered in the folds of her wrinkled skin. In one of her crooked hands, she clutched a torn shred of material. Now she held it against the trunk of the baobab tree. Once again, she keened in some long-forgotten tongue.

Suddenly there was an answering rumble of thunder. A massive bolt of lightning lit the scene. In its lingering flash, Aurore saw the crone, as if in rhythmic fulfillment of some forbidden ritual, stabbing a knife through the cloth and into the bark of the baobab. Horror gripped Aurore as she recognized the material.

It was the fragment slashed from her garment by Leita Ousbane during their struggle!

CHAPTER 2

The sun rays of new morning burst over Ile Celeste like a fine mist of liquid color. The dawning sun in the east was a ball of light so aggressive that it reduced the white colonial buildings of Dakar on the mainland to a blur. To the west, the shoreline of the island was still in shadow, gray sand flowing into quiet, murky waters of deep greens and blues.

Fishermen, Cherif Baye among them, were already lining up their pirogues in the slowly retreating dimness. As they did every morning save Friday, which was Allah's Holy Day, they prepared to catch the outgoing tide at just the right moment. The underwater sandbar that guarded the western beach of Ile Celeste was a daily hazard to be treated with respect. Pirogues had been smashed to bits and men had drowned as a result of underestimating the cruelty of the sandbar.

In the Wolof village, the morning belonged to the women and children. Breakfast was an informal affair: goats' milk and millet porridge with sorghum for the children, and perhaps a mango or coconut to be munched as they played; monkey bread, made from the dried pulp of the sparse fruit of the baobab tree, and coconut milk or orange juice for their mothers. The men had already breakfasted on hot fish and rice, and gourds of thrice-steeped mint tea for warmth against the chill of the early hour.

As the sun rose higher, the villagers who remained behind broke into two groupings. Male children gathered outdoors according to their ages and arranged them-

23

selves in circles to study the Koran under the direction of a *marabout*. The little girls helped their mothers with the scrubbing and beating of clothes at a freshwater stream on the inland perimeter of the village, a daily ritual.

Later, but still well before noon, the women would commence preparations for the communal evening meal. This would be cooked in huge cauldrons over fires in the center of the compound. It might be chicken au yassa, or lamb stew, or couscous prepared with meat, grain, and sauce. Eating it together—women, children, and men of whatever status—was one of the traditions that united the villagers as strongly as any European family.

Ordinarily Aurore, with her mother Odile de Beausoleil and her half-sister Sabine Rama Bakar, would have helped prepare the communal meal and eaten with the group. Today, however, was different. This evening there would be company, and they would serve a French-style repast and dine apart from the others.

Of the three, Aurore's half-sister Sabine was the most excited at the prospect. Her customarily soft and doelike cinnamon brown eyes were sparkling with anticipation. Her usually serene face was agitated as she discussed recipes and ingredients with her mother, Odile. Her long and slender figure was a blur of motion as she raced here and there to be sure their thatched-roof home was in proper condition to receive the guests dusk would bring.

Aurore was amused. Sabine was only two years older than she was, but throughout most of their life together, the difference had seemed greater. Where Aurore was volatile, Sabine was calm by nature. Where Aurore was impetuous, Sabine thought things through before she acted. Where Aurore was rebellious, Sabine had a deep Muslim respect for tradition and authority and the wisdom of her elders.

In older-sister fashion, Sabine did not always approve of Aurore's impulsiveness. Yet somehow she always seemed to understand and never condemned. Judgment would have been foreign to both her culture and her nature. She loved Aurore deeply. And Aurore, who was frequently exasperated by what she perceived as Sabine's stodginess, nevertheless loved her sincerely in return.

"We are out of garlic cloves!" Sabine wailed to Odile.

"Boeuf Bourguignon does not require garlic," Odile replied quietly. Her narrow, pinched face was haggard but quite composed.

"For the salad, Maman! How can I make the dressing without garlic cloves? You know how Amin loves his greens with sauce vinaigrette!"

Amin! Scraping at carrots fresh from the village garden, Aurore tossed her red hair and wondered how her usually tranquil sister could get in such a fret over someone they had known all their life. Amin Baye was Cherif's older brother and not nearly as attractive, Aurore thought, as Cherif was. And surely she didn't get into as much of a dither over Cherif as Sabine did over Amin. Silly goose! Where was the sensible, steadfast older sister upon whom she had always relied? Set aside for the day, it seemed.

"Have you forgotten, Sabine, that you told me the grocery boat from Dakar had no garlic cloves?" Odile inquired of her eldest daughter. She strove to overcome the weariness in her voice, but still there was a slight gasping cadence to her speech.

"Oh, dear! I *did* forget."

"Perhaps you should try Ouna," Aurore suggested. "She uses garlic in her love potions, they say. Perhaps she has some extra. She would overcharge you, but," Aurore teased, "surely money is no object if Amin is coming to dinner."

"No!" Odie said. A spasm of pain twisted her face with the intensity of her reaction. "We do not go to the *katt!*"

"Maman is right." Sabine looked more concerned

for their mother now than for the dinner. "We shall have no barter with Ouna."

"Why?" Aurore looked up from the carrots, surprised at the depth of their reaction. "Has something happened with Ouna that I don't know about?"

Her mother and sister exchanged glances. "No. Nothing." It was Odile who replied, her voice hoarse and shaky and lacking conviction.

Aurore was puzzled. She had not told them of the incident at the baobab tree a few nights before. Once she was safely home it had seemed less ominous to her and more like the silliness of a demented old woman with a granddaughter who was perhaps almost as crazy as she. Besides, Odile was not well and Sabine had been overworked prior to Aurore's return, and so she had not wanted to add to their troubles with an insignificant problem of her own. But why were they so upset at the mere mention of Ouna's name?

"I think I will go to bed for a little bit now." Odile finally had to surrender to her malady.

The pain before had not been fleeting. It was still plainly visible on her light brown face. Seeing it, Aurore forgot about Ouna in a renewed concern for her mother.

"Of course, Maman." Sabine was contrite. "You should not have gotten up in the first place. I could have managed without you."

"Not a *French* meal." Odile forced a smile. "I had years of cooking to please a French husband. Your mother may still have a few cooking tricks for you to learn from her. Even if Amin is all Wolof."

"Except for his appetite." Sabine laughed as she helped her mother from the room. "He and his brother are both crazy about French food. And I have heard a French saying that the way to a man's heart is through his belly."

Sabine returned and began removing long, thin fillets of beef from the spiced palm wine in which they had been marinating overnight.

"How's Maman?" asked Aurore, shelling peas into a large pot on the hearth.

"She is resting." A shadow flitted across Sabine's face. She stared down at the strips of beef silently for a moment.

Aurore didn't notice. "Will she be well enough to join us for dinner tonight?"

"I hope so. She really has been looking forward to it. She is very fond of Amin and Cherif. She has been since they were little boys." Sabine cut the fillets into neat, even cubes.

"She isn't the only one who's been fond of Amin since he was a little boy," Aurore teased.

Sabine smiled complacently. "Nor is she the only one fond of Cherif."

"It's not the same thing." Aurore dumped the emptied jackets of the peas into the mulch pail; later they would be used as fertilizer for the garden.

"Isn't it?" Sabine looked at Aurore with frank curiosity.

"I don't think so. You see, I'm not sure of my feelings toward Cherif."

Sabine nodded understandingly. "Then it is different." She put the cubes of meat in the pot and set aside a bit of suet to sauté the shallots. "I know how I feel about Amin. I love him."

"I should hope so." Aurore made a wide gesture to cover the preparations for dinner. "Considering all this."

Sabine ignored the sarcasm. "Some day you will feel yourself what I feel for Amin. Perhaps you will feel it for Cherif." She studied the spice rack.

"Perhaps. Perhaps not."

"Then we would be doubly sisters because we will have married brothers."

"Has Amin asked you to marry him?" Aurore was surprised. Sabine had not said anything about this before.

"Not yet. But he will." In contrast to her previous excitement, Sabine was quite calm and self-assured now.

She selected bay leaf, peppercorns, and thyme from the spice rack.

"Cherif asked me." Aurore washed some tomatoes in a bowl filled with water she had pumped before. "Sort of," she added.

"He has not spoken to Maman."

"He wants to. He will if I want him to."

"You said no?"

"I said I needed time to think about it."

"How unlike you." Sabine smiled fondly at her younger half-sister. "So mature." She took a pinch of thyme between her fingertips and sprinkled it delicately over the cubes of meat.

"I told him he should think about Leita Ousbane as a substitute." Aurore smiled a Cheshire smile, remembering her impudence. "He didn't like that."

"I should not think he would." Sabine's tone was unusually dry.

Aurore caught it. "Has there been something between Cherif and Leita then?" she demanded. Aurore set the tomatoes down and started slicing them. But her green eyes were intent on Sabine.

"You have been gone four years. You cannot have expected a boy like Cherif not to go near any other girl in all that time."

"But Leita Ousbane!" Aurore chopped viciously at a tomato.

"Except for Leita and you, all the girls on Ile Celeste are Muslim. Being Muslim myself, I can tell you that Muslim girls severely restrict their activities with boys until they are married. I doubt there were any alternatives for Cherif."

"The same thing would apply to Amin!" Aurore said hotly.

"Except that I was here. And he loves me. Not that he would ever raise a finger to defile me, of course."

"Oh, don't be so righteous, Sabine! Nobody could live a purer life than four years in a school run by the nuns of Thiès. I hardly ever saw a boy!"

"I did not mean to offend you, baby sister." Sabine crossed over and hugged her. "I only meant that Leita, not having the inhibitions of a Muslim girl, is perhaps more free with her favors."

"With all the boys?"

"No," Sabine admitted reluctantly.

"Just with Cherif then!" It was not a question. A surge of jealousy went through Aurore. *I'll show him!* she vowed silently. Through with the tomatoes now, she stabbed the knife point-first into the wooden block upon which she'd been working.

They fell silent for a few moments. Sabine prepared the mushrooms to be sautéed later. Aurore began to mix the batter for the crepes they would serve for dessert. "What is it that you love about Amin?" she asked idly.

"Everything." Sabine laughed.

"You want to be a chief's wife?"

"I don't care about that."

"But Amin will be the village chief after his father dies."

"That is not why I fell in love with him."

"You want him to—you know—make love to you?"

"Yes." Sabine's voice was soft and shy, as if she were confessing something to her sister she had not yet dared admit to herself.

"You think Amin will be good in bed?"

"Aurore!" Sabine hastily busied herself cleaning the berries that would be served with the crepes. "But I will tell you something," she said in a whisper after another long silence. "I want Amin so much that sometimes I lie awake at night aching to be his."

"I just lie awake." Aurore sighed.

"You will find someone some day. Cherif. Perhaps somebody else. But there will be an Amin for you, Aurore. Do not worry."

"You're so sweet, Sabine." Aurore was touched. To cover her feelings, she teased her sister once again. "But not like Amin. He's too skinny."

"He is not!"

"Long and thin. Amin is built like a bamboo strip."

"He is beautiful!"

"He's a head taller than Cherif and weighs twenty pounds less."

"I love his body!"

"Aha! I knew it!"

Sabine snatched the spoon from her and raised it high in mock threat. "You'll know something else, younger sister, if you don't finish mixing those crepes! Do you want me to be embarrassed in front of Amin's new friend?"

"Who is this man he's bringing to dinner?"

"His name is Steven Parker. He is an American. Amin has some sort of business dealings with him in Dakar. I'm not sure exactly what. I just know it has to do with why he hasn't been back to Ile Celeste in over a week."

"An American? But the war has been over for more than a year."

"He has been in Dakar since 1943. He was a bomber pilot stationed at Yof airport after the Vichy government in Dakar agreed to cooperate with the Americans in building it. He took his discharge in Dakar and has been there ever since. Amin got the sheet iron for our village dwellings from him."

"Was he in the black market?"

"Is there anyone in Dakar who wasn't after the war?"

"That's true," Aurore granted. "I wonder what this American will be like." She was curious.

Aurore's curiosity was satisfied that evening when Amin and Cherif Baye arrived with the American striding between them. He was taller than Cherif and not quite so tall as Amin. His body was rangy, with that easy midwestern indolence Aurore had come to associate with the heroes of the occasional Hollywood movies the nuns had allowed their charges to attend during the war.

There was indeed a cowboy charm to Steven Parker's awkwardness as he bent over Odile's fragile hand to kiss it. The way he chuckled at his own clumsiness was boyish and self-effacing. Combined with his clear blue eyes and sandy hair, it personified the wartime stereotype of the shy but stalwart Yankee.

He did not attempt to repeat the continental gesture with Aurore or Sabine. He simply shook their hands forthrightly and crinkled his face in a smile that made his freckles dance. He held Aurore's hand perhaps an instant longer than Sabine's, and his quick glance approved of the way her formal white-and-gold *boubou* clung to her ripe figure.

Aurore felt his eyes on her a second time as they all went out to the hard dirt patio in back of the dwelling, where a wooden table had been set formally for dinner. She sensed his approval of the contrast between her tawny red hair and the creamy gold of her skin in the soft light from the candles on the table. How nice! How nice to have Cherif's homage to her allure confirmed by a stranger! And such an attractive stranger at that!

They did not seat themselves at the round dinner table immediately. As was the custom throughout all of West Africa, the evening meal would not begin until about ten o'clock. The French influence on the region decreed an aperitif before dinner.

Sabine went to fetch the drinks. She returned with a tray offering a choice between bissap—a sweet, cool, nonalcoholic mixture of fruit juices—and palm wine, a fermentation of sap tapped from the trunks of palm trees. Steven Parker took a glass of wine. Ignoring a disapproving frown from her mother, Aurore did the same. Odile, Sabine, and Amin all chose the bissap. Cherif hesitated and then took a glass of wine, a certain defiance in his manner.

"I thought Muslims didn't drink alcohol," Steven Parker remarked to Aurore.

"I am not a Muslim."

"But you are perhaps too young for wine," Odile interjected.

"Not for just one glass, Maman."

"Very well. But only one."

"Is it only the French who drink alcohol in Dakar?" Aurore resumed her conversation with Steven Parker. Her green eyes were wide as she looked at him with a certain calculated innocence.

"Well, no," he admitted, laughing. "I've drunk with Wolof friends on more than one occasion. But then Dakar is a very wicked city."

"Is it? How delicious. I haven't been there for a long time. But if it's so wicked, I must arrange a visit soon."

"Aurore!" Odile sighed.

"Perhaps I might escort her to Dakar, ma'am," Steven Parker offered. "I'd see to her safety."

"We will see, Monsieur Parker." Odile was noncommittal.

"What is your religion, Monsieur Parker?" Cherif was jealous. There was a hostile edge to his question.

"I'm a Methodist."

"Are there not Methodists who abstain from alcohol?"

"Yep. Some do and some don't."

"Well, here on Ile Celeste, backward as we may seem compared to Dakar," Cherif told him with heavy sarcasm, "we too have Muslims who do not choose to be bound by old-fashioned religious strictures."

"There is no such thing as old-fashioned or new-fashioned where Islam is concerned." His brother Amin took issue with him. " 'There is no God but Allah; Muhammad is his Messenger,' " he said, quoting the Koran. "And Muhammad forbade intoxicating beverages. A true Muslim does not partake of them!"

"Muhammad taught that all Muslims are equal in the sight of Allah," Cherif reminded him. "Does that not mean those who drink wine as well as those who do not?"

"That is not what he meant! To imply it is heresy!" righteous anger blazed in Amin's long face. "Muhammad—"

"Amin." Sabine put her hand over his and shook it

with gentle, loving humor. "Don't get so excited. Remember the proverb of Ahmadou Koumba: 'If you find favor with Allah, other men will measure their praise.' Let your own observance of the law be enough. You must not judge your brother."

"You are right." Amin looked lovingly at Sabine. "I apologize, Cherif."

"I too am sorry." Cherif put down his wineglass, ashamed at having drawn his older brother into an argument in front of a stranger. He shot a quick, hostile glance at Steven Parker and lapsed into sullen silence.

Aurore was well aware of what was bothering Cherif. She had, after all, known him all her life. Jealousy had always been part of his nature, as it was of hers.

But because she was still smarting from the revelation of Cherif's involvement with Leita Ousbane, Aurore took advantage of Steven Parker's interest to get even with Cherif. She turned toward the American and gave him her full attention, ignoring Cherif entirely. She was happily aware that Cherif smoldered all the while she and Steven Parker chatted.

Sabine and Amin had withdrawn to the shadows and were murmuring to each other in low, tender voices. Odile sat poised and smiling, and yet she seemed withdrawn from the others. Aurore did not suspect that behind her facade her mother was dealing with an increasing physical discomfort.

"Tell me about wicked Dakar," Aurore asked Steven Parker, her voice low and husky.

"Oh, now, I reckon I was exaggerating before, Miss Bakar."

"My name is not Bakar." Aurore explained that Sabine was her half-sister and that she and her mother were named de Beausoleil. "It's confusing," she laughed. "Why don't you just call me Aurore."

"Okay, Aurore. I will." Steven Parker wrinkled his well-tanned brow. "Did you say de Beausoleil?" he asked.

"That's right."

"I believe I've met some of your relations in Dakar."

"I don't think so. We have no relatives in Dakar, do we, Maman?"

"Not that I know of." Odile managed to restore the smile that had faded from her lips.

"A widow lady, still beautiful," he told them. "And her young daughter, a belle of the French *beau monde*. The lady's name is Colette Marie de Beausoleil, and her daughter's called Delphine. In fact, I've had the pleasure of taking Mademoiselle Delphine dancing."

"Maman!" Aurore exclaimed.

"Colette and Delphine in Dakar!" Her mother was as surprised as Aurore. "But why?"

"Well, ma'am, according to Mademoiselle Delphine, Marseilles wasn't too hospitable to them after VE Day, so they came to Dakar."

Aurore was both stunned and fascinated. Could this mean her cousin Blaise was also in Dakar? Her heart skipped a beat. "And Delphine's brother, Blaise? My other cousin? Did you meet him too?" she asked the American.

"No, ma'am. Mademoiselle Delphine mentioned him, but he's not in Dakar."

"Oh." Aurore was very disappointed.

"How did you meet them?" Odile inquired. She dabbed at a thin line of perspiration on her upper lip, the telltale sign of a beginning fever.

"An afternoon cocktail party at the salon of Mademoiselle Minette Fourier. Very fancy. Lots of society hotshots."

"Minette Fourier," Aurore remembered. "I've seen her picture in the society pages of the Dakar newspaper. She's beautiful: long, raven-black hair and porcelain-white skin."

"That's her. Looks a bit like a young Vivienne Leigh. Has just as much clout in Dakar society, too, from what I hear."

"The *crème de la crème*"—Cherif spoke up—"of

white French society.'' His tone was a mixture of irony and contempt.

Aurore ignored him. ''How did my aunt and cousin become acquainted with Minette Fourier?''

''Through your cousin Blaise,'' Parker answered. ''Seems there's some sort of involvement between them.''

''Involvement?'' A flash of unreasonable jealousy went through Aurore.

''Mademoiselle Delphine's expecting them to get engaged. But it seems her brother's dragging his feet.''

Aurore was pleased to hear that.

''Delphine and her mama, though,'' Steven Parker continued, ''they're rooting for Mademoiselle Fourier to hook him. They sort of owe their position in Dakar society to her. I think they're afraid she could dump them just as easily as she raised them up.''

''Just a moment!'' Aurore remembered. ''I'm confused. How could Blaise be involved with Minette Fourier if he isn't in Dakar?''

''According to Delphine, they met in North Africa during the war. Mademoiselle Fourier's father was in the original Dakar Vichy government, but he saw the light and went to Casablanca to make a deal with some Allied brass. She went with him, and that's where she met Blaise. The way Delphine makes it sound, all that moonlight and desert got to them.''

''Are *Tante* Colette and *Cousine* Delphine planning to come to Ile Celeste?'' Aurore was curious to meet these glamorous French relatives.

''Delphine didn't say anything about that. Do they know they have relations here?''

''Oh, yes.'' Aurore remembered her father telling her of the low esteem in which they were held by the Marseilles de Beausoleils. A matter of skin tone, was the way he had put it.

''They also own the château,'' Odile revealed. ''Ownership reverted to them upon my husband's death.''

''Then like as not they'll come out here to look over their property, and all you ladies will get to meet one another.'' Steven Parker grinned an uncomplicated American grin.

Sabine and Amin rejoined the group. "Shall we have dinner now, Maman?" Sabine asked her mother.

"If the gentlemen will join me at table, then you and Aurore might begin to serve."

Aurore brought in the vichyssoise. Both Amin and Cherif were frank as children in their pleasure at the treat of French cuisine. When the Boeuf Bourguignon was served, Aurore took her seat between Cherif and Steven Parker. She concentrated her attention on the latter, flirting lightly with him, testing the allure of her blossoming femaleness. The American responded with obvious interest. She didn't have to look at Cherif to know that his enjoyment in the meal was being spoiled.

Next the sisters brought in the salad. Aurore was happy for Sabine's sake when Amin complimented the delicate flavor of the vinaigrette dressing, despite its lack of garlic. Cherif, she noted smugly, was still sulking.

"Sabine!" Odile had been sitting quietly, not touching the food on her plate. Now, as she spoke her older daughter's name, her voice was tinged with both a reluctance to disturb the dinner party and a surrender to pain. "Could you help me inside?" The beads of perspiration glittered on her brow. "I must ask you gentlemen to excuse me. A slight indisposition."

"Of course, Maman!" Sabine's concerned voice overrode the solicitations of the others. "Is the pain very bad?"

"No. It's nothing. I just feel a little weak." Odile got to her feet. She swayed a moment and might have fallen had not Sabine put her arm firmly around her.

"Shall I come too?" Aurore was dismayed by her mother's condition.

Odile looked pleadingly at Sabine and shook her head ever so slightly.

"It's not necessary," Sabine said. "Maman and I can manage. She just has to rest a little. I can help her to bed while you entertain our guests.'' She led her mother from the room.

Aurore served a platter of cheeses and local fruits, then resumed her flirtatious conversation with Steven Parker. After a while, Sabine returned and cleared the dishes. She was quite subdued, but Aurore was too intent on the American to notice. The sisters brought in French coffee—a rare delicacy on Ile Celeste—and then the crepes suzettes. The three men applauded as the brandy was set afire and flames leaped up around the crepes. They ate them with relish.

Over a second cup of coffee, a heated discussion sprang up between Amin and Cherif. Sabine was too preoccupied with thoughts of her ailing mother to pay attention, but Aurore and Steven Parker stopped chatting to listen.

"Talk is not enough," Amin was insisting with the fervor of an old-time Islamic prophet. "There must be *commitment!*" He emphasized the last word by striking his fist on the tabletop.

"Granted. But commitment to what?" While Cherif's voice was intense, his eyes did not blaze with the same zealous fire as his older brother's. "Commitment to the *imams* and a *jihad*—holy war—for independence from the French? But our *imams* are the very ones who helped the French put the yoke around our necks. Why should we trust them now?"

"Because we are a Muslim people. Eighty percent of Senegal is Muslim. We must follow our Muslim leaders. And it is not fair to label them with the sins of their predecessors. The *imams* of today are not responsible for *indigénat.*"

Aurore remembered her father explaining *indigénat* to her. Originally it meant the right of citizenship as conceded to the natives of West Africa by the French colonial administration. Over the years, the French in Dakar had used the word colloquially to designate the natives themselves. To the Senegalese, however, *indigénat* had come to sum up the hubris of foreigners conceding them citizenship in their own country. To Cherif and Amin, Aurore knew, it still meant the entire body of colonial law by which the French ruled the Senegalese in order to extract the maximum profit from their labor and their land.

"But are today's *imams* different from their predecessors?" Cherif answered Amin. "Or is it just that their aims are different? Not long ago they told us it was Allah's will that we should work like dogs for the French *toubabs*. Now they whisper it is Allah's will that we rise up and throw the French out. But when the smoke clears, will we find these holy men in possession of all the French prizes? Will we now be working like dogs for them because—they will tell us—it is Allah's will?"

"You are impractical, my brother. Have you forgotten that we here at this table are the only people on Ile Celeste who can read and write? Have you forgotten that only five percent of our black children throughout the country attend schools? Our religious leaders are very close to being the only educated people in Senegal. They are the only ones who have the knowledge to lead."

"It is you who forget what is important, Amin. Our father, the chief of our village, has not had formal education as we have. He has studied only the Koran— and that without being able to read it. And yet he is highly respected by his people, his leadership unquestioned. There are many such chiefs in our country. Our people will follow them."

"If we are to enter the twentieth century, we cannot rely on uneducated village chiefs for leadership."

"One day you will be chief. I would follow you, dear brother!"

"How can I argue with that?" Amin's somber face broke into a smile. His lanky limbs unwound as he reached to embrace Cherif.

"But suppose when Amin gets to be chief he's still

following the *imams?*" Aurore deliberately pricked Cherif's logic. "Would you still follow him?"

"By the time he is chief, he will be older and wiser. He will point a better direction for us all.

"Such as?" Amin demanded. His hooded eyes clouded over once again. "Our brave trade union leaders? Those gentlemen who talk of economic security and national independence and then turn to the French labor unions like La Confédération Générale du Travail and Force Ouvrière for instructions? And who runs the French labor unions? The Communists! Would you like it better if the Communists took over our liberation movement?"

Cherif shrugged. "I have nothing against Communists."

"I don't understand young men like you who would trade French *toubabs* for Russian *toubabs.*"

"It was the Communists in the French labor unions—not the Russians—who forced the French government to draw up an Overseas Labor Code that included equal pay for equal work for black Africans, a minimum wage, an eight-hour working day and a forty-hour week, safeguards to protect women and phase out child labor. And what happened? Our own black Constituent Assembly—all those *macacos* serving the red-ears—never even discussed it. And the French National Assembly—in the hands of dedicated anti-Communists—is still postponing a vote on the code."

"Which they wouldn't be doing if it didn't have Communist handprints all over it."

"If it didn't have those handprints, it wouldn't exist!"

"Be careful, Cherif. You are still very young. Embrace Communism in the name of liberation, and you will destroy the very fabric of our way of life."

His younger brother sighed. "I wonder if it's possible to get the French off our backs without doing that?"

"It must be!" Amin's elongated face was transfigured by patriotic fervor. "Even if it should mean *jihad!*"

"Guns? Killing?" Sabine suddenly interjected.

"If that is necessary," Amin responded.

"But don't the French have all the guns?" Aurore asked. "How will it be possible to stand up against them?"

Amin exchanged a knowing look with Steven Parker. "By arming ourselves for the struggle."

"But how?"

"By buying American war surplus guns," Cherif answered. "Isn't that right?" He looked at Steven Parker insinuatingly.

"Not these days." The American didn't seem to notice Cherif's hostility. His tone was calm, informative. "It used to be the main source, but not anymore. After the war ended, all that hardware got snapped up pretty fast. These days there are other connections. Professionals. No more Yankee noncoms getting rich peddling bazookas on the Dakar black market."

"You were one of those black market soldiers, weren't you?" Cherif asked contemptuously.

"Yep. I was every bit as greedy as the next man."

"Only they went home and you're still here."

"That's right."

"And still selling guns illegally!"

"Not exactly. And it isn't the way you're making it sound, Cherif." Steven Parker kept his voice friendly.

"No? Then how is it?"

"I don't think you'll buy it, but I'll tell you anyway. I'm an American. I guess I feel responsible for what happened in Senegal when the war ended."

"Why should you feel responsible?" Aurore wondered.

"We came in here in 'forty-three and we bucked this country up for the war effort. We needed an air base here. We built Yof Airfield. That's a good example. When the war ended, did we turn it over to the Senegalese people? Like hell we did! We handed it lock, stock, and barrel to the French. Not just Yof, but all the improvements we made in Senegal. The French profited, not the Africans. We used the Senegalese, and then we handed them back to the French with an even tighter noose around their necks than they had before.''

"But that was your country's policy. It doesn't make you personally responsible," Aurore decided.

"Not the way I look at it, ma'am. You see, I bought all that garbage about how America was on the side of the underdog. That's why I enlisted. I was sort of naive, I guess. Now I know that rich countries like mine, and like France, don't give poor folks anything for nothing. Poor folks have to stand up and take what's rightfully theirs.''

"Then you're for Senegalese independence?" Cherif asked him.

"Sure am! I'm not exactly sure which of the groups speaks for the people more than the other, but I'm for anybody who'll fight to kick the French out of Senegal.''

"And you're for a holy war?" Cherif persisted.

"The people are Muslim. If that's the route they want to go, then I'm for them.''

"Then you would arm even the religious fanatics?''

"Against the French? Sure!''

"You make yourself sound like quite an idealist.'' Cherif's tone was skeptical.

"I told you I didn't think you'd buy it.'' Steven Parker spread his hands and grinned engagingly.

"I don't. Somehow I can't see a cohort of Mustapha Hakim as an idealist.''

"Cherif!" Amin sounded a warning note.

Steven Parker held up a large hand. "Now just a minute. You really do have it wrong. I'm not a cohort of Hakim's. I don't work for him and I don't work with him. I just do business with him. And for a good cause, too. Ask your brother.''

"Hakim is a Lebanese bloodsucker! The Lebanese are worse than the French! He would sell his grandmother for a profit. You cannot deal with him without becoming tainted from the contact.''

"Cherif!" Amin barked. "*I* deal with Mustapha Hakim," he said deliberately.

"To buy guns for your Muslim revolutionaries?"

"That's not the point."

"It is well known that Hakim is the Dakar connection for American and European gun manufacturers."

"And neither is that!"

"How did you meet the infamous Hakim? Through Mr. Parker?"

"Yes," Amin told him flatly. "And I'm very grateful to Steven for having arranged it. He is a real friend of our people, and I think you owe him an apology."

"Not necessary." Steven Parker waved it away.

"Gentlemen!" Sabine arose, signifying that dinner— and the discussion—were over. "We just have time before the dancing starts to walk to the knoll and show Mr. Parker how pretty the lights of Dakar are from there."

They all stood. Amin helped Sabine carry the coffee cups and desert dishes inside. Then the quintet started up the trail toward the baobab tree overlooking the village.

Aurore and Sabine walked with Steven Parker. Amin and Cherif fell behind them. Aurore couldn't make out their words, but she could sense the whispered urgency in their hushed voices. She guessed that his older sibling was taking Cherif to task for his rudeness to Steven Parker. She was sure she was right when Amin summoned the American to drop back and join them.

"Amin says that Cherif does not trust Mr. Parker," Sabine said to Aurore in a low voice.

"What does Amin think?"

"That Cherif is jealous because of the way Parker flirts with you."

"In some ways, Cherif is still such a boy!" Aurore responded.

"True. But I do not think it is just jealousy. I think he genuinely doubts Parker's motives. After all, why should an American care about the liberation of the Senegalese?"

"Who knows why Americans do anything?" Aurore shrugged.

"Well, this one is showing signs of becoming crazy about you, little sister. I do not blame Cherif for being jealous."

"That's Cherif's problem."

"He will be sure to make it yours."

Sabine was right. When they reached the baobab tree, Cherif drew Aurore aside while Amin and Sabine showed Steven Parker the shimmering lights of the city of Dakar to the east. Cherif's grasp was firm through the silk of Aurore's *boubou* as he propelled her out of earshot of the others.

He came straight to the point. "Why do you flirt with Parker?"

"It's not your business what I do."

"I have spoken of taking you as my wife. Of course it is my business."

"I've agreed to nothing."

"Nevertheless, you know how I feel."

"And I can guess how you feel about Leita Ousbane." Aurore's voice was heavy with sarcasm.

"Leita? What has she to do with this?"

"You speak of taking me as your wife. But have you waited for me, Cherif? Or should I ask Leita that?"

"I am a man, Aurore. You were gone. She was here. Whatever happened is over. But I tell you it has nothing to do with us!"

"And I tell you," Aurore replied sweetly, "that whatever *I* choose to do with Steven Parker also has nothing to do with us!"

"If that is how you want it, Aurore, than I have nothing else to say except—"

"Yes?"

"Fananlen ak diame!"

"Fananlen ak diame." Aurore coldly returned his good-bye.

On the way back to the village, they did not speak to each other again.

* * *

The *sabar* was being held in the central clearing. The area was lit by *fanals*—ornate, multicolor oil-burning lanterns—that had been strung around its perimeter. As the five of them settled themselves on rough wooden benches in the circle of onlookers, the *teujuekat* made his appearance.

He was a small man by Wolof standards, very skinny, but lithe and sinewy. His age was indeterminate. He wore a skirt of long yellow, brown, orange, and green grasses reaching to his shinbones. Under it was a loincloth, above it a short tunic that tied over one knobby brown shoulder, both made of animal skin. His face was covered by a mask with luminous, vaguely beastlike markings. His hair was long and scraggly. His feet were bare, and around his ankles he wore tiny rattles of millet seeds wrapped in leaves. He held a long torch high in one hand. An oblong tomtom was suspended by a thong over his other shoulder.

Anticipation stirred the crowd as the *teujuekat* planted the torch in the ground. He tapped the tight-stretched skin of the tomtom and cocked his ear as if listening to its reply. His masked face nodded, and his long, graceful fingers began to caress the drum.

As many times as Aurore had seen the *teujuekat* perform, she was still stirred by it. Something deep inside her responded to the primal rhythm he drew forth from the tomtom. As the tempo slowly increased, Aurore's blood seemed to pound with it, until she could no longer distinguish her own heartbeat from the throbbing drum.

Now the *teujuekat* began to move. His limbs jerked spasmodically, his masked face bobbing eerily. The crowd started to clap in time with the beat. Suddenly he stopped slapping the tomtom. He waved his arm in a short, imperious gesture. The hands stopped clapping. There was an instant of dead silence. The *teujuekat* leaped high in the air. His skeletal body spun as if suspended there. His calloused heels came together three times before they touched the earth again. As he landed, the *teujuekat* began to beat out a new and driving rhythm on the tomtom.

His gyrations grew even more frenzied as he danced within the circle of onlookers. There was a sensual teasing in the way he paused before one or another as if to lure them with his pounding drum and writhing body. If the person responded, he might carry on the flirtation longer, but in the end, he would move along. Such was the pattern until he reached a middle-aged, rather stout woman wearing a plain brown *boubou*.

The *teujuekat* fell to his knees in front of the woman and remained there, coaxing a less frantic, more suggestive sound from the tomtom. His shoulders, his neck, the mask he wore, all moved in a mime show of courtship. The crowd laughed appreciatively. The *teujuekat* rose slowly and his hips moved with a grinding rhythm that made his grass skirt roll as if under the caress of a gentle breeze. He beckoned to the woman. She got to her feet and danced languorously toward the *teujuekat;* slowly he backed away from her.

Suddenly the woman let out a shriek and leaped. It was a surprisingly high and graceful jump for a woman of her weight. When she landed, she began to dance in earnest. The *teujuekat* retired to the edge of the circle, continuing to supply the rhythm with his tomtom but leaving the stage to her.

Grasping the hem of her *boubou* with both hands, she raised the skirts high and displayed shapely legs in a blur of motion. The crowd clapped to the rhythm, urging her on to wilder and wilder exertions. Eventually her momentum carried her to a young fisherman standing on the fringe of the circle. Sensing her intent, the *teujuekat* slowed the tempo again. She swayed in front of the young fisherman and rotated her ample hips. Slowly he followed her into the center area.

They danced. It began slowly and then once again worked up to a furious peak. Finally the stout woman whirled to the edge of the circle and collapsed. The *teujuekat* now danced with the young man. Then the young man danced alone. Then he selected a young woman with whom he danced until he exhausted himself. The pattern was repeated over and over again.

The *teujuekat* was tireless, and the dancers took their strength from him. The energy level of the crowd seemed to increase like a shimmering cloud of heat rising in the rainbow glare from the *fanals*.

Under her elaborate gold-and-white *boubou*, Aurore's body was drawn taut as a bowstring. Her flesh quivered in response to the increasingly frenetic beat. Her green eyes devoured the flesh of the sensuous dancers. Her blood ran quick and scalding in her veins.

Suddenly, Leita Ousbane darted into the circle and pirouetted up to the *teujuekat*, pausing deliberately between him and the flaming torch he had planted. Swaying before him, the torchlight rendered the thin material of her skimpy crimson *boubou* almost transparent.

Adapting to Leita's rhythm, the *teujuekat* began pounding out a slow, insinuating beat. Leita undulated in front of him, her slender hips swaying under the revealing material, her arms climbing each other like vines twining up the trunk of a mangrove tree. The nipples of her small, uptilted breasts stood clearly erect in the cool night air. Her pelvis began to rotate; her hands fluttered to her eyes as if to convey alarm. But behind her hands Leita was laughing maniacally.

Suddenly she exploded in a series of leaps and handsprings and somersaults. The tomtom accompanied her with a mad flurry, the thunder of stampeding jungle animals. She turned a final handspring and rose in front of Cherif. She struck a pose like an untamed filly bucking on hind legs. Her hands pawed the air like flailing hooves. One of her sandaled feet scuffed the ground. She snorted. She jerked her head, a command to Cherif to join her in the dance. Her dark eyes were hungry and predatory.

Beside Aurore, Cherif rose. He shook his shoulders and advanced toward Leita. He slapped his thighs the way a rider might who was preparing to mount, and pranced into the center.

Leita settled to all fours, her derriere swaying provocatively, the braids of her black hair shimmering like the strangest of manes in the *fanal* light. Cherif, hands outstretched as though holding reins, followed as if jouncing on horseback. The crowd cheered and stamped its feet.

Finally Leita spun to the sidelines. Now Cherif was alone. The audience continued to follow his erotic solo enthusiastically. Aurore, however, was distracted.

Soon Cherif must choose another partner. Everyone would expect him to pick Aurore. But they were not speaking. What would he do?

Cherif whirled around the inner circle toward Aurore. He slowed down in front of her and held out his hand.

She got to her feet slowly. It wouldn't do to appear too eager. She swayed ever so slightly and took a small step toward Cherif. He slid an equally small step backward. Aurore sidled into the center to dance.

Once again, Leita darted from the sidelines. The *teujuekat* moved to restrain her, but Cherif stepped between them. Leita clutched at Cherif and pulled him from the circle. Aurore found herself dancing alone.

The onlookers laughed in good-natured derision. At the back, Ouna the *katt* was fingering a necklace of herbs and charms, and cackling as if she were somehow responsible for Aurore's being scorned by Cherif in favor of Leita. Defiantly Aurore continued to dance. Her angry eyes caught Leita and Cherif watching her from a spot near where Ouna was continuing to chortle.

He humiliated me in front of everybody! The thought flashed through Aurore's mind.

Aurore looked straight at Cherif and Leita. She caught his eye and smiled insincerely, voluptuously. She slid her hands down the front of her *boubou* seductively, caressing her breasts, her hips, her stomach, her thighs. Without turning around, she rolled her hips, a signal to the *teujuekat* to speed up the tempo of the tomtom.

Moistening her lips, she tossed her red hair, stretched her arms to the moon, and began a wordless chant that rose and fell with the drumbeat. She bent her knees, thrusting her hips forward and leaning back so that her firm, generous breasts rose and fell like ripe jungle melons. She could be just as flagrant, just as desirable as Leita! She'd show Cherif! She'd show them all!

Unnoticed, she opened the clasp at the back of her neck that held her *boubou* together. The *teujuekat* was beating a tattoo to urge her back to an erect position. Slowly she started to straighten up. The *teujuekat* danced wild circles around her. Suddenly she straightened, twirled with him, and then dived forward to stand on her hands. The bottom of her *boubou* fell over her hips and for a moment her long, slender, beautiful legs waved in the rainbow light from the fanals, her derriere plump and rippling under French silk panties—Aurore's one secret extravagance, purchased for her by a schoolmate in Thiès.

The audience was shocked. Aurore, daughter of the doctor they had loved and respected, had a status denied Leita. There were even rumors that she might be taken as wife by the chief's second son. What Cherif did with Leita was wild oats. But what Aurore did would not be so easily forgiven or forgotten—especially what followed.

Aurore leaped from her hands to her feet. Her green eyes blazed at Cherif. Then, mockingly, she bent her shoulders forward and curtsied deeply. The bodice of her garment fell away and her red-tipped, cream-colored breasts came spilling into plain view.

An audible gasp swept the crowd. Aurore held the pose as though unaware of what had happened.

"Aurore!"

Her sister Sabine's voice brought her to her senses. Quickly Aurore pulled up her *boubou* and refastened it. Automatically her eyes went back to the spot where Cherif had been. He and Leita were both gone.

The faces watching Aurore were hostile now. She had turned a lighthearted traditional dance into an affront to Muslim morality. Only the *teujuekat*, impassive behind his mask, seemed unoffended. His hands on the tomtom urged her to finish the dance she had started.

Aurore spied the one face not angry with her: Steven Parker was smiling disarmingly. He obviously neither deplored what she had done nor felt obliged to conceal the fact that it excited him.

She drew him to his feet and he danced with her. When she attempted to withdraw and leave him to dance by himself, he wouldn't let her but followed her from the circle. Behind them, the *teujuekat* drummed an *adieu*.

Aurore was still panting from her exertions. Her body was encased in a pocket of heat. Her face was flushed, her eyes feverish, and she felt slightly dizzy. She didn't protest when Steven Parker put his arm around her to support her.

"You are something else again, ma'am," he said with a chuckle. "When you dance, you surely make a guy sit up and take notice."

"I think everybody took notice," Aurore said, and sighed.

"Probably, ma'am. But I'm the lucky one you picked to dance with."

"Does that mean something special in America?"

"Yes—it means this."

She wasn't prepared for his kiss. It wasn't like when Cherif kissed her. There was the lust of a grown man in it, and where his hands touched her body, they touched with the demand of one who had known many women. She didn't know whether she liked it or not, but she did know that there was no stopping it. Steven Parker was not a boy to be teased. She had given him reason—silent but real—to kiss her, and his mouth would not be denied.

"Sweet as cherry wine." He continued to hold her when the kiss was over. Her breasts were crushed against the hardness of his chest; their loins clung together. She could feel a throbbing, a spreading warmth she had not known with Cherif. Helplessly she parted her lips to his second kiss.

A chill ran through her, piercing the hotness of her body. A strange moistness—exciting, unexpected, embarrassing—honeyed her thighs. She was mortified when she felt his hand slide down to grope there. "No!" She pushed away as hard as she could.

He was taken by surprise. He didn't attempt to struggle with her. He just looked at her from narrowed eyes. "I'm not to your liking, ma'am?"

"It's not that. I—I—" Suddenly it was all too much for Aurore. Steven Parker. The *sabar*. Cherif and Leita. Everything. "I just have to be alone now," she babbled. "It's not you. I just have to be by myself!" She turned and fled up the trail without looking back. It was so unexpected that Parker made no attempt to stop her.

Aurore had given no thought to where she was running. After a while, she realized he wasn't following and slowed to a walk, content when the trail led her to the beach. It felt right somehow to stroll there, alone with the roar of the surf and the mysterious turmoil inside her body and the unbidden thoughts that flitted through her brain.

She walked a long way down the shore. The breaking waves, not high but regular, splattered the black-green void with white froth. The fronds of the tall palm trees erased clusters of stars. A three-quarter moon turned patches of sand to gold.

A sound like the groaning of ships at anchor claimed Aurore's ear. But it wasn't coming from the direction of the ocean; its origins were leeward. Aurore went off at an angle through the palm trees toward the sound. She heard it again, much closer now, a mingling of sighs. And then, stepping from behind a tree, she saw the source.

It was Cherif and Leita embracing in the moonlight. She had bared her small, pert breasts. They quivered in his eager hands, the nipples pointy and flame red. Her mouth was stretched wide to his kiss. Her hands were somewhere below their waists, between them; a low bush blocked them from view.

Aurore could only imagine what Leita's hands were doing. Touching him *there*, perhaps? Her heart pounded. Was Leita holding it in her hands, naked and long and hard? Aurore felt a surge of jealousy.

The look on Cherif's face in the moonlight attested to the effectiveness of Leita's caresses. He uttered a long, drawn-out moan, and his head dropped to her breasts, his mouth and tongue licking and kissing feverishly. The flesh of Leita's arms moved in spasm with her unseen hands.

Aurore trembled in the night as if it were her breasts Cherif's mouth were opened to, her nipples he was sucking. She could not stop herself from watching. She had known Cherif all her life; she had seen him aroused; but she had never seen him like this.

Suddenly Leita slid down the length of Cherif's lean body. His naked chest and the top part of his belly were exposed. The area beneath that was hidden from Aurore's view by the underbrush.

She was puzzled. What was Leita doing? Nothing in Aurore's experience, not even the forbidden reading under the covers at school, had equipped her to make anything like an accurate guess. All she could do was look at Cherif's face with his mouth open to the moon and marvel at the ecstasy expressed there.

What was Leita doing to him?

She could see the back of Leita's head from here, the black plaits glistening snakelike in the moonlight. Her arms were stretched high, her hands clawing at Cherif's chest. He seemed not to notice. Then his hands dropped to clutch at the top of her head and he squirmed and writhed and flung a long, drawn-out, triumphal shout at the sky. Then he toppled over and he and Leita rolled on the ground together, laughing mindlessly.

Aurore was slick with perspiration under her *boubou*. A tumult of conflicting emotions and passions racked her mind and body. She turned silently and fled the scene.

Suddenly she was very tired. She made straight for home. The thatched-roof dwelling was bathed in starlight as she approached it.

Unexpectedly the starlight showed a figure on the doorstep. The form bent over and set something down there. Then it straightened up and vanished in the shadows. A high-pitched keening sounded in its wake.

Ouna the *katt!* Aurore was sure of it. She hurried to the doorstep to see what had been left there.

Aurore found a small pouch, hand woven of rough cotton thread and dyed blood red. A drawstring held it closed. When she opened it, a fine dust wafted in a cloud to her nostrils. She recognized it as aloe, a powder made by pulverizing the rare leaves of the baobab tree. In the wake of the aloe, Aurore identified a mixture of aromas including frankincense, orris, patchouli leaves, and sandalwood. The combination was almost unbearably sweet, and her nostrils rebelled at it. Her fingers searched the pouch for something more substantial and came up with a small painted gourd. Feathers had been glued to it, and something was imbedded in it. As Aurore held it up to the moon to try to see what it was, the door behind her opened and Sabine emerged.

Her step-sister gasped when she saw what Aurore was holding.

"What is it?" Aurore peered at Sabine's face in the dimness.

"It means death!" Sabine exclaimed. She reached to take the gourd from Aurore's hand. "Throw it away!"

"All right. But first tell me what this is stuck in here."

"It's the severed and skinned head of a new-killed snake."

"A snake!" Aurore relinquished the pouch and the gourd to Sabine.

"It means death!" Sabine repeated. She put the gourd with its snake skull and feathers back in the pouch, drew the drawstring, and then threw the pouch as far into the surrounding forest as she was able.

"Death? I don't understand. Why would Ouna—?"

"So it was the *katt!*" Sabine interrupted. "But of course! Who else could it be deviling us with this insanity these past weeks?"

"You mean she's left these fetishes before?"

"Oh, yes. And they are more than fetishes. They are omens of death!"

"Sabine! You don't believe that nonsense. Ouna is just a crazy old woman!"

But Sabine wasn't listening. "Omens of death!" she insisted. "Of our mother's death! She didn't want me to tell you, but I must. I can't bear it alone any longer. Maman has cancer! She is dying!"

Aurore looked deep into Sabine's eyes and saw that it was true:

Her mother was dying of cancer!

CHAPTER 3

During the weeks that followed, Aurore devoted herself singlemindedly to the care of her dying mother. Her initial shock deepened into fierce dedication. It was as if through spending every moment with Maman, Aurore believed the sheer force of her love could reverse the course of the disease.

It was to no avail. Odile's condition steadily worsened. Aurore had to accept the fact that her mother, like her father, would soon no longer be there to give her guidance and support and love.

"The will of Allah" was Sabine's answer. Though she was as saddened as Aurore, Sabine had been resigned to their mother's fate for a longer time.

But Aurore was not consoled. That it was God's doing made Odile's terminal illness no more acceptable to her. She continued to exhaust herself doing battle daily with the inevitable.

"You will wear yourself out!" Sabine protested.

"Isn't that what you did while I was away and there was no one to share the burden?"

"It was not the same. I had no choice. And it will not be any relief to me, Aurore, if you become ill and I have to care for both Maman and you."

Finally Aurore heeded Sabine's plea that she take a day away from Odile. She allowed her older sister to pack her a lunch and shoo her from their home with admonitions to "get some sunshine, go for a swim, spend time with young people." But Aurore's despair was such that she could not follow Sabine's advice.

Instead, without conscious direction, her feet carried her toward the château.

It had always been a sanctuary to her during times of stress and heartache. Now, standing midway up the sloping, grassy hill, the sight of the baroque structure that had been her childhood home was like a soothing balm to her spirit. The blazing sun and sea air had bleached its limestone walls and turrets white. The château stood in the morning light like an immense wedding cake, ornate and beautiful.

No one except Aurore ever ventured there; she considered the abandoned château her private domain. Even now its hushed, echoing interior gave her solace. The decaying furnishings were familiar and dear. Aurore knew each room, each corridor, each window by heart. She went up the circular marble staircase swiftly, intending to go to the very top of the westernmost turret. The panorama of Ile Celeste bordered by the wave-tossed sea stretching to the horizon was breathtaking from there, and she knew it would calm her troubled spirit.

Access to the turret was from the master bedroom her parents had once shared. The chamber was as she remembered it—large, square, high-ceilinged, with mote-flecked sun rays cascading through the two large windows. But how sadly the carpet had faded! Its pattern of exotic, bright-plumaged birds had once lifted her spirits; now Aurore could hardly make it out. A patina of dust and sand obscured it, and gaping holes had been gnawed through the weave by rodents. She averted her eyes, glancing from the hand-carved bureau and armoire her great-grandfather André had imported from France to the faded, rose-color canopy of the massive four-poster bed. Her eyes dropped, and—

"Mon Dieu!"

There was a naked white man sprawled across the bed!

Not quite naked, she saw as she moved a step closer. He was lying facedown, asleep, with a small towel around his groin. The ends of it had been tied around his waist to cover his buttocks. The knot, however, had come loose to reveal the sculpted ivory hillock of one hard buttock as well as the deep, well-defined cleft separating it from its mate.

The skin of the sleeping man was ruddy and burnished by the sun. His arms and legs were brawny and bulging with muscle. He had a narrow waist, angling upward to broad, aggressively masculine shoulders. His hair was black and thick and wavy. He was a large man, perhaps not as tall as Amin but taller than Cherif, and much broader in the chest and more heavily built than both.

Aurore stared. The unexpected sight made her heart beat like a tomtom; fevered blood pulsed through her body. The vision of this sleeping Adonis stirred her forcefully.

Who was he? Where had he come from? What was he doing here?

He sighed in his sleep, a deep, self-satisfied sigh, and turned over on his back. For a moment, the towel clung to his groin. Aurore sucked in her breath sharply, her eyes riveted to the shape outlined beneath it.

Then the sleeping man shifted position again. The towel fell to the side, and the crown of his manhood was revealed. Aurore gazed with frightened fascination as the insolent organ was completely exposed. Then, suddenly, it wasn't lying there limply anymore. It was pointing straight up at her!

Aurore backed away from the sight. She didn't see the stout leather boots the sleeper had discarded before taking his nap. She tripped and sat down hard, her derriere hitting the floor with a loud bump.

Aurore's eyes darted to his face, seeing it for the first time. His features were rough hewn and craggy. His black mustache followed the down-turning lines between his nose and mouth. His lips were full and sensual; they hinted of a cruelty that, strangely enough, attracted rather than repelled her. The set of his mouth and chin bespoke a stubborn determination to match Aurore's own. His thick eyebrows had an ironic flare to them. Below them now, his eyes opened in response to the noise of Aurore's fall. The blue eyes focusing on her were piercing and yet clear and warm at the same time. Their initial appraising look helped Aurore find her tongue.

"Blaise!" she exclaimed. "Blaise Honoré de Beausoleil!"

"You have the advantage of me, mademoiselle." He raised one eyebrow quizzically and regarded her intently. A hint of humor lurked in his eyes as they roamed lazily from the frightened curves of her face to the soft, voluptuous contours of her large breasts. "Have we met before?"

"No. No." Aurore was a welter of blushes and confusion.

"Then how do you know who I am?" He stretched luxuriously, his naked chest expanding impressively. His manhood was still thrusting toward her.

"I—I—" Aurore could not keep her eyes from it.

Blaise followed her gaze. A faint smile curled the corners of his sensual lips. "I see." His eyes met hers and held them deliberately. He made no effort to cover his blatantly erect phallus.

Aurore looked away until she felt his gaze claim hers again. Was he laughing at her? She couldn't be sure. There was only that faint irony in the tilt of his eyebrow, that almost imperceptible curl at the corner of his mouth. "Aren't you going to cover yourself?" Finally Aurore managed to get the words out.

His reply was an unconcerned Gallic shrug.

"I'm your cousin," she blurted out, her face on fire.

"First cousin?"

She managed a nod.

"Oh. Well, in that case—" He picked up the towel between two fingers and draped it over his groin with exaggerated care.

She forced her gaze upward. His magnificent chest

rippled with muscles under her glance. A knife scar crossed its expanse from his right collarbone to his left nipple, forming a deep, livid groove.

"What's the matter, cousin? Isn't that better?" There was a teasing note in his deep voice.

"My name is Aurore."

"Aurore, then." His French pronunciation fell deliciously on her ears. "Ah, yes. I did hear that Uncle Justin had a daughter. There wasn't much talk about you, though. My father didn't approve of his brother, and I suppose that extended to his child."

"Because he married an African woman?"

"Probably. My late father was never a candidate for any brotherhood awards."

"And you?" Aurore was suddenly defensive. "How do you feel about blacks?"

"They're revolting!" He paused, then grinned ironically. "Like all the rest of the human race."

Aurore wasn't used to dealing with irony. "Well, I don't like many whites, either!" she snapped at him.

"Then we have a lot in common, Cousin."

"No. You act this way because I'm black."

"What way?"

"If I were a white girl, you'd get dressed properly."

"Why should I discriminate against white girls by hiding my best feature? As matter of fact, I thought you were white until you made such a point of your having black blood. And not much, if complexion is any measurement."

"I'm one-quarter Wolof!" she told him proudly.

"I'm one-eighth German—on my mother's side. It's not something to be proud of these days. Wolof would be better."

"Yes," Aurore agreed without malice. "A Wolof man would dress."

"Ah! I see." Blaise unhurriedly searched the bed and came up with a pair of trousers and a finely tailored silk shirt.

"Why have you come to Ile Celeste?"

"I came to look over the château and see what repairs it needs. As you know, it belongs to me now that both my father and yours have died." Blaise's profile was to her as he tugged at his boots. The angle accentuated the aggressive thrust of his nose and chin; the sunlight glanced off his high cheekbone and threw the carved-out hollow beneath into shadow. There were more lines in his face now than there had been in his youth when the family portrait had been taken, but they only served to heighten his appeal. "My father kept a tight grip on the family holdings," he admitted. "I suppose it's unfair, but—" The wave of his hand expressed a freebooter's morality.

Aurore was as enraptured as she had been by the tales of the bold buccaneers she had secretly read under the blankets at school. She shook her head, dispelling the visions. "It's not unfair," she told him. "We couldn't afford to live in this château now that Papa's gone, anyway."

"You're too generous, Cousin." He crossed to her and took her hand in his. He was so close she could smell his warm, rich masculine aroma—a trace of sweat, a hint of fragrant pipe tobacco, a spicy after-shave cologne new to Aurore. "Much too generous." His other hand, large and calloused, cupped the soft, delicate rose of her cheek with an unexpected gentleness. "You don't have our family's acquisitive knack." His hand moved to grasp a strand of her fine auburn hair. "But you do have the family tresses." He spoke in deep, intimate tones that seemed to caress Aurore's ear. "Like silk," he murmured. "My sister has hair textured like that. Not I, though. Mine is thick and curly, not de Beausoleil at all." Abruptly he bent over and kissed the back of the hand he'd been holding. His lips were warm and slightly moist, and his mustache scratched teasingly. "Greetings from the family, Cousin. And what a pity it is that we *are* cousins."

Aurore pulled her hand from his and moved away,

suddenly confused. Could he be mocking her? "Will you live here?" she asked.

"Yes. After it's fixed up."

"Tante Colette and *Cousine* Delphine? Are they coming to live on Ile Celeste, too?" Aurore babbled with curiosity at the prospect of meeting these glamorous French relatives.

"Yes. I've moved the family shipping business from Marseilles to Dakar. We'll all live here. It's close enough to Dakar for convenience and far enough away to avoid the noise and dirt of the city. The château will properly impress the people I have to do business with, and it should measure up to the entertainment requirements of my mother and sister."

"You'll probably have a lot of parties." Aurore could not keep a note of wistfulness from her voice.

"If I know Maman, we will. Do you like parties?"

"Oh, yes!" she exclaimed, although in truth the only parties she had ever attended were the village *baras*.

"Then you'll be sure to come to ours."

"Oh, no. The French don't ask *Signares* to their parties."

"You're a member of the family," he told her firmly. "You'll be asked, and I hope you'll come. Besides, beauty is always at a premium at any party Colette Marie de Beausoleil gives."

Despite her doubts, Aurore was very excited at the prospect of attending a party of the *beau monde*.

Blaise led the way downstairs. He paused to peer into the large salon where André de Beausoleil had entertained his guests in the nineteenth century. "All this will have to go." His sweeping gesture took in the stiff, brocaded Louis XIV couches and chairs, the ornate tables and their tortured claw legs, and the tarnished silver mirrors. "Maman's a dragon when it comes to interior decorating. I'll just empty the place out and leave the rest to her."

"Then you'll all be moving to Ile Celeste soon?"

"Pretty soon." As they left the château and started

down the path, he took her arm to help her over a tangle of roots. Her skin tingled at his touch. "If you're going back to the village, I'll walk with you," he announced abruptly.

Aurore had promised Sabine she would not return until dinnertime. But that had been before she discovered Blaise. Sabine would have to understand.

"I have to see a man named Amin Baye," Blaise said as they descended the trail together. "His father is the village chief. We've had business discussions in Dakar, but the old man wouldn't commit himself. He says his day will soon be over and then this Amin will be chief, so any decisions should be his."

"Amin doesn't like the French," Aurore warned him.

"Most Senegalese don't. And for good reason, too."

Aurore glanced up at the sky. The sun was at its zenith. The fishing boats would have returned so that the men could take their noon meal. "You can probably find Amin at our house with my sister Sabine," she told Blaise. "They're in love."

"A common folly. Happens to the best of us."

"To you, monsieur?"

"In the past." A shadow flitted across his pirate face. "But experience has brought wisdom."

"Oh? And what about the rumors I hear of you and Mademoiselle Minette Fourier?"

"Minette? Now how the devil did you hear about Minette and me?"

"We are perhaps more *au courant* on Ile Celeste than you think, monsieur." Aurore had no intention of telling him she'd heard the gossip from Steven Parker, who had heard it from Blaise's sister, Delphine.

"And why should you be so interested in my personal life?"

"You're a relative."

"I see!" He threw back his head and laughed, his white teeth flashing in the sunlight.

They continued walking in silence until they reached the house. Amin Baye was with Sabine on the dirt patio in back. Aurore introduced Blaise. The four of them made small talk until Sabine excused herself and went inside to see to Odile.

"I have a business proposition." Blaise came straight to the point with Amin after Sabine left. "I'm moving my family's shipping business from Marseilles to Dakar. The move won't affect our larger ships, but the smaller ones will be standing idle. Now every day the men of your village pole their piroques, loaded with the day's catch, from Ile Celeste to the fish buyers on the Dakar docks."

"My father has told me you have spoken with him about delivering our fish for us." Amin cut Blaise short.

"That's right. Some of my small boats are refrigerated. You lose what—ten percent? Fifteen percent?—to spoilage from the sun every day. Refrigeration would cut that figure by better than half. Also, if your men didn't have to make the trip to Dakar, they could get in two to three hours more fishing, which would decidedly increase the size of your haul."

"But there is no harbor at Ile Celeste, no moorings for motorized boats of the size you imply. There are no docks, no loading platforms, none of the equipment for unloading that Dakar offers."

"I'll build docks with loading platforms off the jetties. I'll supply winches. And I'll hire some of the younger boys who don't go out in the boats to help with the unloading. I'll pay them a fair wage, too."

"French fair is not always Wolof fair," Amin observed dryly.

"I'm not interested in past injustices." Blaise shrugged. "I'm a businessman."

"A French businessman." Amin was cynical. "Still, there is merit to your proposition. What would you charge?"

"A mutually agreed upon percentage of the price each day's catch brings."

"Suppose the entire catch is not bought?" Amin said. "That sometimes happens, you know."

"It happens now because the fish don't keep more than a day or two. They spoil and you have to dump them. That won't happen with refrigerated boats. If I can't peddle your whole catch in Dakar, I'll simply sell it elsewhere. As a matter of fact, if I can get a better price, I'll probably do that anyway."

"No!" Amin was firm. "Our fish are for our fellow Muslims in Dakar. By keeping our prices down, we keep the prices down for them as well. That way Allah smiles on our boats."

"All right. I'll agree to give Dakar priority."

"I will make inquiries," Amin told him delicately.

Blaise understood. "You can check my financial standing with any of the banks or brokerage houses in Dakar. Also Marseilles. You'll find that the De Beausoleil Shipping Company has never defaulted on an obligation. Then come and see me." Blaise handed Amin a business card. "But don't wait too long. If I can't reach an agreement with Ile Celeste, I'll have to make arrangements with one of the other fishing islands."

"Then that will be Allah's Will."

At that moment Sabine reappeared. "Maman has heard your voices," she told them. "She would very much like to meet the nephew of her late husband."

"It will be my pleasure," Blaise said sincerely.

Odile was quite changed from the woman she had been when Aurore returned from Thiès only seven or eight weeks earlier. She had lost much weight, and her body was like that of a child. The bones showed clearly through the thin, taut brown skin of the hand she held up to Blaise, and her once-rich voice was high-pitched and quavery. *"Salaam Alekheim,"* she greeted him.

Blaise returned the salutation and bent low to kiss her hand. "I'm glad that we finally meet, *Tante* Odile," he told her.

"I'm sorry you could not have come while my husband was still alive."

"I'm sorry, too. I would like to have known Uncle Justin."

"He had very strong feelings for his family in Marseilles. No matter the disagreements. His commitment to his family and his pride in the de Beausoleils never wavered."

"I didn't agree with my father's attitude," Blaise told her. "And although I never met Uncle Justin, everything I heard about him only convinced me of what a remarkable man he must have been."

Aurore was surprised at Blaise's tenderness with her mother. He seemed like a different person from the hard-headed businessman who had been negotiating with Amin before. He sat by her mother's pallet, held her shrunken hand gently in his, and spoke of his admiration for the uncle he'd never met.

"I imagined him as a man with a conscience and a heart and a tremendous commitment to the easing of pain," he said, and Odile's ravaged face lit up with a smile of agreement.

Aurore noticed that although he had grown up in the midst of wealth, Blaise seemed completely at ease in the humble surroundings of their home. He didn't care that the "chair" beside Odile on which he was sitting was actually a wooden trunk. He paid no attention to the unsightly tar paper reinforcing the walls. Nor did he, who had doubtless known electricity all his life, remark on the bowls of fish oil with cloth tapers that provided light against the dimness of the interior.

Blaise made his excuses and exited as soon as he discerned that the effort of concealing her pain was tiring Odile. Once beyond her hearing, however, his questions about her condition were searching: When had her illness started? Was its progress gradual or sudden? Did they have medication to ease the pain?

"Only the herbal remedies," Sabine told him. "The *kinkeliba* plant seemed to help in the beginning. But lately it does not alleviate her pain. It is terrible, the way she suffers."

"Morphine?"

"Impossible." It was Amin who spoke. "Such drugs are only available to whites."

"But surely she's been seen by a doctor?"

"Not since her condition was diagnosed," Sabine told him. "She is too weak to travel to Dakar, and even the French doctors who treat blacks won't come to Ile Celeste. Besides, what could they do for her? She is dying of cancer. It is Allah's will."

"At least morphine would make her death easier. I'll get some for you," Blaise said firmly.

"When? Her pain is very bad."

"I'll go now," Blaise told Sabine. "I can be back with morphine by tonight." He turned to Aurore. *"Cousine,* would you like to go to Dakar with me this afternoon?"

"Oh, yes!" She exploded, then quickly got hold of herself. "Why not?" she shrugged. "I have nothing better to do."

Blaise and Sabine both laughed at her inconsistency.

Later, beside Blaise in his speedboat, her red hair streaming behind her as it was whipped by the breeze, Aurore spied Dakar Point, the promontory that deflects the fury of the Atlantic from the harbor. Without Dakar Point, Blaise explained to her, the natural deep-water cove that is the port of Dakar would not exist. Because of it, the largest tankers and ocean liners could be accommodated in the deep waters of this harbor. "And over there are the headquarters of the De Beausoleil Shipping Company." He indicated the docks.

Aurore saw a cluster of huge warehouses, spacious piers, and hulking tankers surrounded by smaller boats. Dominating the scene was a modestly tall, very new office building of gleaming white concrete. On closer inspection, Aurore saw that it was not quite completed yet. Still, a French tricolor flew from a flagpole in front of it and a sign identified it as the De Beausoleil Shipping Company.

Aurore was impressed. How strange it seemed that

such an imposing sight should bear her name! And Blaise owned and operated the company. He must be very, very wealthy indeed!

A few moments later they docked, and the smooth motion of the speedboat was replaced by the jerky, bouncing progress of a taxi on its way to the Hotel Deauville.

Dakar! Its culture-mingling, cosmopolitan atmosphere made Aurore feel alive and tingling. Wicked Dakar, the Paris of Africa, with its wealth of forbidden pleasures which Steven Parker had hinted at and which Aurore longed to investigate with all the pent-up *joie de vivre* of a healthy young girl.

The Hotel Deauville, with its elegant marble facade, its baroque gargoyles, and scampering cupids, would have looked quite natural on the Champs-Elysées. The French doorman helped her from the cab with a light touch of his white-gloved hand. The lobby was sumptuous and serene, with sounds muted by velvet-covered walls and light refracted through cut-glass chandeliers modeled after those of the palace at Versailles. Aurore's sandals sank into deep, rich carpets as they walked past overstuffed couches and chairs on their way to the front desk. Her green eyes widened at such luxury.

Blaise picked up his messages at the desk and guided Aurore to the bank of elevators. "My mother and sister and I have three large connecting suites of rooms here," he told her. "Part of it's for business, and part of it's so that Maman and Delphine can entertain. My mother is visiting friends on Cap Vert today, so I'm afraid you won't meet her. But my sister Delphine is having one of her afternoon salons. We'll look in on her."

"Won't we be intruding?"

"Not as long as I pay the bills we won't. Besides, Minette Fourier will be there."

A flash of jealousy shot through Aurore, though she could not justify it.

"And since Minette grew up in Dakar, she can recommend a doctor to write a prescription for morphine."

Blaise produced a key as they got off the elevator. He opened a door at the end of the hallway and stood aside for Aurore to enter.

Her way was blocked by an Arab manservant in an immaculate white tunic. When he saw Blaise, he stepped back and bowed deeply.

"Abdul." Blaise nodded curtly. "What's happening? Are my sister and Mademoiselle Fourier holding court?"

"No, sir. They are having coffee in the south parlor. I believe they are waiting for more arrivals before joining the guests."

"Good. Then we can catch them before they're knee deep in social chatter. Come along." He led Aurore down a long hallway to another room.

Aurore thought it was the most beautiful chamber she had ever seen. Its pale green striped wallpaper created an aura of coolness that was carried through by the delicately crafted gold and white furniture. At the same time, the beautiful Aubusson carpets with their rose tones lent an air of intimacy. An original Degas hung on one wall and two superb Renoir prints on another. The rich, silk draperies and the cushions on the chairs and sofa reechoed the pale, cool green of the walls.

At the far end of the room, two women were sipping Turkish coffee at a small round table. The demitasse cups they raised to their lips were as delicate as dolls' cups, the rims crested with gold leaf.

"Blaise!" Aurore recognized the brunette who called out his name from her pictures on the society pages of the Dakar newspapers. It was Minette Fourier. She stood and glided toward Blaise with open arms. She was taller than Aurore and had the slim, long-legged figure of a fashion model. There were poise and self-assurance in her every movement.

Grudgingly Aurore thought to herself that Minette Fourier was even more beautiful in person than in her photographs. Her skin was flawless, her violet eyes large and black-lashed, her mouth pouty and sensual. She wore an afternoon dress of the softest chiffon that clung to her small, high breasts and slim hips and showed off her long, silk-sheathed legs. Its fresh, orchid-pink color made Minette resemble an exotic flower.

Minette melted into Blaise's arms. As they tightened around her, Aurore could see the muscles rippling under his silken sleeves. The intimacy of their embrace was such that Aurore knew instinctively that they were lovers. She felt an unreasoning despair.

Delphine smiled at Aurore from the table. In the seven years since the photograph of Aurore's Marseilles relatives had been taken, Delphine had matured delightfully into young womanhood. She was petite and fashionably slim, but her figure had its proper share of feminine curves. The pale blue of her dress matched her eyes—a less aggressive shade than Blaise's—and accentuated the delicacy of her pink-and-white complexion and curly golden hair.

When Blaise introduced Aurore as their cousin, Delphine's blue eyes widened. She moved quickly to Aurore and embraced her. Aurore caught the fragrance of violets.

"Your *cousin?*"

The inflection in Minette Fourier's sultry voice punctured Aurore's composure like a spear. She was suddenly and painfully aware of her bare arms and legs, of her dusty feet in their simple rope sandals. Her *boubou* with its bold orange-and-white pattern was sadly out of place in this hothouse atmosphere. Somehow her very voluptuousness felt vulgar.

"But she's not—!" Minette started to say something else and then stopped abruptly.

White! Aurore had no trouble filling in the missing word. That her skin was almost as fair as Minette's made no difference here; her garb labeled her. To some *toubabs* a few drops of African blood was quite enough to define a "native."

Delphine moved quickly to fill the silence. She put her arm around Aurore's waist and led her to the table.

"How did you two find each other?" she asked, reaching for the samovar and a clean cup and saucer.

It was Blaise who answered. "I went out to Ile Celeste to look over the château. I left early and I hadn't had much sleep last night after that party, so after I went through the place, I stretched out to take a nap in one of the upstairs bedrooms. That's where Aurore found me."

"Sleeping Beauty." Delphine laughed and handed Aurore a steaming, fragile bone china cup perched on a flower-shape saucer.

"Indeed?" Minette raised an eyebrow. "And were you sleeping in the nude as always, darling?"

It was meant both as a reminder of past intimacies and the establishment of a claim. But to Aurore, it seemed so uncannily on target that she swallowed the bitter black Turkish coffee the wrong way and was seized by a choking fit. Her cheeks flushed with embarrassment. It was as if Minette had actually caught her in the act of staring at Blaise's nakedness.

"I see that you were." Minette's eyes sparkled dangerously as she turned from Aurore to Blaise. "I can only imagine what happened then," she added. Her manner was perfectly composed. There was even a look of amusement turning up the corners of her petulant mouth. And yet Aurore could recognize Minette's anger as clearly as if the French beauty had slapped her in the face.

"Nothing happened." Blaise cut her speculations short with a curt reply. "I got dressed. That's all."

"Are you sure, darling?" Minette's tone was light, but the sparkle in her eyes was now a jealous, smoldering flame.

"I'm sure." This time Blaise's tone was backed up by a glance as hard and cold as ice.

Minette bowed her head as if in acceptance of what he said. When she raised it again, her eyes were calm and her composure was restored. "It was thoughtful of you to bring your cousin back with you so that she might make her debut in society," she said lightly.

"Some other time. Right now I need your help, Minette. Can you recommend a doctor in Dakar that I might talk to right away? It's for my aunt on Ile Celeste. Aurore's mother."

Minette thought for a moment. "Aurore's mother." A dimple flashed in her cheek and then disappeared. It was as if she'd had a mildly amusing thought and then relegated it to its proper place. "You're in luck, darling. An old friend of my family, Doctor Pierre Duchamps from Thiès, is visiting Dakar. I told him to drop by this afternoon."

Delphine stood up. "It's time I was greeting my guests," she said. "Come along, Blaise, and Minette can introduce you to the doctor."

She linked her arm with Aurore's and led the way from the room. Aurore cast a frightened backward glance at Blaise, just in time to see Minette take his arm, before she was swept along to the party.

The room they entered was three or four times as large as the one they had left. It was crowded with men in tropical suits and white silk sport jackets and with women in diaphanous afternoon gowns similar in style to the ones worn by Delphine and Minette. A bar and a series of tables stretched out along one long wall. The tables were arranged with displays of crustless watercress sandwiches, hot hors d'oeuvres, petits fours, and an array of bite-size pâtisseries.

Aurore felt like a piece of burlap afloat in a sea of organdy and chiffon. The muted laughter and the polite voices, the combined aromas of ladies' perfumes and cigarette smoke and liquor disoriented her so much that she felt almost dizzy. Her rope sandals kept catching on the thick carpeting, and she clutched at Delphine's arm for support.

Delphine seemed to sense her discomfort, and even as she was greeting her guests she made small talk with Aurore to put her at ease. It was true that this new cousin of hers stuck out like a sore thumb, thanks to the garish colors of that African garment she was wearing. But it was also true that her beauty and her shapely figure would have made her stand out anyway. Aurore sensed that while Delphine was absorbed in her role as society hostess, she was also trying to be kind to her.

When Delphine spoke about Steven Parker, though, it was not because she was trying to put Aurore at ease. Aurore could hear the intensity in Delphine's voice that said her interest in Parker was not merely casual.

"Steven mentioned dining with you and your family on Ile Celeste," she said. "He said you were beautiful. He was right."

"Thank you. He was the one who told me that members of my family were in Dakar." Aurore didn't tell Delphine that Parker had offered to show her around Dakar, or that he had kissed her. Delphine, she suspected, might not be pleased.

"You haven't by any chance seen Steven today, have you?"

"No."

"Oh. I thought he might have stopped off at Ile Celeste. He went fishing with some friends of his." Delphine smiled, and her face lit up like that of an exquisite blond doll. "Ladies not included, so that left me out. I did, however, have the honor of providing the boat. Or, I should say, Blaise did, although he doesn't know it. The boat I loaned Steven actually belongs to the company." Delphine had been talking very quickly in a voice that was somewhat brittle. Now, however, she paused and turned to Aurore and asked seriously, "What do you think of Steven?"

"He was very nice. I liked him. He was so American. And idealistic, too, I thought."

"And attractive?"

"Oh, yes. I did think he was attractive."

"Devilishly attractive!" Delphine's laugh was like bubbles rising in champagne.

Aurore was saved from having to answer by Blaise

beckoning them to join him. He and Minette were standing with a short, dapper, portly man wearing an impeccably tailored off-white suit. The man's pencil-thin mustache flared toward his wide nostrils in a smile as Minette introduced Delphine. The smile vanished when Aurore was presented. Minette looked amused.

"I'm so glad you could drop by, Dr. Duchamps," Delphine told him warmly.

"Call me Pierre." His manner toward Delphine was ingratiating.

"This is the sick woman's daughter." Blaise introduced Aurore. "We'd like you to examine her mother to confirm the cancer diagnosis."

"This lady's mother?" The doctor nodded coldly toward Aurore. The sneer that curled his lips identified the *boubou* she was wearing as a "native" garment. "An African woman?"

"That's right."

"I'm sorry, I don't treat natives."

A look of satisfaction flitted across Minette Fourier's face.

Aurore's cheeks burned. She supposed she should have felt humiliated. She didn't. What she felt was rage.

"I didn't quite get that, Doctor." Blaise cupped his hand to his ear. "What did you say?" His tone was mild, seemingly disinterested.

"I don't treat native patients. It's not that I'm prejudiced, you understand. I just don't practice that kind of medicine."

" 'That kind of medicine'?" Blaise repeated.

"Yes. It's a whole different business treating blacks. They're not like us, you know."

"In what way are they different?"

"It's too technical to go into just now, monsieur. If you're really interested, perhaps we can get together one evening while I'm in Dakar and I'll explain it to you."

"I wouldn't want to spoil your vacation with shop-talk," Blaise said in a voice that was smooth and silky.

"I appreciate your consideration. Come visit me in Thiès sometime, then."

"We'll see." Blaise smiled. Aurore couldn't be sure, but she thought she detected a strange and dangerously savage light in his narrowed eyes.

"At your pleasure," Dr. Duchamps told him.

"There is, however, another favor I'd like to ask you," Blaise said. "I wonder if you could write me a prescription for some morphine?"

The doctor frowned. "Is it for the same native woman?" he inquired.

"Yes."

"I realize that there is a relationship by marriage involved, monsieur, and I would certainly like to help you, but I fear I can't."

"Why is that, Doctor?" The edge in Blaise's voice was so slight that the doctor didn't notice it.

"A matter of principal. I'm not only a doctor, I'm also a Frenchman. I have an obligation to keep narcotics out of the hands of blacks."

"Even sick blacks?"

"There is no guarantee that the drug would stay with the sick woman. Suppose she died? Then the drug might get into other black hands, and the first thing you know, we'd have natives running amok all over Ile Celeste. Perhaps even Dakar."

"Is there a drug problem in Dakar with the blacks?" Delphine asked innocently.

"No, mademoiselle. And you may be sure that the reason there isn't is that the members of my profession exercise the utmost caution. Even at the risk," he added, "of antagonizing the brother of a lady so attractive as yourself."

"I would guarantee that the morphine didn't fall into the wrong hands," Blaise assured him, a restrained note of impatience—and perhaps dislike—in his voice now. "If you will just be so good as to write the prescription."

"You force me to be brutally frank, monsieur. I cannot prescribe morphine for any black, no matter how ill. They are not like whites, you see. They don't have our resistance to addiction. Believe me, monsieur, if you give her morphine, she will be a confirmed addict within just a few days. That's how they are."

"That's not true!" Aurore exclaimed hotly.

Blaise silenced her with a motion of his hand. "Suppose she is?" he said. "She's dying anyway. If addiction to morphine makes her last days more comfortable, what difference does it make?"

"I'm sorry, monsieur." The doctor obviously felt he was being pressured beyond the bounds of politeness. "I don't prescribe for *macacos*. If you'll excuse me." He started to turn away from Blaise.

"I won't!" The two words rang out over the hum of voices in the room like a gunshot. Heads turned.

"Your pardon, monsieur?" The doctor was puzzled. When he looked at Blaise's face, he was suddenly afraid. A thin film of perspiration broke out on his balding scalp.

"I won't excuse you. Not for referring to my aunt as a *macaco*, a nigger. Not for refusing to treat her. Not for being a guest of my sister's. Not for being a Frenchman. Not for calling yourself a doctor when what you are is a disgrace to your profession. And most of all, not for making me angry enough to dirty my hands on you." And so saying, Blaise stepped up to Dr. Pierre Duchamps, took him by the shoulders, twirled him quickly around, and grasped him by the seat of his pants and the neck of his expensive jacket. He lifted him from the floor and propelled him across the room. "Come along, *Cousine*," he told Aurore. "We're leaving. We'll put out this garbage on our way."

The stylish crowd gave way before Blaise. The doctor sputtered incoherently as he was borne helplessly toward the door. As she followed in Blaise's wake, Aurore noticed that Minette did not look quite so pleased anymore.

"Blaise is so damned impetuous," Delphine told Aurore as she left. "If Maman were here, she'd be furious with him for making such a scene."

"I think he's magnificent!" Aurore said truthfully.

"Yes. Well, you're not his sister." Delphine kissed her quickly on the cheek and returned to calm her guests.

Aurore had to hurry to catch Blaise at the elevator. There was an elderly, distinguished-looking French couple in the car as they boarded it. They looked at the doctor squirming in Blaise's grasp and their mouths fell open.

"A sneak thief," Blaise told them. "Caught him rifling my rooms."

The doctor frothed incoherently.

"You should screen whom you let into your hotel more carefully," Blaise called out to the assistant manager behind the desk as he thrust the doctor across the lobby.

"But Monsieur de Beausoleil, Dr. Duchamps is registered here!"

"Not anymore he isn't. He's checking out." As the doorman held open the door for him, Blaise picked the doctor up, held him horizontally by his pants and the nape of his neck, swung him backward, and then threw him out of the hotel so hard that the doctor landed in the pile of garbage further down the block at the service entrance of the hotel. "Get us a taxi," Blaise told the doorman, dusting off his hands.

"Where to, monsieur?" the driver asked Blaise when they were in the cab.

"Sandaga Market."

"Why are we going to Sandaga Market?" Aurore asked him.

"To see a gentleman named Mustapha Hakim."

"I've heard of him." Aurore remembered the conversation between Cherif and Amin and Steven Parker. "Will he sell us morphine without a prescription?"

"The prescription isn't important to Hakim. Only the price is."

"Cherif—Amin Baye's brother—says this Mustapha Hakim is a Lebanese bloodsucker."

"An apt description." Blaise laughed. "But perhaps a bit unfair. Hakim isn't evil, only amoral. He believes that all things under the sun have their value in money. This includes drugs, guns, diamonds, oil, two-hundred-year-old brandy, twelve-year-old virgins, young boys—whatever it is the buyer wants, Hakim's pride is that he can provide it for the right price."

"He sells children for sex?" Aurore shuddered.

"He might tell you that they are better off that way than starving to death. Hakim is amoral, but he does have his rationales. And he may cheat outrageously on the price, but never on the merchandise."

"He still sounds revolting to me."

"I find him rather amusing. I'm intrigued by his Dakar shopkeeper philosophy."

The cab had entered the avenue Jaureguiberry and was crawling up its length. Looking out the window, Aurore saw the panorama of the Sandaga Market. The avenue was lined with booths and stalls with awnings over them as well as plain wooden barrows laden with merchandise and simple mats laid out on the ground to display assorted wares. There were textile merchants offering colorful silks and printed cottons, gold and carnelian dealers, shoemakers, sellers of fresh vegetables and flowers, readymade clothing vendors offering dashikis and *boubous* and English-made suits and loincloths and silk stockings, food stalls groaning with couscous and crepes and other African and French delicacies. She spied the famous Cour des Maures, the area that housed some twenty or more Mauritanian silversmiths, fine craftsmen easily recognized by their bouffant pantaloons and the huge blue or black turbans they wound around their heads.

They got out of the taxi in front of the Sandaga Market Building, a huge, ocher-hued edifice of Sudanese design. As they entered, Aurore's nostrils were assailed by the strongly mingled aromas of human sweat, goat dung, pungent spices and herbs, raw fish and cooked rice and—as everywhere in Senegal—peanuts. Blaise brushed away the insistent tradesmen who tried to detain them as they made their way through the crowd. Everywhere there was the rise and fall of haggling voices. Finally they came to a curtained doorway.

Blaise spoke familiarly to the turbaned young man guarding it. Aurore was impressed by the guard. He was bare to the waist, and his oiled, ebony arms were bulging with muscles. Stuck into his belt was a crescent-shape dagger, its sharp blade gleaming wickedly.

They were admitted to a small, dim room cluttered with cartons, filing cabinets, and safes. The guard remained behind them. Facing them on the other side of the room was a large wooden desk scarred by the butts of many cigarettes and cigars. Leaning back in a swivel chair behind the desk was Mustapha Hakim.

His plump body was encased in a dingy tan linen suit, its vest partially opened. His hands—small, pudgy, beringed—were folded neatly over the rounded bulge of his potbelly. His soft, Arabic features were marked by pouches of dissipation under the eyes and determined jowls. His liquid brown eyes were hooded, their expression dispassionate—incurious, even—as if nothing they saw could surprise them. Aurore couldn't guess his age; he seemed neither young nor old.

"Monsieur de Beausoleil," he greeted Blaise. Then his eyes fell lazily on Aurore and lingered there.

"Mustapha Hakim, Aurore de Beausoleil." Blaise introduced them.

"De Beausoleil? My congratulations. The bride is exquisite. When was the ceremony?"

"We're not married," Blaise told him dryly.

"Ahh! Well, marriage is never the happiest of relationships. So many interesting alternatives . . . Still, the name—?"

"Aurore is my cousin."

"Of course she is. How could I have been so stupid?" One pudgy hand slapped against his forehead. "Cousin is a much more satisfying relationship than husband or wife. Although as for myself, I prefer niece. I have so many nieces whose companionship is a never-ending joy to me—"

"I really am his cousin," Aurore heard herself insisting.

"Of course you are, dear lady," Hakim replied with a cynical grin.

"Well, I am."

"Never mind, Aurore."

"That's right. Never mind, dear lady. Whatever the relationship is, you make a most attractive couple. Where do you find such beauty?" he asked Blaise. "First Mademoiselle Fourier, and now this lady. Which reminds me, how is Mademoiselle Fourier?" His eyes lit up like those of a falcon marking its prey.

"Minette is fine. We just left her."

"I envy you. Please be sure to give her my regards the next time you see her. On the other hand, if you are going to be occupied with your cousin, perhaps I should convey them to her myself. What do you think?"

"I won't be that occupied."

"Ah. What a pity. I'll just have to be patient then, won't I?" He emitted a sigh of resignation and then, quite suddenly, he seemed to bubble with good humor once again. "What can I sell you? Munitions? Documents? Information?"

"These aren't the old days, Hakim. The war is over."

"And may Allah be blessed that the right side won," Hakim intoned piously.

"You'd say that no matter which side won."

"But of course. That is because the winning side is always the right side."

"Hakim and I did some business during the war," Blaise explained to Aurore. "He also did business with the Germans and the Vichy French."

"But you make that sound like such a negative thing,"

Hakim said in an injured voice. "You forget how I cheated them. And you forget that I also did business with the British and the Americans. Ahh, the Americans . . ." He intoned. "So generous. It was always a pleasure to do business with them."

"He stole them blind," Blaise told Aurore.

"How can you say that? Ask any one of them and he will tell you of the bargains he found through Mustapha Hakim."

"I'll ask Steven Parker," Aurore blurted out.

"Ah, so you know young Parker? Such a wholesome American lad, is he not? A friend of your sister's, I believe," he added to Blaise.

"They see each other. But let's get down to business, Hakim. It's getting late. I need some morphine."

Hakim raised an inquiring eyebrow ever so slightly toward Aurore.

"It's not for me," Aurore protested. "It's for my mother."

"Of course it is."

"She's dying of cancer."

"So sad. So very sad." He closed his eyes and sighed. "How much will you need?"

Blaise told him.

"That is not very much. Why don't you take more? I'll make you a special price."

"I don't think I'll need more. If I do, I'll come back."

"The price is going up all the time," Hakim warned him. "Why not take more now?"

"But what for?" Aurore asked.

"You never can tell. Emergencies. A party, perhaps. I'm told it goes very well with palm wine."

"Just sell me what I asked for," Blaise told him.

"Very well." He picked up the telephone on his desk and dialed lazily, his rings flashing. An instant later, he was chattering crisp Lebanese into the mouthpiece. "It will be here in twenty minutes," he assured Blaise when he hung up.

They waited. A wooden ceiling fan whirred monotonously, stirring but not cooling the warm air. The too-sweet smell of pomade wafted to Aurore's nostrils from Hakim's slicked-down hair. The silence was short before he spoke again.

"I understand," he said to Blaise, "that you are negotiating with Amin Baye to haul the fishing catch from Ile Celeste to Dakar."

"How the devil—?" Blaise seemed both amused and impressed.

Hakim smiled enigmatically.

"Parker," Blaise guessed. "Parker must have seen Amin today and then told you."

Hakim shrugged. "Perhaps. It doesn't matter. What does matter is that I think I may have a much more lucrative use for your small boats. And not just the few that are refrigerated, either."

"Such as?" Blaise was noncommittal.

"The shipping rates of the Dakar-Niger Railroad are outrageous!" Hakim changed mood quite suddenly. Now he was righteously indignant. "They get away with it because they have a monopoly on overland shipping. It is breaking the backs of the small farmers who must use the railroad to ship their produce to market! It is a crime!" He pounded the desk with a pudgy fist, then winced at the force of the blow.

"I know how concerned you are with the plight of the Senegalese farmers," Blaise replied skeptically.

Hakim disregarded his attitude. "If you would provide boats to ship produce down the Senegal and Gambia rivers, we could cut into the railroad's business substantially. We could undercut their rates. We could break their monopoly."

" 'We'?"

"But of course. We would be partners. It so happens that I am part owner of a fleet of trucks. Your boats can bring the produce to the river docks, but it would still have to be trucked inland for distribution to the bush villages. You supply the boats. I supply the trucks. We will be partners.''

"We will, will *we?* But tell me, Hakim, how are *we* going to truck produce inland when there isn't a decent road outside of the major cities in all of Senegal?''

"The French colonial government will build the roads,'' He said nonchalantly.

"They haven't built a road since the automobile was invented. Why should they do it now?''

"Progress. They will see that it is necessary to progress.''

"The hell they will. What they'll see is the shares they hold in the railroad and they won't build a bicycle path if it looks like it might cost them a tenth of one percent off next year's dividends.''

"They are like all men and therefore they are greedy,'' Hakim agreed. "But that is the very reason they will build the roads. One has but to know the relevant palms to be crossed with golden shares in our company. I will see to that. The roads will be built. All you have to do is deliver the goods on your boats.''

"I can see it now.'' Blaise was unconvinced. "My boats sitting at various coastal docks and inland river ports all over Senegal, stinking up the air with rotting produce while you're getting the roads built.''

"Why don't you have more faith in me?'' Hakim asked in an injured tone.

"Maybe because I know a few things you haven't mentioned. For one thing, you have a vested interest in a *jihad,* an all-out religious revolution, because your most lucrative operation is the illegal sale of munitions. If you could get the roads built, that's what you'd be transporting over them, not produce. And by fouling up the railroad's distribution of food, you'd make a lot of people hungry, which would speed up the start of the *jihad* and make your gun-smuggling operations four or five times as profitable as they are now.''

"You do me an injustice.'' Hakim didn't seem angry, only terribly sad. "Do you think that I have to do anything to spark a rebellion? High-handed French policy and the insensitivity and stupidity of te administrators will bring one about without outside instigation. No, monsieur. I will not make the revolution. The French will make it for me.''

"You're probably right there," Blaise grunted.

There was a soft knock at the door. The guard took a small package from a hand that reached through the curtains and gave it to Hakim.

"How much?" Blaise inquired.

Hakim named a figure.

"You're out of your mind. Come on, Aurore, we're going. Hakim's greed has made him foolish."

"Don't be hasty!" Hakim told Blaise. "It was a joke. We are friends, aren't we? For friends, I have special prices."

"Name it."

He did. It was half the original figure.

"You want to play games. You don't want to be serious." Blaise started for the door again.

"It is for a dying woman. Isn't that what you said? I am touched with sadness at this circumstance. And so I shall forgo all profit. You can have the morphine for—" He thought for a long moment and then named a figure that was roughly one third of the first price he had mentioned.

"Too much," Blaise told him.

"But how can you quibble when the woman is in pain?"

"It's her pain," Blaise said coldly.

Shocked, Aurore stared at him.

"When the woman is dying!" Hakim said plaintively.

"At those prices, let her die!"

"Blaise!" Aurore exclaimed.

"Stay out of this, Aurore. Here's what I'll pay, Hakim." Blaise offered half of Hakim's last figure.

"It costs me more than that," he whined.

"You're lying through your teeth. I know what morphine goes for on the street."

It took another ten minutes of haggling before the deal was finally concluded. "Please be so good as to remember me to Mademoiselle Fourier," Hakim asked Blaise as he bowed them out.

They left the building and walked toward the outskirts of the marketplace in search of a cab. Aurore was silent. Blaise looked at her quizzically. "You're angry because of my haggling with Hakim," he said. "I'm sorry, Aurore. But it's the only way to deal with him. I could have paid his price and it wouldn't have mattered to me much this time. But next time or the time after, it might matter a great deal and Hakim would trade on my weakness. No, in the long run, I couldn't afford to give an inch. I had to be as unfeeling as he is."

"Well, thank you for getting the morphine for Maman, anyway."

The cab took them swiftly to the docks. It was dusk, and the lights were beginning to go on in the city as Blaise steered the speedboat through the harbor. It had been a long, exhausting day and Aurore dozed in the seat beside him before the boat entered the channel between the mainland and Ile Celeste.

Suddenly Blaise was shaking her awake. "Get down on the floor!" he commanded.

"Why? What's the matter?" Aurore was having trouble orienting herself in the darkness that had fallen. Then she made out the shapes of two boats coming toward them in the pale moonlight. A stream of small, bright, red-and-white lights were trailing the one in front like a swarm of fireflies. "What's that?" she asked Blaise.

"Tracers. From a machine gun. Now get down!"

She did as he said. A moment later, he was kneeling beside her but cautiously peering over the side of the speedboat to observe what was happening. "It's the harbor police," he told her. "And," he added after a moment, "that boat they're shooting at is one of mine!"

The sharp sounds of the discharging bullets receded into the distance. Blaise stood up, and Aurore followed his example. He had cut the motor, and they were bobbing gently in the water. The streaking lights of the tracers were no longer to be seen. It seemed very quiet now. Blaise took a pair of binoculars from the speedboat's glove compartment and focused them on the two boats.

"They've boarded my boat," he said. "They're searching it." His tone was grim.

Aurore was attracted by a sound in the black water. She peered through the darkness of the night. "Blaise!" she exclaimed. "Someone's swimming toward us!"

"Someone off my boat," Blaise guessed. He pulled the life preserver from under the seat, checked that its rope was securely attached to the speedboat, and then stood up to throw it toward the swimming man.

He was too slow. Before he could throw it, the swimmer was at the side of the speedboat, his limbs gleaming ghostly white in the moonlight. His hands sought a grip and he peered up into their faces.

"Howdy, ma'am." The wet, freckled face split into a grin at the sight of Aurore. "You're an angel of mercy come out of the dark night to save my hide, and I want you to know it's a real pleasure to be meeting you again."

As he hoisted himself into the speedboat, Aurore found herself smiling back at a dripping Steven Parker.

CHAPTER 4

The wedding date had been set. Odile's one wish was to see her eldest daughter as a bride, and in view of her terminal condition, Amin's father had agreed to waive the customary waiting period. Sabine and Amin would be married in two weeks.

Excitement swept the village. It was not every day that the eldest son of the chief, the chief-to-be, took an *awa*. There were many preparations to be made, and the time was short. As sister of the bride, Aurore was particularly busy.

She didn't mind the distraction; it kept her from fretting over the three men in her life. Although Cherif was the bridegroom's brother and Aurore the bride's half-sister, they had been avoiding each other since the night of the *sabar*. Steven Parker had made no effort to see her after his narrow escape from the harbor police. And as for Blaise, while he had twice called with more morphine for Odile, his visits had been quite brief and annoyingly devoid of any special attentions to her. On both occasions, he had been in a hurry to check on the workmen's progress at the château and to get back to Dakar and the complexities of his shipping business.

If Aurore was feeling neglected, she could nevertheless look forward to seeing all three men at the wedding celebration. Blaise had been asked as a courtesy after he and Amin signed the agreement for the De Beausoleil Shipping Company to transport the fish caught by the men of Ile Celeste. And Amin had developed a close relationship with Steven Parker that made the American's invitation automatic.

Sabine was concerned about both Blaise and Parker being at the wedding. "There may be hard feelings between them," she told Aurore. "After all, the boat seized by the harbor police belonged to the De Beausoleil Shipping Company, and it was Steven Parker who borrowed it from Delphine."

"Blaise knew that."

"Yes. But he did not know that the boat was being used to transport guns from the mainland to Ile Celeste."

"Really?" Aurore was surprised. "But how do you know that?"

"From Amin. The guns were for him. He bought them from Mustapha Hakim to arm Ile Celeste. He is convinced that a *jihad* against the French is only a matter of time. He wants his people to be ready."

"But Amin does business with the French. He does business with Blaise."

"Yes. And he has even told me that he likes Blaise personally. But it will make no difference if there is a *jihad*. Amin feels too much bitterness toward the French to let personal considerations sway him. And yet my beloved is not consistent. He feels badly about losing the guns, of course, but he also feels sorry that by taking advantage of Blaise's sister, Parker has caused Blaise to lose one of his boats."

"Blaise will probably be able to get it back," Aurore reassured her sister. "He seems to know his way around the *toubabs*. He has influence."

"I hope so." Sabine stood. "I must leave, Aurore. I am going to Dakar with the dressmaker this afternoon, to the Sandaga Market to choose the material for my wedding dress."

These days Sabine was always on the move, darting from sessions with the Ile Celeste seamstress to meetings with Amin to check progress on the dwelling being erected for the newlyweds, and then to endless consultations with Idrissa Baye, the *badyen*, or mistress of ceremonies, for the nuptials. Idrissa Baye was Amin's aunt, the chief's sister. She was a plump woman of middle years with many gold teeth, the harsh voice and determined stride of a drill sergeant, and the sentimental nature of a child. It was she who would coordinate the various aspects of the wedding: the music and dancing; the costumes and movements of the bride, groom, and attendants; and the vast assortment of food and drink for the wedding feast, which would start in the early morning and last all the way through to the dawn of the following day.

All the village women were preparing for the coming event now. Some women worked their mortars and pestles far into the day instead of just at early morning, grinding the kernels of grain into flour that would be used for fritters, dumplings, crepes and cakes. Other women prepared mangrove honey and ginger flavored with various herbs. In the heat of the afternoon, they gathered in the shade to work on their wedding costumes. Yards of bright cotton and silks spangled with silver and gold thread were cut and stitched into snugly wrapped skirts and flowing *boubous*, while the women gave each other advice on which fabric to choose for a contrasting *mousor* or headdress. Little girls strung shells and beads into necklaces, as intent on beautifying themselves as their mothers were.

When her mother took a long nap, Aurore would come out to join the village women and lend a hand where she could. But usually she sat near Odile and put the finishing touches on her own emerald green gown. She was looking forward to the wedding for many reasons, not the least of which was that Blaise would be there. She hoped to dazzle him with her fine green silk *boubou* and the golden bangle bracelets that had been a gift from her father on her thirteenth birthday. She planned to wear her hair in a sophisticated upswept style. She had been experimenting with it in front of the small tarnished mirror over the washtub. With a few wavy tendrils caressing her neck and with a lush, fragrant gardenia pinned behind one delicate ear, Aurore thought her coiffure quite stylish in the manner of the French ladies she had seen at Delphine's salon.

"Aurore, *chérie*." Her mother's faint voice broke into Aurore's thoughts. "You know how pleased I am about Sabine and Amin."

"Yes, Maman."

"If I could see you married as well, then my joy would be complete."

Aurore did not know what to answer.

"One day soon you will be alone, without a father's or a mother's protection."

"Don't speak like that, Maman. The medicine—"

"The tablets cannot cure me; they merely relieve the pain. Please, *chérie*"—Odile held up one thin hand to stop Aurore's further protests—"I do not fear death. It is Allah's will that I die now; I can only accept it. My one worry is for you, so headstrong, so wild, my Aurore. Even when you were children, I thought of Sabine as the lake—calm, placid, self-contained. And you were the waterfall—tumbling, turbulent, rushing heedlessly. And now more than ever I wonder where your wild heart will lead you."

"I don't know that myself, Maman. One day I feel one way, and the next day I wake up feeling completely different and wanting something else. In a way, I envy Sabine because her life is all mapped out for her. She'll stay here on Ile Celeste among friends and relatives who love her, and she'll bear children to a husband who adores her."

"You could have the same thing. Is it not what every woman wants?"

Aurore sighed. "I do want marriage and children someday, and I love Ile Celeste and its people, yet sometimes the thought of staying here in the village all my life makes me panic. I want to see more of the world, Maman, to meet different kinds of people. That day in Dakar was so exciting!"

"What about Cherif Baye?" Odile inquired. "His

love for you shows plainly. I am sure he would marry you if you were willing.''

"I don't know if Cherif is right for me."

"Is he not handsome?"

"Yes, Maman."

"Is he not intelligent, well-educated, ambitious?"

"Yes, Maman." Aurore sighed.

"Did you not tell me many times over when you were children that you felt close to Cherif?"

"Yes, Maman, but we aren't children anymore."

"Do not take that early bond between you lightly, Aurore. Is there no love in your heart for Cherif Baye?"

Slowly Aurore raised her long-lashed green eyes until they met Odile's clouded brown ones. "I do feel a kind of love for him—but it's a calm, tame love; it's not the wild, passionate love I want to know."

"That kind of passion quickly passes, *chérie*," Odile said gently. "It's the calm, steady kind of love that lasts."

"But I don't want to miss it," Aurore cried. "I think I'd rather have the passionate, fiery love for a little while than a lifetime of the tame kind."

"You will be burned!" Odile spoke sharply. "Even as a child you would not stay away from the fire. 'The flames are so pretty, Maman,' you said. And when they singed your little fingers, you came running to me for comfort. Who will you run to when you get burned by this passionate love you hunger for, Aurore?"

"I will dry my own tears, Maman. Don't worry about me, please!" The green silk garment on her lap slid to the floor as Aurore dropped to her knees and buried her face against her mother's breast. "I want to please you, Maman, so much. But I can't marry Cherif when I'm not sure."

Odile resigned herself to leaving this world with only one of her daughters safely married. The other's fate remained a mystery, known only to Allah. She must leave Aurore in His hands. Anyway, she thought drowsily as the morphine wafted her to sleep, may Allah smile on the wedding day of my firstborn.

Allah smiled. The day was bright. From earliest dawn, the village stirred with excitement. Even before the roosters crowed, the noises from outside awoke Aurore—voices laughing, arguing, giving orders. Bare feet pounded the earth outside the house as people ran to and fro on various errands. There was the sound of hammering as the men put the finishing touches on the makeshift platforms and tables and benches they had set up in the central clearing where the wedding reception was to be held. Delicious odors from many cooking pots filled the air, and already the fresh-killed lamb was sizzling on a spit.

"Wake up! Wake up, you lazy thing! It's your wedding day!" Aurore prodded Sabine's sleeping form on the mattress next to her.

Soon their home was part of the frantic preparations as both girls washed their hair and bathed, took care of Odile, and coped with the visitors who kept coming and going. The dressmaker insisted on last-minute alterations. Idrissa Baye, in her element as *badyen*, kept coming in to report on the doings outside, to check on Sabine's intricately braided coiffure, and to offer unwanted advice.

"Sabine, dear one, surely you do not mean to wear *those* earrings. Why, they are not even gold, only brass, and what will people think?"

"They will think that Amin couldn't afford to buy his bride gold earrings," Aurore said impishly.

"Aurore!" Sabine chided her. "As if this beautiful gold necklace Amin gave me was not enough."

"I have a pair of gold earrings you can borrow," Idrissa said, and rushed out to get them.

Another neighbor ran in with the news that the boat carrying the *imams* from Dakar had arrived. Because Amin was the chief's son, the holy men were bestowing upon them the great honor of making the boat trip to Ile Celeste in order to legalize the marriage. "Other boats have arrived also," the woman chattered. "One of them is that speedboat belonging to the *toubab* from the château."

Blaise had arrived! It was all Aurore could do not to squeal with excitement. She peered anxiously into the mirror, pinching her cheeks to redden them and adjusting the gardenia blossom in her hair. She had rushed out to pick it from the bush only moments before.

But Sabine was the important one, and now all the women gathered around to help her into her billowing gown. It was made of pure white silk shot through with silver thread. As its generous folds fell into place around Sabine's tall, slim body, Aurore thought she had never seen anyone so beautiful.

As Aurore reached out to adjust the hemline, Idrissa smacked her hand away. "Take care! You'll wrinkle it, you foolish girl."

Sabine shot her a look of sympathy. "Aurore, why don't you go out and enjoy the party. It will be at least another hour before Amin and I will make our appearance. As you see, I have all the help I need."

Aurore gave Sabine a quick hug before Idrissa Baye could stop her. Then she pranced out into the sunlight and down the path to the central clearing. Even from afar, the brightness of the women's sheer, shimmering *boubous* in hues of brilliant turquoise, magenta, crimson, and gold dazzled her eyes. Gold and silver jewelry gleamed against smooth flesh. The long, slender necks of the women supported head cloths in vivid prints and exotic patterns. The men, some wearing white dress tunics and others in pastel-color pants and waist-length *frocs*, provided a pleasing contrast to their bright-plumaged wives.

The musicians were seated on a special platform, playing their various instruments: the tomtom, with its insistent beat; the *balafon*, a wooden xylophone, with its pleasant rippling sound; the *cora*, a twenty-one-string lute, with its clear and subtle twang. Tiny children joined in the music making, blowing flutes made of millet stalks and shaking the "devil," two crossed pieces of wood with rattles.

Aurore paused outside the clearing, searching the milling crowd for a broad back clad in well-tailored white linen. But she didn't see Blaise. Her attention was distracted by the *griots* poised to greet each arriving guest. Every village had several *griots*—men who were a combination of musician, poet, historian, storyteller, court jester, and gossip and functioned as the village's newspaper and the keepers of its past.

"You're the prettiest girl here today, Mademoiselle Aurore!" Touti, a small, elderly *griot* with the wizened face of a monkey, made Aurore a low bow and led her into the clearing.

Aurore smiled, knowing Touti would greet every female under the age of fifty with the identical comment.

"But where is your dear mother?" he inquired. "We had hoped to see her here."

"Maman will come later, when the bride and groom make their appearance," Aurore explained.

"I hear that dear Odile is much better thanks to the medicine your cousin obtained from the mainland," Touti said with a bright, toothy smile. "Indeed, I have heard that morphine is such a good medicine that some people do not wait until illness strikes to take it." He danced away to greet some new arrivals.

Aurore wandered over to the refreshment tables. Never had she seen so much food amassed in one place. The boards groaned under their load of pots and platters heaped with every delicacy imaginable. All the Senegalese specialties were present in mouth-watering profusion— Chicken au Yassa; Tiebou dienne, a dish of fresh fish; escargots; rice, peppers, and vegetables; mafe, chicken cooked with peanut sauce; Bassi Salete, a couscous of lamb and millet; Dem à la Saint Louisienne, mullet stuffed with a spicy grain filling; accras, rich fritters with a delicate nutlike flavor; and many more.

In case the revelers still had room, there were vats of mangoes, bananas, papayas, and oranges blended with mangrove honey, bowls of spiced ginger slices, and kola nuts. Crowning it all was the cake that three women had spent a whole day creating. It had three tiers and a sugar-cream frosting.

Although it was a Muslim wedding, Wolof hospitality demanded that there be plenty of liquor for those who did not adhere to the orthodox strictures. There were kegs of beer, jugs of palm wine, and bottles of run by the case, as well as several bottles of champagne cooling in a giant bucket of ice water. Aurore had read about this expensive wine that bubbled but had never seen it. Now she stared at the green bottles.

"Have some, *ma petite cousine.*" Blaise materialized at her side, his eyes crinkling in that ironic grin of his. "It's my contribution to the occasion," he added, "and I've been waiting for someone to try it to see if it's as good as the wine merchant swore it was."

"I'm the wrong one to ask," she confessed. "I've never tasted champagne."

"Then it's time you had your first taste."

Aurore raised her head higher and nodded coolly, ashamed of her naiveté.

"Come on. Have some." Blaise removed the foil wrapping from the top of one of the bottles. He took a crisp white linen handkerchief from his pocket and unfurled it with a mocking flourish. He wrapped it around the cork, and with one deft turn of his wrist the bottle was open.

Several people exclaimed at the sudden pop. Aurore jumped backward, but not far enough. A geyser of white froth shot up from the bottle and a few drops sprayed the silken bodice of her green *boubou*.

"Oh, dear!"

"Sorry." Blaise dabbed at the droplets. His fingertips were hard and sure of themselves as they pressed into the softness of her breast. "Cold water will take it right out." He dipped the handkerchief into the champagne bucket and wrung it. Aurore swayed dizzily as one of his icy fingers grazed her hardening nipple. "That's better." His voice was soft and reassuring.

Aurore's cheeks burned with embarrassment at the same time that her breasts betrayed her with their tingling. "I can do it," she managed to say. She reached to take the cold handkerchief from him. For a moment, their fingers met on her breast. Then he surrendered the handkerchief and took his hand away.

Blaise handed her an earthenware cup half filled with champagne. "Here's to weddings and other follies." He touched his cup to hers.

Aurore hesitated.

"Go on. Your first sip of champagne. And then you'll be a woman."

Defiantly Aurore gulped a large mouthful of the bubbling wine. She was unprepared for the carbonation. The fizziness tickled her throat and she swallowed the wrong way, sending the bubbles up her nose. She sneezed and began to choke.

"I said sip, *chérie!*" Blaise thumped her on the back. "Now try again, nice and easy." His blue eyes twinkled below the quirking brows. "That's it."

This time Aurore found the taste and the sensation it produced delightful. By then, others were gathering around, eager to try this strange, bubbly beverage that seemed to explode right out of the bottle. Blaise filled their cups to overflowing, obviously enjoying his role as *sommelier*. Aurore held hers out a second and then a third time.

The champagne, combined with her exciting proximity to Blaise, made her almost late in fetching Odile. With a sigh, she excused herself and left him to round up the boys who had promised to carry Odile to the reception. As they went to get her, they passed the makeshift tent erected for the *imams*. Here they would perform the marriage by proxy, as was the custom. When Amin and Sabine made their grand entrance later, they would already be husband and wife. Then, after prayers and the "enthronement" ceremony, the dancing and feasting would begin in earnest.

Odile was soon installed on cushions in a place of honor in the central part of the clearing. A group of older women gathered around her. They bade Aurore run off and enjoy herself. Odile echoed them. Why should Aurore sit with the elders when she was so glowing with youth and vitality?

Although she would soon have to take part in the ceremony of escorting Sabine to her bridegroom, Aurore nevertheless went off in search of Blaise. Even a few public moments spent with him seemed precious. It wasn't Blaise, however, but Steven Parker whom she encountered.

"Well now, don't you look pretty as a picture!" he greeted her, his freckled face beaming with goodwill.

"Thank you."

"Isn't this something?" His gesture encompassed the party.

"Yes." Aurore looked around her. "I suppose it's very different from an American wedding," she ventured.

"It sure is!" Steven Parker was watching the brightly clad guests dancing to the rhythm of the tomtom and the *cora*. "I can't get over it that the bride and groom aren't even there at the actual wedding ceremony."

"They'll come later."

"Later, in an American wedding, is when the happy couple go off by themselves."

"That will be later still," Aurore told him. "They'll go to their new house. The *badyen* and myself and some other close friends of Sabine will go with her to help her take off her gown and ready herself for her bridegroom. We'll leave when Amin comes to her."

"I just saw him. He's in the chief's hut carrying on some kind of ritual. He's sitting on this mortar thing with an ax handle between his feet. He says it's an ancient custom to assure the bridegroom of potency. He has to stay there in that position until he comes out to claim his bride."

"That's right." Aurore spied the *badyen* signaling to her from across the clearing. "But that will be very soon now," she told Steven Parker. When she excused herself, he asked if she would dance with him later and she accepted.

Aurore and Sabine's other female attendants went to fetch her. As maid of honor, Aurore preceded the bride along the path to the clearing, while the other bridesmaids followed her in a double line. The path was covered with ceremonial cloths. The *griots* walked parallel to them, strumming their *coras* and singing praises to the lineage of the wedding families.

Beside the flower-bedecked throne, Amin waited in a richly embroidered white robe. Following ancient custom, his head was covered with a cloth that also covered his eyes. It would be lifted at the end of the brief ceremony, and then he would be able to gaze with a bridegroom's fervor at this girl he had loved since childhood, this girl who was now his wife.

The *imams* presented the legal document of marriage and gave their blessing to the newlyweds. There was a great stamping of feet and clapping of hands and cries of congratulation. Then the music began again.

Soon it built to a crescendo and everyone was dancing. Fresh supplies of food were brought to the tables, and the serious feasting began. Aurore danced with relatives and close friends, chatted with well-wishers, and sat for a while with Odile. The ailing woman, aglow with excitement, was holding up surprisingly well.

Steven Parker was beckoning her to join him for the dance she had promised. They threaded their way through the crowd toward each other. But Parker stopped as he found Blaise inadvertently blocking his way. Aurore came up behind Blaise without him seeing her. She was just in time to hear the exchange between the two men.

"Hello, Blaise." Steven Parker seemed the slightest bit flustered at the sudden encounter. "I've been meaning to get in touch with you about that business with your boat."

Blaise nodded and waited.

"Just wanted to say I was sorry about the way it worked out."

"Mmm." Blaise's response was noncommital.

"Hope you got your boat back from the harbor police without too much fuss."

"I did." Blaise's manner was courteous. His eyes, however, bored sharply into Parker's. "But they did confiscate the guns. I didn't have any explanation of how they got on my boat. I'm afraid they didn't like that—my not having an explanation. I wondered if you might have one, Parker."

The American cleared his throat and looked embarrassed. Shifting from one foot to another, his freckled face a bright pink, he seemed to Aurore like a little boy caught with his hand in the couscous pot before dinnertime. "I'm afraid I don't, Blaise," he mumbled.

"Well then, we'll just have to forget it. It's not as though I suffered any loss." Blaise's voice was casual, his smile sunny as he turned to walk away.

Steven Parker was returning the smile with relief as Aurore stepped up to him. They were both still looking at Blaise's back when he unexpectedly turned around. "Oh, just one more thing, Parker," he said pleasantly.

"What?"

"If you ever use my sister that way again—" Blaise paused.

Parker waited.

"—I'll kill you." He turned and walked away.

"That is one tough Frenchman!" Steven shook his head ruefully and then grinned at Aurore. "Would you like a drink before we dance?" he asked her.

"I'll have a ginger punch." Aurore thought it best not to have any more champagne.

"Think I'll have something a bit stronger. Be right back."

When they'd finished their drinks, they danced. Steven selected a number with a relatively slow beat, although it was nowhere near as slow as the dance he and Aurore did to it. He didn't dance in the African fashion but rather as Aurore had seen Europeans do. He put one arm around her and held her other hand at chest level. There was no place for her free arm except around his waist. After a moment, his grip tightened and Aurore found herself pressed against him. It felt naughty but exciting, the way his hard body rubbed against hers.

His chest expanded against her breasts and his muscular thighs slid against hers. When he dipped and she swayed backward, his knee rubbed for a moment against the secret place between her legs. The hand around her waist slid downward, and she felt his fingers caressing the top of her buttocks. She was about to protest but forgot to when she realized that the thick bulge pressed against her belly was growing harder and more insistent. Trembling, she closed her eyes and gave herself up to the sensation. The hot breath in her ear became hoarse and irregular. He began to move against her in slow, hard, rhythmic circles.

"No!" Aurore moaned, knowing they should stop, yet not wanting to. "Stop," she said faintly. "Everybody can see."

It was too late. They had already been seen by at least two pairs of eyes. Blaise watched, amused, from the sidelines as a slightly drunken Cherif Baye burned with jealousy.

Cherif lurched over to them. "I want to dance with my new sister-in-law's sister," he said, slurring the words as he pushed Steven Parker aside and put his arm around Aurore possessively.

Steven started to protest.

"Please," Aurore said. The last thing she wanted was to be the cause of any trouble at Sabine's wedding.

Steven shrugged and walked away.

As Cherif guided Aurore from the dancing area, she saw Blaise watching them. She was sure he was laughing at her again. She tossed her red hair defiantly and allowed Cherif to lead her down the path away from the festivities.

"That *toubab* Parker lusts after you like a bull in the mating season!" Cherif exploded when they were alone in the woods.

Aurore shrugged.

"And you encourage him!"

"It was only a dance."

"A dance?" Cherif was furious. "I have eyes! You were making love standing up!"

"Is that worse than kneeling, the way Leita does to you?"

"What do you mean?" Cherif was taken by surprise.

"I saw the two of you on the beach the night of the *sabar*."

"Just what did you see?"

"I'm not sure. But whatever it was, dancing with Steven Parker is no worse."

"You don't know what you're saying, Aurore. And you don't know what you're doing. It's not just teasing like when we were children. You can't tease grown men that way. You can't tease Steven Parker, and you can't tease me. Grown men want more than teasing."

"Do they?" Aurore jeered. "And just what is it that they want, Cherif?"

"This." He kissed her then, and although his mouth tasted of liquor, the kiss was hot and sweet and exciting. "I love you, Aurore," he murmured in her ear. "I want you for my *awa*. I want you! I want you so much that seeing you in the arms of another man is like a knife stabbing my heart. I want you!" He kissed her again, more passionately.

"You want me," Aurore said breathlessly when the kiss was over. "But that's not the same as love, Cherif. You want Leita, too. Wanting—lust—that's not a good reason to get married."

"Don't you want me?" His fingertips began to stroke the areola of her breast through her *boubou*.

"I want something," Aurore admitted, confused and on fire with sensations she couldn't put into perspective. How was it possible to thrill to Blaise's touch, to be aroused by Steven Parker's boldness, and now to burn at Cherif's caress? How was it possible to respond to three men this way all in the same night? "I want *something,* but I'm not sure if it's just *one* someone I want it from," she told him honestly.

"That is the attitude of a *toubab*'s whore!" Cherif said angrily.

"You have no right to say that! It's truly the way I feel!"

"Then you shall have what you want." One strong arm bent her backward while his free hand whipped open her *boubou*. His mouth came down over hers again, forcing her to accept the length of his probing tongue. He groaned with lust as his hand came in contact with the warmth of her naked thighs. He forced them apart, and then he was rubbing the silken crotch of her panties.

Aurore fought to escape, but she struggled to no avail as he began to rub with a steady, circular motion that made her ache and tingle even as she pounded her fists on his chest. "Not this way, Cherif," she pleaded. "Not by forcing me."

"I am a man, not a boy, and it's time you realized it! You wanted something and you don't care from who. Well, here it is!"

Then he was wrestling her down to the ground, his knee between her thighs, prying them open. "No, Cherif! Don't! Let me go!"

They continued to struggle in silence for a moment. Suddenly the silence was disturbed by the whistling of a spirited tune close at hand. "Someone's coming!" Aurore hissed. Reluctantly Cherif let her up.

They barely had time to straighten their clothing before the whistler was upon them. It was Blaise. Seeing him, Aurore realized what it was that he was whistling:

"La Marseillaise!" He whistled the final notes with unmistakable irony.

Aurore and Cherif stared at him.

"Aren't you going to introduce me to your friend, *Cousine?*"

"I—I thought you knew each other. This is Cherif Baye. My cousin, Blaise Honoré de Beausoleil."

"Amin's brother? Well, I'm glad we finally got to meet."

"My pleasure." Cherif managed to reply.

"I—I have to go help Sabine." Aurore ran off down the trail and left the two men to themselves.

"She seems disturbed," Blaise observed.

"I was too ardent," Cherif confessed, blurting it out.

"Happens to the best of us. A bit too much to drink, a beautiful, passionate woman—still, perhaps she's too young for such sport."

"You're most understanding, monsieur," Cherif was far from feeling as composed as he tried to sound.

"My cousin's half-sister married your brother." Blaise grinned at the complexity. "In some societies, that gives me the right to offer all kinds of advice."

"I would be grateful for any you have to give me." Inside himself, Cherif was feeling rather ashamed for trying to force Aurore's affections.

"My advice isn't for you." Blaise was suddenly serious. He paused on the trail so that he might finish what he was saying before they rejoined the wedding celebration. "It's for Amin."

"I will see that he hears it."

"Good. Tell him to be wary of his association with Mustapha Hakim. I've known Hakim a long time. I had dealings with him during the war. He can be useful, but he can also be treacherous."

"But what do you know of these dealings?"

"I know Amin bought munitions from Hakim and arranged for Steven Parker to deliver them. And I know that after he'd been paid, Hakim turned around and tipped off the harbor police."

"How do you know that?"

"I had to bribe the captain of the harbor police to get my boat back. I added a little more and he told me where the tip came from to waylay the boat. You'll appreciate what I'm saying about Hakim when I tell you that the harbor police sold the guns back to him and that he will doubtless sell these very same guns to Amin again just as soon as the opportunity presents itself. A tidy scheme, isn't it?"

"I've cautioned my brother many times about Hakim. But Amin listens only to the *imams*. When they tell him it is time for the Muslims to arm themselves for a holy war against the French-Catholic infidels, Amin goes to Hakim, because he has the guns."

"And you yourself don't listen to what the *imams* say?"

"I don't trust the *imams*, although I am a Muslim. I don't forget that they cooperated with the French invaders who took possession of our country and turned it into a French colony. Now, at long last, the *imams* grow impatient under the French yoke and they tell their followers it is time for *jihad*."

"Holy war?"

"That is what it pleases them to call it. But where were the *imams* when the French used our people as cannon fodder and slave labor for their own wars?" Cherif was bitter. "Many of my people fought and died for the French cause, but now that the war is over, are any of them free?" His eyes blazed as he looked at the Frenchman.

"Why would Amin follow a bunch of religious fanatics with a history of selling out their own people?"

"I have asked Amin the same thing. The *imams* don't have the people's true interests at heart, only their own power. Look at their actions in the past, I tell him. But Amin is good at rationalizing when it comes to the *imams*—and in his dealings with people like Steven Parker and Mustapha Hakim. However, I will try to warn him against them again."

"But not tonight, I trust." Blaise smiled.

"No, I'll leave it to Sabine to take Amin's mind off *jihad* tonight," Cherif said and laughed.

Even as they spoke, Sabine was being conducted to the bridal chamber by the *badyen*, Aurore, and the other female attendants. In accordance with custom, the room was decorated completely in white, including the walls, the ceiling, and the mattress with its fresh white sheets. The women helped Sabine off with her shimmering wedding gown, making ribald remarks that sent blood rushing to Sabine's cheeks.

She went to sponge herself off at the washtub in the kitchen, allowing only Aurore to accompany her. "You seem downcast, little sister," Sabine said as Aurore handed her a cotton cloth with which to dry herself. "Can it be that you already miss your big sister?"

"Yes," Aurore replied. It was true that she would miss Sabine, and she certainly wasn't going to mar her sister's joy by telling her what had happened with Cherif. "I'm a little tired, Sabine, and I *will* miss having you sleep beside me. But I bet you'll enjoy waking up and seeing Amin instead of me!"

"How strange it will be," Sabine breathed, her face radiant. "And how wonderful."

"Delicious!" Aurore whispered intimately. "Here, rub this coconut salve into your skin. I made it myself so that you would be as soft as silk and delicious-smelling for your husband."

"Aurore, you are sweet." Sabine rubbed the salve on her arms and legs. When she straightened up, there were tears welling in her doelike eyes. "I—I feel sad about leaving you and Maman. And I'm so nervous. How do I know I can make Amin happy? What if I do not please him?"

"You will, don't worry. You love him, and he adores you. Once he holds you and touches you, everything will be fine. You'll see," Aurore reassured Sabine as she slipped the fine cotton nightgown over her sister's head.

Sabine's supple brown body showed through the sheer white material alluringly, and all the women assured her that they had never seen such a lovely bride.

"My nephew Amin is a lucky man," the *badyen* said as she led Sabine to the bed.

"Look at her—a picture of virginal loveliness," another woman sighed.

"It's not like some other weddings I could mention, where the *badyen* had to rush in the next morning and kill a chicken so there would be blood on the sheets," one of the women said dryly.

Raucous laughter greeted her remark.

"Hush, Amin is coming," one of the women called from her position near the door.

Laughing and chattering their good wishes, the women filed from the room.

"I wish you happiness tonight and always, dear sister," Aurore said, hugging Sabine.

The all-night *bara* was still going on, but the combined rhythm of tomtom, *cora,* and *balafon* held no further attraction for Aurore. She could not bear to face Cherif again. All she wanted to do was go home, check on her mother, who had been put to bed some time ago, and go to sleep.

Aurore decided to take a short cut around the back of the village. If she went near the clearing, someone might see her and insist that she rejoin the celebration. Lost in thought, Aurore was unaware of being watched. She had forgotten that the dwelling shared by Leita Ousbane and her grandmother lay along the path she was following.

A sudden cackling sound, low, knowing, and sinister, made her start, and she looked up to find herself abreast of the *katt*'s dilapidated home. Pieces of the thatched roof had blown away, and the baked-mud walls were crumbling, but Ouna the *katt* had refused to allow the village men to repair it. Instead, she and Leita had fastened clumps of moss and ragged pieces of canvas over the holes, giving the place a wild, unkempt look that was shared by the old woman herself.

Now Ouna hovered in the doorway, holding back the sack that hung there in place of a door. The sack had been dyed red, and an assortment of fetishes had been sewn to the coarse fabric—animal teeth, clumps of fur, birds' beaks, cowrie shells, and shriveled gray things so repulsive-looking that Aurore didn't even wnat to guess what they were.

"I be waiting here for you, pretty miss," Ouna said in her garbled language, which was part Wolof, part Dyola, and part her own concoction. "I knowed you come. My magic drawed you here."

"What do you want?" Aurore was unnerved by Ouna's demented, staring eyes, her loose, leering grin. Half her teeth were missing; the rest were blackened stumps. Her frizzled gray hair stood out in wild clumps.

"You be evil slut!" Ouna screeched the epithet, her gnarled, misshapen body trembling as with palsy. "I see you with my Leita's man, getting him with fever by slut's tricks."

"He forced me into the bushes!" Aurore drew closer, her fear temporarily replaced by anger. "He tried to rape me!"

"You lie!" Ouna's bloodshot eyes bulged with the heat of her wrath so that it seemed they would pop out of her wrinkled face at any moment. "You after all the mens! Lustful she-goat! I see how you lead them on with your whore body. My Leita, she love Cherif-man. She make him her own. Then you come along! Steal him!"

"I don't have to listen to your lies and your mumbo jumbo! I'm going!"

"You'll wait, whore! Yes you will! If I don't want for you to walk, your feets do not move!"

Aurore stood still. It was as if she were frozen to the spot. But it was because she was curious to hear the rest of Ouna's ranting . . . Wasn't it?

"I put *deume* upon you, whore! Upon you and your whole family. *Ay gaaf,* you hear? Bad luck!" With a savage motion, Ouna took hold of the worn leather thong around her neck and shook it at Aurore. The necklace was strung with fetishes and amulets—bits of bone, hair, feathers, and teeth. These made a grotesque clacking sound as the *katt* jerked them to and fro.

Aurore stared, mesmerized. She shivered in the warm night air, and a cold sweat broke out on her body. With a huge effort of will, she shook her head and cleared it. Ouna was just a crazed old woman whose "magical powers" existed only in her demented mind. She was old and senile, a victim of her own delusions.

"I don't believe in your black magic," Aurore said, tossing back her hair. "Your *deume* means nothing to me. And as for wishing *ay gaaf* to my family and me, all I can say is *Asta Fourlah.* May God forgive you." Aurore turned and went swiftly along the path toward her home, leaving Ouna staring at her retreating back with her crazy, gap-toothed leer.

Although Aurore wasn't superstitious, she couldn't help thinking of Ouna's *deume,* curse, as she tended her invalid mother during the days that followed. Odile grew weaker daily, her body growing even more wasted as her stomach refused to accept the blandest of foods. Even a sip of water made her retch. Aurore didn't know how Odile would have stood the ordeal without the morphine. Her need for it had doubled and then tripled as the pain gnawing at her insides grew increasingly worse. She dozed most of the time, but it was a fitful kind of sleep, broken by moans and sudden muscle twitches that kept Aurore by her bedside in helpless sympathy.

Sabine came by every day, and for her, Aurore maintained a cheerful facade. Sabine was so obviously in love, so thrilled with her new role as wife and mistress of her own home, that Aurore could not bear to disturb her sister's joyful mood with heartache and misery. Dully she obeyed Sabine when she was ordered to go out and revive herself with fresh air and exercise. But instead of seeking the company of her friends, Aurore walked alone in the woods, gathering flowers to brighten her mother's sickroom, or waded in the lagoon alone, her thoughts never far from the sad, inevitable parting that lay ahead.

"Maman is dying." Aurore forced herself to repeat the words aloud, hoping to make the fact real and therefore acceptable. But no matter how often she repeated the sad, terse sentence, it still didn't seem real.

One night Aurore awoke with a pounding heart and a sense that something was terribly wrong. Then she heard it: an unearthly baying sound that sent trills of fear to her every nerve end. It was like the howling of a wild dog, and yet more ghostly.

It sounded again, and Aurore leaped from her mattress and flew across the room to her mother's pallet. She heard her mother's breathing—harsh and shallow— and her heart sank. With trembling hands, she lit the cloth set in its bowl of palm oil.

"Maman, do you need the morphine?"

"No." Her mother's voice was a faint whisper. "Aurore, beware of the *katt*."

"What did you say, Maman?" Aurore had heard the words, but they seemed to make no sense.

"Beware of the *katt!*" This time Odille uttered the warning in a hoarse rasp. "Come closer, Aurore. Remember what I told you about how Justin—your father— came to Ile Celeste and helped us with his medicines and his skill as a doctor?"

"Yes, Maman." Aurore tucked back her hair and knelt so that her ear would be nearer her mother's moving lips.

"Ouna hated Justin. Before he came, the people would go to her for herbs and potions; they believed her powers were magical. But after Justin came, they lost their faith in her as *facc*. She has hated us all ever since."

The baying sound came again, chilling and unearthly.

Her mother moaned. Goose bumps rose along Aurore's arms. "I'll be right back, Maman."

"Beware of the *katt!*" Odile gasped, her eyes staring and her mouth agape.

Aurore ran out into the night, grabbing a stick from the kindling pile as she passed it. The baying continued, now faint, now loud, as if its source was moving. Aurore ran back behind the cluster of thatched houses to the underbrush. She stopped and waited, all her senses alert.

Suddenly the bushes in front of her began to quiver, though there was no breeze stirring. There was a rattling noise. The bushes parted, revealing a sight so horrible that Aurore could not even scream.

The creature before her stood upright, yet its body was of thick fur. Its head was huge and monstrous, the skin a sickly, sulfurous yellow, the eyes beaded and staring, the crimson, cavernous mouth open to a roar with sharp tusks protruding from it. Slung in a rope around its thick neck were several skulls—human skulls.

Aurore's stomach contracted in fear. The ghastly creature began to move forward, toward her. Terrified, Aurore raised her stick to ward the thing off. Just then the demented mind behind the hideous masquerade gave itself away with the mindless cackling that identified Ouna.

"You—you're insane!" Aurore screamed. "Why can't you leave us alone? My mother is sick, and you wake us in the middle of the night with your crazy tricks! I'm going to tell Chief Baye how you frightened my mother and he'll—"

"You has no mother now!" Ouna's words issued from the hideous mask. "She dead, and now the *deume* working on your sister and you!"

"Go to hell!" Aurore screamed. "Hell is where you belong!"

She ran blindly home, ignoring the questions of the sleepy villagers who had been roused by the disturbance. She ran until she reached her mother's house, stumbling inside panting and sweat soaked. "Maman, are you all right?" Aurore bent over the still form.

But there was no answer, nor ever would be again. Odile de Beausoleil was dead.

And so the people of Ile Celeste awoke to sorrow that morning. Odile had been well loved, and the ritual lamentation was loud and heartfelt. Women mourned with their whole bodies, pounding their heads on the ground while their limbs jerked convulsively and wails of grief poured from their throats. Those like Sabine and Aurore, who preferred to keep their mourning more private, stayed in their homes to weep quietly. The men buried Odile that same day, as custom decreed, and those close to her entered upon their forty days of mourning.

As a bereaved Muslim daughter, Sabine stayed secluded from all men, including Amin, speaking to them only from behind a protective screen. She could not sleep with Amin during the forty-day period. Nor could she perform her other wifely duties; neighbor women cooked and cleaned for her.

Aurore was less restricted. She had no wish, however, to exercise her freedom. She chose to sit beside Sabine for most of the day. They talked quietly of their mother, sharing their childhood memories.

"It must be hard for you, staying apart from Amin all this time," Aurore remarked one day near the end of the mourning period. "After all, you haven't been married very long."

"I do not mind," Sabine said. "The time of mourning must be fulfilled, and I take comfort in performing the ritual. I would not want it any other way."

"I guess you're right." Aurore sighed. "I feel comfort during the hours I sit here with you. It's when I go home that I get upset. It's as if she isn't gone at all. I keep thinking that any minute Maman will walk through the doorway, carrying her basket of vegetables fresh from the garden."

"My poor little sister." Sabine took Aurore's hand in

hers. "It is not good for you to stay in that place. After the forty days are over, you must come and live with Amin and me. I spoke to him through the screen the other day, and he wishes it as much as I do."

And so it was arranged. Before long, however, Aurore wished that she had not agreed so readily. It was true that she missed Maman less, being with Sabine and Amin. It was true that she felt less lonely during the day. But at night, listening to the soft whispers and low, intimate laughter of the newlyweds from behind their bamboo screen across the room, she felt more lonely than she had ever felt in her life.

Aurore tried covering her ears with the folded cloth that served as her pillow, but she could still hear them. Amin's tones were husky, amorous, inviting. Sabine's shy giggles melted into desirous sighs and then whimperings of pleasure.

She hid her depression from Sabine, whose attention, in any case, was focused on her virile young husband. She tried to keep busy, pitching in with the work of the village women, but there was still plenty of time left over. She hated being this way; she hated wallowing in misery and self-pity. But she couldn't seem to shake off the despair of her mother's death. She felt desolate and completely alone.

Aurore fell into the pattern of returning to her former home in the late afternoon when there was nothing to do. She would lie flat on her mother's bed and vent her grief. It felt good to be able to wail as loudly as she wished, the way the Muslim women had on the day of Odile's death.

She felt secure in the abandoned house; no one would venture into it because of its association with recent death. Then one day someone did, and Aurore trembled at the unexpected touch of a hand on her shoulder. She shrank away, fearing to find Ouna the *katt* tormenting her with some new trick.

But it was Blaise.

"Aurore, what are you doing here all alone?" His manner was unusually tender.

"Where have you been?" She had not meant to blurt it out, and certainly not in so demanding a fashion, but she could not help herself.

"Marseilles. I had to tie up some loose ends to complete the transfer of my business to Dakar." There was no resentment in his voice at the abruptness of her question, only understanding. "I'm sorry I wasn't here when your mother died. I didn't know her long, but I was impressed by her dignity facing death. A remarkable woman, *Tante* Odile."

"I miss her so much!" It was as if his sympathy wrenched the words from Aurore's throat. And they were followed by free-flowing tears and sobs as if Blaise by his very presence had opened the floodgates of her grief.

Somehow then his arms were around her and her face was pressed against his broad chest, her tears staining the fresh linen of his shirt. He stroked her hair and murmured wordless sounds of comfort, the way a parent does to an inconsolable child. His strength and his tenderness sheltered her in her grief. For the first time since her mother died, Aurore felt safe and protected. For the first time, she felt she had come home.

When the tears stopped, she found herself telling Blaise things she had never thought she would be able to put into words. She told him about her father, and about Odile, and about growing up different from the other children on Ile Celeste, even from her beloved half-sister, Sabine. And she told him how since Odile's death, she had been unable to rid herself of the feeling that there was no place she belonged.

"Sabine and Amin love me and they're wonderful to me," she told him, "but I feel like an interloper in their home. They're just married, and so wrapped up in each other! No matter how polite they are, I always have the feeling that I'm interfering with their lives. But at the same time, I can't stand being alone here with constant reminders of Maman. Oh, Blaise, what shall I do?''

"The repairs on the château are finished. The new furnishings will be here in a few days. My mother and Delphine and I will be moving in next week. Come and stay with us.''

"I couldn't do that.''

"Why not?''

"I'd be intruding.''

"Nonsense! You're a de Beausoleil. It's where you belong.''

And looking at Blaise through the mist of love clouding her eyes, Aurore believed it.

CHAPTER 5

Le Château de Beausoleil was much changed from the musty but comfortable home of Aurore's childhood. The oak floors had been scraped and varnished, their gleaming expanse accented by exquisite Aubusson and Persian rugs. In the parlor areas on both sides and in the back of the mansion, the flooring had been replaced by brightly glazed ceramic tiles from Portugal. In the more formal front rooms, most of the old furniture had been discarded. Only a few choice pieces had been retained and restored to their former glory.

The decor was striking and elegant, the paneling burnished to rich shades of mahogany, the draperies especially designed for the château by a Parisian interior decorator with an appreciation for the purples in African sunsets and the strong white-edged blues of the waters encircling Ile Celeste and the taupe shadings of the drought-scorched earth of the mainland. The successful merging of such individualistic colors was the decorator's tribute to the sharp eye of the patron who had chosen him. Further tribute to her taste was visible in the turn-of-the-century Impressionist paintings—originals by Dégas, Gauguin, Monet—that adorned the walls, and in the Limoges and Chinese vases filled with fresh flowers that were selected daily and that breathed freshness and life into every room. For perhaps the first time since it had been built, le Château de Beausoleil seemed to have attained an integration of its parts with its *bambara* whole. Such was the effect of the decorator's patron, Aurore's aunt, Madame Colette Marie de Beausoleil, upon the mansion.

Tante Colette, like her handiwork, dazzled Aurore. She was possessed of the kind of glamour Aurore had gleaned from the high-society features in French magazines, but which she had never before encountered in person. It both impressed and intimidated her. From the first, it kept her off balance.

Tante Colette's personality mingled a convincing surface warmth with an underlying calculating coolness. The vivacious flush of Gallic beauty lent her an air of ageless allure, while her blue eyes weighed and judged shrewdly. Her charm entrapped like fine gossamer, but when she had left, one was apt to discover a cutting edge to the threads. For Aurore, the young, inexperienced, still-evolving product of an insular world, *Tante* Colette was an enigma dispensing unpredictable and sporadic goodwill.

But *Tante* Colette was also Blaise's mother. It was only natural that she was the one to whom Blaise entrusted the integration of Aurore into the château household. He was too occupied with business to anticipate how the subtleties and complexities of his mother's character might confuse Aurore.

"These flowers will make you feel at home, Aurore." The honeyed concern of *Tante* Colette certainly seemed genuine, and yet it was too readily expressed. Never had Aurore seen quite so gaudy a Wolof clay pot as the one containing the bouquet of daisies and zinnias presented to her by her French aunt. "You will be in *la salle verte*," she told Aurore. All the bedrooms had been christened by *Tante* Colette according to the colors of their newly papered walls. "I hope the bed will be soft enough." *Tante* Colette had entered the room first and smoothed the white counterpane covering the high four-poster bed with its thick mattress.

"I'm used to sleeping on a thin straw pallet on the floor," Aurore had replied guilelessly.

"Quite." *Tante* Colette's smile had the quality of

thin-spun glass. "But we won't find it necessary to mention that again, will we?" Her arm around Aurore's shoulder was certainly meant to be companionable, but it offered no warmth.

"No." Aurore didn't know what else to say.

"Now, I don't see any need to ring for the maid to help with the unpacking." *Tante* Colette looked meaningfully at the cloth bundle containing Aurore's nightshift and two best *boubous*. "We two can manage without help."

"Of course, *Tante*."

"We must see to your wardrobe, Aurore."

"Yes, *Tante*."

"There will be luncheons, evening parties, salons. While your native—uh—*costume* is certainly colorful"— *Tante* Colette paused delicately—"I wouldn't want you to be embarrassed in front of our other guests. They, naturally, will be dressed in the European mode."

"Thank you." Surely *Tante* Colette was trying to be kind. Nevertheless, Aurore felt humiliated. She concealed the feeling by turning away to hang her two *boubous*—including the white-and-gold one of which she had been so proud—in the huge closet.

"We'll have the dressmaker here for you next week." *Tante* Colette was openly solicitous, but with a smooth hauteur that had not been part of the culture in which Aurore was raised. "Meanwhile, Delphine has some gowns she never wears. So wasteful, these spoiled young girls! But so fortunate we have found a good use for them, *n'est-ce pas?*"

Many times in her life, Aurore had worn clothing handed down from Sabine. Never had she felt bad about it. Yet somehow now she felt lessened by *Tante* Colette's gift of Delphine's discards.

As time went on, Aurore felt she should be grateful for her aunt's interest and yet she could not help wishing that *Tante* Colette were less scrutinizingly concerned with her. Aurore simply could not relax in her presence. *Tante* Colette contrived always to make her feel inadequate when she was ostensibly helping her the most. Aurore continually felt she was too tall, too buxom, too brown of skin, too untutored—and possibly untutorable—in the elegant French manner that was *Tante* Colette's forte.

"I tell you things for your own good, Aurore. You are my niece by marriage, and naturally I want you to be accepted in society. You do have potential, my dear. Still, it will take a great deal of work to bring it to fruition." *Tante* Colette's sigh faced the difficulties squarely. "I think of you, Aurore, as a thorny wild flower crying out to be cultivated."

If Aurore did not especially want her beauty pruned and pampered to the hothouse perfection of her cousin Delphine and Minette Fourier, that was beside the point as far as *Tante* Colette was concerned. There was no escaping her aunt's watchful eye.

"Do put on this sun hat, Aurore. The noon sun is the enemy of a woman's skin, and yours has already suffered from overexposure to this pagan climate."

"You must use this pumice stone faithfully during your daily bath, Aurore. It will erase those *parvenu* callouses from your feet and elbows."

"Kindly ask Delphine to instruct you in the use of the curling iron, Aurore, so that your hair does not fly around your face in that wild, unbecoming fashion."

There were so many rules that Aurore was hard put to remember them, in spite of *Tante* Colette's constant reminders:

"Aurore, you have not forgotten to wear the cotton gloves to bed again!" *Tante* Colette would regard her niece reproachfully over breakfast. "Did you at least coat your hands with the glycerin and rose-water lotion before retiring? No, I see you did not. Dear Aurore, how many times must I remind you that the true hallmark of a lady is her hands. Ah well, at least your nails are not so jagged as before. For that we must be grateful, I suppose." *Tante* Colette's blue eyes belied her concern as she continued. "My dear, there are certain things about ourselves that we cannot change, since they are ordained by blood. That is why we must be doubly assiduous in altering those traits we do have control over.''

That particular time Aurore did not restrain herself. ''Are you speaking of my African blood, *Tante* Colette? Well, I wouldn't alter that even if it were in my power to do so! I'm proud of it!''

''My dear, I meant nothing of the kind.'' *Tante* Colette's injured tone questioned how Aurore could have so misunderstood her. ''It was my husband who objected to Justin marrying your mother, not I. Blaise tells me she was a wonderful woman, *très gentile*. Half French herself, I understand. Besides, proud of your heritage as you may be, one would never guess it was mixed to look at you. I have friends in Marseilles whose skin is darker. Actually I think your *café au lait* coloring is quite striking.'' And *Tante* Colette chose that moment to bend gracefully to her dressing table mirror, smoothing a beautifully manicured hand over her own delicate pink-and-white complexion.

Aurore hoped that by submitting to *Tante* Colette's program to mold her, by becoming more cultured in manner and more elegant in appearance, she would entice Blaise to take more notice of her. Originally she had anticipated that the two of them would draw closer together, sharing the same home. But so far, this had not been the case. Much of the time, he was away on business, and when he returned, there always seemed to be so many other people around.

Among these, inevitably, was Minette Fourier. She was the château's most frequent visitor. Her inclusion in virtually every activity was automatic. And she seemed to take for granted her right to Blaise's attentions during his homecomings.

Even when Minette wasn't there, Aurore found it difficult to be alone with Blaise. It seemed that whenever a tête-à-tête might be a possiblity, *Tante* Colette would make an appearance. With an enigmatic smile curving her lips, she would ask Aurore to please excuse them; she simply had to speak to her son about a private matter. She would link her arm through Blaise's and sweep him away, chattering vivaciously. And once again, Aurore would be isolated.

The only one in the household with whom Aurore felt at ease was Delphine. From the day *Tante* Colette had sent Aurore to her daughter's room to go through her cast-off clothing, Delphine had been welcoming and friendly. She made a pointed effort to include Aurore in the picnics and swimming and sailing outings she arranged on Ile Celeste for her mainland friends. Aurore was not yet comfortable with these young sophisticates, but she appreciated Delphine's good intentions.

Their budding friendship was frequently overwhelmed by the appearance of Minette Fourier. The raven-haired beauty made it obvious that she considered Delphine *her* friend and would not take kindly to any intrusions by Aurore. Her dominant personality prevailed over Delphine's peace-loving nature, and so Aurore would often find herself excluded.

Tante Colette confirmed the exclusion. She and Minette Fourier were as thick as thieves. Colette de Beausoleil found in this society beauty a nature similar to her own—complex, sophisticated, clever. In many subtle ways, she made it clear that she considered Minette to be a perfect match for her son. It did not escape Aurore's notice that Colette was quick to leave the room if by her doing so Minette and Blaise would be left alone.

Aurore watched the exchanges between Blaise and Minette, trying to gauge how serious the relationship was. Everyone seemed to accept the fact that there was a relationship of some sort. But Blaise, Aurore was happy to note, seemed to look upon it as quite casual. The one or two times that Minette seemed to be trying to make more of it were shrugged off by him with neither insult nor added commitment.

Aurore thought of Blaise as her champion. Hadn't

Blaise obtained medicine to ease her mother's agonies? Hadn't he stood up to that awful Dr. Duchamps? Hadn't he arranged for her to live at the château? Yes, Blaise was her champion, her protector, her knight *sans* shining armor.

But Blaise was not there to fulfill this function on the day of Aurore's humiliation. He had left on a business trip to Thiès, some sixty kilometers inland from Dakar. Blaise had gone there to confer with the management of the Dakar-Niger railroad line about the possibility of a joint venture to build a processing plant in Dakar. Its function would be to freeze the fish Blaise's refrigerated boats delivered. Then the plant would store the frozen fish until the railroad could distribute it throughout the million square miles of the African continent it serviced. The railroad officials could hardly argue about the efficiency of Blaise's proposal, as compared to the primitive and uncertain drying and smoking techniques traditionally used to preserve the fish. Refrigerated railroad cars would enable Africans in inland villages remote from the sea to add protein-rich fish to diets that now consisted of grains like millet, sorghum, and maize. Instead of falling in with Hakim's questionable scheme to compete with the railroad, Blaise was proposing a joint venture that would provide the railroad with increased business and revenues.

The possibility of the railroad's eventual gain was Aurore's immediate loss. She missed Blaise from the start of that day's festivities in honor of an important visitor. Aurore felt more of an outsider with Blaise not there, and particularly so with both afternoon and evening celebrations on the agenda.

Now she watched as the *crème de la crème* of Dakar society disembarked from the private pleasure boats. Chic young ladies in dresses of crisp piqué, soft dotted swiss, and swirling chiffon strolled with their linen-suited escorts over the rolling lawn and through the lush gardens surrounding the château. Occasionally the couples would stop to listen and sway gracefully in time to the American swing arrangements offered by the hired band. There was general agreement that it was too warm for serious dancing as yet. Brightly striped open tents had been set up to shield the guests from the blazing African sun while they partook of champagne punch, small crustless ddcorated sandwiches, cakes, and ices.

The de Beausoleils were a favorite topic of conversation. Such a fascinating family, were they not? And such a welcome addition to Dakar society! The house and its grounds were so magnificent, and Madame Colette so charming. Mademoiselle Delphine was most agreeable, also, and so pretty. Most of the young ladies, taking their lead from Minette Fourier, simply ignored Aurore, but the young men declared themselves fascinated by her.

"Brought up in a native village, you know."

"A de Beausoleil, and a quarter black!"

"Those green eyes and that honey-color skin—so exotic!"

In spite of her silky auburn hair, now tamed by the curling iron, and her yellow dotted swiss dress designed in the latest fashion, the young men remained convinced that there was something "savage" and therefore fascinating about the de Beausoleil *cousine*. Unaware, Aurore enjoyed the male attention that came her way and basked in the interested and admiring glances. She wandered happily, excited by the festive atmosphere and the prospect of the formal banquet scheduled for that evening.

Tante Colette and Delphine had been planning the menu for weeks. They had agonized over the arrival of delicacies that had to be ordered from France. One entire evening had been spent on the selection of the wines alone.

The banquet was in honor of Duke Alfonso Perriera Alcofarado of Portugal. Internationally known for his globe-spanning import-export business, the duke was an old friend of Colette's. He had done business with her late husband, Maurice de Beausoleil, and during the Vichy years in Marseilles, he had continued doing business with the puppet who ran the family shipping interests.

Over seventy years old now, the duke had lost none of his zeal for making money. With the war's end, he had become heavily involved in exporting peanut oil from Senegal. Now he had plans for expansion, plans that somehow involved Blaise.

"A randy old goat!" Such was the opinion of the duke that Blaise had passed on to Aurore. "He licks his lips over a pretty girl as if she's a Viennese pastry he's about to devour. Still," Blaise admitted, "some women are charmed by his geriatric attentions."

"Indeed, the duke can be very charming." Overhearing Blaise, *Tante* Colette had joined the conversation. "In his younger days, he was very handsome, and even now his looks are quite distinguished. Many a woman has considered herself fortunate to be admired by Duke Alcofarado."

"I'm sure they have, Maman." Blaise's glance had been ironic.

Now, on her way to the pool, where Delphine had organized a swimming party, Aurore wondered when the duke would make his entrance. Most of the young people had already changed into bathing suits and were cavorting in the blue-and-white tiled pool or lounging around it. The pool and the patio surrounding it had been designed according to *Tante* Colette's specifications. She had selected the cushioned lounge chairs and occasional tables and positioned them among the shade trees. There were two large dressing rooms to the right of the pool, one for gentlemen and one for ladies.

Entering the ladies' dressing room, Aurore was taken aback at the sight of Minette Fourier, nude except for a pair of silk panties. Even as Aurore watched, Minette slipped them off and stepped into a sleek black bathing suit of some kind of stretchy material that fit her body like a second skin, enunciating the uptilting breasts, small waist, and slim hips of her elegant figure.

"Oh, it's you, Aurore. Going to join the swimming party?" Minette's tone, as always, was supercilious.

"Yes." Aurore went to the cabinet where she kept her bathing costume. It was a length of cotton printed in a bright Senegalese design. Aurore wrapped it around herself, sarong style.

Minette, busy primping in front of the mirror, paid no attention as Aurore undressed. But when Aurore started wrapping the sarong, she turned around. "What is *that?*"

"A sarong. I swim in it."

"But you can't wear that African rag. Colette will be mortified. You'll embarrass Delphine. You'll ruin her party!"

Aurore stared at Minette. She didn't know how to reply.

"Oh, wait!" Minette didn't bother to hide her annoyance. "I'll find something suitable for you." She rummaged in the cabinets and finally came up with a white, satiny garment trimmed prettily with lace. "Here. Borrow this. It's the latest thing from Paris." Her expression was openly contemptuous as she handed it to Aurore.

Aurore returned frankness for frankness. She made no pretext at a gratitude Minette's haughtiness prevented her from feeling. Still, she was intimidated. She didn't want once again to earn *Tante* Colette's disapproval. And she certainly didn't want to embarrass Delphine, whom she genuinely liked. And so she accepted Minette's offering with the coolest *"Merci"* she could muster. "How do I put it on?" she inquired casually.

"Just hold it by the straps and step into it, one leg at a time." Minette's tone was plainly condescending. "Now pull it up and put each arm through the straps . . . Well, I must say it really does become you," she added grudgingly.

Aurore walked to the mirror. Minette hadn't lied. It fit her perfectly, hugging her round breasts and the full curves of her hips. The leg openings were a bit loose around her upper thighs, but that must be the style, Aurore decided. The straps, threaded with pale blue ribbon, were feminine and delicate, as was the lace trim above the bust and around the legs.

Aurore followed Minette out onto the patio. It was very hot, but there was a fresh breeze from the sea that whipped her hair, making it ripple around her bare shoulders and back. The eyes of the watching, admiring men warmed Aurore as much as the blazing sun. She poised on the edge of the pool and then dove in quickly and cleanly. How wonderful to have her limbs free, to feel the cool water caressing her bare skin beneath the silky material of her suit. Aurore surfaced, smiling. The men gathered on the patio were still watching her as she swam lazily around in the azure water.

Her long hair curled into ringlets when it was wet, and Aurore could see the sun glinting through it, enriching the dark auburn with red-gold highlights. She climbed the pool ladder, feeling blissfully refreshed and eager for more of those hot male glances that confirmed her desirability as a woman. Then, suddenly, her euphoria vanished.

The laughter began in isolated bursts. Then, as the laughers nudged their neighbors, it grew until Aurore wanted to clap her hands over her ears to shut it out. The staring eyes! The pointing fingers! They were laughing at *her!*

One glance downward showed Aurore why. The water had rendered her bathing costume completely transparent! The material clung wetly to her body, enunciating every curve. She might as well have been nude!

Aurore stood frozen as the laughter washed over her in sickening waves. What could she do? Where could she hide? How could Minette have done this to her? For now Aurore understood that the white satiny garment Minette had lent her had not been designed for swimming at all.

With tears of humiliation pricking her eyelids, Aurore covered her breasts with one hand, her groin with the other. Like a sad pantomime of Eve in the Garden of Eden after the serpent had taught her shame, she hung her head.

"Who is this Aphrodite?" A tall, white-haired gentleman materialized to command attention.

"The duke!" A respectful bystander identified him.

Aurore raised her head to see Duke Alfonso Perreira Alcofarado. His fawn-color shantung suit fit his spare frame to perfection. Despite his age, he held himself magnificently erect with the aid of a carved, gold-handled walking stick. He was taller than Aurore by several inches. His silver-white hair was fine textured but thick, his pointed goatee more black than gray. Gaunt of cheek, pallid of complexion, nevertheless his aristocratic features seemed to defy the ravages of age—especially his dark eyes, which were warm, bright, and mischievously alive.

"Come with me, Aphrodite," he said to Aurore. Clasping her upper arm in a surprisingly strong grip with his long tapered fingers, he led her away from the pool. The crowd, silent now, made way for them.

The duke led Aurore to a grouping of lawn furniture set in a shady, flower-filled nook. "And now sit beside me and tell me who you are, my tawny Venus."

"I'm Aurore de Beausoleil."

"Ah, yes. The African cousin." His eyes lingered over her frankly.

"I'd better go and change my clothes." Aurore was still shaken.

"And deprive a nearsighted old man of his voyeuristic pleasure?" The duke's sigh was self-mocking, but his openly admiring gaze at Aurore's still exposed breasts confirmed the wistful sentiment of his words.

"The way they laughed!" Aurore blurted out. "I was so mortified."

"The men laughed to cover their arousal at the sight of your voluptuous charms. They are boors, my dear, with the sensibilities of oafish schoolboys. As for the women, they were jealous, and their mirth was meant to punish you for being so beautiful.''

"People are still staring at me.''

"Let them look, my jewel.'' The duke moved closer to her. She could feel the warmth of his breath in her ear as he spoke. "But don't worry. Already the sun is drying your silken teddie so that it shields your magnificent mammaries once again.'' The duke brushed his fingers over the topmost swell of Aurore's breasts so lightly that it would have been ridiculous to object.

"My—my what?''

"Your magnificent mammaries!''

"No. What I'm wearing. What did you call it?''

"Your teddie? Didn't you know what you were wearing, my innocent?''

"No. I thought it was a bathing suit.''

The duke chortled with delight. "How you refresh me with your sweet naiveté and your unspoiled nature! I feel ten years younger. And believe me, sweetness, it is those ten years that make all the difference to a man. What I would not give to be sixty again, even sixty-five.''

"You don't seem old,'' Aurore assured him. She stood up, saying that now she really must go and dress for dinner.

Such was the prestige bestowed upon her by the duke's attentions that later, when Aurore stepped onto the patio where predinner aperitifs were being served, she knew she had no further humiliations to fear. Although all eyes were upon her, they now expressed grudging admiration rather than derision. Many of the men bowed to her as she passed, and several women complimented her on her dress, a sea-green voile that clung to her figure to the hip and then swirled out like a sea foam around her bare, suntanned legs. She wore her hair upswept in the back, with a few curling tendrils escaping at her temples and the back of her neck. Thanks to the duke, she walked with her head held high.

"Aurore!" He hailed her, then strode directly to her. "Come. I have found the perfect place for us to sit and chat." The duke led her to a marble bench secluded from the other guests by a bank of glowing red bougainvillea. But no sooner had they sat down, the duke staring boldly at her low-cut neckline, than he realized that she had no drink and insisted upon fetching her a glass of champagne.

Alone, Aurore became aware of a whispered conversation coming from the other side of the hedge. She recognized the voices.

"I can't imagine what he sees in the little savage," Minette was saying. "Considering all the attractive young European women here."

"Yourself, for example?" *Tante* Colette's tone was amused.

"What would I want with that senile old lecher? The very thought of those withered old hands pawing at me makes me ill."

"As you very well know, *chérie*, the duke's attentions lend prestige. When a man is that rich, his age means nothing. His gropings are overlooked. His interest in a *jeune fille* dictates society's acceptance. Thus it would seem my clever little niece has eclipsed us all with her choice of bathing attire."

"But it wasn't her choice. It was mine. I told her the teddie was a bathing suit, and she believed me."

"How foolish, my dear. Her body is voluptuous. You put it on dipslay. Knowing men, you might have anticipated that your prank would backfire."

"Only because of that revolting old satyr. He practically drooled when he looked at her."

"I don't doubt it." *Tante* Colette's tone was indulgent. "But the fact remains that Duke Alcofarado's reaction has turned Aurore's humiliation into a triumph."

A while later, Aurore did indeed feel triumphant as she and the duke led the procession into the dining hall. He insisted upon escorting her, paying no attention at all to protocol.

"As hostess, I had hoped for the honor of your arm," *Tante* Colette had murmured with a strained smile.

"This handsome young man will be charmed to escort you, I am sure." Alcofarado blithely paired Colette with a bemused French dandy and cut off further discussion by leading the way with Aurore. Upon reaching the head of the table, he seated Aurore at his right.

"But this is not my proper place," Aurore whispered. "The place card has another lady's name on it."

"No matter." Winking mischievously, the duke quickly switched the offending card.

Even though she had been privvy to the planning discussions between *Tante* Colette and Delphine, Aurore was dazzled by the magnificent banquet setting. The long table was draped in snowy linen, each place marked off by round mats of Alençon lace. The water goblets and wineglasses were of the thinnest, most fragile crystal; they glittered in the light of the tall, ornate gold candelabra set at intervals along the length of the banquet table. Pyramid arrangements of ripe fruit shone like jewels. The delicate bone china, white with an outer rim of pure gold, was complemented by bouquets of fluffy yellow chrysanthemums and white roses.

Footmen in livery distributed elegant handwritten menus. Aurore could hardly believe the profusion of dishes offered. Many of them she had never heard of before. And all those wines! She would surely be drunk by the time dessert was served. Even sober, Aurore didn't see how she would ever be able to cope with the bewildering array of silverware lined up on both sides of her plate.

"I've never seen so many knives and forks and spoons," she confessed to the duke. "Even at our regular dinners, I get mixed up, no matter how hard *Tante* Colette tries to teach me!"

"Don't worry your pretty head about such trifles, my child."

"But I don't want to make a fool of myself. You're the guest of honor, and everyone is looking at us."

"They will soon be too busy swilling wine and stuffing themselves to pay us any attention," the duke assured her. "In any case, it is quite simple. With the silverware, one proceeds from the outside in. For instance, here is the soup, and the proper spoon is on the far right."

"I see." Aurore followed his example.

"Hmmm, quite good," the duke commented after tasting the cream of artichoke soup with hazelnuts. "However, I prefer to drink the champagne. Nineteen thirty-three was a very good year."

The next course was caviar, which Aurore had never seen before, much less tasted. It was served in a huge silver bowl filled with cracked ice, in which a small dish of the pale gray, translucent delicacy was embedded. To go with it, each diner received slices of hot toast wrapped in a napkin and an individual serving of sweet butter on ice.

"What exactly is caviar?" Aurore asked the duke.

"Salted roe from the sturgeon, my dear." When Aurore still looked at him blankly, Duke Alcofarado put it more plainly.

"Fish eggs! I don't think I want any." Aurore made a face.

"You must try it, Aurore. Here, I shall prepare it for you."

She watched as the duke buttered a slice of toast and spooned some of the gelatinous mass upon it.

"Open your pretty mouth and I will feed you." The duke was delighted with his paternal role.

It was so salty! And the eggs slid disgustingly between her teeth. It was all Aurore could do to swallow it.

"You do not like it, sweetling! Ah well, drink your champagne then."

"But I'll be drunk before the banquet is half over,"

Aurore protested as the duke held the tulip glass to her lips.

"Never fear, for I am here to take care of you. Besides, tipsiness becomes you. How your eyes are sparkling! Like precious emeralds! And your cheeks are glowing like ripe peaches."

But Aurore knew that it was not so much the wine but the duke's compliments and courtly attentions that were making her radiant. This man of international fame and untold wealth had eyes only for her. Far from being put off by her ignorance of dining etiquette, the duke was delighted to show Aurore how to manage the turban of sole fillet with salmon and sorrel sauce. To go with it, he refilled both their glasses with the white Bordeaux, Graves, 1937.

Next came an herbed saddle of roast lamb, garnished with baby carrots and pearl onions. The duke showed Aurore how to cut her meat in the continental way, a bite at a time. When she was finished, he took her serviette from her lap and delicately dabbed at her lips with it. Then, reaching under the tablecloth, he replaced it, smoothing it over her thighs, and then smoothing it again until Aurore's flesh began to tingle with the repeated caress.

Startled, she looked up at him. His eyes were sparkling but ever so slightly out of focus. He was partaking liberally of each fine wine as it was served, and now, Aurore realized, the wines were starting to have their cumulative effect. Firmly she removed his hand from her thighs.

"And I thought we were such good friends, *n'est-ce pas?*" His tone was teasing, but his bright, black eyes looked into hers beseechingly.

"We are," Aurore assured him. "Oh, look!" She distracted him. "They're serving dessert before dinner is over." She indicated the lime sherbet in its little glass goblet that had been set in front of her.

The duke smiled indulgently. "The *sorbet* is not the dessert, my pet. It is served between the main courses so as to refresh the palate. I myself consider it a silly custom. My own palate finds refreshment in wine." He refilled both their glasses, drained his own without appreciation of its pedigree, and filled it again.

Already feeling the wine, Aurore ignored this latest glass and savored the refreshing sherbet instead.

It was followed by the entrée, poached chicken mousseline, with a rich stuffing of lobster, cream, and pistachio nuts. The duke seemed to have no appetite for the tempting dish. He picked at it while continuing his steady assault on the wine carafe.

"Aren't you hungry?" Aurore asked him.

"I am *triste*, my dear. I am old, unattractive. It is no wonder that you, in the flower of your young womanhood, should find my slightest attentions repugnant."

"That's not it." He was indeed old, and Aurore felt sorry for him. "I do think you're a very attractive man." After all he had done for her, the least she could do was reassure him. "It's just that some things embarrass me in public."

"In public? But no one can see, *chérie*." His hand was under the tablecloth and back in her lap again. The additional glasses of wine made him bolder. His fingers dug into the soft flesh of her thighs, massaging, squeezing, and moving ever higher.

The fresh salad, served after the entrée in the French fashion, blurred in front of Aurore's eyes as her body betrayed her to the duke's wine-fevered caresses. He had taken her by surprise; she'd had no chance to consider a defense. Without her knowing they would, her thighs parted. His fingertips felt the warm, damp excitement through the material of her dress; Aurore trembled, then gasped.

No! She had to put a stop to this. She removed his hand with both of hers. She squeezed her legs tight closed. Dizzy, she groped for something to say. "Are you and Blaise going into business together?" she babbled finally. She held his hand firmly away from her lap.

The duke managed to focus his glazed eyes. "I do have a proposition for him. Peanut oil. But the details would only bore you, my dear."

"No, they wouldn't. I'm interested. Really I am. Tell me about it."

"All right, *ma petite.*" The duke indulged her. "We will eat our *salad* and drink our burgundy while I explain. You see, at present, the peanuts from which the oil is made are transported to the processing plant in Dakar by the Dakar-Niger Railway, in which I am a major, though not majority, stockholder. But crop production is increasing along with export demand. In a few years, the railroad alone will not be able to move all the nuts from the interior. So I have to plan for alternative modes of transportation."

The duke sipped his wine. "Nuit Saint-Georges. Nineteen twenty-nine. Excellent." he pronounced. "I want to speak to Blaise about two possibilities," he continued. "The first concerns using some of his smaller ships to bring out the peanuts via the inland waterways. My other scheme is more complicated, but if implemented, it would be by far the most efficient means of transportation. I want to truck the peanuts to Dakar."

"But there are no roads, at least none that trucks could run along." Aurore remembered Blaise's pointing that out to Mustapha Hakim.

"Exactly, my dear. But roads could be built. I am hoping that Blaise will see the wisdom of my plan and will want to invest some money in it—an investment that would pay off handsomely. But first, we would have to convince the French colonial government officials to start building these roads for the benefit of the country and its people. Good roads would be a boon to tourism and to commerce. Still, there is always so much red tape involved in these matters. It could take years to get construction underway. Yet for my purposes, it must begin immediately."

"How will you manage that?" Aurore asked.

"Bribery," he told her blandly. "Not that Blaise or I

would dirty our own hands. That won't be necessary. I have already found just the man to act for us—a resourceful Lebanese scoundrel named Mustapha Hakim.''

"But I've met him!" Aurore exclaimed. She told the duke how Hakim had provided morphine for her dying mother when French doctors had refused to prescribe it because she was half black.

"Bigoted fools! Don't they realize that the blending of the races results in the most sensual type of beauty?''

Aurore was forced to set down her fork in order once again to block his questing hand.

"If I were young and handsome and virile," he inquired, downing another glass of wine, "would you let me make love to you?"

"That depends." Aurore had recovered her composure. Quite deliberately she decided to cope with the duke as she imagined *Tante* Colette might have.

"On what, *chérie*?"

"Whether or not we get married first." Aurore's eyelashes flitted so quickly that they cast kaleidescopic shadows over her cheeks.

"Marriage!" The duke snorted. "Had I still my youth, the subject would never come up! How cruel you are, Aurore, to take advantage of a gladiator who has lost the use of his sword! Marriage-indeed! Bourgeois institution! In the old days, you would have been mine with no talk of marriage!''

"By force? How deliciously wicked!" Aurore shook her bare shoulders in a sensual little shiver that successfully aped a gesture she had once seen *Tante* Colette use to captivate an admirer.

At that moment, the salad was whisked away and replaced by a platter laden with several different cheeses. The duke's hands became busy paring bite-size slivers from the wedges and popping them into Aurore's mouth. "The Camembert is divine, so smooth and mellow," he judged. "But for a more pungent flavor, try a small bite of the Roquefort."

"No more! I'll burst! And there's still dessert to come!"

The duke stared at the ripe golden flesh of Aurore's breasts swelling from her sea-green dress. "The dessert I crave is not to be found on any menu." The wine spoke for him even as he poured himself another glass.

"Look. The butler is snuffing out the candles. I wonder why."

The duke did not reply. He drank.

The butler held up his hand for silence. "And now we present the *grande finale*—a cake in homage to the distinguished guest of honor, Duke Alfonso Perriera Alcofarado!" With a flourish, the butler signaled the snuffing out of the last candles to coincide with the entrance of a liveried servant wheeling in a cart bearing a meringue cake in the shape of one of the duke's huge tankers. The snowy confection was surrounded by flames of burning brandy. With the room in total darkness, the effect was of the ship propelling itself through a night sea lighted by flares.

"Oh! I dropped my serviette," the duke exclaimed in a whisper.

Her eyes on the cake, Aurore paid no attention as the duke dropped down to retrieve his napkin. She was only dimly aware of his fumblings in the dark under the table. Then, suddenly, she felt his hand under her dress, between her bare legs!

The wine had gone to Aurore's head. She wasn't drunk, but she had quaffed much more of it than she was accustomed to. Now, in the darkness, with the flaming confection sailing the length of the room so that each of the guests might see it close up, the combination of the alcohol and the duke's sudden impropriety was making her head spin in such a way as to immobilize judgment and suspend action.

Both his hands were on the insides of her naked thighs now. His impeccably manicured fingertips were gently prying the flesh apart. His cheek brushed her calf.

An old man's whim. Surely no more! A prerogative of age. Dizzy, unbelieving, Aurore rationalized her situation to herself. She reached down surreptitiously and tried to push him away. His aging shoulder remained firm as a rock and just as unyielding under her proddings.

He was kneading the tender flesh of her inner thighs now. His hands inched higher. His fingertips grazed a few wisps of pubic hair that had escaped the confines of her panties. His chin rested atop her bare knee, the frothy skirt of her gown a shawl now, draped over the top of his head.

The "oohs" and "ahs" grew louder in Aurore's ears as the flaming ship sailed closer. The flames! Illumination! Light! Everybody would see!

What should she do? What could she do? This was the French high society of Dakar, the *beau monde*, and the man on the floor under the table, between her legs, was a duke!

His fingers, quick and nimble and sure as an adolescent boy's, invaded the soft floss under where her panties were joined. The material was pushed aside and held out of the way by one hand while the fingers of the other hand began to stroke her, plunging ever deeper.

Aurore's eyes filled with tears. Never had she felt so helpless. She could not scream. It would have been unthinkable. She could only endure the caress. Aurore was braver than most girls in difficult situations, but she had not the courage to call attention to the unspeakable liberties the duke was taking. She had not the courage to face the whispers and derision that would be heaped on her as "that native girl who caused all the fuss at the de Beausoleil party."

Chaotically feelings, thoughts, and reactions chased each other through her wine-dazzled brain. And then, suddenly, all were banished as the duke committed the ultimate indignity. His hands suddenly wrenched at her thighs so that they parted widely enough for his head to move up between them, and the hot, velvety tip of his tongue made contact with the berry laid vulnerable by his fingers.

Aurore came very close to swooning. His hot breath was like a match lighted inside her womb. His lips, opening and closing rhythmically, had set the pulses pounding like a drumbeat of desire relayed throughout her body.

Tears trickled down Aurore's cheeks. Her eyes were closed. There was no question of her standing up or attempting to move away. In truth, she was beyond such thoughts now. The duke had forced her into the grip of feverish desire, and she could only react.

The flaming ship had circled the darkened room and was proceeding now toward its final destination, the duke's place of honor. All eyes followed it. All save one violet pair that had been distracted during the cake's first circuit of the table and had continued trying to peer at the distraction through the darkness. Now the return of the blazing confection lent additional light to confirm what had started out as a disbelieving suspicion.

Panting, Aurore's thighs locked around the thin and age-wrinkled neck. Her buttocks rose from her seat, supported by his hands. She was a prisoner now of her own blind and mounting passion.

A bursting nova splashed rainbows of color over the insides of Aurore's closed eyelids. Her seething blood rushed through her body. An unexpected ecstasy squeezed the breath from her bosom and tore a soft cry from her lips. the writhing of her lower body gave way to an impossibly tense stillness, and then a sudden relaxation of honey gushing over the softest and kindest of tongues. The cry melted into a tremulous sigh.

Eternity passed in a shattering moment, and then it was over. The sounds of applause for the cake and for the duke hammered in Aurore's ears. She opened her eyes.

Aurore looked across the flaming meringue and straight into the waiting gaze of Minette Fourier. The chic brunette smiled at her without humor, slowly and cruelly. She said nothing. It wasn't necessary. It was all there in the violet eyes. She had seen enough. She knew. Fate had handed her a weapon, and weapons were meant to be used. Aurore looked away.

The duke was back in his chair. The candles were relit. The duke stood and bowed in acknowledgment of the elaborate cake as the other guests applauded. Ceremoniously he cut the first piece and handed it to Aurore. "You've made an old man very happy," he murmured to her.

The pastry chef had come out of the kitchen. He stood and waited for the duke to taste his creation. When the duke obliged, he could contain himself no longer. "It is to your liking, Eminence?" he inquired nervously.

"Delicious! I have never tasted better!" As he answered, the duke looked at Aurore and licked a dab of whipped cream from his upper lip.

It was too much. Aurore stood abruptly, her cheeks flaming. "Excuse me," she said. "I don't feel very well."

"But what is it, Aurore?" Delphine was concerned.

"My dear?" *Tante* Colette's wise eyes flashed to the duke and back to Aurore.

"I'll be all right," Aurore told them. "Please. Go on with your party."

"Perhaps"—Aurore heard Minette Fourier's malice as she excited—"the meal was too rich for her."

So ended Aurore's first formal dinner party at le Château de Beausoleil. She went directly to *la salle verte*, undressed, got into bed, and fell immediately into a deep, defensive sleep. When she awoke the next morning, for the first time since coming to the château, she requested a breakfast tray in her room. She sat up in bed to pick without appetite at the café au lait and croissants. It was not until afternoon, when the last of the guests had gone, that Aurore left her bed for a warm tub scented with jasmine bath salts. Then she slipped into an afternoon dress of pale lavender batiste with a low, square-cut neckline and soft, puffy sleeves. She was just tying back her hair with a lavender satin ribbon when Delphine knocked on her door.

"Blaise is back, Aurore," she told her.

The lavender knot fell away from Aurore's suddenly trembling fingers.

"He wanted to be in time to discuss business with the duke," Delphine continued, "but he just missed him."

"Then the duke has left."

"Yes."

Good! Aurore did not say it aloud.

"But Blaise ran into Minette just as her boat was about to leave the island. Wasn't that lucky?"

"She decided to stay," Aurore guessed. *Damn!*

"For a few days. Perhaps longer, if Blaise doesn't have to go off on business again . . . Why, what are you doing, Aurore?"

"Undressing."

"But you just dressed."

"I don't feel well. I've changed my mind. I'm going back to bed."

"Is there anything I can do?" Delphine was genuinely disturbed.

"Just make my excuses for me, Delphine. And don't worry. I'll be all right. I just need a day's rest."

"Well, all right, then. But call me if you really feel ill."

"I will." When Delphine had gone, Aurore burrowed into the pillows like a small animal trying to hide from a hostile environment. Blaise and Minette Fourier! . . . Old, lecherous aristocrats who took advantage of their age and their position! . . . The complex rules of the *beau monde*! . . . It was all too much!

It was the middle of the night when Aurore awakened with a bad headache. Probably it was caused by having skipped both lunch and dinner. She got out of bed and made her way soundlessly down the carpeted corridor toward the main bathroom, where the household medicines were kept in a cabinet. She needed no light to find the bottle of aspirin. Shaking out two tablets, she swallowed them down with a half-glass of water.

She had left the bathroom door ajar, and just as she was about to reenter the corridor, Aurore heard another door click open. Shrinking back, she saw a tall, slender figure tiptoe out of Blaise's room, closing the door carefully so that it made no sound. Wearing a sheer nightgown, the figure glided down the hall toward Aurore.

It was Minette Fourier!

Unseen, Aurore stood frozen. Midway down the corridor, Minette turned into the "pink room," her bedroom, and closed the door behind her. Aurore then dashed back to her own room.

She slept no more that night. Her brain was in a turmoil. It was as if a mirror had been held up to her character. Aurore discerned a jealousy so strong and deep that it rendered her sick with herself.

Why did jealousy have such a hold on her? Her young girl's body burned with yearning, while her young girl's brain burned with resentment that everyone seemed privileged to indulge desires save her. The duke? Somehow he didn't count. She wanted lovemaking, not perverse diversion. She wanted a young man, an equal.

But was it any young man? Aurore tried to face the question honestly. Once she had thought it was Cherif she wanted. Also, Steven Parker was decidedly attractive. But in truth, the one her body ached for was Blaise. Blaise! And she had just seen another woman come from his bedroom!

Aurore rolled over and sobbed into her pillow.

Although she got up and dressed and left her bedroom the next day, Aurore still kept to herself. Determining that the others were eating by the pool, she crept into the kitchen and breakfasted with the servants. Then she slipped out the back way and went for a long walk in the woods. Her first encounter with any of the family was when she returned in the early afternoon and, rounding the corner of the greenhouse, bumped into Blaise.

"*Cousine!* How are you feeling? Delphine said you were ill."

"It was nothing. Just tired, that's all."

"You overdid it at the party?" The irony was light but nonetheless present.

"No." Aurore felt her cheeks grow warm. "On the contrary, I left before the dancing started and went to bed early."

"Just after dinner?"

Why was that sparkle of cynicism in his blue eyes? "Yes."

"Did you enjoy the dinner?"

"It was delicious."

"I'm told those were the duke's sentiments as well." There was no mistaking the sarcasm now.

Minette Fourier! Of course, she had told Blaise! Probably between acts of love!

Blaise had begun to laugh but he simply stood now and looked deep into Aurore's eyes for a long moment. She looked back, her heart suddenly pounding, hoping to see a reflection of her own desire in his glance. What she saw instead was concern and kindness mixed with the self-derision of a man who finds himself embarking on an extremely uncharacteristic role.

"You know, *Cousine*, as the only surviving male of our family, I feel a certain responsibility for you." The mockery in his tone was directed at himself, but Aurore thought it was meant for her. "I guess that gives me not just the right but the obligation to offer you some advice. So here goes. First, don't fool around with old men. No matter how rich they are, there's no future in it. Second, don't fool around in public. The *beau monde* thrives on the hypocrisy of savaging girls who let themselves be seen doing things that all the other ladies are doing in private. Third, don't let yourself be sidetracked sexually. There are all kinds of fun things to do, but plain and simple lovemaking is still the ultimate experience to which a virgin can look forward.''

"How do you know—"

"A roué's instinct."

"I'm not a child!" Aurore was suddenly angry at his paternalistic attitude. "Cousin or not, you have no right to talk to me this way! I'm a grown woman!" Her eyes sparkled with green fire.

"A grown woman?" Blaise laughed, then abruptly stopped. "Sorry. I should know better than to laugh at you."

"Yes! You should! And you should know better than to give me advice, which is only a subtle way of trying to dictate my behavior. And nothing gives you the right to do that."

"Well, there is the family name." Blaise was still being ironic. "We can't have it besmirched, you know."

"Then I'd suggest you save your lectures for yourself!" Aurore was furious. Minette Fourier in his bed, and he had the nerve to lecture to her! "From what I know about—"

"My past is nothing to be proud of, I grant you. Still, in this imperfect world, a bachelor's sins are *noblesse oblige,* while a spinster's indiscretions are spelled out in letters of scarlet."

"Spinster!"

"Oops. Sorry again."

Aurore controlled herself. "What you're saying is that you can take your pleasures as you please, while I, a mere *woman,* must be pure and circumspect at all times. That's not only unfair, it's ridiculous!"

"It's nature that's unfair." Blaise was still regarding her in that amused, infuriating manner. "Nature says that the woman must bear the consequences of unbridled pleasure."

"And do you think of that when a woman comes to your bed?"

Blaise shot her a sharp, questioning look and then decided that it had only been an unwitting turn of phrase. "I'm only trying in my muddled way to protect you from a cruel, cruel world, Aurore." Once again, it was himself at whom he was scoffing, and once again, Aurore didn't understand this.

"I really don't need you to tell me about the birds and the bees! I can take care of myself." She turned on her heel and marched away.

"Good advice is hard to find," he called after her. "Take it where you can get it."

His laugh was still rankling in Aurore's ears when she closed her bedroom door behind her. How dare he moralize to her when he was sleeping with Minette Furier? Aurore's face was hot with fury as she brushed away the bitter, unwanted tears in her eyes. She pounded the mattress with her fists. What a two-faced hypocrite he was! What a patronizing rogue, with his brutish body and his evil pirate's face. With his insufferable insolent smirk, and that mocking laugh.

"I'll make him regret it," Aurore vowed through clenched teeth. But whether she meant Blaise's criticism of her moral behavior or his dalliance with Minette Fourier, she wasn't entirely sure.

What seemed to be an opportunity to fulfill her pledge presented itself a few days later when Steven Parker visited the château. He had come to see Blaise about business. It had something to do with the matter the duke had mentioned, involving Mustapha Hakim.

From the moment Parker took Aurore's hand, professing himself delighted to see her again, Aurore knew that the American's interest in her hadn't diminished. This time she would encourage it, Aurore promised herself. And that meant especially when Blaise was present, as he was now.

"I'm delighted to see you again, Mr. Parker." Aurore gave him her most radiant smile. "I've been so *bored* lately." Aurore shot a meaningful glance at Blaise, who, unruffled, winked at her. "But *you're* so interesting, Mr. Parker."

"Well, I'm mighty glad to hear that, Mademoiselle

Aurore. And please, call me Steven. After all, we're becoming good friends.''

"I hope we'll become even better friends." The way Aurore dimpled did honor to the teachings of *Tante* Colette. "Steven," she added.

"Friendship later." Blaise's tone was mocking. "Right now Mr. Parker and I have business to discuss.''

"Steven is staying for dinner, isn't he, Blaise?'' Aurore asked. "I'm sure *Tante* Colette and Delphine would insist if they were here. They left for Dakar early this morning to visit some English friends,'' she explained to Parker. "But they should be back by dinnertime.''

"It's all settled, then. You'll stay for dinner," Blaise said, motioning Parker towards his study. His backward glance at Aurore was one of amusement.

She met it with a blasé smile.

What luck that she had decided not to go with *Tante* Colette and Delphine, Aurore reflected as she dressed for dinner. She chose her most sophisticated gown, a black chiffon with narrow straps and a tight, low-cut bodice glittering with jet sequins. The dress fit snugly to the waist, then flared out around her hips and legs. *Tante* Colette would have thought it a bit much for dinner at home, but it did make her look several years older, especially with her wavy hair pulled over to one side of her face, in the new style favored by Rita Hayworth.

Steven Parker was openly impressed. His light blue eyes missed not one curve. Aurore sat next to him on the bamboo couch in the screened-in sun room while Blaise, still looking amused, mixed cocktails.

She flirted with Steven openly while assuming a distant, almost bored attitude toward Blaise. Her French cousin merely grinned at the two of them. His attitude was that of a schoolmaster pleased that the children in his charge are playing so nicely together.

Nevertheless, Steven Parker's warm, frankly admiring gaze made Aurore feel poised and confident. Here was a grown man who didn't treat her like a backward child. When Steven looked at her, it was obvious that he saw a fully grown, desirable woman.

"Yes, I will have another daiquiri," she said to Blaise, who had bypassed her glass.

He raised an eyebrow and grudgingly poured a few drops into her stemmed goblet.

Aurore immediately drained the glass. "Sometimes I think I should call him Daddy." She made a move as if she and Parker were sharing a private joke.

"There's no telling when Maman and Delphine will get back," Blaise said. "So why don't we just go ahead and eat."

"Blaise doesn't understand that I'm a grown-up woman." Aurore pursued the topic during dinner. "But you do, don't you, Steven." She looked up at him coquettishly.

Steven bent and placed his lips against Aurore's ear. "You're a woman, all right," he whispered. "And a sexy one. If we were alone. . . ."

That circumstance occurred later when Blaise was summoned to the phone during dessert. Pushing his mousse aside, Steven led Aurore out onto the patio. The inviting smile on her lips faded when she saw the way he was looking at her, so intently and so hungrily that her legs suddenly felt weak.

Steven took her in his arms, pressing her back against one of the marble columns that divided the pool area from the rest of the patio. His lips caught hers and clung, opening them to the probing of his tongue. She felt the heat of his long, lean body through their clothing. The sudden pressure between her thighs was rockhard and insistent. Steven's hand moved down her back and over the firm roundness of her buttocks. Suddenly he grasped hold of her bottom and pulled her sharply against him so that his stiffness was embedded at the juncture of her legs.

Yet Aurore had not given herself over completely to Steven's passionate embrace. One part of her mind stayed alert, waiting and hoping that Blaise would appear on the patio and discover them. Intermittently Aurore would peek at the lighted salon with its open glass doors. Finally she saw the silhouette of a figure entering the salon.

"Oh, Steven, kiss me, kiss me," she murmured, allowing her body to curve even more firmly against his.

"Oh!" Her eyes had been tricked by the light. It wasn't Blaise at all. It was Delphine.

Aurore pulled away from Steven. She was going to make a flip remark, but Delphine's face stopped her. Her expression was unexpected and shocking in its intensity.

Delphine's normally limpid blue eyes were filled with pain. Her rosebud mouth was slack and gaping, as if she were about to be ill. She looked utterly destroyed.

"Evenin', Delphine." Steven looked sheepish.

Delphine reacted to the sound of his voice as if it were a slap in the face. She backed away, staring at him. Then, suddenly, she turned and ran, sobbing.

Appalled, Aurore followed. She found Delphine upstairs. She had rushed blindly into her bedroom and thrown herself on the flower-sprigged, quilted satin bedspread.

"Delphine, what is it?" Aurore patted her cousin's shaking shoulder.

Weeping freely now, Delphine could not reply.

"Is it because I was kissing Steven?" Aurore was truly chagrined. "I can't bear to think that I've made you unhappy, after you've been so kind to me."

Delphine fumbled for Aurore's hand and squeezed it. Her sobs abated. "It's not your fault, Aurore."

"You're in love with Steven. That's it, isn't it, Delphine?"

Slowly the golden head turned, and Delphine pushed herself up, facing Aurore. "Yes." She sighed. "Yes!"

Aurore smiled gently at the pretty face so streaked

and swollen with tears. "It's all right then, Delphine. There's nothing between Steven and me."

"He kissed you, didn't he?"

"Yes, but I encouraged it. I was trying to make Blaise jealous. I thought if he saw that a young, handsome man like Steven desired me, it would show him I'm a grown woman and not just a silly child, which is how he treats me."

"Oh, my poor Aurore. And poor me." They put their arms around each other and swayed gently back and forth in a soothing rhythm of comfort and camaraderie. "Poor women everywhere!" Finally Delphine sighed and raised her head. "Men are such bastards," she said, resigned to the fact.

"I don't believe that," Aurore replied truthfully.

But the time would come when she did.

CHAPTER 6

How quickly timed passed, reflected Aurore as she packed the tiny, neatly folded garments into the large wicker basket atop her bed. It was hard to believe that in less than a month, she would be an aunt. Sabine had become pregnant in December, and now her belly was poking out as firm and round as a calabash. How pleased she would be with the handmade baby clothes, Aurore's gift to her new niece or nephew. Naturally Amin was hoping for a son who would one day succeed him as chief, but Sabine had confided that she would welcome a daughter to name after Maman.

Whatever the sex of the child, these tiny shirts and gowns made of the softest flannel and finest lawn and the little sheets hemmed by hand in the tiny stitches Delphine had taught her would be a welcome gift. Delphine was almost as excited about the coming baby as Aurore. The two girls had spent many happy hours sticthing and talking.

Aurore smoothed the beautiful hand-crocheted white coverlet Delphine had made for the baby and placed it on top of the filled basket. The house seemed so empty with Delphine and *Tante* Colette away in Dakar. They were at a weekend house party being given by one of Colette's new society friends. Aurore had been invited, too, but she refused to leave Ile Celeste now that Sabine's confinement was so close. *Tante* Colette had made it clear that she thought Aurore foolish to miss one of the most talked about social events of the season.

Aurore wondered if the real reason for her aunt's

displeasure was that she and Blaise would be alone together at the château that evening. He had just returned from a business trip as his mother and sister were leaving. He had opted for sleep over accompanying them. He left orders not to be awakened until it was time to dress for dinner.

Aurore spent two hours preparing herself for the rare opportunity of being alone with Blaise. She bathed in a tub frothing with a delicious-smelling milk-bath preparation Delphine had recommended, then splashed herself with Chanel No. 5. Duke Alcofarado had sent her a huge bottle of it after his memorable visit. He had sent perfume to *Tante* Colette and Delphine, too, but their gifts had been much smaller.

With a curling iron, Aurore coaxed her shimmering auburn tresses into wavy ringlets that trailed alluringly over her bare shoulders and back. She put on a sun dress of white eyelet that enhanced the creamy tan of her skin and the tawny sheen of her hair. But even if she labored over her toilette all day long, it was doubtful whether Blaise would treat her seriously, Aurore thought as she painted her persimmon-hued lips a deeper red. Still, she had to try.

"Alone at last, *Cousine*." Blaise gave her his customary ironic grin from across the dinner table. "It's certainly a novelty to see you without an amorous swain in tow. Are you sure you don't have an admirer hidden somewhere on the premises?"

"No. Tonight it's just you and me." Aurore smiled at him sweetly over the shrimp-stuffed avocado. Tonight she was going to be mature. She wouldn't become upset no matter how he teased her. "Not a swain in sight."

"How sad," Blaise commiserated, his eyes twinkling. "And how have you managed to survive this woeful lack of male attention?"

"I read. I walk. I do needlework. I've been making clothes for my sister's baby. I'm looking forward to being an aunt."

"How is Sabine? The baby must be almost due by now."

"Uncomfortable. She expects the baby in about three weeks."

"Is that why you didn't go to the party with Maman and Delphine?"

"Yes." The footman removed the avocado and served the main course. "What about you? Will you be joining them later this weekend?"

"No. I have paperwork to do."

"That's too bad. Minette will be disappointed." Aurore couldn't keep the hint of sarcasm from her voice.

Blaise looked at her quizzically over his serving of coq au vin. "I suppose so. But she'll have Maman and Delphine for company."

"Somehow I don't think that will make up for your absence." Aurore took a delicate bite from a dinner roll.

"Really?" Blaise seemed amused at the turn the conversation was taking. "But why not? Minette is a friend of the *whole* family."

"It's said that soon she may become a member of the family." Aurore sipped her dry white wine and regarded Blaise with wide, innocent green eyes.

"It's said, is it?" Blaise laughed easily. "Well, I don't know who's saying it, but until you hear it from me, you can consider it meaningless gossip."

"It's no concern of mine whom you marry." Aurore cut a bite-size piece of chicken and popped it into her mouth.

"How uncousinly of you. I, on the other hand, would be very much interested in your choice of a husband. As head of the de Beausoleil clan, I'd want to be sure he was worthy of you." That mocking note was in his voice again.

Aurore ignored it. "Well, there are no prospects in sight," she told him. "Worthy or not." She sighed and contemplated her mousse au chocolat.

She never got to taste the rich dessert. At that moment, there was the sound of a commotion coming from the hall outside the dining room. Then Khary Saloum, a woman from the fishing village, burst through the double doors, pushing aside the maid who was trying to restrain her.

"Aurore! Your sister Sabine—"

"What's wrong?" Aurore was on her feet.

"She is in labor, but things are not going as they should. She is in terrible pain, and the midwife has run away."

"Why wasn't I sent for sooner?"

"Sabine did not know she was in labor. She thought it was gas pains, because she has been troubled by them often in the last week. Then when she realized the baby was coming, everything was in confusion because of the trouble Ouna started."

"Ouna? What trouble?" Aurore's heart sank.

"Ouna says that Sabine's baby will be born under a *deume*. She calls the baby devil's fruit and says that all who touch it will be contaminated. Old Sula, the midwife, still believes in Ouna's magical powers, and when things started going badly with the birth, she took this as a sign of the *katt*'s *deume* coming true, and she has run away. Idrissa Baye is with Sabine now, but Idrissa has never had a child and doesn't know what to do."

"Is Amin with her?" Aurore asked.

"No. He is in Dakar on business."

"My poor Sabine!" Aurore hurried out of the dining room with Khary Saloun in tow.

"I'll go with you," Blaise said as he fell in with them.

"Thank you."

"But first I want to get something. You go ahead. I'll catch up with you." He went toward the kitchen as they left the house.

He was carrying a small bundle wrapped in a tablecloth when he caught up with them on the trail. Aurore was hurrying ahead. Blaise caught Khary's arm and held her back to ask exactly what had gone wrong with the birth.

"The baby is in an evil position," Khary told him. "Anyway, that is what Old Sula said. She said it will not turn around and it will not budge because it is 'devil's fruit.' The pains were very bad when I left right after Old Sula did. Poor Sabine is in agony. Terrible, terrible agony."

It was true. Pain had rendered Sabine almost unrecognizable, even to Aurore. Her normally nut-brown face was ashen gray and drenched with sweat. Her eyes were slits, her mouth tautly stretched in a grimace of torment. She thrashed from side to side on the mattress, groaning loudly.

"Oh, Sabine." Aurore knelt by the bed, and immediately Sabine grabbed her arm with both hands and hung on desperately, as if to a lifeline. She tried to speak, but all that came out of her mouth were more heartrending groans. Never before had Aurore seen her placid, competent elder sister so out of control. Dear God! What if the *deume* was indeed responsible for this horror?

Blaise squeezed Aurore's shoulder. "Just hold her hands; try to calm her down." Then he spoke to Idrissa, who was standing in the corner, wringing her hands. "Go get a small basin of cool water so that Aurore can bathe her face. And then I'll need a pail of boiling water. Quick, woman! Move!"

Idrissa scampered for the village well.

Blaise set down the bundle he had brought. Then he knelt at the foot of the mattress and grasped both of Sabine's knees. "You have to get control of yourself," he told her in a voice that was firm and yet so tender that Aurore looked up at him in surprise. "Stop thrashing around. Use all your strength to bear down when the pains come. You have to cooperate with me, Sabine, because I'm going to save your baby's life. It isn't going to be easy; we have to work together; together we can do it."

Blaise kept talking, his tone steady and authoritative, kindly and soothing, until Sabine calmed. He asked her to count out the seconds of each contraction, along with Aurore, and this seemed to take her mind off the agony her body was undergoing. Between contractions, Aurore bathed Sabine's face with a wet cloth.

As soon as the boiling water was brought in, Blaise unwrapped his bundle and plunged several kitchen implements into the bucket, then washed his hands vigorously. Aurore watched trustingly as he tossed the crumpled sheet aside and again knelt between her sister's open thighs.

"Damn it! I need more light!" He turned to Idrissa Baye. "Hurry and bring me every candle and oil lamp in the house. Borrow from the neighbors if you have to."

"But, sir," Idrissa quavered, "surely *you* don't intend to deliver the baby!" She gaped at him in shock.

"Someone has to," he snapped. "Now get me light!"

Soon Idrissa and several other village women were holding up candles and palm-oil lamps, shaking their heads and clucking their tongues as Blaise examined Sabine. Aurore's stomach lurched as she saw Blaise's hands disappear for a moment and then appear again covered with blood. Sabine moaned and whimpered, clutching Aurore's hands in a viselike grip.

"Sabine, your baby's in the wrong position," he said. "I'm going to have to turn it around. It may hurt quite a bit, but once I do that, you'll be able to give birth. You'll have to be brave. This is what we have to do to save the child. Do you understand? Now when I start, try not to thrash around. Scream if you want to; don't be shy about that. But try not throw your body around; that will make it much harder for me to do what I have to do."

Blaise stepped back and beckoned to Aurore. The strain showed on his face. "You hold onto her, Aurore," he said. "If she starts to fight, hold her down. Throw yourself on top of her if you have to. She has to lie still. It's the only chance to save the baby. Understand?"

"Yes. I'll do whatever's necessary." Aurore was filled with love as well as admiration for this strange, sardonic, unexpectedly tender man who was about to fight the battle for the life of her sister's child.

It was horrible. Sympathy shone on Blaise's face as his hands disappeared. Sabine screamed as if her body were being ripped in two. Aurore stared mesmerized at the ring of light; she took deep breaths to keep from fainting.

But when Sabine started to writhe in agony, Aurore got hold of herself. It was as if Blaise's courage, or at least some small part of it, had been transmitted to her. She found the strength to hold her sister quiet.

"Lie still, Sabine," she said firmly. "Let Blaise do what he has to do . . . You'll be all right, Sabine. I know you will. So will the baby . . . No, you mustn't fight. You must keep your legs still."

Then Aurore was kneeling next to Blaise. She pinned her sister's legs with her weight. Grimly she watched his hands plunge inside her sister's gaping, bleeding body. She saw the intense concentration on his face as he shifted his arms. She saw the muscles of his thick neck contract as Sabine's screams reached an earsplitting pitch.

"It's turned!" he cried suddenly, his voice exultant. "Now with the next contraction, push as hard as you can, Sabine. For your baby! Push!"

Sabine pushed until beads of sweat ran down her face as fast as Aurore could wipe them away.

"Get behind her and hold her up in a sitting position," Blaise told Aurore. "That might help."

Aurore joined him in urging her sister to bear down. Gradually the voices of the other women chimed in until it seemed that their collective energy and the enthusiasm were part of the birth. And then Aurore saw a miracle! A tiny head emerged.

"You have a son," Blaise announced as the tiny loins and belly came into view.

Aurore could not tear her eyes away from the tiny arms and legs, already kicking and flailing. Both she and Sabine were sobbing with joy and relief. The baby chimed in, its lusty wails issuing from the tiny wrinkled face with the round open mouth.

"He's furious because it took so long." Blaise grinned. "Sorry, little fellow. We did the best we could."

Idrissa, beaming, placed a white cloth on Blaise's knees. He placed the infant upon it, reached into the pail for scissors, and deftly cut the thick blue umbilical cord. Idrissa gave him some string to tie it with, and then she and the other women washed the baby in a basin of warm water.

Soon the baby boy was swathed and nestled in his mother's arms. Shyly Sabine opened her shift, and immediately the tiny mouth latched onto her breast. Tears came to her eyes as he started to suckle.

Aurore felt like crying, too, but there was no opportunity. Well-wishers crowded into the house, beaming and chattering at mother and child, and Aurore had to act as buffer. When she did, they turned to heap praise upon the tall white man who had stepped in as midwife.

Blaise finally sought refuge in the kitchen. He stripped to the waist and began to wash in a fresh pail of water Idrissa Baye had brought him for that purpose. Aurore, passing the doorway, paused to watch the muscles of his back ripple as he bent over the bucket. He looked so boyish with his dark hair all wet and tousled. She was so intent on him that she missed Amin's arrival.

She saw him later when he emerged from his first visit with his new son. "Sabine was wide awake and doting," he said, a note of wonder in his voice as he joined Aurore and Blaise on the patio.

A table and chairs had been set up there, just outside the kitchen. Idrissa Baye had ignored Aurore and Blaise's protests that they had already eaten and insisted on serving them a delicious couscous. They pushed it around their plates to be polite, but they were both glad when Amin ate the lion's share. Aurore's throat was still dry from the emotional experience, and she gratefully drank down two glasses of the tamarind juice Idrissa Baye served them. Its acidy taste was very refreshing, and so she took in a glass to Sabine.

The baby was nestled in a bamboo basket beside the mattress. "He's so beautiful!" Aurore marveled. "My very own nephew." She was surprised at the complexity of emotions the thought aroused.

"Amin is so pleased that our firstborn is a son." Sabine smiled with sleepy contentment. "Still, some day I would like a daughter as well."

"You're already thinking of another? After what you went through? You're truly amazing, Sabine!"

"Not so amazing. If it hadn't been for Blaise—we will never be able to thank him enough. Amin will not rest until he finds a way to repay him."

"Blaise was wonderful." And is, she thought to herself. "Have you decided on a name for the baby, Sabine?"

"Yes. Amadou. And his second name will be Blaise."

"Amadou Blaise Baye. Blaise will be honored. Can I tell him, Sabine, or do you want to?"

"You tell him." Sabine smiled knowingly. "I think I will sleep a little now, Aurore. And thank you, little sister, for everything."

Aurore had promised Idrissa that she would wash the dishes. Now she set to work in the kitchen. Blaise and Amin were seated at the table only a few yards away. Their conversation was easily heard. Instead of talking about the birth and the baby, they were discussing politics. *Men!* Her ears perked up when Cherif was mentioned.

"My brother is in Dakar attending a meeting of a Groupe d'Etudes Communistes." Amin's tone was bitter.

"A Communist study group? Is Cherif a Communist?"

"Not yet. But he is leaning that way. He became interested last year when the Rassemblement Démocratique Africain emerged from the Communist-sponsored conference at Bamako. I have tried to tell Cherif that he is naive to believe that these white French Communists truly have our interests at heart. After all, weren't they in charge when our people were brutally conscripted into the army and into slave-labor battalions during the war? Now, suddenly, they claim to be on the side of those they exploited."

"Hypocrisy and politics always go hand in hand," Blaise observed. "Why expect the Communists to be an exception?"

"Exactly! I believe in Senegalese independence, Blaise. But I am for an independent Muslim Senegal."

"A religious state?"

"If you wish. I am interested in social and economic reforms that are in keeping with Muslim law and tradition. What do Communist aims have to do with us? This I ask my brother."

"And what does he answer?"

"He avoids the question. He says that if the Communists have a contribution to make to the cause of the Senegalese people, he will not let labels blind him to what they have to give. At the same time, he insists that he is not a Communist. His current involvement is with the union of railway workers. It is true that this union is independent of the Confederation General du Travail and also free of the control the Communists exercise over the CGT. But the trainmen's union is grumbling with talk of a strike, which could easily spread to a general strike. The Communists would like nothing better. Through the CGT, they would have a good chance of seizing control of such a movement."

"Maybe Cherif sees the union as a handhold on the independence struggle," Blaise suggested. "A union is a way of bringing together men who may later become fighters for freedom."

"You amaze me, Blaise. You certainly don't talk like a Frenchman. Don't you realize that the first to be thrown out of a free Senegal will be the French? And that means French businessmen like yourself.''

"I'm a realist, Amin. I believe in looking the inevitable squarely in the eye. If you're smart, you'll be realistic, too. An independent Senegal will still need things we French businessmen can provide. I'm gambling that the leaders will see that when the time comes.''

"There is great bitterness.''

"I know that. And the workingmen's bitterness is the greatest of all. That's undoubtedly why Cherif has thrown in his lot with them. He recognizes that the struggle will probably begin with them.''

"Then he is wrong. It will begin with the Muslim faithful.''

"Which brings us back to *your* revolution. How is it going?''

"In some ways, one cannot help admiring the French,'' Amin said with a chuckle. "Who else but a Frenchman would inquire so solicitously as to the movement aimed at bringing about his downfall?''

"One way or another, I'll survive,'' Blaise told him dryly.

"In answer to your question, things could be better,'' Amin confessed. "Cherif delivered your warning about Mustapha Hakim. Despite it, circumstances forced me to ask Steven Parker to buy more ammunition from him. To our surprise, he refused to sell us any more.''

"I'm not surprised,'' Blaise said. "If the railway workers call a strike and a general strike follows, violence will probably break out. If the powers that be found that the bullets killing their soldiers had been sold by Hakim, it would definitely put a crimp in his business. Right now he can't do business at all without French colonial cooperation. Hakim's too smart to give that up until he's sure who's going to win. Besides, by holding back now, he's pushing up the eventual price.''

"That's probably true, although I believe we're a long way from confrontation. Still, I have sent Parker to

Thiès to make arrangements to buy raw potassium nitrate.''

"You're going to process it yourself and make your own ammunition?''

"Yes. Fortunately for us, it's one Senegalese natural resource you French haven't depleted.'' Amin sighed. "Still, I think it will be a long time before it's used. Even if the railway workers go out on strike, what chance have they of winning? They struck in 1938 and were crushed quickly by the French.''

"Hakim remembers that, too,'' Blaise told him. "That's why he won't jeopardize his dealings with the French business community. Still, perhaps this time will be different.''

"You sound almost as if you wish it would be.''

"Perhaps I do. I've always had an uncontrollable urge to root for the underdog.'' His grin was self-mocking.

"Maybe that's why you're the first Frenchman I have ever really liked,'' Amin said candidly. "Even before your invaluable services on behalf of my wife and son tonight, I found myself liking you.''

"Blaise is not the first Frenchman you really liked, Amin!'' Aurore interrupted indignantly as she came out of the kitchen, her chores done. "What about my father?''

"I never really thought of him as a Frenchman,'' Amin apologized. "He seemed so much one of us.''

"All of us de Beausoleils are likable.'' Blaise winked at Amin and got up from the table. "It's time for us to say good night,'' he told Aurore. "The new father should get some sleep, just as his wife and son are doing.''

"I'll never forget what you have done tonight,'' Amin told Blaise as he escorted the two of them out. *"Sidiame dome n'deye,''* he told him as they parted. "Peace be with you, my brother.''

Peace, however, eluded Blaise. When they reached the château, he went directly to the liquor cabinet. "I've earned a drink. You, too, Aurore.'' He took out a full bottle of brandy, opened it, and poured two large snifters almost to the top. He downed one with a swift backward motion. Aurore was still sipping at the rich amber liquid in the other snifter as he gulped a second drink.

Aurore had never seen him so restless. He paced the room like a tiger in a cage. A nerve in his muscular neck twitched spasmodically. He drank a third brandy, baring his teeth after he swallowed as if the strong liquor burned his throat as it went down.

"What is it, Blaise?" Finally she had to ask.

"Delayed reaction, I guess. Delivering babies isn't exactly my *forte*." His lips curved in a grin that was neither cynical nor convincing. "Let's go out on the patio and get a breath of air. It's stifling in here." He took the brandy bottle and the snifters with him. Outside, he faced toward the ocean, breathing deeply as the gentle hilltop breeze stirred his thick, dark hair.

They were silent. Aurore didn't know what to say. His mood was so strange. He refilled his glass again, and then once more. "Sorry. I'm forgetting my manners," he said. "Can I pour you another drink?"

"If you can spare it." Aurore hoped the sarcasm would engage his attention, but it didn't.

Again they drank in silence. Blaise finished the bottle. Only a slight unsteadiness in his gait as he paced the terrace betrayed how drunk he now was.

"It was really wonderful, what you did tonight," Aurore told him sincerely.

"Wonderful?" He went inside and fetched another bottle and brought it out with him. "Wonderful?" He filled the brandy snifter and drank it off. "Would you like to hear a story?" he asked abruptly.

She nodded.

"It could be a true story. And it's touching. Very touching." He drained the snifter and poured again. He swayed in front of Aurore holding the glass. "I think I'm getting drunk," he said flatly.

"I feel a little tipsy, too. All we've been through, and liquor on top of it—"

"Yes, a very touching story." He picked up the thread as if she hadn't spoken. "It happened in Marseilles. Very romantic city, Marseilles. Just the place for a boy and girl to fall in love. The girl was a flower seller, a vivacious urchin in a faded dress and ragged sweater offering scant protection against the winter night. The boy was just a boy, quite ordinary until she looked at him with her large, soulful eyes. Then, for the first time, he felt tenderness for another human being—a fierce, consuming tenderness . . . Well, the boy and the girl approached each other. They spoke. Their hands somehow joined. And—so simply—they went to a small hotel and they made love . . . Do you know what it is to make love?" he asked Aurore abruptly.

"Yes . . . Well no, not from my own experience. But I know what you mean."

"No you don't." Drunk as Blaise was, his voice was very positive. "Man have sex; few—very few—make love. I have done the first many times with many women. But the second with only one woman." His grin faltered and failed like a sob trailing off in the still night. "The boy and the girl made love. They made love that first time, and many times thereafter. But, finally, the boy was sent off to school. The girl went back to her flower selling. The boy did the things that boys do when they're away at school, and while his memory of the girl faded, it did not fade nearly so much as a cynical world would lead us to expect it to fade. The months passed, and then he came back to Marseilles on vacation. And what do you think was the first thing he did?"

"He went to the girl," Aurore guessed.

"That's right. He went to the girl. But she was not selling flowers where she had been. So he went to her room, and what do you think he found?"

"I don't know."

"He found that he had made her pregnant before he

left." Blaise took another drink, but the brandy seemed to be having no further affect on him now.

"I see." Aurore did not know what else to say.

"But the girl had no money, and so she had not received anything like adequate medical treatment. Now, seven months gone, perhaps brought on by the excitement of the boy's unexpected arrival, she went into premature labor. The boy sent the concierge to fetch the nearest doctor. Before they returned, the girl started to give birth. The boy didn't know what to do. He didn't know what to do. He—" Blaise turned away abruptly and took a deep draft directly from the brandy bottle.

"Blaise—"

"When the doctor arrived, the girl and the baby were both dead. The doctor said they could have been saved if only the boy had known what to do. And he told the boy what he could have done. Only by that time, of course, it was too late. Still, the boy remembered what the doctor told him. One day, he thought, it might come in handy. One day it did." Blaise fell silent.

"Oh, Blaise!" Aurore wanted to comfort him, but there was something in his stance that told her the slightest word or gesture of sympathy would shatter his composure. Aurore waited. When he seemed to have a firmer grip on himself, she spoke in what she hoped was a normal tone of voice. "What was the girl's name?" she asked.

"Marie-Anne. But the boy called her Môme—little waif. Of course, the boy has no name." Blaise sat down abruptly. "I'm not *getting* drunk anymore," he said. "I *am* drunk. *Very* drunk."

"I'll help you to bed."

" 'Preciate that." He stood up, swaying.

Aurore slid her arm around his waist so that her shoulder offered support as she helped him into the house. He wasn't stumbling or staggering. He was just a little unsteady as they went up the stairs to his bedroom.

He sank down heavily on the brass bed, his head bowed, his arms hanging slack at his sides. "Shouldn't have told you that story, Aurore. Too sad." His voice was thick but not incoherent.

"It's all right." She knelt in front of him and undid the laces of the black patent leather shoes he was wearing with his dinner clothes. She helped him out of his jacket, and then his shirt. She felt such tenderness for him. Cynical, aggressive, masculine Blaise! Who could have guessed the depth of his pain? Seeing him this way—drunk, hurting, defenseless—Aurore passed from infatuation to a deeper and truer and more compassionate love of her cousin. She unwound the black sash from his waist.

"Môme," Blaise mumbled. "Môme."

"Hush. Blaise." Aurore smoothed the damp, curly tendrils back from his forehead. How he must have loved her! "It was a long time ago." She tried to make her voice calm and soothing as she unfastened his belt.

"Long time ago." His blue eyes, lost in the past, were brimming with tears.

Aurore's chest constricted. He was going to cry. It was too much to bear. What could she do to comfort him?

Blaise fell back on the bed. His shoulders began to shake. The sound of his sobs didn't cross his lips, but they quickly took possession of his body.

"Oh! Blaise! Please don't!" In a kind of panic, Aurore threw herself down beside him. She put her arms around him and tried to hold him to her to comfort him, but he was lying flat and it wasn't possible. Instead, she lay her head on his bare chest.

"Try to sleep," she murmured, as if to a restless child. Unpremeditatedly, guided by the need to comfort him, she pressed her lips to his bronzed flesh in little kisses. Suddenly she was aware of a change in texture, and her eyes flickered open to see the livid, puckered skin of his knife scar.

At that moment, she felt the touch of his hand upon her head. Tenderly he stroked the silky profusion of her auburn tresses, his calloused palms rasping slightly against

the fine texture. She traced the line of his scar with her
lips then, as if to take away any vestiges of pain remaining on the marred skin. His fingers played with the
softly curling ends of the long auburn strands and then
strayed to the bare flesh of her shoulder and upper arm.

Aurore looked up at him. His eyes were closed. The
sobs had stopped. How wonderful it felt to have him
touch her! There was gentleness in his touch, and yet
her heart was pounding like a tomtom. Now his thumb
was rubbing her naked back, working its way up to her
neck. Little ripples of shivery warmth spread from her
nape down to her breasts. Aurore felt her nipples hardening against the eyelet bodice of her dress. He was
playing with her hair again, stroking it upward so that
the silky curls tumbled over his chest. Then he grasped
a handful of her tresses and brought her face up to his.

Without warning, his full, sensual lips were upon
hers, pressing them open so that the warm breath of
their mouths could mingle. She could taste the aromatic
flavor of brandy. He forced her mouth open wider to
admit his eagerly probing tongue. His soft, thick, mustache tickled the tender skin of her moist and quivering
lips.

His free hand brushed over the bare flesh of her
shoulder, sliding the shoulder strap down. His fingers
caressed the swell of her breasts above the snug white
bodice. And then his hand was inside, cupping the
tender mound and making her moan with desire. His
hand closed over hers to help as she reached to pull
down the zipper of her dress. It opened to the waist and
her firm, shimmering breasts tumbled forth. Blaise pulled
her on top of him, his hungry mouth kissing and suck-
ling the hard nipples until Aurore's breasts ached with
desire.

The moonlight splashed over them like molten gold.
It was very late now, and there was the moist nip of
predawn in the breeze cooling their fevered flesh. The
deep red-brown of one of the mahogany stanchions of
Blaise's four-poster bed wavered before Aurore's gaze.

The embossed titles of the leather-bound volumes in the bookcase to the right of the bed swam in a hodgepodge of words that reminded her of hearing *Tante* Colette describe "the masculine and intellectual balance" she had stressed in redecorating Blaise's bedroom.

Blaise's blue eyes were veiled, their depths murky with a mindless—perhaps alcoholic—lust. His mouth was drawn in a thin, cruel line that only relaxed to envelop the pointed nipples of her breasts. There was no hint of what Blaise was thinking, or if he was thinking at all. What he might have been feeling, aside from lust, was not expressed on his countenance.

What has aroused him so? she wondered. Is it me? Or is it the liquor? The memory? Does he really desire me? Or would any female satisfy him now. And then, surrendering herself to passion, she stopped wondering, stopped even caring.

She felt the whole brawny length of his hard-muscled body beneath her, the heat of his flesh burning through their clothing. She moved against him, wanting to be even closer, wanting to merge her whole being with his, and then she felt it, hard and insistent against her inner thighs. How frighteningly huge it had appeared to her on that first long-ago day when she found him sleeping naked.

Now, as she pressed herself against him in an agony of pulsating desire, Aurore was no longer afraid. She hungered with all her being to discover the mysteries hidden within the tower of his erect manhood. She had wanted him for so long, and now at last the miracle would happen. She had been waiting for this all her life.

He growled and shifted, and then his hand was fumbling at his zipper. His thick and rigid priapus sprang out. She touched it hesitantly at first, and then she was stroking it, exploring its entirety and marveling at the velvety softness of the tautly stretched skin.

Blaise lay back watching her, his eyes metallic blue slits, his sensual lips slack, red and moist beneath the downward slash of his mustache. A pulse throbbed at the base of his neck, and his biceps and pectoral muscles rippled beneath his bronzed skin as they changed position. He kissed Aurore's mouth fiercely and thoroughly as his hands moved over her trembling breasts and supple waist. Then he pulled off her white dress completely, tossing it to the floor. The palms of his hands caressed her rounded thighs and the curves of her belly and hips.

His fingertips edged under the elastic of her silken panties and quickly pulled them down. Aurore raised her hips to help him and then looked up at him shyly through her thick lashes, embarrassed—yet still more aroused—by his reaction to her quivering nudity. His glinting eyes raked over her in a slow, piercing way that sent fresh thrills of desire along her nerve ends.

She looked into his eyes, and then his mouth came down on hers again with a force that was almost cruel. The hairs of his mustache bit into her soft lips as he forced them open wider. There was no relief from the unbearable tingles and throbs of sensation that swept over her body, making her whimper and writhe. Now his hand moved down to the base of her belly, the blunt, hard fingers ploughing through the auburn curls to explore her secret cleft.

Aurore could not bear to be touched like this! It was too much, the feeling of his rough finger rolling over and over that shamefully sensitive part of her, now so moist and round and firm.

Finally, making an animal sound deep in his throat, he drew away and lifted himself over her body. She stared up at him, eager and wild-eyed, as his knees forced her legs open wider. His hand was between her thighs, touching both of them as he positioned his throbbing, deep-red erection against her lushly swollen nether lips. She had anticipated this, yes, and craved it, and yet it was a shock, the uncompromising steely hardness and demanding size of him against her soft and vulnerably parted flesh.

The initial shock vibrated through her, sending off tremors and pulsations that boded of the climax to come. She was in upheaval, arching her back, straining her thighs, trembling and shuddering against his force. The pressure was terrible in its intensity, and yet she was fighting with it and not against it, yearning for the dagger of lust, no matter how painful, to pierce her loveless innocence and banish it forever.

And then it struck. She cried out, and yet the pain provided sharp relief from the unbearable pressure. Aurore reveled in it, reveled in the knowledge that it was Blaise who had done it, reveled in the wanton pleasure that followed.

Oh, the bliss of having him move like this, so smoothly and easily! It was more wonderful than she had ever dreamed! To be filled so full and yet have him move in and out so effortlessly with this slippery, sensuous rhythm! She wanted to tell him how wonderful it felt, but her lips would not move to frame the words. She would tell him without words then, by kissing his rough cheeks, the crisp curls of his sideburns, and most of all, his deliciously cruel mouth. She would tell him with her arms, hugging him tight against her rhythmically moving and joyous body, and with her hands stroking the smooth skin of his broad, muscular back as their passion mounted with the steady, soothing motion of ocean waves.

But then a storm came out of nowhere, heralded by her wildly pounding heart and a pulsing beat in her loins that made her hips strain frantically against him. She was being sucked downward in a vortex of rushing, swirling sensation that made her fight for breath. His every thrust was pushing her deeper into her own molten center. Flames sprang from the hot core there and licked at her unmercifully until she felt as if she were glowing with an incandescent fire.

Aurore writhed and strained against Blaise, her nails raking his back, her teeth sinking into the flesh of his shoulder. He loosed an angry growl, and then he was looking down at her, his face swarthy and demonic in the predawn light. His eyes were narrowed, his lips drawn back from his clenched white teeth, the muscles of his square jaw clenched.

Slowly, deliberately, thoroughly, Blaise thrust and withdrew and thrust again. Aurore could feel the power, the strength behind each motion. She braced herself and accepted them mutely, her mouth open, her eyes unfocused as she stared up at his rugged pirate's face. She lay quite still now, savoring each blow as it resounded inside her. Her body was open and unmoving in response to the ferocity of his latest assault. It was as if she were trembling on the peak of a sheer cliff and the slightest motion might push her over the edge and into the abyss.

Then his thrusts came faster and harder until she could remain still no longer. Something erupted deep inside her, and Aurore began pitching and tossing uncontrollably, meeting his thrusts as if to challenge his primacy, to clutch him to her womb and beyond. She wanted more! If he stopped now, she would die!

Finally time stood still as Aurore realized her squeezing, shuddering climax. Ecstasy, aching pleasure washed over her in warm, delicious waves as she held Blaise inside her, clenching and unclenching until she felt the hot geyser of his release. His wordless roar of triumph mingled with her soft cries of joy.

Slowly Aurore's eyes refocused. Over Blaise's shoulder, she saw the orange-yellow disc of the sun burst over the horizon. Its dawn rays danced with shimmering rainbow hues. The graying veil of the night sky parted to disclose silver and violet clouds lighted by shocking streaks of scarlet and saffron. The morning light invaded the open windows, and Aurore closed her eyes against its glare. Then, as it bathed the lovers in its rosy glow, she and Blaise both fell into a deep and blissful sleep, their limbs entwined about each other, Blaise's head cradled on Aurore's breast.

When she awoke, the sun was as its zenith, burning

the skin of her shoulder and back, dazzling her eyes. She sat up, momentarily disoriented by the unfamiliar surroundings. There was a raw and burning sensation between her legs, and a stickiness . . .

Aurore remembered then, remembered everything with a rush of joy and embarrassment and erotic yearning all combined. She looked at Blaise beside her, his magnificent furnished body sprawled in abandoned slumber.

She smiled and nestled closer, a delicious anticipation stirring her lower body. Blaise looked so much younger asleep, with the downward lines of his mouth smoothed out and that stubborn jaw relaxed. His mouth seemed softer and almost innocent beneath the brigand mustache. How demanding that mouth had been last night! Her own mouth was still swollen from their kisses.

How she loved him! She always had, ever since she had first seen his photograph and heard tales of his exploits. But that love had been unreal, the kind of crush all young girls have on unattainable male idols. And for so long after she met him in the flesh, Blaise had still seemed unattainable, separated from her by his wealth, his worldliness, and, most of all, by his insistence upon treating her like a child.

Thank goodness that barrier was broken down. Blaise could certainly not deny that she was a woman now, not after what had happened between them. Aurore stretched luxuriously. *A woman!* She reached for his half-erect phallus with a curled hand.

His eyes flickered open lazily, then widened, staring into hers like two blue marbles. "Jesus Christ!" He sat up, pulling away from her hand. He took in her tumbled auburn hair, her creamy, rose-tipped breasts, the ripe, naked curves of her hips. He reached down for the sheet that lay wadded in the center of the bed and pulled it up over his loins. The movement revealed a bloodstain on the bottom sheet. "Jesus Christ!"

Aurore was suffused with embarrassment. "I'm sorry," she started to say. "I couldn't help—"

"You're sorry!" His laugh was a humorless mixture of contempt and disgust.

Aurore didn't realize that both were meant for himself. She thought that she was the object of his displeasure. But why? What had she done wrong? How had she disappointed him?

"I get blind drunk and deflower my innocent young cousin, and *you're* sorry!"

There was more bitterness than irony in his voice, but such nuances escaped Aurore. To her, the words were like ice water splashed over all her warm, tender feelings for him. Whatever last night had meant to her, it was obvious that Blaise took no joy in what had occurred. "I only meant to say that I was sorry you didn't enjoy it," she uttered stiffly.

"Didn't I?"

"You don't remember?"

"I was very drunk. If I hadn't been, I might have drawn the line at incest!"

"Incest?"

"That's what they call it when first cousins make love. In some places, it's a crime. Marseilles is one. I don't know about Senegal."

"A crime," Aurore repeated numbly. "You think it's a crime?"

"Not really. Still, when I asked you to live here, I assumed a responsibility for your welfare—for your innocence, if you like. Once before in my life I betrayed such a responsibility." Blaise shook his head as if to banish painful memories. "Last night, I repeated that betrayal with you. I didn't think it was still possible after the life I've led, but I'm ashamed." He looked at her directly then, and his words were a pledge. "I promise you it will never happen again."

Aurore fled then. She didn't stop to put on her dress, only wrapped it around her trembling body and rushed from the room. She ran to the bathroom and locked the door behind her.

She ran a tub of water as hot as she could stand it.

Then she kept the water running in the washbasin to hide the sound of her sobbing as she scrubbed herself. She had to remove every vestige of what had happened. He had ruined it! Obviously it had meant nothing to him. Only shame!

Aurore climbed from the tub and dried herself. Her whole body was sore and aching as she dragged herself to her room. She flung herself across her bed.

Why? What had she done? Had she been too wild and wanton? Too uninhibited? Too easy? Perhaps a lady was supposed to restrain herself. Perhaps he had expected her to be more reluctant. Perhaps she should have protested and fought to retain her virtue.

Aurore began to shake and tremble. She bit into the pillow, choking on the sobs that rose like nausea in her throat. Her fist formed and slowly began to beat with futility into the unresponsive mattress. Gradually Aurore's despair changed to anger and then to a quiet, cold, determined rage.

Blaise didn't want her. He had only made love to her because he was drunk. He had no intention of possessing her again. He found her repulsive.

Very well then. She would face reality. Her virginity was lost, and Blaise was lost with it. But she wasn't going to let it destroy her. There were other men. They found her attractive. She would not deny herself the joys of sex. She had nothing more to lose and only pleasure to gain. She would have other men.

Hatred now was her response to Blaise's rejection of her. Yes! She hated him! That was all. He had killed the love she felt for him. She would never feel it again.
Never again!

CHAPTER 7

The loss of innocence is an inescapable part of human development. Sometimes, as in Aurore's case, this is the lesson for the seduced. And sometimes it is a lesson for the seducer, the rapist, the colonizer. The French rulers of Senegal began to learn it on October 10, 1947, when the black railway workers on the Dakar-Niger line went on strike.

Running from Dakar in Senegal to Bamako in Mali, the Dakar-Niger Railroad was one thousand miles long. It linked one million square miles of the African continent. The Senegalese and other Africans called it the Smoke of the Savanna.

The name had originated not in fondness for the steam engine chugging across the once-barren continent but rather in bitter recollection of how the French had built the railroad. They had seized ancient tribal lands along most of the track length and killed the tribal warriors who opposed them. In the Bamako area, by depriving tribes of their farmlands, they had brought about a famine. This resulted in disease of such epidemic proportions that the populations of entire tribes—men, women, and children—were wiped out.

"The Smoke of the Savanna" had burned out fertile lands and denied sustenance to those who lived there for generations to come. It had effectively created a food shortage so that it could distribute food—and other products—at a profit. It was a classic example of how Europeans brought "progress" to Africa. The Senegalese would not soon forget this example.

But if African memory was long, French memory was not. Indeed, it reached no further back than the beginnings of paternalism. Thus the *toubabs* of the railroad were genuinely puzzled when their "children," to whom they had brought and were still bringing "the benefits of Western civilization," proved so ungrateful as to go on strike.

The railroad management took the position that first the strikers must go back to work, and then—perhaps—they would deign to discuss the workers' grievances. The *toubabs* announced that some grievances—the matter of family allowances, for instance—would not be discussed under any circumstances. The Muslim practice of polygamy and the high black birth rate made it impossible to consider providing Africans with family allowances like those given French railway workers who were monogamous and Christian.

Management took offense when the strikers did not acknowledge the benevolence of their position and return to their jobs. They prevailed upon the colonial government to issue an order to each individual striker that drafted him back to work on the railroad. Most strikers ignored the order. The government could not put them all in jail, but some were arrested as an example. A few of the strikers went back to work. Unofficial union squads were formed to punish these "scabs." Finally the railroad brought in white railway workers from Europe to run token trains once a week. These carried passengers only and bristled with government troops assigned to protect them.

The reason the trains carried only passengers and not produce had to do with the railroad's determination not only to break the back of the strike as they had done with the previous strike in September, 1938, but also to destroy the union permanently. They had many strategies toward this end. They infiltrated the union to keep abreast of its plans and activities. They tried repeatedly to buy off the leaders of the strike. They even strove to build up a faction among the strikers that would break away and create a rival union under the secret control of the company. But their primary—and most effective—tactic was starvation.

It was a two-pronged tactic. On one hand, it cut off the strikers from any support in the rural agricultural areas of the country. Watching their produce rot for lack of transportation to take it to market while the railroad agents, the government representatives, and the French-trained native officers of the army and militia all assured them that it was the strikers who were responsible, many farmers turned militantly antiunion.

On the other hand, the cities of Senegal—Dakar, Thiès, St. Louis, and others—were at the mercy of a rigidly French controlled distribution of foodstuffs, administered by colonial officials pledged to aid the management of the railroad in ending the strike. It was a simple matter to feed the French while starving all the Africans except the colonial troops guarding the border between the two areas.

The French recognized that poor urban blacks would support the strikers, perhaps even with food, and decided that to drive a wedge between them and the strikers, they would have to starve the native populace as a whole. Armed convoys carried foodstuffs through the black districts to the plush French quarters of the cities. All deliveries of meat and fish, rice, millet, and maize to markets in the native areas were forbidden, depriving the residents of the staples of their diet.

The inevitable result was a black market. It was only natural that it should be run by the Lebanese foodsellers who had always flourished as the merchant class between the French rulers and the Senegalese workers. Black markets, however, can't be run on credit.

Food had always been bought on credit by the poor blacks of the cities. By extending credit, the sellers had been able to keep prices up without being challenged. Now, deprived of the ability to buy food on credit, the city blacks faced starvation. The French let it be known that the black market would be halted and credit reinstituted just as soon as the strikers went back to work.

The pressure was intense. Adults grew thinner with starvation as they watched their children's bellies swell. In Dakar, the French cut off the pipeline providing the main water supply, letting through only a trickle at unannounced intervals. Water joined food as a black-market luxury. In Thiès, there was a confrontation between strikers and troops that resulted in five wounded and one dead. In Bamako, the African women who worked in the market refused to sell produce to European households.

With the aid provided by other unions both in Senegal and France, the railway workers' union undertook a regular distribution of food to strikers and their families. But there was not enough to go around. Many of the men were polygamous, and so they gave the food allotment to one wife and her children one week and a different wife and family the next week. In the interim, the various families had to exist as best they could. Native women began selling their most prized possessions to moneylenders at a fraction of their value in order to purchase food on the black market.

Ile Celeste was removed from the direct impact of these events. Nevertheless, the people of the island could not help but be affected. Nearly all the Wolof islanders had family connections or friends in Dakar. The island fishing industry was seriously threatened. It was the plight of the island economy that led to a business meeting at le Château de Beausoleil one warm and balmy morning in late November when the strike was little more than a month old.

Aurore was breakfasting late and alone on a terrace overlooking the pool when Steven Parker and Mustapha Hakim arrived. Just as she rang for coffee for them, Blaise appeared. He nodded curtly to Aurore, whose return greeting was equally brusque, and ushered the two men to a group of brightly cushioned rattan chairs arranged in the shadiest area of the patio. Aurore could see and hear them clearly from where she was eating, but she was excluded from their discussion. Coffee was being served to them when Aurore spied Amin Baye climbing the path leading to the château.

She went to greet her brother-in-law halfway. "How is Sabine?" she inquired. "And how is Chief Amadou?"

Amin smiled at this reference to his son's heritage. "Sabine is fine," he told Aurore. "So is Amadou, although Sabine complains that he is a glutton who nurses twenty-four hours a day. He has already grown so much that we are making him a larger basket in which to sleep."

"Tell Sabine I'll be down to see them both soon." Aurore smiled at the prospect as they reached the terrace and she parted from Amin to resume her breakfast.

Amin returned her smile, but his face turned serious as he joined the three men waiting for him. He accepted a cup of coffee and sat down in one of the rattan chairs. He nodded to Steven Parker and greeted Hakim: "Thank you for coming." Then he turned to Blaise.

"You didn't tell me that you'd asked these gentlemen to join us," Blaise said bluntly.

Aurore sipped her second cup of café au lait, making no effort to hide her interest in the men's conversation.

"I told Steven our situation," Amin replied. "I thought he might be of help. So did he. And so I asked him to join us."

Blaise glanced quizzically toward Mustapha Hakim. Amin shrugged to indicate that he was as puzzled by the Lebanese's attendance as Blaise was. Hakim sat complacently unembarrassed, showing no inclination to enlighten them as to the reason for his presence.

"I asked Mr. Hakim to be here." It was Steven Parker who spoke. "I reckoned he might make things easier for both parties."

"Oh?" Blaise looked amused. "Is that so, Hakim? Are you prepared to bring the strike to an end for our convenience?" he asked sarcastically.

"How much would it be worth to you, monsieur?"

Hakim inquired with equanimity. "All things are possible if the price is right."

Blaise threw back his head and roared with laughter. "I believe you, Hakim. I really do believe you. With enough money, you could have bought off Adolf Hitler himself and prevented the Second World War."

"Or Churchill," Hakim suggested. "Or Stalin. Or Roosevelt, although that might have been very expensive indeed."

"If the pacifists had only had enough money," Blaise said innocently, "you could have bribed the various harbor patrols to confiscate all the arms shipments before they could be used for war."

Hakim glanced quickly at Amin and Parker and then back at Blaise. "As usual, monsieur, your *bons mots* are too clever for my poor wits. I am only a humble Lebanese businessman and not up to the banter of the *beau monde.*"

"And how does this 'humble Lebanese businessman' propose to solve our present dilemma?" Blaise inquired.

"Wait!" Amin interrupted, holding up a hand. "Before we get into that, Blaise, I'd like to know if you've come to a decision regarding our arrangement."

"Yes." Aurore could not miss the note of reluctance in Blaise's voice. "I'm afraid I have. I'm going to invoke the escape clause in the contract I have with the fishermen of Ile Celeste."

"That seems mighty harsh!" Steven Parker sputtered. "These fishermen didn't come chasing you for a contract to tote their catch. It was the other way around. And now you're set to pull out and leave them with tons of rotting fish!"

"Like Hakim, I'm a businessman." Blaise shrugged.

"Blaise has been a good friend to me." Amin cut Parker off in anticipation of the heat of his response. "But business is business, and when I negotiated the contract with him, I insisted on certain provisions which— as it turns out—are now working to Blaise's advantage. That is not his fault. Nor can we blame him for invoking the escape clause against the losses he would have to take if it were not there.''

"Excuse me. I don't mean to pry,'' Hakim interjected. ''But I am not familiar with the contract to which you refer. If it is not confidential, might I know its terms and the details of the escape clause you've been discussing?''

"There is nothing secret,'' Amin answered him. ''It is a simple contract. It gives Blaise exclusive rights to haul each day's catch of fish from Ile Celeste to Dakar for a percentage of the price the catch brings. It specifies that the catch is to be sold to food buyers for the black section of Dakar. If Blaise sells the fish elsewhere the escape clause allows us to terminate the contract. If he can't sell the fish as specified, it allows him to terminate it. Now that the Dakar colonial government has imposed an embargo on food sold to the blacks of the city, he has the right to exercise that option.''

"Steven told me that,'' Hakim replied. ''I just wondered about the specifics.''

"Well, now you know,'' Blaise told him.

"Contract or not, it's a cruel step to take!'' Parker said bitterly.

"What is cruel,'' Amin told him, ''is the French strategy aimed at starving out the strikers.'' A muscle in his jaw jumped angrily. ''And they call us savages!'' he added. ''They call us savages and they starve our children!''

"But there are so many, many children,'' Hakim observed blandly.

"I do not think I follow you.'' Amin looked at him with eyes like burning coals.

"It is the Muslim curse,'' Hakim explained calmly. ''Remember, monsieur, that while I am a Lebanese, I am also Muslim just as you are. We both know that when a Muslim finds himself with extra money, his impulse is to acquire another wife and beget another tribe of children. While it is delightful to have such connubial variety, it does result in a staggering birth rate. It is hardly surprising that the French don't look kindly upon granting their Muslim workers two or three family allowances while their Christian workers receive only one.''

"Children are a gift from Allah! If it pleases him to bless a man with many offspring, it is His will and must not be questioned!'' Amin's voice was heated now.

"Then it must be Allah's will that they starve.'' Hakim shrugged complacently.

"No! The strike is not Allah's will!'' Amin told him. "The *imams* have told us as much. If the Muslim workers would listen to them instead of to the Communists, then their children would have food.''

"We're not here to discuss politics,'' Blaise reminded them. He turned to Hakim. "If you have any practical suggestions to persuade me not to invoke the escape clause, Hakim, then let's hear them.''

"Monsieur Amin Baye has been a good customer of mine,'' Hakim replied smoothly. "Perhaps now it is my turn to become a good customer of his. If you, Monsieur de Beausoleil, will continue to deliver the daily catch of fish from Ile Celeste to the Dakar docks, I will buy it.''

Blaise looked at Hakim through narrowed eyes for a long moment. "At what price?'' he asked finally.

"Let us say an average of the price you have been receiving over the last six months.''

"An average of the price over the last six months!'' Blaise snorted. "And with fish up fifty percent since the strike cut off the meat supply!''

"We are all good friends.'' Hakim was not insulted. "Why don't I add ten percent to my original offer?''

"Why don't you add the whole fifty?'' With his teeth bared that way, Aurore wondered why Blaise didn't look as much like a deep-sea shark as Hakim with his plump face did.

"My friend! My friend! Now it is you who forget the hardships imposed by the strike. I will have many distribution costs stemming from the government's attitude. I will have to function *sub rosa,* so to speak.''

"Sounds reasonable to me," Steven Parker grunted.

"It may sound reasonable, but it isn't," Blaise told him. "Our good friend Hakim here won't have any problems at all in disposing of the fish. If there were problems, he wouldn't be here. He made sure they were all solved before he came. Isn't that true, Hakim?''

"Warmth spreads from my toes to the roots of my hair at the closeness of our relationship, Monsieur de Beausoleil. To be known so well is indeed a compliment. Of course, there is truth in what you say. Still, what does it matter? We are all businessmen. If I have taken pains to be sure my part of this arrangement will bring me profit, why should that bother you?''

"Why should it?" Steven Parker echoed.

"Because," Blaise explained, "what our good friend Hakim means to do is to buy the fish from us at wholesale rates—below wholesale rates if I hadn't challenged him—and sell it at profiteer prices to the merchants of the European community in Dakar.''

"Is that true?" Amin demanded.

"The entire catch, which you insisted must feed Dakar blacks, will be eaten by wealthy Europeans whose meat supply has been restricted by the railway strike," Blaise told Amin. "That's what will happen if it's sold to Hakim.''

"Suppose that is true," Hakim said. "The islanders of Ile Celeste will still catch fish. You, Monsieur de Beausoleil, will still transport it. If we agree on a price, it will be business as usual despite the strike. Why quibble over whose plate the fish graces?''

"Whose plate the fish graces is the whole point of the escape clause," Blaise told him. He turned to Amin. "If you're willing to have the catch sold to the French, we don't need Hakim. I can arrange that kind of deal without any help. And probably at a much higher price without a middleman.''

"No." Amin sighed. "I don't want to do that. I am

sorry to have taken up your time,'' he apologized to Hakim.

"It is of no importance. Besides it is always a pleasure to receive the hospitality of Monsieur de Beausoleil."

Blaise bowed ironically in acknowledgment of the compliment.

"I shall have to seek another solution," Amin said.

"You're not thinking of that hare-brained scheme of Cherif's!" Steven Parker exclaimed.

The look Amin flashed him, Aurore was sure, said that he should hold his tongue. There was an awkward moment's silence. Hakim broke it.

"I saw Cherif Baye in Dakar," he said. "With the strikers." His voice was without inflection.

Amin nodded nervously and didn't comment on this information. "If you will excuse us," he said to Hakim and Parker, "I should like to speak to Blaise privately."

Blaise and Amin moved to the other side of the patio, where they could be seen but not overheard. The expression on Amin's face testified that the conversation was serious. Steven Parker and Hakim watched them for a moment and then turned to each other and made small talk. Aurore, however, continued to watch Blaise and Amin.

Doing so, she missed the entrance of Minette Fourier as the French *fille* stepped through the salon door and onto the patio. It was the scent of heliotrope that announced her presence to Aurore. When she did focus on Minette, she couldn't help admitting to herself that the society girl looked especially beautiful this morning.

Minette wore a print dress of blue and lavender chiffon. Its stylish cut showed off her slim, elegant figure to perfection. The colors enhanced the striking violet hue of her black-lashed eyes. Her shoulder-length hair framed her face, with its voluptuous scarlet mouth and classically chiseled features, like a soft ebony cloud.

"Business again!" Minette's voice was petulant and teasing at the same time. "A woman might as well be old and fat and ugly for all the attention you men pay to her.'' She acted as if Aurore were invisible. ''Well, far be it from me to intrude. I'll just take my morning stroll alone.''

''Allow me.'' With an agility at odds with his usual indolence, Hakim was on his feet and offering his arm to Minette. ''I should welcome the opportunity to see the grounds in such charming company, Mademoiselle Fourier.''

Minette's expression, Aurore noted with some satisfaction, betrayed that Hakim was not the companion she had had in mind for her walk. ''I don't really know my way around very well,'' she objected weakly.

''Then perhaps we shall get lost together.'' Hakim clasped her arm.

Minette flinched, then tossed her black hair, slipped her arm through Hakim's, and bestowed her most dazzling smile on him. ''Somehow I don't think we shall.''

''Let Allah decide.'' Hakim's manner was proprietory as they moved off together, the flat, polished top of his pomaded head barely reaching Minette's shoulder.

At that moment, Aurore happened to glance at Blaise. He was still talking to Amin, but his eyes were on Minette and Hakim. He watched them until they disappeared down the hill, one eyebrow lifted quizzically.

Is he jealous? Aurore wondered, made jealous herself at the thought. Why else would he stare after them in that intent way? But how could such a repulsive little man be competition for Blaise?

''Okay if I join you?'' Steven Parker stood beside Aurore's table. ''I'm getting bored all by my lonesome.''

''Of course. Sit down.''

He eased his rangy body into a wrought-iron lawn chair. ''Beauty and the beast,'' he said idly, nodding in the direction Hakim and Minette had gone. ''Although I suppose Mustapha's not all that bad.''

''She didn't have to go with him. She could have made some excuse.''

''The lady couldn't exactly do that to an old friend.''

''Are they friends?'' Aurore was surprised.

"If coming to the aid of a lady in distress is friendship, they are."

"What kind of distress is Minette in?"

"Financial. A ways back, she went to Hakim asking for a loan. He gave it to her, bought up her unpaid bills, and has been underwriting her fancy duds and lavish parties ever since."

"How do you know all this?"

"Sometimes, close-mouthed as he is, even Hakim has to talk to somebody. A lot of it I know from Delphine. I guess it's just a matter of putting two and two together."

"I thought Minette's family was wealthy."

"They were before the war, when her daddy was alive. He was a real smart wheeler-dealer, from what I hear. Played footsie with Vichy and the Free French, all the angles. But when he died, it turned out he had all his money tied up in artworks that the Nazis confiscated when they took over France. These were classic paintings, masterpieces, and they're back in Paris now. Supposedly Minette is going to get some kind of settlement for her daddy's investment. But that could take years. Meanwhile, Hakim foots her bills."

"Why? Charity isn't like him."

"Well now! Aren't you just the most naive little lady?"

"You mean—" Despite her dislike for Minette, Aurore shuddered at the idea.

"I don't think Minette sleeps with him, if that's what you're thinking. But my guess is Hakim means to let her get in so deep it'll come to that in the end. Unless he means to marry her. Providing, of course, that your cousin Blaise doesn't get hitched to her first."

"Do you think he will?" Aurore's heart sank.

"I don't know what to think. It appears Blaise is dragging his feet more that somehwat."

"Really?" Aurore was relieved.

Her relief didn't last long past Steven and Hakim's lunchtime departure. It was replaced by jealousy again when Blaise took Minette sailing that afternoon. The idea of the two of them alone somewhere in the middle of the ocean was painful for Aurore to contemplate.

It had been like this for Aurore ever since the night Blaise made love to her. She had vacillated between wanting him and hating him for rejecting her, between being jealous over his ongoing affair with Minette and so eager to repeat the physical joy to which Blaise had introduced her that she would have given herself to any man who wanted her. No small part of this last feeling was the suspicion that in some peculiar way, it would punish Blaise for his treatment of her.

Blaise's attitude toward her was circumspect. He carefully avoided being alone with her. He was considerate but distant. When, at rare moments, their eyes met, it was to Aurore like a physical caress. But Blaise would simply look away, adding one more small rejection to the major one he had inflicted. Thus Aurore learned to live with that pain which is the other side of the coin of love.

Still, the pain was easier to handle than the incessant yearnings of her body. Blaise had opened the Pandora's box of her passion, and it would not be closed. The hungry flesh of her young woman's body burned for fulfillment.

So it was when she returned to her room after lunch. It was quite hot, and she was so restless that even the touch of the linen sheet against her flesh was unbearable. The walls of the room seemed to close around her so that she could hardly breathe. She had to squeeze her eyes shut against the imaginary vision of Blaise and Minette locked in lovemaking on the sailboat, but her mind would not let go of them.

Perhaps a swim would refresh her, calm her down. But not in the pool where *Tante* Colette and some guests were already splashing. No, she would swim in the ocean.

Aurore undressed and took a bright, flower-printed *pagne* from one of her bureau drawers. Instead of wrapping it around her waist, as was the Senegalese custom, she tied it around her breasts and let it cover her thighs sarong-style. She slipped from the house unnoticed.

At the bottom of the hill, she began to jog. The slow, steady running motion soothed her jangled nerves. She ran under the palms at the edge of the sand for over a mile before cutting across the beach toward the water. None of the château guests ever came this far. She was about halfway to the fishing village; she need have no concern about shedding her *pagne* and stepping into the sea naked.

How delightful the cool waves felt against her over-heated skin! The water was so clear that she could see her toes on the sandy bottom. She swam and then floated face upward so that all she saw was the crystal blue sky, and all she heard was the soft, lapping sound of the ocean washing the shoreline.

Finally she emerged from the sea, a honey-skinned Venus, her dark red hair a mass of shimmering ringlets dripping bright beads of water upon her full, rose-tipped breasts. She spread her *pagne* on the sand and lay facedown upon it. The sun's pulsing heat on her back and buttocks seemed to throb under her skin itself as it warmed her coursing blood. How gloriously free she felt! She relaxed fully, burrowing her breasts and hips into the sand.

What a comfortable bed the sand makes, Aurore thought dreamily. The sun gleamed red behind her closed eyes; her flesh continued glowing under the radiant kiss of its rays. Every pore of her body was open and avid for penetrating—as open and avid as she had been for Blaise's embrace that night three long months ago. She shivered suddenly, remembering the feeling of his tongue upon her stiffly aroused nipples, the sensation of his fingers probing her flesh.

Aurore was suddenly distracted from her reverie by the sound of footsteps thudding on the beach. She sat up. The approaching figure was running quickly along the golden sand.

"Cherif!" Hastily Aurore wrapped the flowered *pagne* around her naked body. More than a year had passed since Sabine's wedding, when Cherif had taken her into the bushes and tried to make love to her. This was the first time they had been alone together since then. "Why are you running so fast?" she greeted him awkwardly.

"Not so fast. I pace myself. It relaxes me."

"Running relaxes me, too." Aurore felt strangely uncomfortable with him. She didn't know what to say. "I thought you were in Dakar with the strikers," she managed finally.

"I was with them." Cherif threw himself down beside her. He wore only a pair of khaki shorts. His gleaming chest rose and fell rapidly from the exertion of running. "I came back to see your cousin Blaise. But he isn't here."

"He went sailing. He should be back by dusk, I imagine."

"I have business to discuss with him and with my brother."

"Business about the strike?"

"Yes."

"Blaise and Amin are concerned about selling the catch."

"I know. I think perhaps I may have a solution."

"To sell the fish to the strikers illegally?" Aurore guessed.

"You ask too many questions."

"I'm sorry."

An uncomfortable silence fell between them. Cherif finally broke it. "I did not mean that you should stop talking altogether," he said.

"I don't know what to say."

"Then go ahead and ask me questions if that is the only conversation you can make."

"All right." Aurore thought a moment. Then—"There is one thing I'd like to ask you," she said. "Why are you, a fisherman, involving yourself with the railway workers?"

"Because they are the only ones standing up to the *toubabs* at the present time," he told her without hesitation. "One day we must all do that. The strike is a beginning."

"But their concerns aren't your concerns."

"Yes they are. And mine are theirs. We must all share each other's troubles until we have driven the French from Senegal. Besides, the demands of the railway workers are just. Equal wages for equal work, sick benefits, family allowances, and a pension plan—all benefits the white workers receive; all benefits to which the blacks are entitled."

"But the strike is illegal. The French say that if the demands are just, the workers have legal ways of getting them."

"Legal ways?" Cherif snorted derisively. "Let me tell you about legal ways. The Overseas Labor Code was a legal way. It contained every reform the strikers are demanding. It was drawn up by the French government itself. But it is not law. The French see to it that it never gets to the floor of our noble Black Constituent Assembly for discussion and that the French National Assembly continues to postpone voting on it. Without the enactment of the code, a strike was inevitable. So much for legal ways!"

"Sabine says that Amin is afraid the Communists are behind the strike."

"Amin listens too much to the *imams*. They serve the French well when they throw up their hands in horror and scream 'Communist!' The *imams* kiss the asses of the *toubabs* to hold onto their own power."

"But the Communists are involved, Cherif. You know that. Amin didn't make it up."

"He distorts it. Look, I do not deny that the most powerful trade unions in Senegal, led by the Confédération Générale du Travail, are Communist. But the union of railway workers is not one of those trade unions. It is independent. Completely. It has stayed independent in the face of great pressure from the CGT to affiliate with them. The railway workers did not require Communist agitators to get them to walk out. Their grievances and French arrogance and stubbornness were reason enough.''

"Isn't the CGT financing the strike?"

"They are helping, it is true. But what is wrong with that? If the railway workers win, it will be a blow against the French for all Africans. The CGT knows that. And the strikers know that they must take help wherever they can get it and leave the ideological questions for later.''

"Ideological questions." Aurore couldn't help smiling. "You've changed, Cherif. That doesn't sound much like the boy I used to know."

"I am not a boy anymore, Aurore. I am a man."

"Yes. I suppose you are." Aurore scowled.

"You do not like it that I am a man?"

She shrugged.

"You are thinking of my behavior at the wedding a year ago?"

Actually, she hadn't been. She had been thinking of Blaise. She had been thinking of him as a man who acted like a man, and she had remembered what Delphine once said: "All men are bastards!" If Blaise was typical of men, then that was true. Still, why was she taking out her feelings toward him on Cherif? Aurore shook off her resentment and answered Cherif. "No, I wasn't," she told him. "I long ago forgave you for that. You'd had too much to drink, I think."

"Yes. I had. But it was also that I was jealous. And that I was burning with desire for you."

"Or perhaps just burning with desire, period." Her tone was not unkind. "After all, there was Leita." She held up a hand to cut off his explanation. "It's all right. If I didn't understand then, I do now."

"Leita was never anything but a substitute for you."

"Poor Leita. It's not very nice of you to talk that way

about her, Cherif. Not after the way you've been together.''

"No. It is not very nice. But I did not mean it as gossip or as an insult to Leita. I only meant it as the truth. You are the one for whom my flesh has always yearned.''

"Oh, Cherif.'' Aurore was touched.

"You are like a fever in my blood.''

"My poor Cherif.'' She reached out a trembling hand to stroke his cheek by way of comfort.

There was longing in his soft brown eyes as they locked with hers. A muscle twitched above his lean jawline. His long, tapered fingers entwined with hers, trapped her hand and held it to his cheek. "Remember how it used to be?'' he murmured.

Aurore remembered. She recalled the days of their youth when they had explored each other's bodies. "I remember.'' She sighed deeply, knowing that he was about to kiss her and content that it should happen.

She leaned closer to meet his lips. Her wavy, sea-dampened mane of hair fell forward, providing a curtain from the blazing sun as his mouth met and clung to hers. It was a loving and deep and hungry ritual. Cherif kissed her as if her mouth were an exotic fruit he must taste and taste again before consuming it. His hand stroking the supple skin of her neck and the swelling rise of her bosom was as tender as his kiss and as demanding. Then his fingers were sliding under the knot of her *pagne*, and Aurore's nipples were tingling expectantly as he caressed the softness of her breasts. The ardent probing of his tongue was both a thrill and a promise.

From a nearby grove of lemon trees, the aroma of citrus filled the air, mingling with a heavier perfume of hibiscus. The shadow of a tern in flight swept over them and spread its wings as the bird glided closer to the romantic scene below. Somewhere in the distance, a child laughed freely, the sound like a dispensation of innocence borne on the warm and rippling summer breeze.

Cherif undid the knot of her *pagne* and spread the garment out so that they might lie upon it. Aurore saw the reflection of her sun-drenched nakedness in the smoldering depths of his eyes. Her heart beat faster, and she felt mesmerized by the intense desire of his gaze.

As he bent to close his lips gently over one of her tender nipples, Aurore closed her eyes to savor the sensation. When she opened them, his hand was moving over her belly and down to her pubic curls, glinting red in the sun. Now his finger was dabbling in her secret moistness, teasing the hidden petals to unfurl. Gently her legs opened wider to his touch. She longed for his fingers to probe deeper.

Suddenly Aurore realized that if she let Cherif continue, he would find out that she was no longer a virgin. How would he react to the knowledge that she had given that which he wanted so badly to another man? Would he be disgusted with her? Would he leave her and never return?

Aurore didn't know the answers, and she was afraid of what they might be. She panicked at the idea of having to see that realization in his eyes, of seeing disgust, perhaps rage, or the devastation of rejection! No! She could not stand another rejection!

Instinctively, she reached out and ran her hand over the long bulge in his shorts. Cherif groaned and unbuttoned his fly. An instant later, his erect manhood nestled in her palm.

Aurore knelt over him. Her breasts swayed, and one of the ruby tips grazed the crown of his manhood. She trembled with the thrill it sent through her and grazed it once again.

She backed away a little and bent her mouth to his arching flesh. Her lips brushed against the pointed tip. She parted them gently, tentatively, and took in the raised, heart-shaped head. Cherif groaned and his hand reached out to stroke her silky, windblown hair.

Perhaps it was the blood rushing to her bent head and

perhaps it was the thrill of performing this intimate and forbidden act that made Aurore so dizzy. Her heart pounded wildly, as if trying to burst free of her body. When she closed her eyes against the faintness, a fire-works display erupted behind the lids, a dazzling rock-etry of bursting colors.

How easily and fluidly he moved inside her cheeks. It was as if nature had designed a woman's mouth especially for pleasuring a man. With every downward swoop of her head now, she took him in deeper until the burning *O* of her lips pressed against the firm twin bulges at the base of his member.

Cherif was groaning and thrusting upward. His rhyth-mic movements were in perfect harmony with her mouth. Any second now he would erupt and bestow upon Aurore's palate the nectar provoked by her deliciously erotic sucking.

Before that could happen, however, a shadow fell across the sun and a shrill, rage-filled shriek pierced Aurore's ears. "Frenchie whore!" Leita Ousbane loomed over them, quaking with righteous jealousy.

Aurore and Cherif scrambled apart. Cherif pulled up his shorts and buttoned them. Aurore pulled the *pagne* around herself and retied it. Leita watched, feet planted solidly, arms akimbo, looking down on them with eyes that were wild and angry and accusing.

"What are you doing here, Leita?" Cherif demanded.

"I see what you do with this one!" The finger Leita pointed at Aurore quivered like a dagger that had found its mark.

"You followed me!" he accused. "You are always following me. Just as when we were children. But it cannot go on anymore, Leita. You must stop it."

"You are my man!" she insisted.

"No."

"Yes! I do it first! I do it best! And when I do it, you are my man! You say so!"

"I do not say so, Leita. I am not your man."

"You do say so! You say many love words all the

time in the dark when I pleasure you. And now you show her things I show you!"

"You've been watching us all the time!" Aurore exclaimed.

"High and mighty!" Leita screeched. "What you think you are? I hear you tell Cherif how you watch us the night of the *sabar*. So why shouldn't I watch you, Mam'selle High-and-Mighty Frenchie Whore?"

"I stumbled on you by accident. I didn't sneak around spying!"

"You should maybe spy more. Maybe you learn something," Leita jeered. Her shiny black braids stood up straight in a wild crisscross of trembling indignation interlaced with gleaming scalp. "The way you do, his long, stiff serpent shrink to a little mouse!"

"That's not true!" Aurore retorted.

"I am best! I please Cherif! Not you! Is that not so, Cherif?" She turned to him for confirmation.

"It is crazy to argue over such a thing. Please, Leita, go now. Leave us in peace!"

"Not until you tell her I do it best!"

Although Aurore knew better than to let the deranged girl get to her, she was furious. In her anger, she unconsciously adopted the manner *Tante* Colette had been trying to instill in her, the cool arrogance that Minette Fourier so frequently displayed toward her. "Perhaps you are better," she told Leita haughtily. "After all, you've had so much practice." And then the coup de grace delivered in *Tante* Colette's most offhand tone: "Going down on your knees to every man in the village!"

Even more than the words, the snobbish tone enraged Leita. "Filthy half-breed!" she screeched. "Throw yourself at every man what comes along, Wolof or *toubab*. At the *sabar*, you drop your *boubou* and jiggle your big, naked melon breasts at all the men! At the wedding of your own sister, I see you with that straw-haired American, grinding up against him for all to see! And now with my Cherif!"

"He doesn't seem to think he is *your* Cherif." Observing how her hauteur was infuriating the black girl, Aurore spoke with even more aristocratic nastiness than before.

She did not realize, however, just how far that tone would push Leita. The island girl had not the sophistication to deal with it as Dakar society *filles* did. Her reaction was direct and immediate. With a wordless scream of rage, Leita flung herself at Aurore.

"Red-ear slut!" she shrieked. Like a maddened cat, she crouched and sprang at Aurore again. She grasped handfuls of wavy, auburn hair and tugged viciously.

"You—you—" Beside herself with pain and rage, Aurore delivered a stinging slap that caught Leita full in the face.

Blook trickled from Leita's flared notrils. She let out an injured yowl. Then, her sharp white teeth bared, she went for Aurore's throat.

With a cry of fear, Aurore kicked out, pulling back to avoid the bite of the teeth at her jugular. She blocked her throat with her arm and rolled over, taking Leita with her.

From the beginning of the fight, Cherif had been trying in vain to separate them. Now, finally, he managed to grip Leita under the arms and drag her off Aurore. Hissing and spitting like a wildcat, the black girl tried to pull loose. But she was no match for Cherif's sinewy strength. He threw her over his shoulder like a sack of cornmeal. The look he shot Aurore was a helpless and reluctant farewell. Then he started off in the direction of the village with his struggling and cursing burden.

Aurore lay on the sand, sweat-drenched and panting, and watched them out of sight. Then she threw open her *pagne* to let the ocean breeze soothe her sticky skin.

Suddenly, from behind Aurore, came a dreadful cackling that sent the adrenalin of panic racing through her body. It was the demented laughter of Ouna the *katt!*

Even in its shrillness, it was knowing, derisive, and eerily threatening.

With shaking hands, Aurore drew her *pagne* around her and stumbled to her feet. For one horrifying instant, she caught sight of a grizzled mop of hair and a witchlike face peering from behind the trunk of a coconut palm. Then she was running along the sand, fleeing from the crone and her evil mischief.

Aurore didn't slow her pace until the château was in sight, its pearl-white limestone turrets gleaming above the shade trees and flowering bushes surrounding it. She slipped inside unnoticed and went directly to her room. Soon she was immersed in a luxurious warm bath.

Afterward, she put on a jade-green silk dressing gown, went down the hall and rapped on Delphine's door. Delphine had been keeping to her room lately. She seemed uncharacteristically listless and depressed and complained of migraine headaches. Aurore had not seen her at all that day and was concerned about her.

Aurore knocked again. "Delphine? It's me—Aurore. Can I come in?"

Delphine opened the door. Aurore was shocked at her appearance. Her cousin's normally porcelain-clear skin was blotched and reddened and swollen around the eyes. Obviously Delphine had been weeping.

"What is it?" Aurore asked. "What's the matter?"

Delphine let her in and closed the door behind her. "I—I have a headache," she said in a small, choked voice.

"If the pain is this bad, perhaps you should go to Dakar and see a doctor." Aurore followed her to the pink-canopied bed and sat down on the edge beside her.

Delphine's shoulders were hunched as if against a sudden chill. "I have seen a doctor." Without makeup, she looked like a forlorn gamine, young and helpless and vulnerable.

"What did he say?" Aurore took Delphine's hand in hers and squeezed it sympathetically. "Is it serious?"

"Yes. It's serious." Delphine emitted a bitter little laugh. For a moment, it seemed as if she weren't going to say anything else. Then the words burst from her lips as if she could no longer hold them inside. "The doctor says I'm pregnant."

Aurore was too stunned to do anything except look at Delphine with all the tenderness she felt for her. "Who's responsible?" she asked finally. "You don't have to tell me," she added quickly. "I don't mean to pry."

"I have to talk to someone." Silent tears ran down Delphine's cheeks. "I have to tell someone or go crazy. But I can't talk to Maman. She's so contemptuous of him. And somehow Minette—" Her gesture conveyed the fact of Minette's self-centeredness. "You're the only one I can talk to, Aurore. You don't make judgments." Delphine took a deep breath. "It's Steven," she told Aurore. "Steven Parker."

"Have you told him?"

"Yes." The word came out harsh and clipped, like a pistol shot.

"What did he say?"

"First let me tell you what he didn't say. He didn't say 'Let's get married.' "

"Oh, Delphine!" Aurore hugged her and smoothed her tousled blond hair.

"What he did say was that he would arrange for an abortion. Coldly. Very matter-of-fact. But he's a man of his word, my sincere American. He's done just that."

"Have you told your brother? Perhaps if Blaise talked to him—"

"No!" Delphine was quite agitated at the suggestion. "I haven't told Blaise, and neither must you. Promise me, Aurore!"

"All right. If that's what you want," Aurore soothed her. "I promise. But why not, Delphine?"

"I'm afraid of what Blaise might do. He might hurt Steven. Or he might force him to marry me. I don't want either of those things."

"But surely Blaise would be more understanding than that. He's a man of the world."

"I've known Blaise all my life, Aurore, and I've learned one thing about him. You never can predict what he might do. He has a strange sense of family, and of honor."

Aurore wondered. Would Blaise think himself obliged to punish Steven Parker for doing what he himself had done? Did he make a distinction in his mind between what another man might do with his sister and what he did with Minette Fourier? Or with Aurore herself?

It struck Aurore forcefully that only chance kept her from being in Delphine's position. Suppose Blaise had made her pregnant. Would he have married her? Of course not! They were cousins, he would have said, and so marriage was out of the question. And he doubtless would have arranged an abortion for her just as Steven had for Delphine. Indeed, all men were bastards!

"When is the operation?" she asked Delphine.

"A week from Tuesday. In Dakar."

"Will Steven go with you?"

The cynicism that distorted Delphine's face as she answered wasn't pretty. "No. He'd like to, of course," she said with heavy sarcasm, "but he can't. Tough luck, but he has to go to Thiès on business. Too bad. So he's arranged for me to go to Mustapha Hakim, who will send me by car to the place where it will be done." Delphine wrung her hands in despair. "Still, Steven was very reassuring. He told me it's really no worse than having a tooth pulled. So earnest! So American! You know, I think he believes it." Delphine's high, brittle laugh broke into a series of uncontrollable sobs.

"My poor Delphine." Aurore comforted her. "Don't worry. I'll go with you. It will be all right."

"I'm so afraid!" Delphine confessed through her tears.

"Of course you are! Who wouldn't be? But it will be all right. I promise you."

"You're a good friend, Aurore." Delphine dried her

tears. "And God knows I need a friend right now. I wanted to ask you to come with me. I'm so afraid to go alone."

"You won't be alone, Delphine. I'll be right there. And you needn't be so afraid." Her lips framed the appropriate words of comfort and reassurance.

Nevertheless, Aurore was fearful for her cousin. After all, women did die from abortions. It had happened even in the remote little village of Ile Celeste.

CHAPTER 8

The stench of fuel and the stuffiness in the closed cabin of the cruiser the de Beausoleil women used for their excursions to the mainland were making Aurore a bit queasy. "I've got to go out on deck," she told Delphine. "Maybe you'd feel better in the fresh air, too," she added.

"No. I'd best stay near the bathroom." Delphine, her face pale and drawn, pressed a lace-trimmed handkerchief to her lips. It covered her attempt to smile away her apprehension. "You go ahead."

Alone at the railing, Aurore breathed in the fresh, salt-scented air and felt better immediately. The breeze tumbled her tawny curls and molded the creamy linen of her dress against her body. The dress was in the latest French fashion and had been selected for Aurore by *Tante* Colette. Although she was tired of her aunt's sartorial meddling, Aurore liked the frock and appreciated how becoming it was to her.

Thinking of the dress made Aurore think of *Tante* Colette. She had been concerned about Delphine's "migraines" and therefore was glad to hear that she felt well enough to attempt a shopping expedition to Dakar with Aurore. She had even swallowed her resentment when Delphine told her that just this once she would like to pick clothes for herself without her mother's interference. Aurore smiled wryly to herself. *Tante* Colette was so wordly wise, so sophisticated; yet it had been easy to deceive her as to the real reason for the trip.

They were nearing Dakar. As the cruiser glided across the large harbor, she could already see Goree Island, for centuries a major port for the slave trade, on their seaward side. Now the idyllic, tropical beauty of the island belied its turbulent and tragic past. It was always an emotional sight for Aurore. She would never forget visiting it with her mother and father and Sabine when she was a child.

"Thank God we're almost there." Delphine joined Aurore at the railing. "I just want to get it over with; the quicker the better."

But there were delays, first in obtaining a cab, and then, after making their way through the Sandaga Market, its bustling ranks of dealers and customers markedly reduced by the railroad strike, they were informed by the guard outside Mustapha Hakim's office that he was busy. The ladies would have to wait.

"Tell him that Mademoiselle Delphine de Beausoleil is here," Delphine demanded.

"He left orders not to be disturbed." The turbaned guard eyed them insolently.

Delphine's blue eyes took in the muscled magnificence of his oiled ebony torso, the crescent shape dagger in his belt, his folded arms and unyielding stance. Here at Mustapha Hakim's doorway, it was obvious that white skin and a fancy-sounding French name carried no special privileges. Defeated, she turned back to Aurore. The two of them withdrew a few yards to wait.

Finally the curtained doorway parted, and two black men wearing baggy pantaloons emerged. From their clothing, the scars on their chests and arms, and the dye marks on their faces, Aurore knew immediately that they were not Wolof. Probably they hailed from one of the warlike mercantile tribes of the interior. Such tribes had once prospered by raiding more peaceful villages for slaves, killing those who resisted, and selling their prisoners to slavers for shipment to America. They were merchants of the flesh, traders in human misery.

"What's that they're carrying?" Delphine inquired of Aurore.

Each man balanced a long pole across his shoulders. On both ends of the pole were large jugs sweating beads of liquid. To Aurore, it was the evidence that they had not changed their ways since the days of slavery.

"Water," Aurore told her. "They're water sellers."

"Sellers? But who would buy water?"

"People who don't have any. People who are thirsty. Whose children are thirsty." Aurore explained to her how the French had shut off the water supply to the working-class district of Dakar so that now there was a black market in water.

"But what are black-market water sellers doing here?" Delphine wondered.

The guard snickered openly.

"Getting their supply of water from Hakim, I expect," Aurore told her.

"But where does he get it?"

"From the French *toubabs* who cut off the supply of water." Aurore was as sophisticated as any native Senegalese in her cynical awareness of just how colonial victimization worked. "If you don't believe me, here's your chance to ask him."

The guard had stepped aside and motioned them to enter. Aurore and Delphine went into the cluttered little room. Its warm air was a malodorous blend of pomade, cigar smoke, and hidden, fetid wetness.

"Ladies! Welcome! Come in, come in." Greeting Delphine, Mustapha Hakim was as bouncy and genial as a host at a social gathering. "Mademoiselle de Beausoleil—" He bobbed at Aurore. "What a pleasant surprise! I am *doubly* honored!"

"You were expecting me?" His bubbly manner confused Delphine, who was in any case quite jittery.

"But of course. Of course." He might have been reassuring her of a dinner invitation. "Your visit was not only expected but most enthusiastically anticipated."

"Then you know why I'm here?"

"Certainly, dear lady," he said and beamed. "Our mutual friend was most specific in defining your—ahh—need."

"Can we get on with it?" Delphine was holding herself together very carefully, and there was more to the edge in her voice than mere impatience.

"May I speak freely?" Hakim's brown eyes floated over Aurore and back to Delphine.

"Yes. Aurore knows all about it."

"No offense, mademoiselle," he assured Aurore. "Very well then." His manner became slightly more businesslike as he turned back to Delphine. "Our friend reports that your problem is of only a few weeks' duration. Are you certain of that, mademoiselle? I inquire only because the woman who will conduct the proceedings has a rule against becoming involved in matters beyond a certain point. Because of the risk, you understand."

"I understand." Although her hands were clenched tightly to keep from wringing them, Delphine's jaw was firm. "I'm only a few weeks pregnant." Her directness was a rebuke to Hakim's elaborate euphemisms.

"I admire your frankness." Hakim's hooded eyes were indeed lazily approving. "And I shall be equally frank. When this is over, come and see me again and I shall—for a purely nominal fee, I assure you—recommend a medical gentleman who will arrange for a device whereby the next time you will not find yourself in such a predicament."

"You call that equally frank?" Despite her nervousness, Delphine laughed. "Thank you. But that won't be necessary. There isn't going to be any next time."

"After the first time, there is always a next time." Hakim folded his hands over his belly, and for a moment, he looked very much to Aurore like pictures she had seen at school of statues of Oriental buddhas.

It was, however, Hakim's words more than his pose that affected Aurore. Her face flamed as if the remark had been directed at her rather than Delphine. Already her body had confirmed the depth of its truth. How her flesh hungered for a next time!

Aurore pushed the thought from her mind. Concern for Delphine had to take precedence over such matters. "You mentioned a woman," she said to Hakim. "We thought that arrangements had been made for a doctor."

"I can assure you that Madame Sophia is more skilled at her work than any doctor in West Africa. She's the best. Some of the most distinguished ladies of French Dakar society have availed themselves of her services. You would recognize their names, I am sure, mademoiselle," he told Delphine. "But naturally I am honor-bound not to mention them."

"What do you think?" Delphine asked Aurore.

"What he says is true. A Senegalese woman who performs this sort of operation is probably more experienced and skilled than a white doctor would be." Aurore turned back to Hakim. "The arrangements were supposed to be for tonight," she said. "Are they?"

"But of course, dear lady."

"Where?"

"At Madame Sophie's domicile. Near the railroad station."

"That's all the way on the other side of Dakar," Aurore realized. "It's the district where the strikers live."

"I've heard there's violence there," Delphine added, worried. "Isn't it dangerous?"

"I've arranged for a car and chauffeur to take you there." Hakim was reassuring. "And my connections in the constabulary assure me that all is calm and under control in the district."

"That's not what I've heard—" Aurore started to protest.

"It doesn't matter. I have no choice," Delphine decided.

"A wise conclusion," Hakim said approvingly.

"One other thing, monsieur." There was insistence

in Delphine's voice. "My mother and my brother are not to hear about this!"

"I am distressed that you think it necessary to invite such reassurances." Hakim's tone was dramatic, even tragic. He struck his breast with a plump fist by way of a solemn pledge of confidentiality. "Discretion has always been my watchword. The more delicate the matter, the more discreet I am. I ask you—" Suddenly he reverted to the businessman. "Would I still be in business if my behavior were otherwise?"

"As long as it's understood." Her tremulousness showing now, Delphine rose to go.

Aurore took her arm to steady her.

Hakim came from behind his desk to see them to the waiting Mercedes limousine. "Will you be seeing Mademoiselle Fourier soon?" he inquired of Delphine, his manner a little too offhand to be truly casual.

"Minette? I suppose so."

"Would you do me the kindness of delivering a message to her?"

Delphine nodded.

"Tell her that I'm sorry to report that the news from Paris is not good." Hakim didn't seem sorry. On the contrary, the smile on his full lips smacked slightly of gloating.

"That's all there is to the message?"

"She will understand."

Aurore thought she understood, too. If what Steven Parker had told her was true, then this must mean that Minette's settlement from her father's art investments was being delayed. Much as Aurore didn't like Minette, she didn't envy her remaining in debt to Mustapha Hakim.

Hakim left them at the limousine. The uniformed driver greeted them courteously. He helped them into the wide backseat with its soft, cushiony upholstery.

Aurore had never before seen a car like this, much less ridden in one. The outside was so polished and shiny she could see her face in it, and inside it was like being in one's own private world. Thick glass separated them from the chauffeur, and they could have drawn the maroon velvet curtain for further privacy if they had wished. Even the large side windows had curtains, drawn back with tiny golden cords. How heavenly to lean back against the plush cushions and be driven through this most cosmopolitan of cities. The ride was so smooth that the passing scenery was the only indication of motion. The engine purred soothingly as a pussycat as the driver guided the sleek vehicle from Sandaga through the French business district. They glided past gleaming white office buildings, elegant shops, and posh restaurants that catered to the wealthy whites, and grassy, flower-dotted squares designed to refresh European senses.

Aurore became aware of the silence in the Mercedes. She glanced at Delphine. The blond girl's delicate features were tense and drawn; her blue eyes stared straight ahead, their fixed expression perceiving nothing. Her attention was drawn inward, her body stiff and rigid on the cushioned seat. One she sighed. Aurore patted her hand.

The scenery began to change. Immaculate skyscrapers were replaced by desolate dirt lots covered with heaps of twisted, rusted metal and dry, stunted weeds. The smooth asphalt avenues turned to narrow lanes of packed dirt more suited to bare feet than to the heavy impression of whitewall tires. The limousine raised clouds of choking dust that fouled the windows and turned the shiny black paint job to gritty gray.

Naked children squatted by the road. Their black eyes, huge in their pinched brown faces, stared listlessly at the elegant limousine. Perhaps if their swollen bellies had been filled with rice and meat, the exotic vehicle might have excited them. But in the midst of their hunger and hopelessness, it was out of context, surrealistic, as meaningless as a melting clock in a Dali landscape.

The homes of these children were cabins of wood and

tar paper or shacks of mud and straw reinforced by old fishing nets or, in luckier cases, zinc sheeting. The fences that strove to separate one shapeless hovel from its neighbor were fashioned of flattened tin cans.

In a vacant lot, a stray dog, its bones poking pathetically through its mangy, dun-color fur, nosed the piles of debris, hoping to find a scrap of something edible. Nearby, a toddler sat stuffing something into her mouth. Aurore watched the tiny fist move down to the ground and pick up a handful of dirt. Then, with an automatic movement, the fist moved upward to the open mouth. The hungry child—little more than a baby—was eating dirt!

Aurore looked away, her throat constricting with pity and outrage. If these were the living conditions of the black railway workers and their families, no wonder they were desperate enough to go on strike! True, the strike had worsened their poverty; before, the child eating dirt might have had a bowl of rice and lentils. But perhaps if the strike succeeded, her father would be able to afford to provide an occasional meal of chicken or beef. Unless, of course, the French starved the strikers into submission first.

Suddenly the limousine, which had slowed its pace because of the narrowness of the streets and the pedestrians spilling out on them, came to a stop. The driver stuck his head out of the window, impatiently asking a group of people to step aside. Aurore moved closer to the window to see what was causing the delay.

At first, she thought the angry, excited women blocking the street were quarreling among themselves. Their fist-clenched gestures were violent, their voices shrill with emotion. Some had babies in slings clinging to their backs and toddlers clutching at their skirts. All seemed to be carrying containers of one type or another—jugs, pans, bottles, or jars—and beyond them, on the ground, stretching in a line to a stone street fountain, were still more containers—huge earthenware jugs and tight-woven baskets, pottery bowls, and ornamental vases.

Aurore understood before the chauffeur turned and rolled down the glass partition to explain: "They are angry because the authorities have shut down the fountain and there is no water for them. I'll get out and see if I can't persuade them to move out of our way."

"I still don't understand," Delphine said. "Don't they have faucets in their homes or wells of their own?"

"No," Aurore told her. "There is only a communal fountain for each black neighborhood in Dakar. And the government controls it. It's a whole system, you see; a factory to purify the water so there is no disease; miles and miles of pipes to carry it to the different parts of the city. All of this is owned by the French. The very spigots on the fountain belong to them. And they have chosen to withhold the water to punish the strikers."

As they watched from the Mercedes, a woman mounted the hard clay platform—which had been formed by an endless succession of wet feet pounding the earth—that encircled the fountain. Grimly she turned the pump handle. Then she bent and placed her ear where the rusty pipe entered the ground.

"Do you hear anything?" a chorus of women's voices inquired.

The woman straightened up, shaking her head sadly.

"Not a gurgle?" A young woman with a baby in her arms cried out. "The milk in my breasts is drying up for lack of something to drink."

"The *toubabs* have the power to dry up even our breasts!" another woman shouted angrily. "Soon we will have no tears to shed no matter how they make us suffer!"

"Tears will do nothing anyway!" an old woman snarled. "What we need are weapons to fight with! How much longer can we stand by while they kill our children?"

As if in confirmation, the tearful voice of a child speaking in Wolof was heard: "Mama, I am so thirsty. Why don't you fill the jug so we can drink?"

There was a brief silence. "What I would not give

for a bath!'' a tall, ebony-skinned woman cried finally, breaking it.

"May Allah forgive us, we cannot even purify our hands and feet before we pray,'' said another.

"Try the pump handle again, Hanta,'' someone urged.

"Why? So I can lose my body's last bit of moisture in senseless sweat? Let someone else try,'' the woman said, stepping down from the fountain. "Look how filthy the trenches have become,'' she said, grimacing as she pointed to the tiny channels that radiated outward from the clay platform. "Filth and rags and rat carcasses where once clear water ran. It's a wonder we aren't all dead of disease!''

The crowd of women began to disperse, querulous and discouraged as they carried their empty containers home again. The narrow road cleared, and the driver climbed back behind the wheel. He hadn't had the heart to shoo the thirsty women and children out of the way after all.

Looking back as they drove on, Aurore saw that the fountain was deserted except for the oddly assorted line of vessels left as place markers, and one little girl perched atop the stone fountainhead. She was waiting to give the word in case the officials decided to release a trickle of water. How lonely and pathetic she looked, with her small, graceful head bent toward the fountain, her thin brown limbs folded in an attitude of waiting that was almost like prayer.

Now their progress through the narrow, dusty streets was agonizingly slow. The way was frequently blocked by groups of hostile-eyed, gossiping women, raggedy youngsters, and assorted stray animals. At one point, a tall, scarred, ebony-skinned man balancing a pole with two heavy earthenwear jugs across his shoulders veered in front of the limousine in order to evade several buxom middle-aged women who were pursuing him, one of them brandishing a flatiron. Aurore recognized him as one of the water sellers they had seen leaving Hakim's.

"You will give us that water, son of a pig," the woman screamed. "You will!" She let fly with the flatiron, which grazed the water seller's arm.

"You cannot meet my price," the man brayed. "I must go all the way to Pikine to get the water," he lied. "Five and twenty francs is not too much to ask."

"Not too much to ask? It's robbery! Even a *toubab* would not dare to ask such a price of thirsty people! And your skin is as dark as ours! I will pay you ten francs for half a jug, godless cheat that you are."

"I sell only by the jug." He was safely shielded by the limousine now. "'Twenty-five francs. *Kio dieu n'da n'do?* Water, water, who will buy?"

"*Bambara!*" The woman cursed him for a bastard.

"Water sellers!" a second woman growled bitterly. "They are all *bilakoros*—unclean infidels!"

A third woman ran around the car and fell before the water seller in the dust, seizing his hand. "Give me just enough to boil my children some rice," she begged. "They have not eaten in two days."

"And how will my children eat if I give my water away for nothing?" The man trudged away as the limousine moved forward again.

A moment later, there was an indignant shriek. Aurore looked back to see the women surrounding the water seller. One of them clawed at his baggy pantaloons until his bare buttocks were exposed. Another gave him a vicious jab between the legs with her knee. The water seller let out a second scream, and the balancing pole slipped off his shoulders. The jugs would have spilled but for the quick reaction of a third woman. She quickly caught the pole, hoisted it, and waddled back across the road with the water just as fast as her chubby legs would carry her.

Similar incidents further delayed them. Delphine became nervous. Night was falling, and despite Hakim's previous assurances to the contrary, it was obvious that the section of Dakar they had ventured into was far from safe. "Driver, how much further is it?" she asked anxiously.

"Just a few blocks after we turn the next corner, mademoiselle."

"Please hurry."

The driver stepped on the gas, only to lurch to a stop midway down the block after the turn. *"Spahis!"* he exclaimed. "Mounted soldiers."

Aurore moved over to the side window. The hulking shapes of the horses and riders were barely discernible in the twilight. Their elaborate uniforms and flowing burnooses were a darkening blur of red and white and gold. They were moving into the street single-file, and their centaur shapes might have been a mirage save for the dull thud of hooves on the dirt road and the muted jingle of spurs and stirrups and bridles.

Delphine told the driver to move on.

"But more *spahis* are coming into the street, mademoiselle!"

"Then they will give us safe escort. Find the French officer in charge. He's probably at the head of the column."

The Mercedes inched past the single column of black riders. At their head, two officers—one black, one white—rode side by side. As they approached, Aurore got a close-up look at the *spahis*. Arrogance was their hallmark. There were few Wolof among them. These troops hailed from places far from Dakar. The French were too clever to use local cavalry to enforce their rule. All that the soldiers and the subjugated had in common was their skin color. They didn't even speak the same language.

As Delphine rolled down her window and called to him, the white captain of the troop reined in his magnificent chestnut horse. "What is the trouble, *capitaine?*" Delphine said as she smiled up at him.

The captain twirled his mustache in an old-fashioned, traditional cavalry gesture of appreciation at Delphine's beauty. "Nothing serious, mademoiselle. Some women broke into the local native chief's coop and stole three of his chickens. Bold as brass they were about it, too!''

Inside the car, Aurore nodded approval to herself. Everyone knew that the so-called chief of this district, one El Hadji Assitan, was nothing but a French-picked toady who was doing all in his power to help the *toubabs* break the strike. There were half a dozen such black officials like him in Dakar. Without the French, they were nothing, and with them, they were little more than that. To those they supposedly "ruled," they were known as *toubabous dyions*—slaves of the Europeans.

"All these soldiers just to get back a few stolen chickens?" Delphine was saying. "It seems a bit much, *capitaine.*"

The French officer leaned down from his horse so that the black officer could not hear what he was saying to Delphine. "You are right, mademoiselle. There is a bit more to it. What happened is that the nigger police went in to retrieve the chickens and some black wenches attacked them. Routed them, they did. Threw half a dozen of them in a latrine drainage ditch, begging your pardon, mademoiselle. So we've come down here to arrest the ringleaders."

"I see."

"The native quarter is in a stew tonight, mademoiselle. You really shouldn't be down here." The look on his face made no secret of the fact that he thought Delphine attractive.

"We're only going a few blocks up this street." Delphine fluttered her eyelashes. "Couldn't we drive beside you?"

"My pleasure to be of service to you, mademoiselle." He gave her a very smart salute and indicated that the horsemen behind him should fall back so that the Mercedes might have an escort.

The driver maneuvered the limousine into the empty space, the headlights illuminating the gleaming chestnut hindquarters of the horse immediately in front of them. The headlights also lit up the rows of standing women on either side of the street. For a moment, Aurore assumed they were merely inhabitants of the crude dwellings behind the makeshift fences and mud walls, who had come out to watch the passing parade of cavalry. But something in the tenseness of their attitude and in the solemnity of their dark and brooding faces made Aurore aware that they were not there just to gape at soldiers on horseback. She noted other details as the limousine crawled along. Virtually all the women were holding things. Here an iron pot of live coals gleamed red in the darkness; there a group of women held twisted sheaves of straw in their arms or clutched bottles or tin cans to their chests.

The French captain signaled the driver of the limousine to stop. He reined in beside and bent to address Delphine again. "The nigger officer thinks he's spotted one of the ringleaders," he told her. "See. Down the block there."

Like Delphine, Aurore looked where he was pointing. She saw a young Wolof woman in a chemise top that did little to conceal her jutting breasts and a tightly wrapped *pagne* that accentuated her lean hips and pertly rounded derriere. Perched atop her elaborately braided hair at a rakish angle was a red fez. It was unmistakably a policeman's fez.

The black officer rode over to her. "You there!" His voice was harsh with authority. "Where did you get that?"

"This?" She snatched the scarlet fez from her head and held it aloft. "It's a souvenir!" Her voice, rich and resonant, rang in the tension-fraught air like a tolling bell.

An older woman beside her cackled loudly. Some of the other standing women broke their silence to join in the laughter.

"If you don't believe me, ask my mother," the young woman with the fez told the *spahi* officer.

"That's right!" The older woman's high-pitched laugh sounded again. "It is a souvenir my daughter found in the drainage ditch. It was covered with policeman's *caca*, but we cleaned it off.'' Her short, stocky body quivered with the pride of a bantam rooster as she stepped between her daughter and the black *spahi* officer.

''No policeman would lose his fez in such a way!'' The black officer was humorless.

''He would if he fell in the latrine!'' the mother told him.

Again the laughter of the other women joined her cackle.

''Don't waste time talking,'' the white officer interfered. ''Arrest them!''

''Arrest us?'' The daughter now stepped between her mother and the black *spahi*. ''What for?''

''Interfering with a policeman in the performance of his duty,'' he told her.

''Duty? What duty?''

''Investigating a theft.''

''He means the chickens of El Hadji Assitan,'' the daughter told the mother.

''The district chief,'' the black officer contributed.

''Chief?'' The mother spit. ''Traitor, you mean! He makes pilgrimage to Mecca, kisses the behinds of the *toubabs*, and sells us out just as often as he is able!''

''Nevertheless, it is against the law to steal his chickens.''

''Nobody stole his chickens.'' the mother replied. ''His coop was left open, that is all. The chickens left of their own accord. Some of the ladies encountered these chickens in the public street and—''

''And cut their throats and popped them into the stew pot. Is that it? Well, that is still stealing!''

''What would you have had these ladies do?'' The daughter spoke now. ''Feed these chickens their last grains of millet while they waited for their owner to claim them? And the chickens so plump already they could hardly waddle!''

''No!'' her mother said. ''These ladies got down on their knees and praised Allah for sending food to fill the swollen bellies of their children! And you call that a crime?''

"It is a crime. And I am placing you two under arrest for it!''

"We two?'' The daughter was indignant. "Some ladies did this. Some ladies, we said. But not us. Some other ladies.''

"That fez is all the proof I need.'' The black officer called to a sergeant behind him. "You take the old lady. I'll take the daughter myself. Dismount first and give her a leg up.''

The sergeant grabbed hold of the young woman and started to drag her over to his superior's horse.

"You let go of my daughter!'' The old woman rushed forward, drawing a stout, gnarled baobab branch from the folds of her *boubou*. She raised it with both arms and brought it down hard on the sergeant's back. With a howl, he let go of the young woman. She ran to a group on the sidelines who were bent over a pot of live coals, lighting twisted sheaves of straw.

One of them handed her a flaming torch. She ran back to the black *spahi* officer. With a warlike cry, she flung the torch in his face.

He screamed, beating at the flames that licked at his scalp and the shoulder of his uniform. His horse, feeling fire upon its flanks, began to whinny and rear. Unable to control his mount, the black officer slid off his back and writhed in the dust, in danger of being trampled by the women moving in now from all sides.

All along the cavalry line, torches sprang to flaming life, setting ebony and copper skins aglow before being flung at the stunned *spahis* and their terrified mounts. Other women beat on tin cans, raising a clamor to frighten the horses. Bottles weighted with hard sand arced through the air. One bottle hit the French officer full in the face, the force of the blow pushing him back in the saddle as blood spurted from his nose.

Some of the *spahis* had drawn their swords, only to find them useless against the sailing bottles and flaming bundles of straw. But one soldier had dismounted and was slicing out at the women, aiming his sword at their bare brown arms and quivering breasts. Suddenly an old woman, her toothless mouth framing screams of outrage, came at the swordsman. By some miracle, her scrawny, scarecrow body managed to evade the slashing blade. She held her bundle of burning straw high in the air to lure the sword, then as the soldier hit out at it, she lashed it downward and jabbed it between his uniformed legs. He screamed as the hungry flames licked at his groin, and dropped his sword. Gleefully the old woman seized it and attacked one of the horses.

Aurore was frightened as she and Delphine huddled together in the back of the car. They had rolled up all the windows, but the sounds of the lurid scene still came through the glass loud and clear. The neighing and whinnying of the bucking, heaving horses, the curses and grunts of the *spahis*, the shrieking of the women as they fought with fire, the sound of glass shattering, the metallic drumbeat of tin cans—such as the cacophony of the women's rebellion.

The plush interior of the limousine offered no illusion of safety as the car was buffeted by panicked horses, smacked with swords, and crawled over by soldiers and women alike. The white officer, their supposed protector, was nowhere to be seen now. Suddenly their view was obliterated by a bursting torch of straw someone had flung. It landed on the car's hood and licked at the metal and glass. The closed car became hotter, stifling; it was hard to breathe.

"My God, Aurore!" Delphine cried out. "We're going to be killed!"

Everywhere Aurore looked, there were scenes of violence and destruction. A horse plunged by, the whites of its eyes rolling in its head while froth dripped from its mouth. Its rounded flanks and graceful legs were not covered with glossy chestnut hair anymore but with flames.

To their right, a young woman screamed and fell to

the ground. The child she was holding, a toddler of about two, tumbled from her arms. Then, its face distorted by confusion and fear, the baby began to crawl toward the panic-stricken horses.

Aurore did not stop to think. She flung open the car door and dashed out into the torch-lit darkness. A horse reared up in her path, and she jumped to one side in the nick of time, still keeping her eyes riveted to the child. He was still crawling, still miraculously unharmed. Aurore bent over and plunged through the sea of bodies separating her from the baby. Then she was upon him, grabbing him up in her arms and running with him to his fallen mother. She lay on the side of the road, her eyes open but unseeing, her blouse ripped to reveal her slack and blood-smeared breasts.

Aurore pressed the baby's round head to her shoulder so that he should not see his dead mother. She then turned, intending to get back to the car with the toddler. However, so suddenly that she felt it before she saw it—flaming heat against her face and then a bright, bursting wall of fire as the wooden shacks and straw huts ignited one by one, expelling the old women and young children sheltered inside—the conflagration cut off her path to safety.

"Fire! Fire!" The cry went up as women turned from the battle to search for their children and to try to save what possessions they could from the crackling, hungry flames already starting to devour their homes.

The sheets of tar paper and oil-smeared timbers from the railroad yard that the people had used to construct their dwellings gave off acrid clouds of black smoke as they burned. The zinc roofs and the fences of flattened tin cans reflected the flames, intensifying the heat until people staggered under its impact. The very ground underfoot became intolerably hot.

"Water! Get water!" voices screamed, until they remembered that there was no water. The *toubabs* had turned it off.

Where in this blazing inferno was the car? Aurore

looked desperately around as the child clung to her, a dead weight shrieking now with terror. But the Mercedes was nowhere to be seen.

Aurore made her way to the entry way of a home beyond the conflagration. Here she and the baby were out of the way of the rushing people and horses. But they were safe for only a little while.

Soon Aurore was watching the row of dwellings across the street fall like a house of cards. The fire consumed one tinderbox structure in a fiery gulp. Then the leaping flames licked hungrily at the roof next door, and the fire devoured another whole building with its crackling dragon jaws. Aurore saw a straw hut illuminated red from within, saw it swell with impossible heat and then burst open like a seed pod, spewing sparks and fireballs into the milling crowd.

She watched as a young woman became a human torch, her *boubou* bursting into flames, her braided hair catching fire like dry twigs. The victim ran, screaming and demented with pain, until someone tackled her to the ground and tried to extinguish the live firebrand that was her body in the dust. A few minutes later all that was visible was a charred bundle of rags that could have been anything—a mattress, a tarpaulin wall, a piece of furniture.

Until now, the strike had been just a phrase to Aurore, an idea she had been trying to grasp. She had heard so many different viewpoints expressed in the last few months. She had heard Cherif defend the strike passionately, praising the Communists who supported it as the only whites sympathetic to the black railway workers' struggle for equal rights. She had heard Amin denigrate the strike and his brother's stand. She had heard *Tante* Colette deplore the strike as an insufferable inconvenience to herself and her French friends.

But it wasn't until now, trapped in the middle of the holocaust, that the strike became real to Aurore. She understood now that the people living in this section of Dakar—the railway workers and their families—were desperate. To undergo such privations in the struggle for their rights! To live without water and without food! To risk their very lives by fighting the French-commanded *spahis!* Surely such determination could not be stopped!

Using Senegal's natural resources and indigenous labor force, the French had made progress and improvements—and then had denied the native population a share in them. The people who lived in the fishing village in Ile Celeste were relatively untouched by modern-day progress, and yet their living conditions were much better than here. It was profit, not progress, that defined the French rule in Senegal.

Aurore remembered the Slave House on Goree Island. She saw again in her mind's eye the dungeons where the captured Africans had waited, already in chains and doomed to spend the rest of their lives—if they survived—doing the white man's dirty work. But now a new breed of African was being forged in the fire! Now there were men and women who had decided to fight against their enslavers rather than live in the thralldom of poverty.

"Colonialism will not survive much longer," her father had said. "By the end of this century, the African nations will all be independent," he had predicted.

Was this strike, with all its violence, a step in that direction? Aurore wondered. Was it indeed a first step on the road to Senegalese independence?

A sudden crash set the rough wood floor planks of the doorway shaking. The heat became more intense. Hugging the toddler to her breast, Aurore saw with a surge of terror that the fire had crossed to her side of the street now! Even as she watched, a ramshackle mud-and-straw dwelling three or four doors down burst into flame.

Men rushed by with shovels and wheelbarrows of sand. What else could they use to fight the fire? There was no water.

Aurore realized she would have to leave her place of refuge with the baby before the fire reached it. But in the street, people were running in every direction, their eyes streaming tears from the thick, acrid smoke. The air was alive with sparks that at any moment could ignite one's hair or clothing.

"Come on! This way!" a man shouted, beckoning to her.

Before Aurore could act, however, the porch collapsed. The fire had sneaked through the house from the rear. The baby added his terrified shrieks to the pandemonium. A huge railroad tie used as a wall brace crashed down in front of her, blocking the doorway. To go forward would have been suicide; she was facing a sheer wall of flame. Aurore turned back, only to see tongues of orange fire flickering at her from behind and from the right and left. Dear God, the fire was all around her! She stood there with the child, helpless, terrified. She couldn't breathe or see! Her ears were filled with the roaring sound of fire. In a moment— less—it would consume them.

Suddenly strong arms were gripping her, lifting her bodily with the child and swinging them up, high above the flames. They were set down on solid earth again and then she was being pushed roughly along the dirt-packed street. The air changed, growing clearer, breathable, delicious. Her smoke-inflamed eyes could see again. There was a moon, cool and crystal-white in the night sky. The roar of the fire was in the distance, and now, truly, she and the child were safe.

The man who had saved her still had his arms around her shoulders, steading her from behind. She looked back, curious now, then gasped in disbelief.

"Blaise!"

"At your service, *Cousine*." He made a sweeping, ironic cavalier's bow. "Where did you get the child?" he asked. "Cute little tyke. Here, give him to me."

"Oh, Blaise." In spite of what she had just been through, Aurore found herself smiling at the way he grimaced when the child wet him. Then she stopped smiling. "The poor little thing," she remembered. "His mother was killed, and he would have been trampled by the horses if I hadn't picked him up.''

"But what do we do with him now? I'm half tempted to take him home, except that he probably has relatives in the neighborhood.''

The little boy leaned back contentedly against Blaise's broad shoulder. Aurore found it somehow touching that this man, so ironic and forbidding at times, could be so natural and at ease snuggling a child in his brawny arms. He patted the child's back with his large hand and was rewarded with a sigh and a burp.

They walked up and down the streets, stopping to ask people if they recognized the little boy. But in the end it was the child who recognized his father with a little shriek of glee.

"Touti, my son! My son! Praise Allah, he is alive! When they told me about my wife, I thought Touti had been taken, too. *Alham doulilah!* He lives!'' Shaken and weeping with emotion, the man took his son from Blaise's arms.

"It is for him that we strike,'' he said in broken French, a black man wanting to explain it so that the whites who had saved his son would understand. "So that he may have a better life. I told my wife to stay in the house where it was safe. But she and the other women, they do not listen to their husbands anymore. They go out and fight like the men.'' He shook his head slowly. "And they die like the men. It is a high price to pay for a better life. But at least Allah in his mercy has spared my son.''

When the man had taken his son and left them, they made their way through the turmoil of the flaming streets in silence. Blaise's jaw was set firmly, his face grim at the destruction and human misery around them.

Aurore was wondering about Delphine. Had the limousine managed to escape the quarter before the conflagration got out of hand? Had Delphine—French, white, wealthy; a symbol of all that the strikers and their women were rebelling against—avoided becoming a target of their wrath? It was impossible, Aurore knew, that she should have reached Madame Sophia's and gone through the abortion in the midst of all this chaos. But was she safe? Was she unharmed?

Of course, Aurore could not mention her fears for Delphine to Blaise without risking the betrayal of Delphine's secret. She could justify her own presence in black Dakar. But there was no reason Aurore could think of why Delphine should have come here. And so she said nothing of the concern now uppermost in her mind.

When Blaise spoke, it was as if his thoughts had paralleled Aurore's. "How do you come to be here at a time like this, *Cousine?*" he asked as they reached the relative safety of the main road leading out of the devastated area.

"I was on my way to visit an old friend from the convent school," Aurore improvised. "The taxi driver lost his way, and then we were trapped by the fighting."

"Maman said you'd come to Dakar to go shopping with Delphine."

"I did originally. But I got bored with the shops, and so I decided to look up my friend."

"And Delphine? Where is she?"

"I don't really know." Aurore shrugged. "You know Delphine. She probably met one of her beaux and went on to a party or something. And what brought you down here?" she asked quickly to forestall any further questions about Delphine.

"I came to keep an appointment with some of the union officials. Cherif set it up."

"Is it to bring the fish from Ile Celeste here? I hope so. These people are starving."

"Yes. Amin knows they're starving, and although he's opposed to the strike, he'd rather the strikers have the fish than the rich Europeans."

"Did you keep your appointment?"

"Yes. It's all arranged. It's smuggling and it's illegal, but we'll get the fish to them."

"I'm so glad!" Aurore looked up at him in the faint glow from the blaze receding behind them now. "You should feel proud to risk running the French blockade to help these people. After all, you're a Frenchman. If it comes out, your own people will say you betrayed them. It's such a—a—*humane* thing to do."

"It's good business, that's all," Blaise told her gruffly. "I'm going to make a lot of money from this arrangement. I'm not concerned with humane acts."

Somehow, adamant as his tone was, Aurore didn't believe him.

They caught a taxi on the avenue de l'Arsenal. It carried them along the waterfront to the pier where Blaise kept his speedboat. His large hands grasped her under the arms and swung her lightly aboard.

It wasn't until Dakar Harbor was behind them, a ring of fairy lights glinting silver on the black water, that the full impact of her narrow escape hit Aurore. Until now, her senses had been numbed. Now she saw before her again the sheer wall of fire that had closed her in, the snaking flames that had licked at her as if to caress her flesh before consuming it.

She had almost been burned to death!

Aurore bent forward in the leather seat, hugging herself with her arms. The cream linen frock, now soot smeared and raveled beyond recognition, had been suited to the warm afternoon temperature. But now it was night, and the swiftly moving mahogany craft, skimming the water as effortlessly as a dragonfly, was generating a stiff, cool breeze. She was suddenly quite chilled.

"Are you cold, Aurore?" Blaise was unexpectedly solicitous.

She nodded her head. Her teeth were chattering too much for words.

Aurore expected him to offer her his linen jacket, but he didn't. Instead, he moved closer to her and slid his arm around her shoulders, drawing her close, deliciously close. She rested her head in the hollow formed by his neck and shoulder; she felt his chin resting atop her head as he guided the speedboat with his free hand. Her auburn curls whipped against his face and, laughing a little, he smoothed them down, tucking them under his sheltering arm.

It felt so good to have him hold her. She could feel the heat of his body right through the linen suit, warming her, soothing her. Aurore wriggled, pressing her rounded thigh against his hard and muscular one. She sighed with contentment, rubbing her cheek against the sunburned skin of his throat. She felt like a cold and hungry stray kitten taken into a warm place, fed with milk, snuggled and petted by its new owner. She would purr if she knew how.

But after a while, Aurore became aware that her needs were not as simple as a kitten's. She did not fall blissfully asleep against the warm body of her new master. She did not rest content in the closeness of his embrace. Instead, the comforting warmth turned into a demanding hotness that made her stir and sigh. Her breast against his side began to burn and tingle. She felt the heat of desire throbbing in the pulses of her body. There was an aching heaviness in her loins.

"Blaise." It was a sigh.

His face turned to look down into hers. "Did you say something?" He bent his head down to her, and she raised her face so that their lips met and clung.

His lips were alive and demanding, his mustache prickling and tickling. She touched the roughness of his cheek with her fingertips. Her senses were reeling with the spicy male scent of him, the intimate taste of his mouth, the pressure of his hard, muscular body.

Aurore brought his hand to her breast, pressing it to where her hard cherry nipples were thrusting against the material of her dress through the bra she had taken to wearing with the French frocks *Tante* Colette acquired for her. She guided his hand under the neckline of the dress. She shrugged her shoulder until the bra strap fell.

An instant later, she gasped as she felt the bare nipple in the stroking clutch of his fingertips.

How her body cried out to him from every curve and crevice! How it longed for the sensations, the delights he had introduced on that first magical, unforgettable night! How much she wanted him again!

Her body belonged to Blaise; surely he must know it, feel it. Yet she could sense his tenseness, his holding back. She must show him that there were no barriers to reliving the ecstasy they had known.

She took his hand and moved it down her body, trying to reawaken his erotic memory. She guided it up under her skirt, along the ripe, quivering contours of her thighs. She shivered as his blunt fingers grazed the fevered, sensitive flesh through the silk of her panties.

Still Aurore could feel the reluctance of his caress. Even as she forced his hand under the elastic of the panties to the moist and secret place of velvety warmth, the initiative remained hers, the invasion no more than a passive aquiescence. But Aurore was too excited to let his lack of enthusiasm stop her.

She dropped her hand between his thighs, finding the stiffening bulge, caressing it hungrily. She fumbled for his zipper, writhing against his hand, open, longing for the plunging thrusts to fill her pulsing sheath. Then it was in her hand—so large!—stiff and throbbing, ready to be enveloped by her.

"Cut the motor!" she gasped. "Let me lie down! Oh, God! Oh, please!"

Without waiting for him to comply, she slid down on the seat, shifting her body to make it accessible to him. Her thighs, slippery with desire, opened to receive him. With both her hands, she grasped the erect root of his manhood and tugged him over her.

"That's enough!" His voice was like a crack of thunder. He moved away from her. Roughly he stuffed his erection back into his pants and jerked up the zipper.

"What?" Aurore was dazed at the suddenness of the rejection. "What's the matter?"

"Fix your dress," he said harshly. "Sit up like a lady."

It hurt so badly she couldn't believe it. "Why, Blaise?" The words burst from her constricted throat. "Why?"

"We've been through this once before," he reminded her. "As I recall, I made you a promise then that it would never happen again. I have no intention of breaking that promise, no matter how you may tempt me, *Cousine.*"

"How I may tempt you!" Someplace deep inside Aurore, fury replaced frustrated passion. "On Ile Celeste, a girl who leads a man on and then denies him is called a tease," she snarled. "In France, it seems it must be the men who are teases!"

"Not all Frenchmen—" Blaise started to say.

"I don't know about all Frenchmen," she interrupted him. "But I know about you, Blaise. You are more of a tease than any girl could ever be!"

"I'm sorry if I led you on, he said stiffly, but with a trace of his old irony.

"Oh, Blaise!" Tears sprang to Aurore's eyes, cooling her anger. "Can you really look at me and tell me that you don't want me?" she pleaded.

His eyes looked into hers. His gaze was direct, determined, but a muscle twitched at the side of his mouth—a small but distinct betrayal of his words. "I don't want you!" he said, pronouncing each word distinctly and with an almost studied brutality.

Aurore turned away, facing into the wind, glad of the way it whipped her hair against her flaming cheeks and dried her tears even as they emerged. The wind also prevented her from hearing the rest of what Blaise said:

"I can't afford to want anyone—to love anyone—that way ever again!"

No, Aurore didn't hear these words. All she heard was the rejection. And now all she could hear was the roaring inside her head as her shame was welded once again to her hatred for Blaise Honoré de Beausoleil!

CHAPTER 9

Shaken gently awake the next morning, Aurore's eyes opened on a welcome sight. It was Delphine. The two girls hugged each other.

"Thank goodness you're all right!" her cousin exclaimed. "I was so worried."

"So was I." Aurore saw that Delphine was still wearing the same dress she had worn the previous day. "What happened to you?"

"Nothing really. When you vanished, I had the driver wait for you to come back for a while, but then the situation became impossible. We had to get out of there or risk being set afire by the rioters. The chauffeur found a back street that was relatively clear, and we escaped from the quarter. We went back to Sandaga Market, but Hakim wasn't there. I stayed the night at the Hotel Deauville. I saw Hakim this morning, returned to Ile Celeste, and here I am. Now tell me what happened to you."

Aurore told her about saving the baby and being rescued in turn by Blaise. When she had finished her story, she asked Delphine if Hakim had made other arrangements for her to see Madame Sophia.

"He couldn't," Delphine replied. "Madame Sophia's house has been destroyed. She's evidently left Dakar to stay with friends on Cap Verde. Hakim said it would be too involved and take too long to try to find her. He advised me that an abortion in Dakar will be out of the question now with all this turmoil."

"But what will you do?"

"Hakim will arrange an immediate operation by a woman in Thiès. He says it can be done next Monday."

"Thiès? But that's seventy-five kilometers inland from Dakar. With the railroad strike on, how will we get there?"

"Oh, Aurore, I'm so glad you said *we*." Delphine embraced her. "I was hoping you'd come with me to Thiès, but I was almost afraid to ask after all that happened last night."

"Of course I'm coming with you. But you haven't answered my question. How will we get there?"

"The railroad is still running one passenger train a week from Dakar to Thiès. It's symbolic, I suppose. Just to prove they can do it despite the strike. European personnel—mechanics and engineers—operate the train."

"Scabs!" After what she had seen the previous evening, all Aurore's sympathies were with the strikers. "But I know about that weekly train, Delphine. What I don't see is how we're going to get aboard it. Even though strikers and their wives and children are forbidden to ride the train—no matter the emergency—it's still jammed. Ten people try to get aboard for every one who succeeds. Even two out of three Europeans are turned away. What makes you think we can do it?"

"Don't worry. We'll be on that train. You see, the superintendent of the Dakar terminal is a good friend of Maman's. A *very* good friend."

"*Tante* Colette?" Aurore foresaw problems. "But how will we explain our going to Thiès to her? A shopping expedition to Dakar is one thing, but such a long trip, and in times like these—what excuse could we possibly give her that she would believe?"

"No excuse." Delphine compressed her lips into a thin line. "I'll just have to tell Maman the truth."

The scene with *Tante* Colette later that day was not nearly as difficult as Aurore had anticipated. Delphine had asked that she stand by her while she told her mother. Aurore had done so with some apprehension. For one thing, *Tante* Colette made no secret of the fact that she looked at Steven Parker as an impertinent American parvenu possessed of neither breeding, wealth, nor social connections. And for another, *Tante* Colette had little if any tolerance for the gaffes of others—particularly if those others were related to her, as in the case of a niece or a daughter.

Nevertheless, Colette was a worldly woman. Her sophistication took precedence over her intolerance of female stumblings and forbade her the indulgence of mouthing moralities. "Even a little Boy Scout knows enough to be prepared," she told Delphine wryly, allowing herself just that much sarcasm but no more. "Didn't it occur to you, my dear? Or to your partner in foolishness?"

"Do you really want the sordid details, Maman?"

"I suppose not." Colette thought a moment. "Your partner—it was that deplorable American, I suppose?"

"What difference does it make, Maman?"

"Only that he may prove helpful to us. This is not the time for womanly chivalry, Delphine. Besides, he doesn't deserve it."

"No, he doesn't," Delphine said and sighed.

"Then it was Steven Parker?"

"Yes, Maman."

"All right, then." Colette glanced from Delphine to Aurore and back. "I will arrange for you two to have seats on the next weekly train to Thiès. That scoundrel Hakim will, I presume, have made all the necessary arrangements for the—ah—operation. Still, you will need a place to stay for a few days to recuperate. You can't just get back on the train and come back. You might do yourself harm."

"Besides," Aurore interjected, "there is no return train for a week, *Tante* Colette."

"Quite right. Therefore, I will telegraph my friends the du Mauriers that you are coming to Thiès and would like to stay with them for a few days."

"Won't they wonder why I'm coming to Thiès in the middle of a strike?"

"Of course they will, my dear. I shall say in my telegram that you have come to visit your American fiancé because you could not bear the separation from him for one moment longer."

"Maman!"

"I do remember correctly, do I not? This Steven Parker is presently in Thiès on business?"

When Delphine didn't reply, Aurore answered for her. "Yes, he is."

"But he is not my fiancé, Maman!" Delphine protested.

"No matter. The least he can do considering his responsibility in this matter is to accept the honor."

"We are not planning to marry, Maman."

"But of course not! I wouldn't hear of it! Marriage to this American nobody? Perish the thought! At some later date, we will simply inform the du Mauriers that you have broken the engagement. It's a common practice with girls your age. So flighty. They will think nothing of it."

And so it was decided.

Only to Sabine did Aurore reveal the true reason for their journey to Thiès, and only after she had secured Delphine's permission to do so. After all, she could not simply disappear and leave her half-sister to worry. Sabine had enough to worry about. That was obvious from the conversation Aurore had with her.

"It is Amin," she confided. "He has become quite deeply involved in the Muslim revolutionary movement. As the son of a chief who will himself one day be chief, his role will be an important one. But right now it is merely an increasingly dangerous one."

"Why dangerous? I thought he wasn't involved in the strike," Aurore replied.

"He treads a very careful line regarding the strike. He does not support it because the Imams do not support it. At the same time, he did not hesitate to arrange through Cherif to have your cousin Blaise deliver the entire catch of the Ile Celeste fishermen to the union strike committee every day. That is illegal, and they could all go to jail for it—Cherif, Blaise, Amin—all. Still, I could wish that was the most dangerous activity my husband was engaged in. Unfortunately, it is not.''

"Then what is?''

"His involvement with Steven Parker. If that goes too far, both he and Parker might well face execution at the hands of the French.''

"For what?'' Aurore had rarely seen Sabine so worried.

"After Hakim cut off the supply of munitions the Imams will need to wage a *jihad*, Amin—with the help of Steven Parker—set out to find a source of potassium nitrate so that the revolutionaries could make their own ammunition. Parker, through his former wartime black market contacts, located such a source in Thiès. This source is a band of thieves who stole the potassium nitrate from the loaded freight cars piled up at the railroad yards because of the strike. But before they will part with it, according to Parker, they want payment in cash.''

"But surely it's very expensive. Where would Amin get such a sum of money?''

"Yes. It is very expensive. But he has obtained the money. Most of it the Imams have supplied. The balance Amin has borrowed from Hakim at an exorbitant rate of interest. And now he must take this cash himself and deliver it to Thiès.''

"Couldn't he send it with someone? Since I'm going to Thiès, perhaps I could take it for him.''

"No. You know Amin. He would never risk your safety. And he would neither trust anyone else with this mission nor risk someone's life on it. He will go himself. He will be on the same train that you are taking.''

"But how will he manage that? We only got our seats through a high railroad official that *Tante* Colette knows.''

"Perhaps Mustapha Hakim knows the same official.

At any rate, it was he who arranged a seat for Amin—for a substantial fee, of course.''

"If Amin's mission is so delicate, then I don't imagine he'll want to sit with us on the train," Aurore said. She was relieved. It would have been difficult to justify the journey to her brother-in-law.

"I think he would prefer it if you did not even recognize him."

Aurore followed Sabine's advice. Three days later, when she spied Amin in the overflowing crowd at the Dakar terminal, she made no effort to approach him. She didn't even call his presence to the attention of Delphine.

The French girl seemed overwhelmed by the masses of humanity among whom she found herself. Even the presence of the uniformed railraod official, assigned to expedite their boarding by the superintendent of the terminal, could not do much to relieve the chaos around them. The building was filled to overflowing by people waiting and hoping for a place on the one train out of starving Dakar that week. Some of these people had been encamped there for days with their pitiful possessions.

Aurore was not as appalled as Delphine, but she did feel guilty. While the black soldiers under their command manhandled the crowd, the French military officers filling in as stationmasters bowed low to Aurore and Delphine and processed their papers quickly. While the soldiers held back the crowd with unsheathed bayonets, the two girls were waved through the gates to the train platform. Blacks were still pleading to be allowed to board as they were shown to a private compartment.

But it was not private for long. By the time The Smoke of the Savanna finally got underway, every inch of available space, including their compartment, was jam-packed with people. Aurore and Delphine were soon as hot and sweaty and dust smeared as everybody else. Any feeling they might have had of special privi-

DRUMBEAT OF DESIRE 233

lege was gone. Only their clothes and their complexions set them apart from the others in the compartment.

"See if that window beside you will open any further, Aurore," requested Delphine. "It's so close in here I can't stand it."

As Aurore struggled with the window, yet another passenger squeezed into the seat on the other side of Delphine. The man carried a rickety string-and-wood crate containing two roosters. When he set it on his lap, their red beaks poked out to snap at Delphine's bare arm. She cringed and pushed away so hard that Aurore was wedged solidly into the corner.

Now the only thing private in the compartment was their conversation. They were the only passengers speaking French. In any case, jammed into the corner as they were, they couldn't be overheard.

The journey seemed to stretch on endlessly, until both Aurore and Delphine lost track of time and distance. Dazed by the hot and stifling air of their crowded compartment, Aurore found her mind wandering from Delphine's conversation to the confusing and traumatic events of the past few months. Would she ever understand men?

Some time later, she was abruptly jolted back to reality as the train shuddered to a halt, its brakes screeching. The door of the compartment opened, and a chubby black conductor entered. Behind him were a uniformed officer and two soldiers.

"That one there." The conductor pointed at a toffee-skinned woman sitting across from Aurore. "Her husband is one of the ringleaders of the strike. Throw her off the train."

"You filthy traitor!" the woman screamed. "You voted for the strike along with the other men. You received money from the union to live on, just as they did. Then you sneaked behind their backs and went back to work for the *toubabs*. Now you inform on us. Allah will curse you!"

The rest of her tirade was lost as the soldiers hustled

her out of the compartment. They pushed her off the train so roughly that Aurore could hear her falling down the steps.

"There is another one." The rotund black conductor pointed at an elderly woman.

"Oh, please, monsieurs," she begged as the soldiers grabbed her bony arms. "My daughter in Thiès is very sick. They tell me she may die. That is the only reason I am on the train. Be kind to an old woman," she wailed frantically. "Do not throw me off the train in the middle of nowhere!"

But that is just what the soldiers did to her, as well as the other women who were known to be relatives of the striking railway workers. Carrying their baskets and bundles, some of them with babies and children in tow, they were being ejected from every car on the train. Craning her head out the window, Aurore watched the process.

Soon there were clusters of the dispossesed stretching all along the right-of-way. Beyond them were flatlands covered with brush and nothing else, no sign of human habitation. They were being abandoned about midway between Dakar and Thiès. How would these people manage the journey on foot either back to Dakar or forward to Thiès under the blazing sun? Aurore was filled with indignation and pity at their plight.

About two cars down were parked several jeeps painted in military colors. As Aurore watched, a group of soldiers disembarked from the train with a handcuffed prisoner in tow and ushered him toward the vehicles. He was tall and slender, with velvet-black skin. His posture and bearing were familiar.

"Amin!" Aurore recognized her brother-in-law. Without stopping to explain to Delphine, Aurore rushed from the compartment and scrambled down the train steps. She ran the length of her car, then another, catching up with the soldiers just as they were about to put Amin in the back of one of the jeeps.

"Wait!" Out of breath, she addressed the young

black officer in charge. "Why are you detaining this man?"

The eyes of the officer took in her white skin and her Paris frock. There was a certain amount of respect in his tone as he answered her. "He was passing himself off as a farmer, but he has been recognized as a fisherman whose father is a chief on Ile Celeste. Also he is carrying a great deal of money, which he has not explained to our satisfaction. Obviously there is some sort of fraud involved. Therefore we are taking him for questioning. And now, mademoiselle, might you be good enough to tell me why you have made this matter your concern."

Amin's face was blank as he looked at Aurore. Nevertheless, the message in his eyes was clear to her: Do not involve yourself!

Aurore ignored it. "He's my brother-in-law," she told the officer, noting the immediately raised eyebrow that questioned how a woman with white skin might come to have a brother-in-law with skin that was darkest black. "Do you think that I could talk to him alone for a just a moment?"

The black officer shrugged. "But only a moment, mademoiselle." He backed away from his handcuffed prisoner a bit to give them some privacy.

"How can I help you, Amin?" Aurore asked him.

Amin answered her in a low voice for her ears alone. "Steven Parker was to meet me at the train station in Thiès. Tell him I've been arrested with the money. Tell him I think it was Mustapha Hakim who betrayed me."

"Hakim? But why? How?"

"It was he who arranged for a seat for me on this train. He was the only one who knew of my mission, the only one who knew how much money I'd be carrying. And he has betrayed us before."

"That's true." Aurore remembered the incident with the harbor patrol.

"Tell Sabine that I love her as always," Amin added

in a louder voice as the officer moved in to end their conversation. "And give Chief Amadou a kiss for me."

"I will." Aurore watched as the soldiers hustled him into the jeep. "Where are you taking him?" she asked the officer.

"The police station in Thiès," he told her.

"You won't mistreat him."

"We won't," the officer promised. "But the police in Thiès are another matter. Feelings are running very high because of the strike. The French control them, the Thiès police. If you have any influence with the prisoner, then advise him to cooperate, mademoiselle."

"I have no influence with him." Aurore blew Amin a kiss as the jeep pulled away. Then she reboarded the train.

A little more than an hour later, they arrived in Thiès. Aurore and Delphine had thought that the conditions on the train were bad, but nothing could have prepared them for the sights and sounds and smells that greeted them at the Thiès station. Every single bit of floor space was occupied by men, women, and children who lay sprawled out or crouched like stone statues. Most of them had been waiting day after day, many week after week, for a train that would finally have room for them.

Since they were unable to move for fear of losing their places, the people performed even their most intimate functions right where they were. Spit, stained red from cola nuts or black from chewing tobacco, covered the walls and floors. Flies buzzed ceaselessly over the remnants of food that lay scattered around. The stench of urine and feces hung in the air, creating a foul miasma. Babies cried, children whined and stumbled aimlessly over the boxes and baskets and rolls of matting and animal skins that hemmed them in.

The luckier would-be passengers were camped out on the covered porches and platforms surrounding the station house. Those swarmed around the train from Dakar, waiting for the soldiers to allow them to fill the vacated places on the once-a-week train as it continued on to Bamako in Mali. There was no porter to be found. Aurore and Delphine struggled through the closely packed bodies, carrying their suitcases themselves. They were eager for a breath of fresh air. But outside the station, more people were waiting, their eyes fixed dazedly on a group of strikers who were demonstrating a few yards away.

Some carried rough wooden boards with slogans lettered in bright red: WE DEMAND FAMILY ALLOWANCES and FOR EQUAL WORK, EQUAL PAY and PROPER HOUSING IS OUR RIGHT. Others marched and chanted about the strikers' right to collect sick benefits and old-age pensions. It was a peaceable demonstration until a platoon of police arrived.

They immediately began to disperse the demonstrators with billy clubs and strong-arm tactics. The strikers resisted. Rocks and sand-filled bottles sailed through the air, hitting several police officers. Incensed, they drew their guns and began to fire into the mob. The terrified strikers ran every which way. Aurore and Delphine, who had been on the sidelines, were rapidly swamped by panic-stricken demonstrators trying to escape the gunfire.

They clung together, determined not to become separated this time. The gunfire grew louder. They were about to throw themselves to the ground, as many others had done, when suddenly Aurore noticed a tall, blond-haired figure striding through the melee. He had a pistol in each hand held high in the air. He was firing them by turn to clear a path through both police and demonstrators. In his broad-brimmed panama hat and tight-fitting jeans, he reminded Aurore of a cowboy in the American Western movies she had seen as a schoolgirl. As he came closer, the broad-brimmed hat disclosed the blue-eyed, freckled face of Steven Parker.

"Come on, ladies. Follow me," he suggested with his easy, lopsided grin.

Still firing his pistols into the air, he escorted them

through the crowd. It quieted down to watch the flamboyant American-style rescue operation with open mouths. Even the police were staring.

He led them through the open square in front of the station, around a corner and down a quiet street. At the end of it was an open-air café. Here Steven proposed that they pause and have a cool drink.

Delphine, obviously ill at ease in Steven's company, declined the chair he offered her and said she was going to the ladies' room. Steven gestured for the waiter and ordered himself a gin and tonic. Aurore ordered *bissap*.

She was trembling and shaken from the ordeal, but she managed to return Steven Parker's smile. "Thank you for getting us out of there," she said, drinking her fruit juice thirstily.

"My pleasure entirely," Steven answered in his folksy way. "But I'm afraid I'll have to be leaving you now." He drained his drink. "I was supposed to be meeting a certain party back there at the station. By now, I reckon he'll be wondering where I've got to."

"He isn't there." Aurore told him what had happened to Amin.

"Sometimes luck just ain't no lady nohow." Steven exaggerated his drawl to point up the irony. "Well, I'll just have to hightail it over to the police station and see what can be done."

"Will they hurt him?" Aurore was worried. "I've heard stories—about beatings and torture."

"Probably all exaggerations, little lady." He was trying to reassure her, but she could read the truth in his eyes. The police were not likely to be gentle with Amin.

"The army officer seemed mostly concerned about the amount of money he was carrying," Aurore remembered.

"I'll tell the local gendarmes it was dough raised by strike sympathizers to buy food for the strikers' starving children."

"Will they believe that?"

"Probably not. But they'll keep the money anyhow. And maybe if I grease their palms a bit more, they'll let him go."

"I hope so." Aurore glanced around the shaded patio of the café. "I wonder what's keeping Delphine."

"Likely she's avoiding me. Wants me to keep promises I never made, and now her nose is out of joint 'cause I just plain won't do that." He shook his head ruefully. "You'd think now that her little problem's taken care of she'd let bygones be bygones."

"But it hasn't been taken care of. It couldn't be done in Dakar. That's why we've come here. A woman here is going to do it this afternoon."

"I see." His voice was flat and noncommittal.

"Oh, Steven!" Aurore reached across the table and took his hand. "Come with us! It would mean so much to Delphine to have you there!"

"Whoa there, little lady!" Steven got to his feet.

"Please, Steven! You wouldn't have to make any commitment. Just be there."

"I can't really do that." He tipped his hat politely. "You're forgetting that I have to get to the police station to see about Amin before those boys get carried away with their job. Sorry." He smiled his laconic cowboy smile at Aurore, and then he was gone.

Men! They were quick enough to enjoy the pleasures of a woman's body! But when it came to facing the consequences of such actions, there would always be some more pressing matter to which they must attend, she thought bitterly.

Aurore's bitterness recurred that evening as she sat at Delphine's bedside and watched the pale and shaken girl fall into a fitful doze. Delphine had gone through a horror of fear and pain and blood. The woman who performed the abortion was the sister of a striking trainman who had been brutalized by the French-controlled railroad police. She made no secret of this fact. Nor did she bother to hide her dislike of French white women. It was in this hostile atmosphere that the abortion had been performed.

After the long and painful ordeal, they had taken a taxi to the du Mauriers, the friends of *Tante* Colette with whom they would be staying. The du Mauriers were a well-to-do French family who lived in the European section of Thiès. Alain du Maurier held a high position in the management of the railroad, and he and his pretty wife traveled often to Dakar on business and took part in the social life there, which is how *Tante* Colette knew them.

They had been shocked by Delphine's appearance. Aurore explained that her cousin had been taken ill on the hot and crowded train. Madame Adèle du Maurier, a buxom, auburn-haired creature with the chirpy voice and the nervous movements of a little bird, had taken them directly upstairs to the guest room they would share. She suggested a doctor, but Delphine said it was unnecessary, that a night's rest would suffice.

"It's my time of the month," she told Adèle du Maurier. "It took me by surprise, and what with the heat and the overcrowding on the train, I became weak and faint."

"You poor dear," Adèle sympathized. "We're delighted to have you here, of course, but we did think it a foolhardy time to travel. Still," she chirruped, *"l'amour, l'amour!* When one is young and in love, one lets nothing stand in the way. Isn't it so? But where is the young man? Your fiancé? He knows you've come, does he not?"

"He met us at the station." Aurore answered quickly to save Delphine the effort of improvising lies. "But he couldn't come with us. Business. He's very busy. So he saw us safely to a taxi and here we are."

"But the train pulled in hours ago." Adèle looked bewildered.

"Young lovers." Aurore made her voice conspiratorial. "You know how it is, madame. They needed some time alone."

"Unchaperoned?" Adèle looked scandalized.

"Not at all. I was there."

"But I thought it was the train trip that made Delphine ill. She should have come straight here. Her dear mother would have wanted her to, I'm sure."

"And so she should have," Aurore agreed. "I told her so, didn't I, Delphine. But no. She had to see Steven first. And now just see how she has fatigued herself."

"Well, I don't know." Adèle was still dubious as to whether the proprieties had been fulfilled. "I just don't know."

"How have you fared here in Thiès since the strike began?" Aurore seized the moment of doubt to change the subject.

"We've had no real trouble. Still, there have been incidents. Even on our quiet little street. Alain and some of the men who are our neighbors take turns patrolling at night. Alain takes his pistol, and he's careful to load it. After all, who can tell what these savages might do in a situation like this?"

"Who indeed?" Aurore murmured, careful to keep the sarcasm out of her voice. Obviously *Tante* Colette had not thought it necessary to inform Madame du Maurier of her niece's Wolof heritage.

Adèle left them then. Aurore sat up and watched Delphine, still fearful as to what the aftereffects of the abortion might be. Still, when Delphine dozed, Aurore drifted off, sitting up in the chair beside the bed. She awoke with a start at a movement beside her.

It was Delphine, getting back into bed. "I've just been to the bathroom, Aurore. The bleeding is much better. I can sleep now. You too. Get into bed and stop worrying about me. Everything's all right."

Aurore did as she suggested. She was asleep in moments. And she did not wake until long after the sun had lit the blue African sky.

The next few days had a pleasing, soothing rhythm of their own. Life in the European section of Thiès where the du Mauriers and the other railroad officials and their families lived was easy, lazy, and, despite the strike, uneventful. The little enclave was well outside the city, far from the railroad station and the train yards.

The homes were all alike—prefabricated roofs, small balconies, fenced-in porches, an abundance of spare rooms. Only the pastel tints of their facades varied. In front, they boasted well-kept lawns and orderly gravel walkways; in back were lush gardens of rose bushes, daisies, and chrysanthemums, shaded from the blistering sun by tall hedges of bougainvillea.

The somnolent rhythm of the days was broken only by the meals and teas which the du Maurier's servant girl seemed always to be serving. They took tea in the rear garden, seated in the circle of lawn chairs, always with one or two neighbor couples, the men balancing cups and plates uncomfortably on their meaty thighs. Conversation was dominated by the strike and the threats it posed to the du Mauriers' and their neighbors' easy, pleasant way of life. The men were thinking of organizing vigilante committees so that if it came to defending their homes and gardens against a group attack, they would be prepared.

On the fourth night of their visit, Aurore was awakened by the sound of gunfire. She leaped up and ran down the hall to the upstairs balcony. Leaning over the concrete balustrade, she saw the tall, gray-haired form of Alain du Maurier stretched out on the lawn. Standing over him, gun in hand, was the hulking shape of another man. She was about to rush back inside to summon help by telephone when the shadowy form straightened up, his face illuminated by the porch light.

"Blaise!" She recognized him instantly. "What happened?" she called. "Is Monsieur du Maurier all right?"

"He's just stunned. He mistook me for an intruder and fired. I rushed him before he could do any damage. In the process of disarming him, I'm afraid I gave him a nasty punch in the jaw. He's coming around now. Make an ice pack. I'll get him inside before the whole damned neighborhood descends on us with their swords drawn and their muskets at the ready.''

A few minutes later, Alain du Maurier sat at the kitchen table holding a cold compress to his injured jaw. His wife bustled around fixing a sandwich and coffee for their newest guest. Aurore eyed Blaise nervously. Why had he come? Had he found out about the abortion? Did he know that Steven Parker was the responsible man? If so, what would he do?

"My apologies." Blaise was explaining to his host and hostess. "I would have called first, but there's been some trouble with the phone lines between here and the company airfield. I'm told the strikers have cut them in five or six places—at random, it would seem."

"They're like children." Adèle du Maurier shook her head sadly. "Vandalism like that can't do them any good. It's just like a child throwing a tantrum and breaking things because its parent won't give him what he wants when he wants it."

"No, my dear." Alain du Maurier disagreed. "They are not children. They are beastly savages. And they know exactly what they're doing. The beggars bloody well know that by cutting communications between where we live and where we have to function for the railroad— not so much the airfield, but the switching yards and the loading platforms and so forth—they make our jobs much harder." He turned to Blaise. "You flew in?" He seemed puzzled. "On the company plane?"

"Yes."

"But I thought our pilot was in the hospital in Dakar having his appendix removed."

"He is. I flew myself. I'm a licensed pilot," Blaise told him. "Duke Alcofarado arranged for me to have the use of the plane through the president of the board in Dakar. He wanted a message delivered to you and to the other top management officials in Thiès."

"I see." Alain du Maurier glanced quickly at Aurore and then back at Blaise. "Is it confidential?" he asked.

"Not at all. As you know, while the duke is a large

stockholder in the railroad, his major business in Senegal is exporting peanut oil. He and other stockholders with similar interests have formed a little group—quite friendly, you understand—to make their thinking known to railroad executives such as yourself.''

"Peanut oil." Alain du Maurier nodded as if he knew what Blaise was going to say next.

"The growing season will soon be over. The groundnut harvest has to be brought to the factories for processing before it rots, or the whole Senegalese economy will go down the drain. The only way to do this at present is by rail. The duke's stockholder group doesn't want to meddle. He wants you to understand that. Nevertheless, they think that perhaps the time may have come for railroad management to think about seeking some accommodation with the striking workers.''

"Some accommodation!" Alain du Maurier sounded bitter. "These beggars won't go back until their outrageous demands are met in full. How would the duke and the other stockholders feel about that when it comes time for the next dividend to be declared and it's half what the last one was?''

"You'll have to ask the duke that yourself. I'm only the messenger boy.''

Was that true? Aurore wondered. Would Blaise have come merely to deliver a message for the duke? The answer was obvious. Of course he wouldn't. When Blaise spoke again, she knew she was right.

"And now I think I'd like to say hello to my sister,'' he said.

"Of course." Adèle du Maurier replied. "I can't imagine why she hasn't come down.''

Because she was afraid that Blaise knew everything and had come to take some sort of action. That, Aurore knew, was why Delphine had remained in her room.

"Nor can I,'' Blaise replied dryly.

"I'll take you to her room." Adèle du Maurier rose from her chair, the full sleeves of her peignoir fluttering like wings.

Aurore watched them go up the stairs. A moment later, Alain du Maurier said good night to her and went to his room, still clutching the cold compress to his swollen jaw. Aurore decided she might as well go to bed herself.

It was perhaps half an hour later and she was lying awake staring at the ceiling when the knock came at her door. It was as if she had been expecting it. She didn't have to ask who it was. She opened the door, and Blaise entered without requesting permission. He closed the door behind him. His eyes were flashing and angry as he stared at her in the dim light from the small lamp on the nightstand beside the bed. Aurore felt a chill at his expression. Her arms crossed over her breasts as if to draw a wrap around her body. But there was no wrap, only the skimpy material of her nightie, a Parisian import ordered by *Tante* Colette, stretching revealingly against her full breasts.

"Well, *Cousine!* And I was worried about defiling your innocence!" His voice was cutting, cold, sarcastic. "It seems I should have directed my concern closer to home."

He knew about the abortion. There could be no doubt about it. But what did he expect her to say? What could she say? Nothing. Aurore remained silent.

"Why didn't you come to me and tell me about Delphine's problem?" he asked when she didn't speak.

"She made me promise not to. She was afraid of what you might do."

"Did she think I wouldn't have understood?" His tone was a little softer now. "She must know that I've seen something of the world. Did she think that I would be her judge? My own sister? That I would punish her?"

"I don't think she thought you'd punish her." Despite his hostility, Aurore found her heart going out to him.

"If Maman didn't think better of me than either Delphine or you, I might never have found out."

"I think well of you," Aurore said in a voice that was suddenly, inexplicably close to tears. "It's you who don't value me."

Blaise didn't pick up on her reply.

"Maman didn't know who the man was who was responsible," he said.

At least *Tante* Colette had withheld *that* information!

"And Delphine won't tell me. So that leaves you, *Cousine*." His eyes were like shards of blue ice cutting into her.

"I don't know who the man was." Aurore wasn't close to tears anymore. The look on Blaise's face made her understand completely now why Delphine hadn't wanted him to know. The snarl on his lips belonged behind dueling pistols of a bygone era.

"I don't believe you," he told her bluntly. "But I'm not a stupid man, Aurore, regardless of what you and my sister may think. I have eyes in my head, and sometimes I keep them open. Where Delphine is concerned, one candidate stands out above all the rest."

"And who might that be?" Aurore asked, knowing the answer.

"Steven Parker."

"And what does Delphine say to that?"

"She denies it's Parker, of course. But then that's what I'd expect her to do. So I'll just go ahead and pay a call on Monsieur Parker anyway."

"I wouldn't if I were you."

"Oh? Why not?"

"Because Steven Parker isn't Delphine's lover. He's mine." Aurore lied smoothly.

"What?" It was the first time since they'd known each other that Aurore saw Blaise's composure shaken. "Do you expect me to believe—"

"I don't really care what you believe. But you'll embarrass Delphine for no reason if you go to Steven. You see, I haven't told him about why she came here."

"Parker is your lover," Blaise said as if he was trying to comprehend the fact.

"Yes. Why are you so surprised? You didn't want me. Did you think every other man would turn away from me as well?"

"I thought you'd have the good sense to—"

"To live a celibate life? The way you do?" Aurore laughed harshly.

"No. I suppose not." The old cynicism was back in Blaise's voice. "You'll have to forgive me. I'm an incurable romantic when it comes to young girls."

"Are you?" Aurore inquired sweetly. "Does that mean you expect them all to become nuns after you deflower them? Or does inaction eventually enable them to grow new maidenheads?"

"*Cousine*, you are growing up." Blaise threw back his head and laughed. "You're acquiring the art of repartee."

"*Merci*." Aurore curtsied elaborately.

But his laugh wasn't the same. It wasn't! There was something missing—humor? Tenderness? Happiness? There was a quality to it that was weary, resigned.

"I'm going to bed, *Cousine*," he told her. "I'd suggest you do the same. I'm flying you and Delphine back to Dakar in the morning." He left her room.

Aurore waited until she heard the door to his room close. Then she slipped into Delphine's room. She informed Delphine of how she had told Blaise that Steven Parker was her lover and not the man responsible for making Delphine pregnant. Then she bid Delphine good night and went to bed and finally to sleep.

There was an alteration in plans the next morning. The strikers had gotten onto the airfield during the night and sabotaged the plane. A messenger had brought Alain du Maurier the news. So now Aurore and Blaise and Delphine would have to travel by railroad. Fortunately they would still be able to leave that morning. This was the day the train stopped in Thiès on its weekly journey back to Dakar from Bamako.

The crush outside the railroad station was just as bad,

if not worse, than it had been when they arrived. Blaise led the two girls around the station building itself and along the barbed-wire fence to the narrow gate being guarded by a quartet of soldiers. Blaise showed the sergeant in charge the authorized pass he had obtained from Alain du Maurier. They were passed through to the waiting train.

After a half hour or so, as had been the case in Dakar, the train began to fill rapidly. Soon all the saets in their compartment were filled. Even after all the seats on the train were taken, the anxious people continued to come.

They were amazingly docile and polite, despite the crush. They sat on their bundles in the aisles and kept crowding closer and closer to make room for new arrivals. The closeness became unbearable.

Flies buzzed in the stifling air of the compartment. Blaise had given Aurore and Delphine the two window seats. Now he stood and leaned over them to wrench the window open wider.

When he sat down, Aurore leaned out to gulp a few breaths of air. The whistle sounded. The huge locomotive began to shudder and shake.

Suddenly Aurore spied a familiar, blond-headed figure loping down the platform. He saw her and waved frantically. It was Steven Parker, and obviously he wanted to talk to her. Aurore excused herself. She left the compartment hurriedly and pushed through the packed aisle to the open vestibule. Parker was already standing outside the doorway where the steps led from the train to the platform.

"It's Amin," he told her. "He escaped from the police. But he's been shot. He's hiding in the native quarter. He may die."

"Amin," Aurore repeated automatically, taking a moment to catch up to the horror of what Steven Parker was telling her.

"I went out to the du Mauriers to tell you, but you'd

DRUMBEAT OF DESIRE 249

already left. They said you were taking the train. So I came here.''

"Did you say he was dying?" Aurore shook her head to clear it.

"No. I said he *may* die. It's a bad wound. The doctor just doesn't know. He says with good nursing . . ."

"Take me to him." Amin! She would never be able to face Sabine and Amadou again if she didn't do everything she could for Sabine's husband.

The train was starting to move. She leaped from the steps and Steven caught her in his arms. He held her a moment to steady her.

She looked up and saw Blaise staring down at them from the window. There was no opportunity to explain anything to him. His cynical gaze took in their embrace, and then he shrugged as if to confirm that he didn't care, had never cared.

Aurore averted her eyes and found herself looking at Delphine. The French girl appeared surprised, then hurt. Oh, dear! Delphine was bound to mistake her sudden departure for a betrayal. She would think what Blaise thought: that she and Steven Parker were lovers.

Aurore felt awful that Delphine must believe this, but she was through caring what Blaise Honoré de Beausoleil thought about her!

That's what Aurore told herself as The Smoke of the Savanna disappeared around the bend.

CHAPTER 10

Almost three months had passed since the day Steven Parker brought Aurore to the small wood and tar-paper cabin in one of the poorest sections of Thiès, where the badly wounded Amin lay on a straw pallet. His skin had been a sickly gray, his breathing shallow and ragged. The bullet had caught him in the upper chest. Steven had used Amin's shirt to fashion a tourniquet and bandage to staunch the bleeding.

They had to disinfect the wound and somehow pry out the bullet. Neither of them had any real medical knowledge. Aurore didn't know what they would have done without the help of the family to whose compound the cabin belonged.

The Diop family—some eighteen members in all, ranging from ancient grandmothers to tiny infants—were distant relatives of Amin's mother. The fact that they hadn't seen Amin since he was a boy made no difference. When Steven appeared with him, they had taken in their wounded cousin immediately, prepared to share what little they had. The Diop men, like most of the men in the neighborhood, worked for the railroad. The strike had hit the family hard.

While Steven was out buying disinfectant, the women of the Diop family came to the hut where Amin lay. They brought what few comforts they could offer—a jug of precious water, some clean rags, a gourd of rice gruel from their dwindling store. They exchanged introductions with Aurore.

"Your sister is the wife of Amin Baye?" It was all

they needed to know. From then on, Aurore was considered one of their own, a sister.

Steven returned. He managed to extract the bullet from Amin's upper chest with a kitchen knife. Aurore poured peroxide over the wound and bandaged it. Finally Amin slept, but fitfully. Steven left, saying he would be back the next day. The women brought in a piece of straw matting and a coverlet for Aurore. But she couldn't sleep. She sat up most of the night, sponging Amin, watching over him.

The next morning, instead of being better, he tossed and moaned under the onslaught of a high fever. The wound was festering; infection had set in. The following week was a nightmare during which Aurore, her own body suffering the effects of too little sleep and food, fought to keep Amin alive. He was often wild-eyed and delirious and had to be restrained. He had no idea where he was; he recognized neither Aurore nor Steven, who came and went, bringing aspirin he obtained on the black market for the fever.

But Aurore could see that aspirin was not enough. Each day the wound became more swollen with pus. Draining it provided only temporary relief. "I don't know what to do," she told Steven one night. She was close to tears with anxiety over Amin.

"Only thing that might help is sulfa drugs."

"The new drugs you Americans used during the war?" Aurore had heard of them and of their miraculous curative powers. "But where could we get any of them? Only the American military had them. Or does the black market—"

"No. Right after the war you could get sulfa on the black market, but no more. Oh, if we were in Dakar, sure as shoot Hakim would find us some for a price. But here in Thiès, the only one likely to have it is the French doctor who works for the railroad."

"You think the railroad doctor might have some?"

"They used to stock it in the infirmary in case one of their execs had an accident."

Aurore thought a moment. "If they have it, maybe we can get it," she decided. "Do you have a pen and some writing paper?" she asked Steven.

"Guess I can scrounge some up." He fetched it for her and waited, curious, while she wrote a note. When she was done, she handed it to him.

"Monsieur le Docteur," he read. "I am in need of enough sulfanilamide, or one of the other suitable sulfa drugs, to treat an infection from gunpowder sustained by my brother-in-law as a result of the railroad's current troubles with the strikers. If you will be good enough to give an adequate amount of this drug to the bearer, my family and I would be most grateful. Thank you for your cooperation." The note was signed *Aurore de Beausoleil* with a flourish that owed less to the nuns who had taught her handwriting than to *Tante* Colette.

The ruse worked. The de Beausoleil name was evidently known to the doctor. Nor did it hurt that the messenger was an American. Steven returned with the precious drug.

The sulfa turned the tide of the infection. The angry red swelling around the wound diminished; the healing process began. A week passed, and then one morning Amin awoke completely lucid, the fever gone. In spite of his subsistence diet of rice, supplemented only occasionally by cassava roots and monkey bread, the fibrous fruit of the baobab tree, Amin continued to improve.

He was still confined to bed, but since he no longer required constant care, Aurore was able sometimes to leave the tiny cabin to spend time with the other women in the Diop family compound. This compound included the main house, a large wooden structure containing several rooms. Its tile roof was extended outward by zinc sheeting to form a shaded verandah. Surrounding the large house were several small huts of mud and straw, as well as five wood cabins, including the one in which Amin lay convalescing. A wall extended around the entire compound, and in front of the gate stood a latticework screen, the *m'bague gathie,* "protection from dishonor.'' This shielded the central courtyard where the men congregated from the eyes of passersby.

The women spent most of their time in the smaller courtyard behind the main house. The lean-to used as a communal kitchen was here. Aurore joined the Diop women in their various household chores here—preparing the meager meals, washing the clothes, trying to distract the small children with stories and games to take their minds off the ever-present gnawing in their bellies.

Because of the strike, life had been reduced to its most elementary function—survival. All the produce from the local gardens had been eaten long ago; every edible plant and root and tree fruit had been consumed. The Middle-Eastern storekeepers had cut off credit to their local customers and would sell foodstuffs only at exorbitant prices. Little by little, the strikers' prized possessions had been sold—an almost-new blanket vanished from a child's bed, a silver bangle left a brown arm bare, a bolt of fine-spun silk cotton saved for a wedding dress was offered up for cash.

Now the Diop women lamented the lack of buyers for the few marketable items they still possessed. Even the finest head cloths, even the waist cloths fashioned by the most skillful weavers of the city, symbols of the women's virginity when they married, were offered in vain. No one had money left for such finery.

Twice each week the women went to collect the ration of rice distributed by the union to the strikers' families. At first, the rations had been given to the men, but this caused too many problems because of the multiple wives who vied for it. The squabbles that arose were so frequent and so serious that the union leaders feared the men might return to work in order to escape the ire of their womenfolk. Now rations were given directly to the women from tables set up in an open field near the union building. The wives lined up in front of a table, where a union official checked their names off his list. He then sent them to a second table, where three women volunteers dug two-pound scoops into the big rice sacks behind them. They poured the rice into whatever container each woman had brought with her.

The waiting women exchanged news, gossiped, joked, and occasionally quarreled. Seeing their children hungry, knowing that four pounds of rice per week was far from adequate to feed their large families, caused a constant strain. And what made it worse was that there was no end in sight.

The strike had been going on for four months. The women not only had to contend with hungry children but also with discouraged husbands whose masculine role as breadwinners was in abeyance. It was only human that the women watched the measuring scoops with eagle eyes, fearful that one of the servers might favor a relative or friend with a more generous portion.

Aurore understood why some of the waiting women at first eyed her suspiciously. They were wondering what she, with her light skin and glossy red hair, was doing in their midst. But as the time of her visit with the Diop family lengthened, she became a familiar figure. Since she showed no signs of trying to appropriate a single grain of precious rice, the other women came to accept her. Pale-skinned or not, the faded, threadbare *boubou* one of the Diop sisters had lent her proclaimed her position to be as desperate as anyone else's.

Some nights the desperation was eased by a bit of meat to flavor the rice. The teenagers occupied themselves with setting handmade traps to capture small animals or birds. Slingshots were also used. The whole compound celebrated on the evenings the boys came in with a good haul of crows or magpies or hummingbirds. Occasionally a foray into the French section would result in the capture of a chicken that had strayed from its roost.

After clearing away the dishes, the women would gather in a circle on the cool earth of the inner courtyard. One after another, they would sing, improvising verses that concerned both the privations they were enduring and their hope for a better future. By the end of a few weeks, Aurore felt comfortable enough to take her turn in the improvised singing. It was a great relief to express one's innermost thoughts and feelings in this way; it seemed to give the strength of spirit necessary to face yet another day of hunger and thwarted hope.

The women told Aurore that in the first month or two of the strike, the evening gatherings had been much more spirited. Old ceremonies had been revived, with the women dyeing their hands and feet with henna and coloring their lips silver-white with antimony. They would dance until well after midnight. The men, wielding staffs or sticks, would perform the ancient ritual of saber duels. The beating of the tomtoms had resounded from every courtyard and street corner, proclaiming the people's unity and their resolve to overcome the tyranny of the *toubabs*. Now the drumbeats still sounded in the cool night air, but they were softer and slower, and no one had the energy to dance, or to act out ritual duels.

Amin, however, seemed possessed of an inner energy. It showed itself as a restless and burning desire to get on with his mission. Once he was out of bed, there was no restraining him. He paced the small cabin and the large courtyard, stretching and limbering up his long-limbed body, heedless of Aurore's admonitions that he was overtaxing himself.

He was impatient for Steven Parker's visits. When Steven came, they would sit in the cabin until late at night, talking *jihad*, making plans. Their discussions were of how to replace the money that had been confiscated by the police. Without it, there would be no potassium nitrate; without potassium nitrate, there would be no ammunition; and without ammunition, there would be no holy war against the *toubabs*. But from where was the money to come?

"The *imams* couldn't put up the whole bundle last time," Steven pointed out. "So how can they make up what we've lost? Maybe we should go to Mustapha Hakim again."

"Never again!" Amin made a face. "He has betrayed us once too often. I would not consider borrowing from him at usurious rates so that he can then arrange to have the money he lends stolen from us. Never again!"

"There's cash coming in from de Beausoleil for the fish," Steven reminded him.

"That belongs to the people of Ile Celeste. Only they can decide to contribute to the *jihad*. Someday perhaps they will. But the time has not yet come to ask them to decide this. We are still a long way from that."

"Then where'll the money come from?"

"There is only one source we have not yet tried—the Muslim leaders of Algeria. Before this happened, I was in contact with them. They are involved in an ongoing struggle with the French. Eventually it must end in independence and a Muslim state."

"But why would they put up money for a Senegalese independence struggle? Why wouldn't they conserve what dough they've got for their own use?"

"Because they are pragmatists," Amin told him. "If by supplying money to us, they can bring about the day of a Senegalese uprising, which will make it necessary for the French to move troops from Algeria to Senegal, and if French wealth and power are drained fighting in Senegal, then this will make their own struggle easier and save Algerian lives in the long run. But they are religious Muslims first and Algerian politicians second. They will only deal with other Muslims—Muslims they trust."

"Do they trust you?" Steven asked.

"They do not even know me. My contact with them was through a group of Imams. They might provide the funds to them, and then the *imams*—in view of the potassium-nitrate situation—might give it to us. But first, we have to contact the Imams here in Thiès. I'll write a letter. You can deliver it."

The letter was quickly answered. The Thiès *imams* were anxious that the available potassium nitrate not slip through their fingers. They agreed to send a representative to Oran to arrange a loan from the Algerian Muslim leaders.

At first, during the day that followed, Aurore was glad to see that Amin's spirits were high. He was excited about resolving the problem of the potassium nitrate so that he could return to Ile Celeste, and to Sabine and little Amadou. But as the days and nights passed without delivery of the necessary money, Amin became restless and anxious. He cursed the *ay gaaf*— bad luck—that made it necessary for him to remain in hiding. Because of his arrest and subsequent escape, he was a wanted man, and Steven had impressed upon him the danger of leaving the Diop compound.

For Aurore, it was like being caged with a restless and ill-tempered panther. More and more frequently Amin's irritability drove her from his presence to the inner courtyard with the other women. She was sitting there one night when Steven Parker arrived, waved a jaunty hello, and went inside to visit Amin. Only a few moments later, Amin called to Aurore to join them.

One look at his face told Aurore that the news was good. He waved her to one of the mats placed just inside the cabin door to take advantage of the cool night air. "The money has come," Amin announced.

"And I've nailed down the deal for the potassium nitrate," Steven added. "Soon as the dough's delivered, it'll be loaded into a truck and headed for the processing factory on the outskirts of Dakar."

"I am leaving with it," Amin informed Aurore.

"But is that safe? Suppose the police—"

"I've crossed the palms of the Thiès police with more silver than is good for them," Steven reassured her. "Amin will be safe until he's outside the city limits. Then the truck has to make a run for it, anyhow. Militia patrols are the big danger. The truck will have to travel without headlights. But I don't see any other way to get Amin back home. And sooner or later, they're bound to close in on him and pick him up if he stays here."

"I'll go along," Aurore decided.

"Too dangerous." Both men spoke at once.

"I could never face Sabine if I let anything happen to her baby sister," Amin added. "You have done too much already, spending all this time nursing me."

"But I want to get home. There are no trains anymore. The latest violence by the strikers has stopped the French from making even weekly runs. Besides, if it's not too dangerous for you, then why is it for me?"

The two men exchanged looks. It was Steven Parker who answered. "There wouldn't be enough room," he told her. "We have men riding shotgun on the truck, just in case. There isn't even room for me to go along."

"You're not going?" Aurore was surprised.

"Nope."

"You're staying behind to make more deals for more stolen potassium nitrate," she guessed.

Both men laughed. "She's getting smart fast," Parker said.

"I shudder to think where woman's place will be after the revolution," Amin agreed.

"Equal," Aurore told him flatly. "We're ready for our independence, too. And we're ready to take risks alongside the men."

But her arguments were to no avail. Amin would not be budged. He insisted there was no room for her on the truck; he would not hear of her making the trip with him back to Dakar.

"I can't stay here living off your relatives." Aurore voiced her final argument. "They don't have enough food for themselves."

"That's true," Amin granted. "But Steven has made alternate arrangements for you—and for himself."

"What alternate arrangements?" Aurore wanted to know.

"You can go back to stay with the du Mauriers," Steven told her. "Madame du Maurier says she'd be tickled to have you."

"The du Mauriers!" Aurore was astonished. "How—"

"I've been staying there myself these past weeks." Steven grinned at the expression on Aurore's face. "Well, why not?" he asked her. "After all, you and Delphine did go and pass me off as her fiancé. I just followed up on it. And I tell you, Aurore, the food's a lot better there than here. Meaning no offense to your relatives," he added to Amin.

"No offense," Amin assured him. "You will be safe with these *toubabs*," he told Aurore. "And the first thing Sabine will ask me is about your safety."

"But how can I take advantage of their hospitality like that? How can you?" she asked Steven indignantly. "It's so hypocritical!"

"Really?" It was Amin who replied. "After all the advantage the French have taken of the Senegalese, am I supposed to worry that they are the ones being taken advantage of now? And in such a small way? Also, let us not talk of hypocrisy as regards the French."

"Those are my sentiments, too," Steven chimed in with a cynical grin. "The du Mauriers have been on the people's backs just as long as they've been in this country. If I can freeload off them as Delphine's intended, and you can freeload off them as her cousin, it doesn't add up to a hill of beans considering how they've been taking the Senegalese in the name of almighty commerce."

And so it was decided. Once again, Aurore found herself under the comfortable wing of the du Mauriers. Kind as the Diop family had been to her, she could not help but find the soft bed with its smooth, clean linen sheets a welcome relief from the straw mat on the earth floor. Her palate responded enthusiastically to the warm, fresh croissants and raspberry preserves and scrambled eggs the du Mauriers served for breakfast, and to the pâté and fresh salad and onion soup they ate for lunch, and to the sumptuous, deliciously filling dinners.

Aurore could not help but feel guilty about all the food she savored while only a few miles away the Diops, who had accepted her as a sister, were practically starving. But she couldn't stop herself from eating, either. She also felt guilty about the pretty dresses and underthings Adèle lent her to wear. But they were such a welcome change from the threadbare *boubou* she had worn during her stay with the Diops.

Had she lost the African part of herself completely, Aurore wondered. Should she feel ashamed to respond so eagerly to European comforts? But no. She knew these comforts and amenities were only surface luxuries. Her Wolof heritage, bequeathed by her dear Maman, was secure deep inside her, in her heart. So she reasoned, but still she had doubts.

Did she even know her own heart anymore? She had been so torn these past two years. She had lost her father, and then her mother. Sabine had been parted from her by marriage. She had been uprooted from the village like a seedling and transplanted into the newly and richly fertilized soil of le Château de Beausoleil. She had exchanged her *boubous* for brassieres and lace-trimmed camisoles, for chic dresses of linen and lawn and lace. She had been taught to coax her flyaway hair into sleek waves and silky ringlets; she had been taught that bare feet were vulgar and had endured the pain of leather pumps and high-heel sandals. She had learned to hold her wild nature in check and to behave in the correct French fashion, *comme il faut,* as *Tante* Colette was always saying, "as is proper."

But she wasn't proper at all—not deep down. She had made love with Blaise at the first opportunity. How stupid she had been! She had assumed he loved her as she did him. She had given him her virginity, with all the passion that was in her, and in return, she had received insults and rejection. In spite of this, she still cared for him, still loved him—when she didn't hate him, that is.

Finally, just to add to her myriad ambivalent feelings, she had been plunged headlong into the violence and tumult of the railroad strike. First in Dakar, then in Thiès, she had seen the terrible privations of the people and had shared in them. She had learned to curse the toubabs and to share the strikers' indignation at their arrogance—this despite the preponderance of French blood running in her own veins.

Would her French blood always be at war with her Wolof heritage? Was she destined always to have the turmoil of Senegal mirrored inside herself? This period she was going through, this time of feeling torn, conflicted, confused—was it an interlude that would pass? This was what Aurore asked herself one sleepless night— one of many—as she paced the expensive carpet of the floral decorated guest bedroom.

It was useless to try to sleep. Despite the cross-ventilation, it was close in the room. Aurore put on a cream-color, beribboned peignoir over the low-cut nightgown she was wearing and tiptoed the length of the upstairs hall. At the far end was a screen door leading to a balcony overlooking the grounds. It would be cooler there.

When Aurore opened the screen door, however, she found Steven Parker on the balcony. With paranoia spreading throughout the French quarter, all the men had been standing guard over their property. Steven was spelling Alain du Maurier at sentry duty.

"Hello, Steven. I wanted some fresh air." Aurore went over to him and leaned on the balustrade. She looked up at the starlit sky and blinked at its magnificence.

"It's ages since we've been alone, Aurore." Steven was looking at her warmly, his light blue eyes taking in the swelling curves of her silk-clad body with frank appreciation. "It was on the patio of the château. Remember?"

Yes, she remembered. She remembered the way his lips had pressed hers open. She remembered the way he had held her so tightly that the hard and insistent bulge of his manhood had embedded itself in the softness between her thighs, burning through the layers of their clothes. But she also remembered Delphine and the rotten way Steven had treated her.

"Yes, I remember." She moved away from the warmth of his upper arm against hers. "I also remember how terribly hurt Delphine was when she walked in and found us kissing. If I had known you were so deeply involved with her, I would never have let you kiss me that way."

"We weren't deeply involved," Steven protested. "If Delphine said we were, she was exaggerating. We had a casual affair. That's all it was."

"Maybe for you it was casual. But not for Delphine. She was in love with you. And the least you could have done was to go with her for the abortion. It was horrible and painful, and she was frightened."

"I couldn't go. I had to see about getting Amin out of jail."

"You didn't want to go. You didn't want to be bothered. You didn't want to be involved. And that was rotten of you, Steven. After all, her predicament was at least half your fault."

"Maybe." His freckles in the starlight accented the sincerity of his expression. "But maybe not. I'll never know for sure, and neither will Delphine. You see, I wasn't the only one she was with around that time. She wasn't any more faithful to me than I was to her. Even so, I stood by her the best I know how. I arranged things with Hakim. I even shelled out his price. Truly, Aurore, I calculate I paid in full whatever obligation I had."

Perhaps he had, Aurore thought. After all, Delphine had admitted to having had many lovers. Steven's version contradicted nothing that Delphine had said. Perhaps it was simply a case of unrequited love. And anyway, Aurore thought, who was she to pass judgment on Steven Parker? Who was she to pass judgment on anyone? If she had learned anything since leaving the convent school, it was that life was too complicated for such judgments. She said as much to him then, apologizing for her presumption.

Steven smiled, his dimples making him seem more boyish, more innocent. "I'm relieved," he announced. "For a long time now, I've been afraid something fierce I'd never have your good opinion again."

"Is it so important to you?" Aurore was surprised. Steven always seemed so casual and offhand to her that she hadn't thought he cared very much about anything or anyone.

"Yes, ma'am, it is." His hand moved to rest lightly on her upper arm; his thumb caressed the silk-sheathed flesh gently, rhythmically. "I've been attracted to you since the first night we met at your mother's house on Ile Celeste," he told her frankly. "You were just so beautiful in that white outfit with your green eyes all asparkle and your red hair down your back like tumbleweed in the breeze. I think I fell for you right then."

"I don't know what to say." Aurore was touched. His openness and sincerity embarrassed her, but at the same time, she couldn't help feeling both warmed and flattered. "I like you, too, Steven," was all she could think of to add.

"It's more than 'like' with me. Even that first night—you were like a goddess! The way you danced! Just like a goddess, with the firelight flickering over your beautiful breasts when you bared them to the rhythm of the beating drums."

"I shouldn't have—" Aurore started to say, her face aflame with the memory.

"I wanted you then, Aurore." He cut her off. "And I want you now. I'm not a man for mincing words, nor for thinking up pretty speeches. I surely don't mean to insult you. But I want you, Aurore. Now!"

Except for the duke, no man had ever voiced his desire for Aurore so openly. But the duke had been old and foolish. Steven was young and handsome. His lean body was hard and virile; his eyes were wide and guileless, but in their depths was a desire so demanding that Aurore's pulse quickened with her comprehension of it.

Her reaction showed in her face. Steven waited for her neither to confirm nor deny it. He took her in his arms and his mouth covered hers like a warm, moist blanket of passion.

Aurore's tongue fluttered under his like a butterfly. His hand holding her arm was pressed against the soft outer curve of her breast now, and his roving thumb stroked there insistently. Her breast swelled at the thrill of his touch. She swayed against him, letting him pull her own timid tongue into his mouth where his teeth held it in gentle, tantalizing thrall.

Hot and fierce, the kiss continued. Steven's hand moved between them, over her breast, its firmness a reminder that save for the thin gossamer layer of Aurore's nightgown, the breast was bare. Her nipple quivered and hardened against the palm of his hand.

The caress outlasted the kiss. Aurore moaned under its sweet torment. She felt herself pulled more firmly against him. His lean hips strained against the softness of her belly as he wedged himself between her thighs. They clung together that way for a long moment, savoring the heated sensation.

A breeze ruffled the hair at the back of her neck; a shiver swept down her body from the light, tickling touch. The close aroma of a man aroused filled her nostrils; the scent replaced the air in her lungs; her breasts strained to hold its sweetness. Suddenly there was music: the tender trill of a night bird; the obbligato of its mate; and then a duet that blended so truly that an unanticipated lump filled Aurore's throat.

"Aurore." The voice was a murmur in her ear. It was an American voice with a prairie twang and an intrinsic friendliness, but it was not the voice Aurore might have hoped to hear under these romantic circumstances. It was not Blaise's voice.

Without thinking, she pulled back from him.

"Aurore?" Now her name was a puzzled question.

"I'm sorry. I—"

"Oh, no. You did that once before and I let you run away from me. But not this time." Steven kissed her again, firmly, demandingly. His arms were like steel bands holding her to him.

It was Blaise she wanted—but he didn't want her. His rejection had been clear, final! And her pulses were pounding with a desire that only a man could silence.

Her mouth opened hungrily to his kiss once again. Aurore's skin was alive with sensations—now flushed with heat, now tingling with shivers. Steven's hands moved down from her waist to her hips, his muscular arms still holding her prisoner. His palms cupped her derriere, stroking and kneading its roundness. Unthinkingly, she writhed against him.

Steven's fingers fumbled with the satin bows of her peignoir, and it floated open. He slid the narrow straps of the nightgown off her shoulders. The low bodice fell away, revealing her breasts, firm, creamy, shimmering in the soft, muted light from the hallway behind the screen door. His neck arched and he kissed each of the taut, rose-hued nipples in turn. He caught one between his lips, sucked it into his mouth, and continued licking and sucking with such tender vigor that thrills shot like electric currents down Aurore's body to her moist and swollen cleft.

Aurore's face was raised to the heavens as if in gratitude. Her eyes teared with the brilliance of the star-filled sky. It was as though she were melting to the heat of the stars, to the amorous abrasions of this boyish—yet so manly!—American, to the release of the long pent up passions within her woman's body.

Finally her sensitive flesh was too tortured and bruised to tolerate his mouth anymore. She fought to stand upright. She both trembled and thrilled at the expression of lust that could no longer be denied in his eyes.

"I want you, Aurore! *This* wants you." He took her hand in his and spread it over the throbbing protuberance beneath his trousers.

Then Steven dropped her hand. With a savage motion, he yanked down the zipper of his pants. Aurore gasped at the sight of the erection springing from the confines of his shorts.

He guided her hand to his arching phallus. Of her own free will, Aurore's other hand joined it. Her fingers investigated the velvet-soft length of him. The pulse between her own thighs quickened; a honeyed balm parted the furled petals of her womanhood.

Now his hand was moving up her bare legs, raising the diaphanous skirts of both peignoir and nightgown. It moved to the inside of her thighs, his fingertips savoring the young-girl softness of her flesh there. His fingers dipped between the petals, delighting in their moistness.

Clutching at him, Aurore closed her eyes to the intricate fingerings. Somewhere far in the distance, a Wolof tomtom was measuring a primeval rhythm. From the du Maurier garden, a mingling of transplanted blossoms released a stirring effluvia of unmistakably French perfume. The taste of desire was tart and sweet on Steven's animal-harsh breath.

His fingers nestled in the floss of her pubic curls; their tips vibrated like tentative bees scouting the secret recesses of a pollen-drenched flower. He tickled and teased until she was weak-kneed and moaning. Then, finally, there was a firm probing and a hard, masculine pressure that gradually filled her taut and aching void. The palm of his hand closed over her nether mouth, sealing two fingers within.

Aurore's hands moved more quickly over his erection, pulling and pleading mutely for it to replace his fingers, to grant her fulfillment. But his first response was to change the way his fingers were moving—where they had been pumping, now they rotated and stirred—a maneuver that sent shooting sparks of delight into her most private crevices.

"Do it, Steven," she panted aloud.

Her moist and molten interior was drawn back like a

bow, and yet it was a willing target, too, a target waiting for his rigid arrow of flesh to plunge and pierce her to the quick. She sank to the cement floor of the balcony. Steven freed her of the peignoir, ripping it in his eagerness. Lying there, the nightgown was just a gossamer strip gathered at her waist. Her large, tremulous breasts were bared to the flower-scented night air and to his lips as he bent to kiss them once again.

"Darling," he murmured. "My lovely, eager, waiting darling!"

"Oh, yes, my sweet!" She blotted all thoughts of Blaise from her mind. "I'm ready for you, Steven."

His open shirt revealed his sun-reddened chest with its sprinkling of freckles and tufts of sandy hair. He kicked his trousers free, and then his knees were between her thighs, forcing them wide so that he could lie between her legs. He paused for a moment. Then, with one finger, he deliberately manipulated the pointing, pulsating nub that was the fount of all her passion. Aurore gasped and writhed, feverish and frantic for release.

Her body arched up against his tormenting hand. She bit her lip; her head tossed wildly from side to side. There were blinding red flashes, then brilliant white stars—like those in the African sky above—behind her closed eyelids. Her whole body began to shiver.

"Oh, please!" she begged him. "Stop! . . . No, don't stop! Oh, my God! . . . My God!"

Steven lowered himself upon her. Aurore reached around him and dug her nails into the hard, muscular plumpness of his buttocks. Her teeth sank into his shoulder. The heart-shaped head of his phallus pressed hard against the sensitized, blood-filled portals. Heart pounding, Aurore waited for the thrust that would fill her and make the culmination of her desire complete. But her passion would once again be denied.

A sudden shadow loomed over them. It came not from the doorway but rather from the top of the concrete stairway that led up to the balcony from the grounds at the rear of the house. "Steven!" The starlight was blocked from Aurore's view first, and she screamed.

"A thousand pardons." Aurore froze at the familiar, ironic tone. "For the indiscretion," the voice added. The figure moved and came into focus.

"Blaise!" she exclaimed.

"De Beausoleil!" Steven realized.

"Chagrined at being an interruption. And very embarrassed," Blaise apologized blithely.

His *savoir faire* was all the more disconcerting to both Aurore and Steven. She scrambled out from under Steven, adjusted her nightgown, and searched in the shadows for her peignoir. Steven pulled on his pants.

"Here, *Cousine*." Blaise, still seeming amused, picked up the peignoir and handed it to her.

Steven was completely discombobulated. He stumbled over his words and almost stumbled over his feet as he tried to excuse himself, telling Blaise he would see him in the morning. His exit was marked by its contrast with Blaise's relaxed and inscrutable demeanor.

"Why are you here?" Aurore demanded when Steven was gone. She was quite shaken herself.

"I came to rescue you, *Cousine*." Blaise spoke the words with a sort of disbelieving wonder at his own naiveté. "You see, Delphine told me that you lied about yourself and Parker. I believed her. She's been my sister for twenty-three years, and still I believed her," he added sarcastically.

"She told you the truth."

"That's what I thought. You lied for her to protect Parker from my brotherly wrath. That's what she said. And of course when I heard through Sabine that you had been nursing Amin, I told myself that was why you stayed behind. It wasn't Parker at all."

"That's right," Aurore said dully, knowing it was hopeless. "That's the way it was."

"Yes. And so I came here to get you out of Thiès.

No trains running, but I was able to arrange for the plane again. This time it's under guard.''

"Blaise—is there anything I can say? Anything at all?''

"About what, *Cousine?* You mean that little scene with our American friend? But it is I who should apologize to you. I did apologize, though, didn't I? To Parker, too. Not that he deserves an apology. I mean, he was supposed to be standing guard, wasn't he? Protecting the household—the host and hostess and guests? Ah, Aurore, don't underestimate the potency of your charms. If I'd been a revolutionary run amok, everyone might have been massacred while you seduced the sentry.''

"I didn't seduce him," Aurore said with a sigh.

"Whatever." Blaise shrugged as if he didn't care.

"Blaise—'' Desperate, so desperate that she had to try even though she knew she was doomed to failure, Aurore reached out for his hand. "I'm sorry about what you saw tonight. I know how it must have looked. I can't excuse it. I don't really want Steven Parker. It's you I want, but you reject me. And so—Blaise, please believe me. I love you, Blaise.''

"Poor Parker. Nobody wants him. He makes love to my sister and she becomes pregnant, but she tells me that she doesn't want him. If she did, I would see to it that she got him. And now you, Aurore. He makes love to you and you acquiesce, and you don't want him. Poor unwanted American.''

"Blaise, please. I don't want to talk about Parker. I want to talk about you and me. I love you, Blaise.''

"Go to sleep, *Cousine.*'' There was suddenly a weariness in Blaise's voice, the weariness of a man who has seen too much of human behavior to have any illusions left. "You'll have to get up early. We're leaving at seven sharp for the airfield.''

"Blaise—'' Then, suddenly, not knowing what to say, Aurore burst into tears. She groped blindly for the screen door. She ran down the hall and slammed the door to her room behind her.

Why did she feel so guilty? It was Blaise's fault if she'd been driven to lovemaking with Steven Parker. He had rejected her. What did he expect?

Aurore threw herself on the bed, burying her face in the plump feather pillows to muffle the sound of her sobs. Her fists pounded the mattress in a paroxysm of frustration. Was she never to know fulfillment again?

And love? What of love? Gone! Destroyed by the iciness of Blaise's tone, lost in the cold blue depths of his uncaring eyes. She could not, would not face that again.

Blaise meant only one thing to her now: rejection. But she didn't have to accept it. There was a choice to be made. She didn't have to fly back to Dakar with him in the morning. And she wouldn't!

In one way or another, each of the three men in Aurore's life had failed her. Now she turned from them in her thoughts and remembered the comfort and solidarity she had felt with the women of the Diop household. In the compound, they had spoken as women to women, with the values of women and with no need for any direction or judgment by men. They had been brave in the midst of hardship and generous with each other in sharing what little they had. They had joined voices in the songs of their female souls, and they had found a sustenance in the music that was beyond food, beyond the gnawing pain in their bellies.

Men—Blaise, Steven, even Cherif—brought pain. Bitterly Aurore summed up her experience. Yes, it added up to frustration and suffering for her. Well, then, she would forgo men. If she must suffer, then let it be in the company of other women and let it be for a worthy cause like the strike. Aurore went to the closet and took out the faded, worn *boubou* she had worn before seeking a second sanctuary with the du Maurier family. She took off her nightgown and put on the *boubou*. A few moments later, she slipped silently from the house and made her way out of the French quarter.

It was shortly after dawn when Aurore reached the Diop family compound. Rena, the *awa* of the eldest Diop brother, spied her first. "Our sister has returned," she called to the other women.

They came running to greet Aurore. "We have missed you," they told her sincerely.

Missed her! They had not enough food for themselves and their children. To them, she might have been just another hungry mouth to feed. But she wasn't. She was their sister! Aurore wanted to cry, and to keep from doing so, she blurted out what she'd been thinking about how her return might just be an extra burden on them.

But Rena waved it away. "If you have chosen to share our *kassirane,* our poverty, then we welcome you with open arms." Rena moved to embrace Aurore warmly. She was followed by the other women.

How good it was to see them all again—Patha, the ancient, toothless grandmother who worked her mortar and pestle out of habit now that there was no grain to grind; Liane, the frail and lovely young bride who had scarcely even seen her husband since the wedding ceremony; Arona, an intelligent teenager with intense black eyes who had proudly demonstrated to Aurore her ability to read and speak both Wolof and French; Melami, a robust, cheerful mother of eight who had somehow managed to maintain her rolypoly proportions in spite of the meager rations; Aby, thin, angular, ill-tempered, who hated the *toubabs* with a fierce passion and described her blood-drenched dreams of revenge with relish; Katina, with her harelip and voluptuous body, who veiled herself on certain nights and went in search of men, causing some of the women to curse her as a whore and some to bless her for the food she earned and shared.

Their clothes were more ragged, their cheeks more sunken, and their limbs more wasted than when Aurore had left. When the greetings were over, Aurore noted an apathy about their words and movements that hadn't been present before. She sensed that if the chronic hunger continued for many more weeks, turning the children into brown skeletons with big, sad eyes and swollen bellies, the women would lose hope altogether. They might even pressure their men to go back to work out of desperation.

Aurore noticed another change in the next few days—the teenage boys now stayed in the compound most of the time. They looked bored and restless. Always before, they had been away scavenging and hunting, armed with their rubber slingshots and homemade traps. She asked Melami, the mother of two of them, why this had changed.

Melami's normally cheerful face hardened. "The boys were getting into trouble, wandering into the *toubab* section and shooting pebbles at their cars and the glass windows of their houses. It is because there is nothing for them to catch anymore—no birds, no animals. There is not even any more monkey bread from the baobab trees. Everything has been eaten up, and only the dust and the lizards remain. There is nothing for the boys to do now but make mischief, and all the *toubabs* are carrying guns these days. Some mothers still let their children run wild; they have no energy to discipline them." Melami sighed, glancing at the four or five boys aimlessly tossing small stones at the zinc siding of one of the huts. "But it is dangerous," she added.

"The strike will be over soon." Aurore tried to comfort her. "Then the boys will be back at the rail yards learning a good trade."

Melami shrugged and moved her heavy body over to a scrap of shade, where she began to nurse her youngest child. She was one of the few women whose malnourished bodies still managed to produce milk for their babies. The rest of the infants had to make do with rice water. Some of these had died.

One afternoon not long after her conversation with

Melami, Aurore heard a commotion coming from a neighboring compound. Along with the other women, she went to see what had happened. There was already a crush of people blocking the entrance when they got there. The air was thick with cries of grief and pity and outrage. It was Rena who found out what had happened from a neighbor woman and returned to inform the rest of them.

"Theo, the son of our neighbors, has been killed, along with another boy," she told them. "Theo was only ten years old, the other boy twelve. They were shooting pebbles with their slingshots at a French flag that was flying outside the home of one of the railroad bosses. When the *toubab* came to the door, some of the pebbles hit him. He shot both boys dead with his shotgun."

Looking at the faces around her, Aurore became afraid. It was too much. Since coming to Thiès, Aurore had always thought the du Mauriers and the other French were paranoid in their fears of a native uprising. Now, as the mutterings of shock and indignation hardened into grimness around her, for the first time, Aurore knew that such violence was really possible. A people, no matter how peaceful their tradition, can be pushed only so far. There comes a point when they will not budge one centimeter further. With the killing of the two boys, the blacks of Thiès reached that point.

Not that anything happened. Nothing at all did. But the bereaved silence of the next few days was more ominous than any action would have been.

The railroad officials of Thiès must have realized this. They had ignored Blaise's message from the duke and the other stockholders to settle the strike quickly. But they did not ignore this silent threat hanging in the air. They sent word to the union that the officials of the Dakar-Niger Railway were ready to meet with the representatives of the strikers.

The news was received in the Diop compound as gratefully as rain upon the parched earth. The day of the meeting, the women and children joined with the women and children of other compounds to form a crowd outside the building where the historic confrontation was taking place. Aurore, caught up in the high hopes of the other women, waited with them all day in the hot sun. Patiently they waited in the heat, waited to be told that at last the long strike had been resolved.

At sundown, the union delegates emerged from the building. Their dark faces were set in bitter expressions of defeat. The company had refused to accept any of their demands. No raises in salary; no paid vacations; no pensions; no payment of back wages; no parity with white workers. And, most significant of all, no family allowances.

"Muslim marriages are barbarous," said the union speaker, quoting the company *toubabs'* opinion of polygamy. "They call our mothers and our wives whores! They call our children bastards!"

It was at this moment that a young, ebony-skinned woman with a tall, graceful body and a face distinguished by the purity and nobility of its purpose climbed up on a wooden box and claimed the crowd's attention. "Whores! Bastards! We who have suffered during this strike as no grown Frenchman has ever suffered! Women of Thiès! Hear me! The time has come to show the *toubabs* what we are made of. They have felt the determination of our men. But they foolishly think that the weakness of their women will make them surrender. Let us show them how wrong they are! Let us abandon our fires and our cooking pots. The fires are cold and the pots empty. Let us show them we are through rearing children to be starved and spit upon and shot in cold blood! Let us, the women, end this strike! Let us see to it that the demands of our men are met! Let us, the women, march to Dakar and confront the most important railroad *toubabs* of all! Let all of us march, mothers and daughters, wives and sisters, old and young. Let us show the lordly Dakar *toubabs* that nothing can stop the women of Thiès! Not hunger! Not thirst! Not even bullets! Let us meet here tomorrow morning and start on our march to Dakar. And I say to you that all women capable of walking must join in this march. On to Dakar!" She raised a fist high and shook it in the air. "On to Dakar!"

"On to Dakar!" the women shouted back. "On to Dakar!"

Never had Aurore been so stirred. Nor was she alone. All the women were inspired to action by the speaker's words. And the men were moved as well.

The speech confronted the men with the fact that the extraordinary hardships of the strike had wrought a change in their once shy and submissive women. In the crucible of the strike, a new kind of Senegalese woman had been forged. She was a force to be reckoned with, a force to be weighed in the struggle for equality.

Now these women were asking each other if they would join the march to Dakar. And with few exceptions, they were telling each other that they would. The spirit of the march moved through the women like a flash fire. All were touched by the flame.

"Will you come with us, Aurore?" The question was asked of her several times by women that she knew. "Will you march to Dakar?"

"Yes," she told them, her face transfigured, as their faces were, by belief in the rightness of their cause. "I'm marching to Dakar." She felt exhilarated, hopeful, and prouder of her Wolof heritage than she had ever been in her life.

Aurore was an African woman, and she would march. She would march for the future of her people and her country. She would march for women everywhere!

CHAPTER 11

The women started out in high spirits. After so many months of straining to make a handful of rice feed a whole family, the march offered a blessed alternative to the stagnation of slow starvation. Under the blazing blue expanse of early morning sky, the road to Dakar was a glittering asphalt ribbon of hope rolling out to the horizon.

They sang at first, the impromptu verses passing from group to group and woman to woman in an inspiring march-time rondelet. The singing cemented the unity of their purpose. The words were a message to the *toubabs* from the women of the strikers: The union must prevail!

The fireball African sun rose higher. It beat down on them as mercilessly as the lash of an Arab slave master. Aurore, like the other women, wore a head cloth as a shield against the scalding rays.

These head cloths varied from snowy white to gorgeous hues of peacock blue, emerald green, damson purple, and watermelon pink. They contrasted with low-cut cotton blouses over tightly wrapped *pagnes* patterned with black and red checkerboard squares, or intricate batik designs, or with airy, billowing *boubous* in abstract patterns of turquoise, saffron, or magenta. The poorer women, whose finery had been sold long ago, wore bleached-out tunics and simply cut skirts of mattress ticking. Many of these were brightened by a colorfully embroidered or lavishly fringed waist cloth preserved from some long ago wedding day. En masse the women were a moving patchwork flung out over the dun-color landscape.

There were so many of them that the road could not accommodate all their marching feet. The procession had to fan out. Some women walked in the dust by the side of the road. Others trod the dry grass of the plain itself.

By afternoon, the cruel sun had stopped the singing. There was no more lighthearted joking and gossiping. The women marched in silence as if struck dumb by the fiery rays. Long skirts were hiked up to waist level; underskirts were removed. They stopped under a sparse clump of trees to rest and take a mouthful of water. But a few minutes after resuming the march, it was as if this respite had never been. They began to comprehend the enormity of the task they had undertaken. They walked. They sweated. They looked in vain for a sign of civili— zation in the distance, but there was nothing. Only the sky, the sun, and the parched earth, stretching on forever.

"We have to stop!" Melami spoke. Aurore turned to see agony etched on her chubby face. "My feet are swollen to twice their size," she groaned. "I can't go on. I can't."

"You have to." Rena's voice was stern. "All of us are suffering, Melami."

"It's because she's so fat." Katina, of the harelip and the beautiful body, spoke scornfully. "I saw her stuffing her face with rice cake. That food was meant be shared equally among us. There'll be nothing left!"

"Shut up, slut! You who can only get a man veiling your ugly face! The rice cake I ate was mine from my husband's own ration." Melami advanced Katina menacingly. "You should not even have been allowed to come with us, unclean one! There has been deume on you since birth! You will bring ay gaaf down upon us all!"

"You lie! I am not cursed!"

Aby, the skinny spinster woman who thrived on

sension and violence of all kinds, laughed shrilly, her beady eyes avid with the expectation of a fight.

"Calm yourselves, sisters." Rena stepped in front of Katina, whose slender body was poised like a cat about to spring.

"Of course Katina isn't cursed. You know better than that, Melami." Aurore placed a comforting hand on the heavy woman's shoulder. "We're all hot and tired, but we have to keep going."

"She's right!" Arona, the intense and intelligent teenager, stepped forward, her arm around Liane, the frail young bride with the doe eyes. "We have to show the men we are not weak and powerless just because we are women. Liane is the weariest of us all—in body. But in her mind and spirit, she is strong. She has almost fainted twice now, but she refuses to stop. She is determined to go on, aren't you, Liane?"

"I will get there if I have to crawl!" Liane answered, her soft eyes brilliant with an inner light. "All my life I have wanted to be strong. When I walk into Dakar, I *will* be strong."

Liane's spirit inspired them. Katina turned back to the road first, her body still tense with anger transformed into energy to propel her shapely, dust-caked legs. The others fell into step behind her—Liane and Arona, Aurore and Rena, Aby with a black umbrella held over her head. Melami brought up the rear, her feet slapping the dust, her lips mumbling with a pain that would soon become as familiar to them all as the scorching rays of the sun.

They trudged and plodded and limped over the dead landscape. Commencing in October, the strike had coincided with the dry season, which would not end until June. Not a drop of rain had fallen since the men walked off their jobs, and now the savanna was a desert of dehydrated dirt stretching as far as the eye could see. The parched soil was as ridged and cracked as the skin of a hundred-year-old man, and regeneration seemed as remote a possibility as a return of youth. If clumps of wild grasses and the sere, stunted stalks of plants remained standing, it was doubtless because their buried roots had stiffened into a rigor mortis that kept them in place like grave markers. From time to time, the women passed patches of earth that had once been cultivated by farmers. Now there were only the dried and colorless stumps of what had been corn or millet, grim reminders that it was the drought that had ultimately reaped the scarecrow harvest.

But in this hostile soil where the hardiest plant had been unable to survive, the gnarled and twisted baobab tree, forty feet high and thick of trunk, thrived like a parasite on a blood-filled host. All during the rainy season, its roots had sucked in water, to be stored indefinitely in the interior of its spongelike trunk. Yet the *baobab* hid its liquid secret well. Its torturously jumbled, thorny branches and its elephant-skin bark looked as dessicated as the landscape itself.

There was one other tree that survived on the parched plain—the cade. Growing in clumps, splayed-out branches a ghostly dead-white, the cades resembled upended skeletons. The women cringed from these weird and bonelike configurations that offered neither shade nor sustenance. According to the legends of old, the cade tree was the symbol of death.

At nightfall of the first day, the women came to a village. The inhabitants, with traditional Wolof hospitality, invited the women to share their food and make use of their water. How heavenly it was to lie on the softness of the dusty earth and feel the cool evening air upon her freshly bathed skin, Aurore thought gratefully. With her belly full and her swollen feet wrapped in wet cloths, even Melami seemed at peace.

At dawn, the march leaders woke them—to aching muscles, sore feet, and the road that seemed to have no end. They walked all that day, their throats parched, their bodies drenched with perspiration. They no longer bothered to communicate. The steady stomping motion, unbroken by any human comforts, had turned them into dumb beasts. All they could do was move, as if driven by a whip across their flanks. Life had been reduced to putting one foot in front of the other.

They forced themselves to keep going until it was dark. Then they threw themselves on the ground and slept until the first light of day. And then the interminable march resumed.

At noon of the third day, with prostration from the heat thinning the ranks of the march, the leaders agreed to a longer rest stop than usual. The women stretched out on the ground; many took off their skirts and *boubous* to rig makeshift tents to protect their small groups from the sun. Under one of these, provided by Rena, Aurore wiped at her perspiring chest and arms, making a face at the reddish dust that came away from her skin. She reached to loosen her auburn tresses, but instead of the smooth and springy waves she was accustomed to feeling, her hand encountered a coarse, tangled mass that was matted from lack of brushing and sticky with sweat. She was too tired to cope with it. She closed her eyes against the white-hot disc glowing through the unrelieved blue of the sky. She slept.

Aurore awoke to the delicious sensation of cool air caressing her skin. She stretched luxuriously, then raised the skirt of her *bouboy* to feel the blessed coolness on her thighs. She felt a strange sensation, one she had not known since the last rainy season. She had shivered!

The tingling chill made her smile, but it also stirred her curiosity. Why was it so dark? Surely she could not have slept past nightfall!

Around her, other women began to stir. She saw Melami's bulk shifting itself into a sitting position. "Look at the sky!" Melami's soft, heavy features took on an expression of terror as she pointed upward.

Ragged black clouds smudged the bright blue canopy like charcoal. The dark streaks scudded swiftly over the face of the sun, casting shadows that swept over the women like giant bat wings. A gale wind set skirts billowing and sashes and head cloths fluttering.

"Tialaverd!" The cry moved from one group of women to another, as if flung by the wind. *"Tialaverd! The whirlwind is coming!"*

There was no shelter to run to, no place to hide. The women huddled close to each other, bundling their few possessions underneath them. All across the savanna, the dried grasses bent to the earth before the wind, giving off crackling noises. Dry leaves and twigs whisked through the air as if fleeing a demon. Only the giant baobab trees stood firm, their thick trunks and stout branches immune to the assault.

"Tialaverd! Here it comes! The whirlwind!"

Aurore had heard of the savage windstorms that swept across the savanna when certain weather conditions prevailed, but she had never before seen one. Now her eyes widened at the huge columns of dust writhing skyward as they skimmed swiftly over the flat surface of the plain. The whirling shafts of dust were headed straight toward the women.

With cries of fear that were quickly swallowed by the wind, the more knowledgeable turned on their bellies and flattened themselves against the dirt. But others panicked and decided to run for a small, bowl-shaped gully several yards away, where some women had already taken refuge. "Don't move!" Arona shouted, hoping to prevent any of the Diop women from making this mistake.

Too late! Katina had already started for the gully, her body bent almost double against the wind's force. Aurore knew the exact instant the whirlwind struck her by the way Katina's body jerked violently as if under the crack of a horsewhip. The thin fabric of her flame-colored *boubou* billowed out until it was filled with air like a parachute. It rose higher until it covered the tragically flawed face and displayed the perfection of the lithe and shapely chocolate-color body. Then, with a sudden sucking sound, the red-orange material was devoured by the cyclone.

Her head was thrown back, her malformed pink mouth

agape as the wind seized her orange-printed head cloth. One end whipped loose, and the head cloth unwound in a sudden spiral. Her tightly plaited black braids sprang free and stood out straight, tiny quivering snakes. And then, eerily, as if by some supernatural force, the braids were demolished and Katina's black luxuriant hair stood out straight in a giant ruff around her face.

Aurore was distracted by a scream. Liane, her frail body no match for the whirlwind, was being dragged away from the others. Young Arona scrambled after her. She flung her own wiry, compact body on top of her delicate-boned friend. Their skirts fluttered wildly, revealing Arona's compact rump and taut belly as she pressed against Liane's cinnamon-skinned slimness in an attempt to anchor her to earth.

In the force of the gale wind, gravity was overpowered. Like a bully who enjoys taking playthings from smaller children, the whirlwind snatched the women's few possessions. Aby's ancient black umbrella, an article she prized above all else, was almost torn from her bony arms. But she refused to loosen her grip, hanging on with her spiderlike fingers even when the whistling air inflated the black silk folds and lifted the umbrella. Aby went with it, her tiny brown body skimming across the wind-whipped surface of the soil as she screamed out furious curses that no one could hear.

Aurore turned from Aby and saw, horrified, that the final corkscrew column of dust was headed straight toward her. She dug her hands and feet into the hard-packed dirt and hid her face under one arm. And then Aurore was being whipped by hundreds of tiny, stinging lashes that bit into her skin, stung at her scalp, and tore the thin cotton of her dress to ribbons. A strange, vibrating hum in her ears grew in intensity and rose in pitch until it was a banshee scream echoing inside her head. A sudden force reached under her and lifted her into the air. Her insides lurched painfully, and it felt as if her limbs would be torn from her body. She had been sucked into the furious center of the whirlwind itself.

Then, with the capriciousness of a spoiled child, the whirlwind rejected her like an outworn toy. She was flung to the dirt, discarded.

Aurore landed on her back, her tattered clothing offering no protection at all from the swirling dust. Her exposed breasts were bombarded by tiny stinging pellets. She had no strength to close her open legs, and the gritty grains bit into the soft flesh of her inner thighs. Aurore moaned and tried to turn on her side. She could not manage it.

After what seemed a very long time, the shrill screech of the wind became less painful to Aurore's ears. Was the whirlwind truly abating? Or was it just that she was weaker? Still dazed, she wondered.

"The storm has passed. Aurore, are you all right?" It was Rena.

"I think so," she told the older woman.

"Look at poor Melami there, half buried in the dust."

Aurore looked. Melami was sputtering with the grit that filled her mouth. She was like a huge statue in sandstone that had suddenly come to life.

Fortunately none of the women marchers was seriously hurt. They reformed their ranks as the funnels of dust receded from view. Soon they were on the road again.

Shortly before nightfall, they came to a village, the last they would stop at before reaching Dakar. The people were expecting them. Beating drums heralded their arrival, and children came to meet them with jugs and pots of water. Word of the march had spread like wildfire over the last few days. The villagers told them that even the radios and newspapers were reporting upon their progress.

"We're famous!" Melami's fat face spread open in the wide and happy grin Aurore had despaired of ever seeing again. Arona and Liane began to dance to the drumbeats and *cora* music being played to welcome them. Aurore joined them as the other Diop women clapped hands.

That night, after washing thoroughly and repairing their clothing, the women attended a huge *bara* in the village square. Two sheep had been slaughtered in the marchers' honor, the first meat many of them had tasted in months. They dug into heaping bowls of thiou à la viande, a stew of lamb chunks, sweet potatoes, turnips, onions, and cabbage wedges flavored with thyme, coriander, and tomato paste. They feasted on dundu oniyeri, fried spiced yams, and akara, delicious patties made of white beans, salt, and cayenne pepper, as well as light, sweet fritters made of bananas and crushed peanuts. For dessert, there were sweet, juicy mangoes and papayas to suck at their leisure.

Strengthened by the feast, revived by their baths and all the water they could drink, the marchers joined in the dancing. The beating of the drums and the melodic twang of the *cora* and *balafon* were a goad to uninhibited movement. The ceremony of dance was an exorcism of all the hardship they had suffered. From these primal rhythms sprang a new hope and faith in the future.

The next morning, when they resumed the march, the women sang as on the first day. They felt strong again. Their numbers were increased by the village women who had joined them. Still more women joined them as they neared Dakar.

They knew their destination was in reach when the salty breeze of the Atlantic reached them. A little later, they could see Goree Island, a dark speck on the shimmering blue-green stretch of sea. They passed groundnut processing factories, and then the houses of the suburb of Hann. The women walked faster, spurred on by rumors of the gala welcome that the people of Dakar were preparing for them.

And then, just as they were approaching the entrance to Dakar, word came that soldiers would block their way. The march leaders quickly circulated among the women to reassure them: they had come much too far to turn back now; they greatly outnumbered the small contingent of soldiers; their friends were waiting; their men depended on them.

The women pressed onward, arming themselves with stones and sticks of wood—just in case. On the crest of a small hill, Aurore first spotted the bright red, brimless caps, *tarbooshes,* worn by the soldiers. In front of her, at the bottom of the hill, she saw the leaders of the march halt. Fists were raised. Some of the soldiers raised their rifle butts. A scuffle ensued. And then, with a sinking feeling in the pit of her stomach, Aurore heard shots fired. Two distant figures, tiny dolls in bright-colored boubous, crumpled to the dust.

"Oh, God! Not more killing!" Melami exclaimed.

"Where are the men of Dakar, that this should happen?" cried Aby.

"I didn't come all this way to be shot down like an animal," Rena said loudly. She was quickly seconded by Katina.

"But we didn't come all this way to turn back, either! Did we?" The blood was pounding hotly in Aurore's veins. She felt she could take on the soldiers single-handedly. "I'm going on!" she announced. "We've come too far to let anything stop us—even bullets!"

"Come on, women!" Arona joined Aurore. "Let's show them what we're made of."

"Look! The women are rushing past the soldiers!" Liane jumped up and down with excitement. "The soldiers are running away!"

There was no hesitating now. The women were like a human river pouring into the streets of Dakar. Thousands of black people had turned out to greet them. As the women passed, they whistled and cheered and waved handkerchiefs and head cloths in the air. Then, as if moved by a common impulse to honor these brave women in a special way, the people of Dakar laid down their head cloths and waist cloths and handkerchiefs and robes to form a riotously colored carpet upon which the marchers could walk. In the old days, before the French came to Senegal, this was the honor given to returning warriors.

Aurore had never felt so proud; she was bursting with it. Some of the little children threw flowers in their path, and she picked up two scarlet frangipani blossoms and tucked them behind her ears. It had been worth it! Every minute of parching thirst and gnawing hunger, every mile of scorching sun and stifling dust had been worth it. All the sweat, and the aching muscles, and the swollen feet had been worth it. Even the deaths of the two women leaders had been worth it. The French—yes! Even the French!—must see now that the strikers could not be ignored, that their women would let them settle for no less than victory and equality. Victory! Equality! This was the message of the women's march!

It was a message the strikers of Dakar accepted jubilantly. Union representatives and members of the strike committee stood at attention to pay homage to the marching women. Like her black sisters, Aurore strained to walk tall as she passed them. But then her composure was shattered by the shouting of her name.

"Aurore!" From behind the union dignitaries where the minor strike officials were, Cherif Baye stepped forward and hailed her again. "Aurore!" He elbowed his way to where she was and drew her from the ranks of the marchers, urging her to one side. "What are you doing here?" He didn't hide his surprise at seeing her.

"I marched here from Thiès with the women." Aurore laughed at the amazed expression on his face. "What are you doing here?"

Cherif ignored the question. "I am impressed," he told her. "The last time we spoke of the strike, you weren't even sure it was ethical. Remember?"

Aurore blushed. In truth, she didn't recall the details of their discussion of the strike at all. But she remembered all too well the interplay between them on the beach the last time she had seen Cherif. She put that out

of her mind and explained how her extended visit to
Thiès had persuaded her of the rightness of the strikers'
cause. "Now tell me why you're here," she said when
she had concluded her explanation.

"I work with the strike committee. I am the liaison
man with Blaise de Beausoleil. I arrange with him for
different delivery destinations for each day's catch from
Ile Celeste. Between the two of us, we have managed to
stay one jump ahead of the French harbor patrol."

"Is Blaise back from Thiès?" Aurore asked all too
casually.

"Yes. And Steven Parker with him. They flew back
together."

"Oh!" Aurore could just imagine the cozy chat between the two of them on that flight. *Men!*

"I cannot get over your being on the women's march."
Cherif grinned at her as he had when he was a boy. "It
is nice that we are on the same side at last."

"Yes. But I'm still not a Communist."

"Nor I. But I am not an anti-Communist either.
Without Communist help, the strikers could never have
held out this long. All the branches of the Confédération Générale du Travail in France, Guinea, and Dahomey
have been contributing money to help feed the strikers.
And that support is more important to me than the fact
that the CGT is Communist controlled."

"France? Guinea? Dahomey?" Aurore had spoken to
women who were knowledgable about the strike during
the march, and she had learned from them. "But what
about the CGT right here in Senegal? Why are they
dragging their heels?"

"It is a complicated situation," Cherif admitted. "The
Senegal CGT controls the dock workers, the miners, the
metal workers, the masons—just about every major
union in Senegal except the railway workers. Only they
are independent, and they have gone on strike without
even consulting with the CGT. Naturally the noses of
the leaders of the CGT are out of joint. But in the end,

they will back us. Their differences with the railway union are mere quibbles.''

"Not such quibbles,'' Aurore contradicted him. "I've heard it said that if the railway workers' leaders don't agree to bring the union into the Senegal CGT, then the CGT will refuse to call a general strike. And without a general strike, the Dakar-Niger *toubabs* won't give an inch as far as the railway workers' demands are concerned.''

"You have come a long way." Cherif was impressed. "And your information is correct, too. But the CGT will call a general strike whether or not the railway union insists on its independence. How can they not? It would put them on the side of the *toubabs* and in opposition to the black workingman if they did not do so.''

"But they can stall. That's what they've been doing. Why shouldn't they just go right on doing it?''

"Because they are men of conscience, that is why. You have listened too much to talk of the Communist bugaboo, Aurore. The CGT will call a general strike. Business will come to a standstill throughout the country. The *toubabs* will be brought to their knees. And they will turn on the managers of the railroad and force them to give in to the workers' demands.''

"That sounds wonderful. But when, Cherif? When?''

"This afternoon.'' He grinned at her again. "There is to be a meeting at the racecourse. The railway union leaders expect the CGT to announce a general strike at the meeting.''

"What kind of meeting is it? Who'll be there?''

"It is a meeting to discuss the impasse that has been reached. Just about everyone will be there—the French governor-general; his black lackey, our beloved mayor of Dakar; the Grand Imam of Senegal; several other *imams* representing the most important mosques in Dakar and Saint Louis and Bamako and Thiès; a dozen of the more important tribal leaders, including my father; the heads of all the unions affiliated with the CGT; the leaders of the strikers; the leaders of the women's march. These will be the dignitaries. But the meeting will be open to all, and it is sure that all the strikers, all the women marchers, all of the French who have any connection with the railroad, or with the government of Dakar, or the government of Senegal, and all the blacks who can crowd onto the racecourse will also be present. Not to mention the newspaper and radio reporters who are following up on the meeting as a climax to the women's march. Even the fishermen from N'Gor, Yoff, and Ile Celeste are taking the day off to attend. By the way," Cherif added, "did you know that the fishermen of Ile Celeste voted to donate a full day's catch to the women marchers from Thiès. And—this of course is off the record—Blaise de Beausoleil has arranged for us to 'borrow' a refrigerator truck from one of his warehouses to transport the fish to Thiès."

"That's wonderful. The strikers' families in Thiès are close to starvation."

"We know. In Dakar, there are many ways of circumventing the French blockade. But Thiès is too remote and too completely in the hands of the railroad and the police."

"Speaking of the Thiès police," Aurore remembered, "what news of Amin?"

"He is still a wanted man. He dares not return to Ile Celeste. He has been hiding out here in Dakar."

"Poor Sabine. She must be so lonely. How is she? And little Amadou? How he must have grown since the last time I saw him. It's been months!"

"Amadou is a swaggering giant with a mighty war cry. A credit to his uncle Cherif." His eyes shone with fondness and pride as he spoke of his nephew. "And Sabine may be lonely, but she abides. She knows that Amin will return when he can. She is content that Amin's well-being is in Allah's hands."

"I can't wait to see them—the baby, Sabine, and Amin, too."

"You do not have to wait long to see Amin. Come to the racecourse with me. I am meeting him."

"You mean Amin is going?"

"Yes."

"But is that safe?"

"He insists that it is. He says that in such a large crowd, one black man will hardly be noticed. He is probably right. The French make little enough distinction among us."

"But if the police are after him—"

"The police will have enough on their minds with the size of the crowd that's expected without worrying about an escaped prisoner from Thiès. That is what Amin insists. And you know how stubborn he is." Cherif linked arms with her. "Come with me to the meeting, Aurore. Seeing you will be a happy surprise for Amin. He has told me more than once since his return that he owes his life to you."

"He exaggerates. But I'd really like to see him, too."

"Then let us go." Cherif guided her through the throng.

The streets were jammed. In spite of the long ordeal of the Senegalese workers, now a carnival atmosphere prevailed. Tomtoms beat from every corner, and there was much spontaneous dancing. The women of Dakar had bedecked themselves in whatever finery remained in their depleted wardrobes and walked proudly beside their men. The inspiration of the women's march from Thiès had spilled over to spark faith in the outcome of the racecourse meeting. The *toubabs* would have to save face, of course—saving face was very important to the white man—but surely the meeting itself must signify their readiness to deal with the strikers on a reasonable basis. Such was the feeling that ran through the crowd.

"Over there." Cherif nodded toward a doorway in a side street. There, leaning against the trunk of a transplanted and somewhat stunted baobab tree, sat Amin. Steven Parker was with him.

Aurore and Amin hugged each other wordlessly and with intense emotion. Finally Amin spoke. "My sister." The words conveyed the depth of the love and gratitude he felt for Aurore.

"Howdy, Aurore." Steven Parker's greeting was more casual. It seemed quite free of any reminiscence of their passion the last time they had been together.

Aurore was content that it should be this way. So much had happened since that night. She had been through so much, and she had changed and grown. Her ideas about life and her understanding of people had broadened. She knew what it was to commit herself to a cause and to suffer hardship and deprivation in fealty to that commitment. Yes, she had outgrown Steven's glib charm. She knew without putting it to the test that she would find his masculine persistence resistible now. And she was glad that Blaise's unexpected arrival had aborted their lovemaking when she had not had the strength to resist it.

Such were Aurore's thoughts as the four of them proceeded to the racecourse together. When they reached it, Aurore was struck by the stringent security measures the French had taken. Soldiers and police were posted at each of the entrance gates, at points all around the field, and at the foot of the grandstands. The grandstands had been cordoned off and divided into two sections, the smaller one reserved for European and Senegalese dignitaries and speakers, the larger one set aside for "whites only."

Despite all the guards, Amin had no trouble passing through the gates. They found four seats together with a good view of the speakers' platform, with its French tricolor bunting and array of microphones. Aurore sat between Cherif and Amin.

The occasion was marked by pomp and pageantry, interspersed with moments that genuinely moved Aurore. Shortly after sitting down, she observed the arrival of the Grand Imam of Senegal and his coterie of disciples and servants. The Grand Imam was a truly imposing figure, his lofty height augmented by an ornate satin turban, his well-fed body arrayed in a richly embroidered and intricately draped white tunic. The medals and decorations studding his broad chest gleamed in the tropic sunlight. The sun's rays were kept from his round face by an officious follower with an umbrella. Due to the Grand Imam's long stride, the holder of the umbrella was forced to jog to keep pace with him.

If there was a comic opera aspect to the Grand Imam and his retinue, it made no dent in the reverence Amin granted Senegal's religious leader. His respect for the Grand Imam was written plainly across his face. Aurore noted it and also noted that Cherif refrained from challenging it. He would show his older brother the courtesy of listening to what the Grand Imam might have to say in support of the strikers.

Aurore observed that Cherif's own admiration broke through with the arrival of the officials of the CGT. They joined the Grand Imam on the speakers' platform, while the delegates of the various unions affiliated with the CGT took their alloted places in the rear of the main grandstand—behind the white section. Aurore wondered if Cherif was right. Would the CGT speaker announce a general strike? And if he did, what would be the official Muslim attitude voiced by the Grand Imam? If there was solidarity between the trade-union leaders and the religious leaders, the railway workers couldn't lose. An agreeable side effect would be the resolution of the differences between Amin and Cherif.

For Aurore herself, the highlight of the arrivals was the entrance of the Thiès women marchers. They filed onto the field singing, ten abreast, shoulders squared, pride shining in their faces. Their banners were held high, and the words on them were angry: THEY CAN STARVE US! BUT THEY CAN'T STOP US! and MUSLIM WOMEN DEMAND FAMILY ALLOWANCES! and EQUAL PAY FOR OUR BLACK MEN!

They were followed by the striking men themselves. The railway-union leaders led them to their seats. As with the leaders of the women, they sat with their followers. None of them went to the speakers' platform. Aurore noticed that Amin looked puzzled and Cherif scowled at this circumstance.

The raggedness of the strikers was underscored now by the dramatic arrival of the French governor-general of Senegal, the black mayor of Dakar, the president of the board of the Dakar-Niger Railway, and sundry other high government and railroad officials. Shrill whistle blasts from the police guarding the gates heralded their coming. A contingent of the "Red Guard," a troop of mounted soldiers clad in striking scarlet-and-white burnooses that flowed over the backs of their glossy, jet-black horses, preceded these dignitaries. They cantered briskly onto the field, the sun reflecting from the gold stars emblazoned on the troopers' *tarbooshes* and dazzling the eyes of the onlookers. Then, at last, came the slow-moving shiny black limousines bearing the crème de la crème of the French colonial administration and the businessmen they represented.

Aurore, however, couldn't take her eyes off the ebony steeds of the "Red Guard." Their appearance finalized her commitment to the strikers. With the possible exception of the Grand Imam and the mayor, these horses were undeniably better fed than any black person at the racecourse.

The thought was stored in her mind as the meeting was called to order. The crowd became quiet, expectant. They paid respectful attention as the first speaker, the Grand Imam of Senegal, strode to the bank of microphones.

His voice boomed out. It was a powerful voice, and yet his opening words seemed obsequious. They were words of gratitude to the governor-general and the mayor for deigning to be present at this—the implication was quite clear—*unfortunate* occasion.

Then he spoke about "dangerous influences from

overseas," implying that the strikers had been duped by alien Communists. Aurore felt her jaw clenching against her outrage in much the same way Cherif's was. As if "outside agitators" had "stirred up" the strike! As if the overworked and underpaid Senegalese had required an *agent provocateur* to goad them into action!

Finally the Grand Imam praised the *toubabs* for bringing "progress" to Africa. He preached that the Senegalese people should be grateful to the "civilized" French for conveying specialized technical knowledge and scientific "gifts" to their "backward and needy land." The Grand Imam's grand finale was a rousing castigation of the "ungrateful" strikers for biting the generous white hand that had fed them and led them.

As he left the microphones, there was scattered applause, mostly from the whites present. Aurore's eyes met Cherif's in mutual bitterness. Neither of them had the heart to say anything to Amin. They didn't have to. He said what there was to say himself.

"That is not the word of Allah!" He was quivering with disappointment and anger. "That is the voice of treachery!"

Cherif reached across Aurore to his brother and hugged him. "I am sorry," he said. "I am truly sorry. I know what Islam means to you."

"My faith in Islam has not been shaken. Only in the false prophets who speak in the name of Allah."

"But Amin—" Steven Parker started to protest.

Amin held up a hand to silence him as the next speaker approached the microphones. This was the governor-general. His tone was kindly and paternal and condescending. He spoke of the strike as a "misunderstanding" and counseled patience as a necessary step toward progress. He advised the strikers to return to work while he personally studied their grievances.

He was followed by the mayor, who rephrased the same sentiments and who also spoke French, a language more than half his black listeners didn't understand. He advocated faith in the fairness of the governor-general.

Then he spoke straight from the shoulder—but still in French—to his fellow blacks. The strikers, he said, were irresponsible and ignorant malcontents who had "spoiled things for themselves and others" by their ill-considered action. Now there was no water to drink and no food to eat because of them. Furthermore, he had heard rumors of plans for a general strike. As mayor of Dakar, he forbade it! As mayor of Dakar, he had given his word that the railway workers would return to work the next day. Only then could negotiations begin. The mayor of Dakar went back to his seat to the accompaniment of the kind of good-natured belly-laughing a local audience always bestows on its favorite hometown comic.

The laughter turned to boredom as a representative of the Dakar-Niger Railroad spoke. The president of the board didn't even deign to speak himself. The spokesman said what had been said from the first. The railroad would only agree to discuss the strikers' demands if they went back to work first.

Like everybody else, Aurore's attention perked up when a high-ranking official of the CGT rose to speak. Cherif nodded at her hopefully. Even Amin wanted this most powerful Communist in Senegal to undo the harm done by the Grand Imam and announce a general strike. It was the hope of many, including Aurore as she strained to hear the historic announcement Cherif had predicted.

It did not come. Instead, the spokesman of the CGT explained that since the union of railway workers was independent, the CGT could not in good conscience back their strike. He called the strike, now in its fifth month of suffering, a "political stratagem." He defined the railroad workers' union as a "separatist" movement that could only cause a deep schism in the Senegalese labor movement. Therefore the CGT, he said, would maintain its judicious "wait and see" policy toward the strike. The strikers must prove that their action was good for *all* the workers of Senegal. Such was the Communist decision.

A growl of disappointment rose up from the strikers and their families as the CGT spokesman returned to his seat. Aurore felt like crying. Beside her, Cherif was pounding his fist on his knee, violent in his bitter disillusionment. "The *imams* are not the only traitors," he snarled to Amin. "The black workingman and his family are evidently expendable to the Communists, too."

"It seems that we have both put our faith in false leaders," Amin sympathized. "Still," he added, "does it not seem altogether too pat to you, Cherif?"

"What do you mean?"

"I never thought that I would hear myself admit it, but I do not doubt that the Grand Imam has been bought off by the French in one way or another—perhaps directly, perhaps indirectly. The mayor is a pawn and a joke, of course. But the CGT? Is it possible they arrived at some agreement with the *toubabs?* Is it possible that they too were paid off to withhold their support by refusing a general strike? What do you think, Cherif?"

"Ask me another time. Right now I am too disgusted with the Communists to think anything but the worst of them."

"What Amin is suggesting is the worst!" Aurore exclaimed.

They stopped talking as the crowd around them began to chant. The strikers were demanding that a representative of the railway workers' union be allowed to speak in order to refute the one-sided arguments that had been made. On the platform, the dignitaries sat impassively, ignoring the demand. No representative of the union was on the roster of speakers. Certainly they couldn't change the program in the middle.

It was, however, changed for them. A leader of the railway union suddenly leaped to the platform with the easy grace of a leopard. He ignored the dignitaries ensconced in the row of chairs there when they protested that he was not scheduled to be heard. He grabbed one of the microphones and held up a hand to silence the crowd's roar of approval.

He spoke in Wolof, simply and sincerely. His words cut through the righteous rhetoric of the previous speakers like a scythe. He told the strikers that what they had always known was still true. They were in the right, and the time had passed when they could afford to be swayed by empty promises or betrayals in the name of ideology or threats of violence. He exhorted them not to lose their bargaining lever by returning to work before their demands were met. And finally he had them on their feet, cheering and echoing the vow to stand fast until they had won, while he repeated it in French for the benefit of the *toubabs*.

On this note of resolve, the historic racecourse meeting ended. Nevertheless, Aurore was left feeling depressed. Nothing had been settled. The strikers' hopes had once again been dashed. The French overlords still had all the power. They still refused to concede a crumb of food or a drop of water to the strikers and their families.

As the four of them rose to inch their way out of the racecourse with the rest of the dense crowd, Cherif was still muttering his disillusionment with the CGT. "Black means nothing to them until they can turn it red," he acknowledged to Amin.

"And the only color the *imams* are interested in would seem to be the color of money." Amin put his arm over Cherif's shoulder. "How naive we are, my brother. How eager to believe in leaders when there is only Allah Himself to believe in."

"And the people," Aurore added. "Not the leaders, but the people themselves. It's the lesson I learned on the women's march."

"Yes. There is truth in what you say." Amin smiled wanly. "But most certainly not in leaders who say they are planning for *jihad* while they are preaching to the people that they should lick the hand of the French master. Such leaders may well turn the guns—guns and munitions we have risked our lives to procure—on our people in the end."

"I don't agree." Aurore was struck by the strangeness of Steven Parker's tone. His usually lazy and good-natured manner seemed suddenly querulous and shaky. A whine had crept into his voice, like that of a child who has been promised a sweet only to be told that it is too close to bedtime to have it now. "One measly speech doesn't change anything. Shoot, Amin, the Grand Imam is just a politician. Nothing new about that; nothing you didn't know. That's no reason to back off from our commitment."

"It is every reason, Steven." Amin spoke gently to him, as if to alleviate his childish disappointment. "Especially if the Grand Imam and the other *imams* are politicians who are manipulating in the interests of the French against the black people of Senegal."

"Well, what about the holy war then?" Steven Parker's voice was sulky.

"It will have to wait. I no longer trust the *imams* to do what is right for my people."

"And what about all the dough tied up in the guns we've already bought and—more important—in the potassium nitrate and the plant we've set up to process it?"

"I will not turn the guns and munitions over to the control of the *imams*. I shall hold onto the potassium nitrate and the factory until the day comes when the Senegalese people rise up of their own accord. Then we shall turn the potassium nitrate into bullets for them. But until then, I will not risk my people's lives for hypocrites who talk holy war and then use all their influence to support the status quo."

"What about the assurances I've given to the folks that supplied the money to you?" the American demanded angrily.

"What about their assurances to the people?" Amin countered softly. "The money was gotten through the *imams*, was it not? But the *imams* have not acted for the people as they said they would. Instead, they have betrayed them. Look, Steven, we have all been fooled. Ask yourself this: What better way to protect oneself against a revolution than to finance it in such a way that one controls the armaments? That way one may determine which way the guns will be pointed and end up on the winning side. I fear that is the only true faith of our *imams*, and their only motivation for financing us. In answer to your question, Steven, the *imams* will have to forget your assurances as the people must forget theirs. Should the time come when they prove their good faith to the people, I will be happy to back up your good faith in dealing with them.''

"You're just plain ditching me, Amin. You're leaving me out there in the cold with egg on my face and no answers. And I don't come out with anything for all I've done for you and your people."

"Steven, Steven," Amin said and sighed. "We are friends. But even in the name of that friendship, I cannot place the welfare of my people second to your interests. Have we not always said that what we were doing was for them, and not for our own profit? Do not make me feel guilty for standing by that. Do not make it a choice by which I must lose a friend."

Listening, Aurore was touched by Amin's plea. After all, hadn't it been Steven Parker who stood by him when he escaped the police in Thiès? Hadn't it been Steven Parker who fetched her, and later carried her note for sulfa drugs to the railroad doctor? Without Steven Parker, there was a good chance that Amin might not have survived his wounds. And yet, now, perceiving the mingling of disappointment and greed and anger on Steven Parker's face as he evaluated his position in light of Amin's decision, she had a sudden strong intuition that the sincere feeling of friendship Amin had expressed for him was not reciprocated.

"I know when I'm being shafted!" The American turned a deaf ear to Amin's plea. He turned abruptly on his heel and walked away from them. A moment later, he was swallowed up by the crowd.

"I should have been wiser, more tactful. I could have prevented that." Amin was distraught.

"Perhaps he will cool off in time," Cherif comforted his brother. "After all, you and I have resolved our differences."

Somehow Aurore didn't think Steven Parker's anger would cool so easily. It wasn't the same. Amin and Steven Parker weren't brothers. And there had been that look on the American's face.

"Yes, we have done that," Amin responded to Cherif. "At least some good has come out of this day." The brothers joined hands in a fistlike Muslim handshake.

Aurore looked from one to the other, smiling. "I can't wait to tell Sabine of this *concorde*," she said. "How happy she'll be that little Amadou won't have to grow up listening to his father and his uncle arguing like stubborn hyenas."

Still trapped in the slow-moving crowd, they were proceeding an inch at a time toward one of the gates leading out of the racecourse. Aurore was slightly in front of the two brothers, who were walking with their arms about each other's shoulders, enjoying their *rapprochement*. Suddenly she caught sight of Steven Parker again, his straw-color hair and ruddy complexion standing out from the masses of black faces and head cloths crowding past the guards at the gates. He was talking to someone she couldn't quite make out until they drew a little closer.

Then she recognized the man to whom Parker was talking. He was a white man, French. Aurore remembered meeting him at one of *Tante* Colette's parties. Out of politeness, Aurore had listened while he described his position with the French colonial government of Senegal. It was to coordinate actions of Dakar's black police force and certain units of the Senegalese black armed forces with units of the white railroad police. Now Aurore watched as Steven Parker directed this man's attention to the three of them.

"Amin!" She realized immediately that he was being betrayed by the American. She stepped in front of him and Cherif and pointed out to them what she had seen, telling them who the man was with Steven Parker. Even as she did so, the Frenchman was issuing orders to black policemen, who started pushing through the crowd toward them with pistols drawn.

"I can't believe that Steven would—" Amin was dazed.

"No time for that." Cherif was appraising the situation. "The gates are hopeless. They're too heavily guarded, and now they'll know to look for you. We'll have to go back through the crowd to the grandstand and then try to get out back of them where the paddocks are. Come on." He turned and led the way, against the direction the crowd was moving.

The crowd thinned out near the grandstand, and it was no longer so difficult to make progress against its flow. As they mounted the first tier, Aurore paused to look back. The black policemen set on them by Steven Parker and the Frenchman were still stuck in the throng. With luck, Amin would be gone from the grandstand by the time they reached it.

"Go down that aisle and through the stables," Cherif told his brother. "I'll stay here and delay them."

"You'll get into trouble," Amin protested.

"Do as he says. I'll stay with him. They won't dare shoot if a white woman is in the line of fire. And they'll have to slow down to be polite to me," Aurore backed up Cherif.

Amin gave the two of them a look of gratitude. He ran for the back of the grandstand as they tried to gauge where the policemen would emerge from the crowd. When they had them pinpointed and Aurore turned around to see what sort of lead Amin had, her brother-in-law was out of sight.

"I think he's safe now," she told Cherif.

"I hope—"

Cherif's words of agreement were cut off by the sound of a volley of bullets from behind the grandstand. He and Aurore looked at each other with the thought they dared not put into words written plainly on their faces. Then they both started running in the direction of the sounds of gunfire.

No! Tight bands of steel squeezed Aurore's breasts as she ran. *Not Amin! Please God! Not Amin! He has so much to live for—Sabine, Amadou; he has so much to contribute to his people. Don't let him be dead! Not Amin!*

He was lying in the dirt. A circle of men stood around him—white men. They were holding shotguns. Their Dakar-Niger Railway caps were their only uniform. They were the railway police. The Frenchman Aurore had seen with Steven Parker was voicing his approval to the man in charge of them. Cherif, somewhat in advance of Aurore, started to push through them toward his fallen brother. They stopped him with deliberate roughness.

"You there!" Aurore heard her own voice crack out over the hubbub to claim the attention of the Frenchman she had met. "You remember me! I am Aurore de Beausoleil! Tell these men to let us through! The man you have shot is my brother-in-law!"

Emotions chased one another over the Frenchman's face. He knew, of course, that Aurore had some black blood. It had been discussed in titillating fashion among all the men who attended the de Beausoleil parties. On the other hand, she was a de Beausoleil, and that name had come to carry considerable weight in white Dakar society. "Let her through," he decided. What was there to lose?

Amin lay flat on the ground. Blood was pouring from his stomach and chest. He was dazed but conscious. Cherif knelt beside him and tried to staunch the flow with his tunic. Standing over them, Aurore could see that it was no use. She turned her face away so that he might be spared her tears.

"Aurore." He managed to speak her name. When she turned back to him, a ghost of a smile was playing over his grayish lips. "No nursing this time."

Cherif slipped his arm under Amin and cradled his head. Aurore sank down beside him and took his hand, weeping openly now. Amin spoke again, these words for his brother:

"My time is over. Allah in His wisdom has decreed it. You will be chief after our father has joined me, Cherif. Promise me that you will lead with restraint, and that no man or woman of Ile Celeste shall shed blood needlessly."

"I promise."

"Perhaps I was wrong about the *jihad*. Think on it."

"I will think on it. I promise."

"Sabine—Amadou—" The blood bubbled from Amin's lips.

"I will look after them always. I swear it, my brother." Cherif stared deeply into Amin's eyes. "As Allah decrees," he added meaningfully.

"As . . . Allah . . . decrees." Amin struggled to flatten his hands one against the other in the traditional Muslim prayer position. *"Sidiame dome n'deye.* Peace be with you, my brother." His head fell away from Cherif's cradling arms.

"Fananlen ak diame. Good-bye." Cherif passed his hands over his brother's eyes and closed them.

Aurore stared at him pleadingly. It was no use. Cherif could only shake his head.

Amin was dead.

CHAPTER 12

During her first few days back at Ile Celeste, Aurore made the grief of Sabine her own. Observing the Muslim custom that separated women mourners from men, she stayed with her half-sister night and day. By the end of the third night, however, Sabine had sought solace in a deep retreat of Islamic religiosity beyond Aurore's grasp. There was no further comfort Aurore could offer that would be as healing as that which Sabine found in her religion.

"Nevertheless, I'll return tomorrow," Aurore told Sabine that evening after sunset as she prepared to leave for le Château de Beausoleil. "At least I can look after Amadou for you."

Aurore wanted to go back to the château for fresh clothing. All her things were there. And in truth, after the hardships she had been through, she was looking forward to the luxury of a warm bath in a tub and a night's sleep in a soft featherbed. As she started up the wooded inland path that led from the village to the château, Cherif hailed her.

It was the first time she had seen him since their arrival. While she was with Sabine, he had been mourning Amin with his father, the chief, and the other men of Ile Celeste. Now as he walked toward her in the moonlight, she was struck by the difference between the image of the adolescent playmate that always came to her mind with thoughts of Cherif, and the reality of the grieving man.

Grief had bestowed dignity upon Cherif. His once

carefree, loping gait was a purposeful stride now as he came toward her. The playful light in his eyes had been shrouded with pain from the loss of his brother, and the pain had deepened into the maturity of reflection and the acceptance of responsibility. The boy had become a man.

He asked where Aurore was going, and when she told him, he fell into step with her. "I have something I want to say to you," he told her, and then fell silent without saying it. When he finally did speak again, Aurore sensed that it was not straight to the point but rather an oblique approach to his topic. "You have changed a great deal in these past few months, Aurore," he said.

"We both have. I was just thinking that."

"Yes. That is true." Cherif allowed himself a small smile. "Still, I shall miss the frank vanity of the young girl I loved. I remember how you were always tucking fresh flowers behind your ears and peering at yourself in the mirror of the pond, as if nature itself were obliged to confirm your beauty."

"All young girls are vain. They think the world revolves around them. A flower exists to enhance the complexion, and a blemish is a catastrophe. But a girl grows up. I have. I've learned that there are things more important than the curl of my hair or the drape of my *boubou*."

"And what is important to you now, Aurore?"

"Other people. Making the world a better place. My world. Our world. Oh, I know that sounds high-flown. I know that one girl can't have much effect on events. But I do intend to have what little I can."

"Toward what end, Aurore?" Cherif seemed to be asking the question as much of himself as of her.

"First, the winning of the strike. Second, education and medical care for all the people of Senegal. Third, independence from the French."

"But you yourself are three-quarters French."

"That doesn't matter. For every good man like my

father who came to Senegal to help the people, there are ten Frenchmen who came to squeeze the wealth from the land and use the black people's labor without paying them even a living wage in return. The French must go.''

"Yes." Cherif nodded. "That was what Amin believed. It is what I believe, too.''

"You will have the power to help bring it about. Now that Amin is gone, someday you will be chief. You will be a leader of our people.''

"I am not worthy." Cherif's eyes seemed to be looking inward with self-recrimination as he said this. "Amin was a man of God. He walked with Allah always. I have been too casual with my Muslim faith.''

"You are a good man, Cherif." Aurore squeezed his arm. "Better than you know. You will find the Path of Allah if that is what you wish to do.''

"It is what I wish to do." His voice was very low. "But it is very difficult." He took a deep breath. Then, seemingly, he changed the subject. "I have always wanted you for my wife, Aurore.''

Was he going to propose to her again? "Perhaps this is not a good time to speak of such things, Cherif,'' she told him gently.

"The time is right." He said it flatly. "Hear me out, Aurore.''

Before he could continue, however, their attention was diverted by a sudden hissing sound and then the crackling of dry underbrush. A split second later, Leita Ousbane emerged from a thick clump of proposis trees. She darted onto the trail a few yards in front of them, her *boubou* all twisted, her braids sticking out like porcupine quills, her eyes staring and wild, her sharp white teeth bared to emit a strange hiss from her distorted mouth. Then, like some wild jungle creature that fears the approach of the hunter, she ran across the path and plunged back into the sheltering thicket once again. Something had been writhing inside the sack she carried.

Aurore felt a surge of pity for the demented girl. She knew how it felt to be rejected by a man who had used you for sexual pleasure and then denied you further intimacy. Blaise had treated her in this fashion. And Cherif had behaved perhaps even more cavalierly toward Leita. He had slaked his lust with her countless times. Discarded now, it was no wonder Leita was running through the jungle like some dispossessed spirit, hissing out her hatred at the man who had used her and was now about to speak of marriage to another woman.

"I must do penance for what I have done to Leita." Cherif's thoughts had paralleled Aurore's own. "I have not behaved toward her in the way that a man who is someday to become chief should behave toward a woman."

"That's true." Aurore agreed.

"Perhaps what I am about to say to you, Aurore, is part of that penance." Cherif sighed. "It has to do with marriage between us. It is a very painful thing, that which I must say. I cannot ask you to be my wife, Aurore. I have decided to live my life by the Muslim faith as Amin would have done. I cannot marry outside that faith. I shall love you always, but—" His voice broke.

"It's all right." She touched his cheek with her fingertips. His skin was tight and dry and burning. "It's all right, Cherif. I understand." They were at the foot of the hill trail leading up to the swimming pool and patio in back of the château. "I can go the rest of the way by myself from here," she said to relieve the awkwardness of the moment. "Thank you for walking with me, Cherif. *Fananlen ak diame*. Good-bye."

"*Fananlen ak diame*." He took her by the shoulders and kissed her. Then he was quickly gone around a bend in the trail.

Aurore knew that this would be the last time Cherif would kiss her in just that way. He had made a choice. He had rejected her. And yet Aurore didn't feel rejected. She felt released. It was somehow all part of what she had been saying to Cherif. Painful or not, the time had come for first love to be discarded. *"Fananlen ak diame,"* she repeated softly, sadly to herself as she started up the steep path. She went slowly, suddenly realizing how exhausted she was, both physically and emotionally.

The sound of laughter coming from the swimming pool made Aurore pause in the shadows as she reached the patio. She recognized Blaise's deep, throaty chuckle. And those little gasps and feminine trills of merriment identified Minette Fourier. Aurore was in no mood to cope with them, their banter, Blaise's sarcasm, Minette's barbs. She stayed where she was, out of sight.

Chinese lanterns with candles inside them illuminated the patio. Small, multicolored, revolving spotlights rainbowed the swimming pool. It took a moment before Aurore's eyes adapted to the light.

When they did, she focused on Blaise kneeling on the edge of the low diving board with an open bottle of champagne in one hand and two goblets in the other. He was wearing bathing trunks as black and wet as his curling hair. Beads of water glistened on his tanned flesh, and the hair on his chest was matted. Obviously he'd just come out of the water. It had pasted the trunks tight across the muscular globes of his buttocks.

Minette was treading water in the pool just below him. Her aristocratic kitten face looked up at Blaise. Her gaze never wavered, although she was turning her head from side to side. Long raven hair clung in wet tendrils to the alabaster skin of her graceful back and shoulders. Her pert breasts were floating, sharp-tipped emerald globes in a tight, strapless green swimsuit.

"Don't tease me!" Minette pouted as Blaise poured the sparkling wine into one of the goblets and proceeded to sip from it. "I want some, too."

"Then reach for it." Blaise poured champagne into the second glass and held it tantalizingly out of reach.

Unexpectedly Minette swam to the side of the diving

board and jumped straight up in the air. She grabbed hold of Blaise's trunks and tugged. "You give me my champagne, or I'll pull off your bathing suit," she threatened.

"Promises, promises." He set down the bottle and glasses far back on the board and dived in after her.

There was much splashing and laughter then. Blaise's strident guffaw and Minette's silvery giggle mingled in suggestive, intimate bursts, livening the sweet-scented evening air. Listening, observing, Aurore realized they were a little drunk. Perhaps more than a little. They were playing tag in the pool now, water sprites flickering in the watery light.

Watching, Aurore's heart was thudding in her breast at the sight of Blaise. The uncontrollable surge of feeling was the Achilles' heel of her new maturity. The sound of his voice was still—even now, even after all she had endured, all the growing up she had done— quite enough to reduce her to a lovesick schoolgirl once again.

Aurore was afraid that if she tried to cross the patio to get into the house, she would be seen. It would be embarrassing to confront them. Yet to remain where she was left her vulnerable to the even greater embarrassment of being discovered in the act of eavesdropping.

In her confusion, Aurore opted for greater concealment. She glided across the edge of the patio toward the pool, her sandaled step an unheard whisper on the bright blue ceramic tile. One side of the swimming pool was shielded by huge glazed flowerpots containing scarlet bougainvillea and blue-violet African lilies. The thickly massed flowers screened Aurore from view. She watched the cavorting couple through an eye-level opening between the fragrant blossoms.

They were playing a wild game of tag. Minette was swimming and diving frantically to escape Blaise's determined pursuit. With his drenched hair hanging over eyes slitted against the chlorine in the pool and the soaked hairs of his mustache askew above his spouting mouth, Blaise conveyed the impression of some sinister species of sea creature risen from the deep to frolic with his silverfish Circe.

Minette paused, out of breath. Blaise closed in on her. Only a few feet away, he dove—strong, tanned, hairy, straight legs rising perpendicular to the water for an instant—and vanished in the depths.

Then, suddenly, Aurore saw the heaving bulk rise up from underneath Minette and force her out of the water. Blaise's head appeared between her slim white thighs; Minette's elegantly rounded derriere was supported upon his shoulders. The sudden upheaval had displaced the tight, molded cups of Minette's strapless bathing suit. The top had slipped down so that her milky breasts with their uptilted rosebud nipples were exposed.

Aurore felt a sudden spasm of jealousy deep inside her as Minette giggled wickedly, bent forward, took her breasts in her hands and repeatedly brushed the rosy tips against Blaise's tousled hair until the nipples were pointing out stiffly. Blaise's large, tanned hands moved up the tender skin of Minette's inner legs and disappeared behind the juncture of his neck and her bottom. Aurore ached with passion as the French girl's delicate white teeth bit down on her full underlip and she gave herself up to the pleasure of Blaise's intimate caress.

Then Minette leaned back and coyly covered her naked breasts with her hands. "I somehow don't think that is what Colette had in mind when she so tactfully contrived to leave us alone. Do you?"

"That's difficult to say. Maman is, after all, a woman of the world. I doubt she'd be shocked to learn where the waves of champagne have wafted us."

"But it was not her intent." Minette stressed the point.

"Oh?" Blaise seemed amused. "And what was her intent?"

"To leave us alone so that you would have an opportunity to propose to me."

"But I have proposed to you," Blaise said. Aurore's heart took a sickening lurch. "I have proposed all sorts of wild and wondrous activities. I've been proposing them all night." He reached up and firmly removed her hands from her breasts. "And I've got another proposal for you right now." His tone implied that this was a familiar game. He leaned forward and murmured in Minette's ear.

"You beast!" Minette went for him with her long nails. "You know I come all unstrung when you talk to me like that!"

"But so many things unstring you, *chérie*." As if to prove his point, Blaise held her hands away from her breasts and bent to them again. His mouth opened over one breast, engulfing both nipple and areola.

Minette emitted a helpless little moan. If Blaise's object had been to put an end to talk of marriage proposals by focusing the champagne-muddled Minette on her erotic appetites, he had succeeded. She pulled her breast away and offered the other one to Blaise's expert mouth, digging her fingers into his thick black hair and whimpering with excitement, her tongue too thick with lust now to give any further voice to her marital ambitions.

Aurore was glad that he had sidestepped the issue. At the same time, she was fiercely jealous of the sight of him kissing and caressing Minette. Mesmerized, Aurore recalled the musky taste of manflesh, the texture, the pricklings of coarse curls against her nostrils. The earthy aroma that had so aroused her.

Aurore watched as Blaise teased her rival with his skilled hands and tongue, and she wondered how the French girl could endure another moment of his love-making. Finally he drew Minette up on the patio and climbed out after her. He eased off her bathing suit and poised himself above her, his knees forcing her thighs still wider. He entered her. Wisp of a girl that Minette was, her struggles were no less amorous and strenuous than his own.

Tears came to Aurore's eyes, testifying to the aching emptiness inside her. She felt almost faint with lust, and yet she could not turn away. She could almost feel each thrust with a *déjà vu* of desire that was startling in its clarity and immense in its longing.

How could he do it to another woman? Was Minette better at it than she?

Her hurt and hungry woman's heart screamed the questions silently into the soft, perfumed air. Her love for Blaise was so strong! Nothing could kill it! Couldn't he feel it at all? Dear God!

Aurore watched as Blaise collapsed upon Minette's slim and sinuous form. She stroked his midnight hair. They lay now with the stillness of satiated lovers. Aurore saw that their eyes were closed. They would not catch sight of her now as she moved toward the house. She crept along the hedge of flowers, a shadow, then flitted across the patio to the doorway to the lounge. A moment later, she was starting up the stairs.

All Aurore wanted to do was throw herself upon her soft white bed in *la salle verte,* her green bedroom, and fall into the dark oblivion of sleep. When she awoke, perhaps the painfully erotic scene she had just witnessed would seem like no more than a bad dream. Perhaps cool sleep would dissolve the hot bile of jealousy in the pit of her stomach.

In her hurry along the upstairs corridor to her room, Aurore didn't notice the door to the hall bathroom opening. By the time she saw *Tante* Colette emerging into the hall in her lace-trimmed peignoir, it was too late. She collided with her head-on.

"*Mon Dieu!* It is you, Aurore!" There was a note of relief in the recognition. "Have you no sense at all, to come charging through a civilized home like a rampaging bull?"

"*Pardonnez-moi, Tante* Colette. I didn't see you."

"You vanish for months and then reappear only to knock me down!" *Tante* Colette shook her head disapprovingly and brushed a stray blond tendril from her forehead.

"Let me help you." Aurore took her aunt's arm and supported her as she struggled back to her feet.

Tante Colette allowed Aurore to lead her into her own room, *la salle blanche,* with its white carpet and furnishings, its wallpaper striped in white and gold, and its canopied bed covered by an ivory satin quilt embossed with golden *fleurs de lis.* She fumbled at her white and gold dressing table and came away with a lace handkerchief soaked in eau de cologne. Daintily she dabbed at her temples. She then sank back upon a gold brocaded chaise longue and sighed wearily.

"Delphine has run away." Unexpectedly her tone of voice made it a shared confidence. "To France, with that ne'er-do-well lover of hers," she added.

"Steven Parker?" Aurore had not thought it possible that she would ever feel sorry for her aunt, but at this moment she did.

Tante Colette nodded. "In the note she left, Delphine said that Monsieur Parker has made some kind of arrangement with the railroad administrators and is currently in their employ. I have no way of knowing whether this is the truth or whether she was trying to make her scoundrel of a lover more acceptable to me. In any event, I have no doubt that it is Delphine's money he is after. Her father left her a generous settlement in her own name, you know." She shrugged, more with bitterness than resignation.

Aurore too was bitter. "I imagine Parker has made an arrangement with the French who run the railroad," she reassured her aunt. "He has done them a service, and I imagine they have indeed rewarded him." She did not explain that the service Parker had performed was the betrayal of Amin, which caused his death. Of course Parker would have asked to be sent to France by the railroad. To remain in Dakar after such a treachery would have meant risking his life to the vengeance of Senegalese patriots. Aurore pitied Delphine for loving so despicable a man. And she sympathized with her aunt, whose snobbery in this case had proven more than justified.

"You young girls are all alike." *Tante* Colette ignored Aurore's reassurances about Parker. "Foolish infatuations! Headstrong follies! You simply plunge ahead and do what you like with no regard to consequences. I wash my hands of all of you. So!" Her smooth, white, beringed hands fluttered in a gesture of dismissal.

"Don't be too hard on Delphine, *Tante* Colette. Love blinds many women to their own best interests." Aurore herslf was well acquainted with the obsessiveness that made this so.

"It is not just Delphine. It is also you, Aurore. I had hopes for you, truly I did. And what have they come to, my hopes? You run wild in the street with unruly natives!"

"They are my people," Aurore reminded her quietly.

"Well, they are not mine! I hate this land, this Senegal. I hate this pitiful excuse for an island! This railroad strike has been the last straw, depriving me of life's comforts, preventing me from seeing my friends. It has turned you, Aurore, back into a savage with wild hair and that ragged native dress. And this after all the time and trouble I took to teach you the civilized French mode of manners and appearance. If you have any sense left in that perverse head of yours, I advise you to stay here where you can benefit from my teachings and perhaps become a lady instead of reverting to your former ways."

"I am going back to the village tomorrow, *Tante*," Aurore told her. "And now I'm going to bed. Good night." Aurore got up to leave.

"Aurore."

"Yes, *Tante?*" Aurore paused at the door.

"Forgive me if I have spoken harshly. My nerves are in a terrible state, what with this native uprising and Delphine running away with that—that—American! I scarcely sleep at night, fearing that the house will be set on fire or broken into by some half-crazed revolutionary. I have not known such fear since the war ended in Marseilles.''

Aurore looked more closely at her aunt, surprised at this revelation of weakness. Anxiety and sleeplessness had left their marks on the delicate porcelain complexion. There were dark shadows under the blue eyes and deep lines around the rosebud mouth. For the first time since Aurore had met her, *Tante* Colette looked old.

"The strikers are in Dakar, *Tante*. There's no reason for them to come here." Aurore spoke gently, wishing there was something more she could say to console this sad and bitter woman whose domineering nature had finally shown a more vulnerable side. "Besides, Blaise is here," she added. "He'll see to your safety."

"Have you seen him?"

"He and Minette are swimming in the pool." There was a certain hurt irony in Aurore's voice at the memory of how much more they were doing than swimming.

"Ah. Yes." *Tante* Colette's face brightened. "Perhaps there will soon be happy news concerning my son and Minette. One of my children, at least, will make a suitable marriage."

"Yes," Aurore replied, choosing her words with pain and anger and sarcasm, but carefully keeping these emotions out of her voice. "I am sure that Blaise and Minette are most deserving of each other." And then, not sure that she could maintain this blasé attitude which came so unnaturally to her, she bid her aunt good night with finality and went to her own room.

Sleep, however, did not wipe out the hurt of the scene Aurore had witnessed between Blaise and Minette. Nor did it erase her fear that *Tante* Colette's wishes of marriage between the two might well come true. All it did was translate the hurt and fear into the language of dreams.

Aurore dreamed that she was chasing Blaise down a long corridor lined with doors of different colors. Blaise's boots pounded the marble floor with a heavy, thudding tread, while her sandals moved silently. As hard as she ran, Aurore could not keep up with him. Blaise kept disappearing into the various doorways, but she could never tell which until later, after he had departed. Then the doors would be open, their occupants revealed. But no one noticed Aurore or spoke to her. It was as if she were invisible.

A blue door stood open to reveal Delphine and Steven in a passionate embrace. Further along, a white door stenciled in gold *fleurs de lis* was ajar. *Tante* Colette was standing inside, wearing a beautiful ivory satin gown. There was a purple cloak over her shoulders and a jeweled crown upon her head. In her hand was a golden scepter, which was pointed menacingly at a little black girl who crouched on the floor at *Tante* Colette's feet, her ebony limbs barely covered by a ragged dress. *Tante* Colette was angry at the little girl. She was lecturing her, but Aurore could not hear the words or discern exactly what the child had done wrong.

Behind a partially open rose-color door, Minette posed voluptuously in front of a canopied bed. She was wearing a sheer black teddie that displayed her elegant figure to perfection. Her thighs were open seductively, her pointing nipples were erect; her lips were swollen and bruised as if she had been kissed long and passionately. Her head was thrown back, her sleek black hair fanning out over her bare white back. Although she took no notice of Aurore, she laughed mockingly and derisively, as if to confirm that Aurore would never catch up to Blaise.

Aurore ran faster, catching sight of the back of Blaise's head and a portion of his broad back before he vanished behind yet another door. Her heart was pounding; she could feel rivulets of sweat trickling between her breasts. She was panting harshly.

She paused at a half-open door made of bamboo. Inside, there was a wicker throne, its back fan-shaped and decorated with peacock feathers. Upon it sat Cherif, his black body naked and gleaming. Between his legs knelt a woman, her head moving in an unmistakable rhythm. First the hair on her head appeared dark red, like her own, but Aurore knew it couldn't be herself kneeling there. Then, as she watched, the head grew smaller and the dark red ringlets metamorphosed into tight black braids that quivered and writhed like inkworms. Suddenly from behind Aurore came the demented cackling of Ouna the *katt*.

Aurore fled down the long hallway until she came to another open door. This room, however, was empty. It was her room, *la salle verte*. She went into its cool greenness and lay down on the bed and closed her eyes. She left the door open behind her. Perhaps Blaise would come. Perhaps . . .

In her dream, a kind of voluptuous lethargy came over her. She was not asleep, but her eyes were closed to focus upon her wishes. And when they began to come true, she did not open them for fear of dispelling her vision of Blaise.

Surely that was him sliding the sheet down over her breasts. Surely that was his touch, light and airy, which was making her nipples tingle and harden. He had found her! He *had!* Yes, he had finally entered *her* room, preferring it to all the others. And now his large, hard hands would grasp her, arouse her, press her to the hardness of his chest. But the sensation that occurred was not what she anticipated. Instead it was dry, and smooth, and somehow repellent.

In her dream, she opened her eyes. Blaise wasn't there. Nothing was there. Yet the pressure on her chest remained. And something invisible continued to move, to slide, to squeeze her breast.

A sickening dread possessed Aurore then. So terrible was her fear that she fought her way out of the dream and back to wakefulness. Her eyes flew open. She was truly awake now. But the horror was still there. It was still there and it was no longer invisible. Wide awake now, in the cold white clarity of the moonlight, she saw it.

A snake was coiling around her breasts!

This was no dream! This was reality! The dry, sliding weight on her chest was not a nightmare! The snake was truly there!

Aurore fought down the scream that was tearing at her throat. She forced herself to lie still. An eternity of seconds ticked by as she stared at the serpent in frozen terror.

It was a bright green snake, marked here and there with black scales. It was long—about five feet—and very slender as it writhed over her sensitive flesh. Aurore recognized it as a *boomslang,* or tree snake, the deadliest of all African vipers. She knew that its venom was lethal.

The snake, poised now between her breasts, lifted its blunt head and stared at her with its round, yellow-green eyes. *No! She must not scream or move.* Slowly, lazily, the snake slithered again. In a chill sweat of horror, Aurore felt its dry scales caressing her flesh. It slid sinuously over her breasts and coiled itself in the hollow between her body and her outspread arm. *It wasn't touching her anymore!*

With infinite care, Aurore edged her body a few inches away. She planned to raise herself up and throw herself clear of the bed. But first she must move her arm away from the bright green coil.

The instant she raised it, there was a sharp, searing pain at the tip of her shoulder. Alarmed by the sudden movement, the deadly snake had reared sideways and struck. Now its neck and breast were puffed and spread like a lady's green evening fan as the deadly fangs at the back of its mouth locked over her shoulder flesh and released their venom.

Aurore screamed, and screamed again.

Finally *Tante* Colette appeared in the doorway, a small lady's pistol in her right hand. The hand was shaking as she tried to aim the pistol at the *boomslang.* Nor did it stop shaking as she released the safety catch.

The venom had been drained from the snake's fangs, and now it released its grip from Aurore's shoulder. As the blunt head darted upward, through the daze of her pain, Aurore knew that *Tante* Colette was going to fire. Aurore closed her eyes, positive that the bullet would strike her rather than the *boomslang*.

"Wait!" Instead of the shot, there was the sound of Blaise's voice.

Aurore opened her eyes. Blaise was standing beside his mother in a brocade dressing gown that looked frivolous on his rugged, pirate's body. He had taken the gun from Colette.

"Don't move!" he said in a very low voice to Aurore. He crooked his left arm, steadied the gun below the bend, and sighted down the short, feminine barrel. When he fired, the sound was like a bombshell in the small room.

Beside Aurore, the *boomslang* leaped into the air, a long, green spiral, and then hit the floor with a thud. Headless, it writhed there a moment, and then it was still. Blaise walked over to it.

"Jesus Christ!" He groaned deep in his throat. "It's a *boomslang!*" He turned to Aurore, a sick look on his face. "Did it bite you?" he demanded.

"A moment ago." Aurore nodded weakly. "My shoulder."

Blaise looked down at the twin puncture wounds at the tip of her right shoulder. The two small holes were oozing blood. "Get Abdul!" he barked to his mother. "Hurry, Maman."

He knelt beside the bed. His dark, tousled head bent to the wound. Aurore breathed in the scent of his cologne—sandalwood spiced with citrus—and the musky aroma of his flesh. She felt his lips purse gently over her shoulder. It was like a kiss. And it was not a dream. It was real. Aurore smiled.

When Blaise began sucking at the wound and then spitting, Aurore realized that her mind had been playing wishful-thinking tricks on her. His lips were not bestowing the lover's caress for which she longed. He was trying to suck out as much of the venom as possible in order to minimize the amount infiltrating her bloodstream.

Aurore was beginning to weave in and out of consciousness when Blaise stopped sucking the snakebite. She realized vaguely that he was speaking to Abdul, the manservant. He was telling him to take the speedboat to Dakar and fetch the doctor who lived near the harbor and worked for the De Beausoleil Shipping Company.

Only fragments of the conversation registered. "A matter of life and death . . . snakebite; a *boomslang;* antivenin serum . . . whole blood for a transfusion if necessary . . . Hurry! . . . Hurry! . . ."

There was anguish in Blaise's voice, anguish for her. Aurore managed a weak smile and gave herself up to the waves of faintness engulfing her.

Some time later, Aurore again regained consciousness for a short period. Blaise was beside her bed, holding her hand, his eyes closed so that he didn't notice that hers had opened. The look on his face was almost as if he was silently praying.

Behind him Aurore saw *Tante* Colette in the doorway. There was another woman with her, but she was in the shadows. When she spoke, Aurore recognized the voice of Jeanne, a downstairs maid who had come with the family from Marseilles.

"I had trouble sleeping and went to the kitchen to fix myself some warm milk," Jeanne was saying. "Coming back, I heard the sound of running footsteps on the main staircase. I went to investigate and saw this girl—a black girl—hurrying toward the front door. I asked her what she was doing in the house, but she didn't answer. She just laughed in a crazy way and stared at me with big eyes that were popping out of her head. She said something in a language I couldn't understand, and then she ran out."

"Why did you not inform me, or my son, of this intrusion?" *Tante* Colette demanded.

"I—I—" Jeanne floundered.

"Well? Why do you hesitate?"

"Sometimes the male servants entertain native girls in their rooms at night." Jeanne's voice was low, embarrassed, reluctant to inform on her co-workers. "This girl I saw had braids sticking out of her head every which way. Her clothes were disarranged. I thought—"

"I see!" *Tante* Colette's tone said that she would soon put a stop to such goings-on.

Oh, God! Even in her delirium, Aurore realized who the girl was that Jeanne had seen and what she had been doing in the house. It was Leita Ousbane! And it had been she, poor demented Leita with her outdated jealousy, who had put the *boomslang* in Aurore's bed! That was what had been writhing inside the sack Leita had carried when Aurore and Cherif encountered her on the trail earlier that evening.

The realization was too much for Aurore. Once it had penetrated, the thick haze moved in over her mind again. She felt heavy, as if she were sinking into the soft mattress. She fell once again into a doze that was heavier and darker but also more fitful than sleep. She emerged from it a few times, but when she did she was only vaguely conscious of her surroundings.

Blaise was all she could focus on at such times. He was always there, sitting beside the bed, standing over her, treating her wound with compresses soaked in a purple solution of potassium permanganate, poultices meant to draw the poison from the blood, she supposed. Once Aurore tried to turn her head to him, tried to smile to show how grateful she was. She wanted to tell him that she could face anything—even death—if he was there beside her. But this moment of awareness, so long to her, was merely the instant between the opening and closing of her eyes, the tiny time of wakefulness between two periods of unconsciousness.

Later, much later, she came to again for a longer period. She heard an unfamiliar male voice. She felt her body being poked and prodded.

"See the dark patches on her abdomen, and on her

hip and her thighs? That's coagulated blood. It's a sign of internal bleeding." The doctor spoke.

"I know. There's been bleeding from her nose and mouth too." Blaise's voice was grave. "I sucked all the venom I could from the wound, but it had already entered the bloodstream. Perhaps I should have enlarged the puncture wounds with a knife and bled her that way."

"It probably wouldn't have helped." The doctor had a nice voice; kindly, efficient. Aurore tried to open her eyes to look at him, but they wouldn't open. "I'm going to inject the antivenin serum now," he told Blaise.

Aurore felt the coolness of alcohol being applied above and below the wound. She felt a stinging pain in her arm, then another in her shoulder, but they came from far away, like everything else. The pain was remote and seemed to have nothing to do with her.

"Now we wait," the doctor said. "If there's more bleeding, we'll have to give her a transfusion. I brought two units of O blood—the universal donor. It was all I had." He sounded worried. "I'm not sure it will be enough," he said almost in a whisper.

"I'm Type O," Blaise told him. "I'll donate all the blood you need."

It was the last thing Aurore heard before darkness closed in over her again.

She awoke to terrible pain. Every part of her body felt as if it were being attacked with sharp needles. She threw herself from side to side, kicking off the sheet, which was like a lead weight on her tortured flesh.

"She's allergic to the antivenin. There's extensive swelling of her arms and legs. More coagulation under the skin also." The doctor sighed. "I don't know whether to risk another injection of the serum. The reaction could kill her."

"And if you don't give her the injection?" Blaise asked.

"The internal bleeding could become worse. The

venom could have a fatal effect on her kidneys and other vital organs.''

"Sweet Jesus!" Blaise sounded so upset that Aurore wanted to comfort him. But she did not have the strength to speak. Darkness closed over her again.

Aurore alternated between sleep and wakefulness more frequently now. The pain would lift and then come back with such renewed fury that she would wake herself screaming. Once she woke to a burning pain in her arm. When she tried to pull away from the pain, she found that her arm wouldn't move. She whimpered with frustration.

"It's all right, Aurore," Blaise said quietly.

She turned in the direction of his voice, and her flickering eyelids saw a dark rubber tube joining his arm to hers.

"I'm giving you blood," he said. He smiled at her.

It was all right then. She would bear the pain. Blaise was giving her his own blood! The thought made her strangely happy, soothed her.

She didn't see the worried looks that Blaise and the doctor exchanged. She had lost consciousness again. The doctor took Aurore's pulse and listened to her heartbeat. He stepped away from the bed.

"If she's Catholic, you'd better send for a priest," he said.

In Aurore's dream, she was running down the corridor again. This time Blaise stood at the end, his arms held open, ready to catch her, hug her, hold her close.

It was like the gates of heaven opening.

CHAPTER 13

No priest was summoned. Instead, Blaise sent a servant
to fetch Sabine. Despite the fact that she was still in
mourning for Amin and supposed to stay secluded according to Muslim doctrine, Sabine came at once. She
had loved Aurore from the day she was born, and she
would not forsake her half-sister now. She had to bring
little Amadou with her, of course, and was grateful
when Blaise arranged to have a servant look after him
so that she might remain at Aurore's bedside.

Aurore was in a deep coma. The doctor frankly
admitted that there was not much he could do. If her
allergy to the antivenin was so strong as to make her
system reject it, then no matter how many blood transfusions were given her, Aurore would die. "It is in
God's hands," he told Sabine, and there was not very
much hope in his voice.

"Allah's will be done!" Sabine replied. Unlike the
doctor, however, her tone belied the fatalism on her
words. Faith and hope had always been the cornerstones
of Sabine's religious belief, and now, in the struggle for
Aurore's life, they translated into prayer and expert
nursing care.

"Where did you take your training?" the doctor
asked Sabine, impressed by both her devotion to the
patient and her professional demeanor.

"My stepfather taught me all that I know."

"He was a physician?" It was practically impossible
for a black man in Senegal to receive training in the

professions. The doctor's tone of surprise was a comment on Sabine's skin color.

"Her stepfather was Dr. Justin de Beausoleil, my uncle," Blaise told him.

Sabine took pity on the doctor's confusion. "I used to go with Papa on his calls," she explained. "I watched him treat people and I helped him with bandages and salves and sometimes with the preparations of medicines. At one time, I had the dream of becoming a nurse."

"Why didn't you?"

"I was in love. It would have meant my leaving Ile Celeste, leaving Amin, the man I was to marry. I would have had to be away a very long time, first for training, then for working."

"It's too bad you gave it up. You have a real talent for nursing."

"I did not mind giving it up. I wanted to marry Amin more than I wanted to be a nurse."

Sabine didn't mention that one reason she had not gone to nursing school was that she had remained on Ile Celeste to care for her mother, Odile. She did not like to think of this. Odile's death had been so long, so drawn out, so painful. And in the end, inevitable.

Fiercely Sabine insisted to herself that it did not have to be so. True, Odile had died. Yes, and Amin had been killed. But this did not mean that she must always lose those dear to her. It did not mean that Aurore must give up her life.

Sabine would not let it mean that. She would not let Aurore die! With Allah's help, she would not!

The coma had started on the first day after the snakebite. It persisted for the next week. During that time, Sabine and Blaise rarely left the sickroom. Aurore did not regain consciousness again, not even when she received additional transfusions of blood from Blaise.

Then, on the seventh day, Aurore's eyelids fluttered open. Her green eyes, however, did not focus. They wandered from Sabine to Blaise to the intravenous feeding tube in her arm without making any distinction.

The doctor came and examined her. By then Aurore's eyes were closed. To all outward appearances, she might have sunk back into her coma once again. But the doctor said this wasn't so. While she was in a state somewhere between sleep and outright unconsciousness, she had in no way retreated to the depths of the last week. The doctor was still cautious, but more optimistic than he had been before. The coma seemed to be over. The patient's body seemed to have accepted enough of the serum to counteract the venom of the snakebite. Her respiration and pulse were stabilized. She would be ill for a while, and she would have to take it very easy during an even longer convalescent period, but her chances were much improved. "Mind you, she is not out of danger yet," the doctor said. "But with proper care—"

"She will get the best care," Sabine assured him, her eyes brimming with tears of relief.

"Yes." The doctor voiced his respect for her. "I'm sure she will."

The weeks that followed were like a long, slow, confusing journey back to life for Aurore. She was frequently delirious. The doctor, hearing her babble on one such occasion, told Sabine and Blaise that she was hallucinating, having visions.

The visions were recurrent. They were rooted in the dream she had had before she awoke to the horror of the *boomslang*. Endlessly she moved through those rooms now, always seeking—seeking what? She never seemed quite to know—and never finding. Each room's promise was shattered. In her fantasy world now, the occupants of the rooms were mirror images of herself, reflections confirming her unworthiness and her disappointment.

At such times, Aurore's despair was obvious to Sabine and Blaise. Sabine's ministrations did not calm these deliriums. It was only when Aurore called out for

Blaise, her voice the voice of a child seeking the reassurance of love, that she was open to the balm of tranquility. When he would answer her call and take her hand, she would relax. And Blaise was always there to answer. Indeed, he slept in the easy chair next to her bed.

Finally there came a day when Aurore's eyes were clear. She was still weak, but the doctor confirmed that she was out of danger. The two figures who had moved through her hallucinations these past weeks took on form and substance and became real to her. "Blaise. Sabine." Her voice was weak, but she spoke their names clearly.

A few days later, Sabine left Aurore's bedside. Reluctantly she turned over the responsibility of Aurore's convalescence to Jeanne, the French maid. She was not truly comfortable with the redecorated sumptuousness of the château, and besides, she wanted to take her son back to his own home. The crisis was over now, and there was nothing to keep her.

The day after Sabine left, Blaise came into Aurore's room. Jeanne had gone to fetch her a luncheon tray, and so they were alone. Aurore looked at him with adoring eyes.

Blaise seemed embarrassed by her gaze. "You're feeling better, *Cousine?*" he asked. There was no trace of the old mockery in his voice.

Aurore missed it. "Much," she told him.

There was an awkward pause. The love shining from her eyes did not seem to be making it any easier for him. "I have to go away on business," he told her.

"I'll miss you," she said sincerely. "First Sabine has deserted me, and now you. It almost makes me wish I'd get worse again."

"You're well on your way to recovery," he told her with an abruptness that was almost cold. "I'll see you when I return." He turned on his heel and started out of the room.

"Blaise!" Her voice stopped him.

"Yes?" He didn't turn around.

"Thank you for everything."

"You're welcome."

"And Blaise—" She spoke quickly before he could leave.

"What?"

"I love having your blood running in my veins. It's almost as if—"

"Not now, Aurore!" His voice was harsh as he cut her off.

"We have to talk, Blaise! We have to!"

"Yes. But not now!" And then he was gone.

Two weeks went by without Aurore seeing him again. She agonized constantly for some explanation of his attitude, his absence. Surely his constant devotion during her illness proved that he loved her! That was what she had thought when she began to get better. It had been that thought that had speeded her recovery. He loved her! He must!

But perhaps he didn't after all. Aurore had to face that. Perhaps it was simply his goodness of heart, usually kept under cover, which explained his concern for her. But—but—each time Aurore arrived at this conclusion, she instinctively rejected it.

She struggled to come up with other explanations. Could his involvement with Minette be of such a nature that he was committed to her in some way that honor would not let him repudiate? Had the experience he had told Aurore about with his dead sweetheart left him desolate of the ability to acknowledge his love for another? Had he treated Aurore so badly and rejected her so often that now he found it impossible to reverse himself? Was it still that he felt responsible for Aurore and guilty for having betrayed that responsibility by taking her virginity? Was it the taboo of sex between first cousins that still bothered him? Or was it a combination of these—or perhaps none of them, perhaps some other, hidden reason of which Aurore had no hint?

Whatever the reason, his absence hurt Aurore. It hurt

even more when, her first day out of bed, she learned inadvertently from *Tante* Colette that Blaise had been coming home nights from Dakar. He had been home, and he hadn't even come in to see her!

She was up and about every day during the following week, but still she didn't encounter Blaise. Finally she had to face the fact that he must be purposely avoiding her. It was a bitter nostrum for her convalescence.

It was during this convalescence that Aurore heard from Jeanne, the maid, of the history-shaping events that had transpired during her illness. Just after the meeting at the racecourse, the rank and file of the Communist-dominated CGT trade unions had rebelled against the leaders who refused to back the striking railway workers. In defiance of the Communist brass, the trade unionists had shown their solidarity with the railway men by calling a general strike. In vain did the mucky-mucks protest. The rank and file had spoken.

The French powers that ruled Senegal looked on in horror as all commerce in the country came to a halt. It took only ten days of the general strike for the management of the Dakar-Niger Railroad to react to the pressure being brought by the other French interests in Senegal. At the end of that period, they resumed negotiations with the striking railway workers, this time displaying a great deal more good faith and elasticity than in the past. The result was that on March 19, 1948, the director of the railroad signed an agreement with the union delegates that granted all their major demands.

It was a great triumph, not just for the railway workers but for all the people of Senegal. It was the first time since the colonization of that country that the blacks had won a major victory against the Europeans. Any knowledgeable observer—and Aurore's experiences had made her quite knowledgeable—could see that this was the first step on the road to Senegalese independence from the French.

There would be diehards, of course, but generally speaking, even the French colonials recognized that independence was inevitable. The doctor surprised Aurore by conceding this one day and telling her that he was already making plans to return to France. "You should, too," he told her, still judging by her white skin. Although she liked him, Aurore didn't bother to enlighten him.

The doctor also told Aurore that he was very pleased with the way her convalescence was progressing. She had been asking him each time he called when she would be well enough to walk down to the village. Now he told her that if she proceeded slowly, she might visit her sister that very day. Aurore gave him no chance to change his mind. She started down the trail before he'd even left the château.

Entering the fishing village, Aurore caught sight of Sabine standing outside her thatched-roof home. Little Amadou was in her arms. Aurore's instinct was to run to them, but she checked it. After almost six weeks, she still hadn't regained her strength.

"Aurore!" It was Sabine who ran, with Amadou giggling at the bouncing motion and stretching his chubby arms out toward his aunt.

Aurore threw her arms around both of them and then took little Amadou. He grinned at her, displaying his newest acquisitions, four pearl-white teeth, two on the bottom and two on the top. "He's so much bigger—and heavier," Aurore marveled.

Sabine smiled with a mother's pride, then stepped back to survey her sister. "You look better, Aurore. Have you been eating?"

"Like a vulture."

"Still, you look just a bit peaked. Perhaps the long walk has tired you. Come and sit down. I always set the table outside under the bamboo awning. We can have lunch whenever you like." Solicitously she took Amadou back from Aurore.

Then Sabine led Aurore through her small home and out to the patio with its packed-dirt floor and bamboo roof supported on wooden posts. Sabine had planted flowering vines, which now grew up around the posts and festooned the bamboo awning with bright blossoms and trailing greenery. Around the edge of the patio, she had put in a border of zinnias and snapdragons; a bowl of these sat on the plank table, which was covered with a bright, printed cloth.

"How pretty it is here, Sabine! So shady and restful. And all these flowers! You've inherited Maman's green thumb."

"I am lucky anything is left of the garden with this little fellow around." Sabine looked at Amadou, who was struggling to get down from her lap. Sure enough, the minute she set him free, he crawled to the bed of flowers and began to crow joyously as he uprooted them.

"Amadou, no," Aurore scolded, laughing.

"It keeps him busy. When he is finished, I just stick them back into the ground." Sabine smiled and shrugged.

"You're such a good mother, Sabine. Of course, I always knew you would be."

"Not really. It's just that taking care of Amadou leaves me no time to brood." She jumped up to take away a pebble Amadou was about to pop into his mouth. "Do you see what I mean?" Sabine smiled as she came back carrying her frisky son.

"I can see that he's a comfort to you," Aurore said.

"I can never thank Allah enough for sending me this precious little boy. He is my comfort and my joy. And I can never thank you or Blaise enough for helping me bring him into the world." Sabine smiled affectionately at her sister.

"While we're on the subject of giving thanks, I will never forget the way you took care of me while I was ill, Sabine."

"It was nothing. I was glad to do it." Sabine spoke with her customary modesty.

"It wasn't *nothing* for you to break your forty-day mourning period to come to me and stay with me and care for me."

"I knew Allah would understand. I knew it was right for me to be with my baby sister when she needed me. You were so near death!" Sabine shuddered.

"But you pulled me through, Sabine. You, with your prayers, and your love."

"Perhaps I helped. I hope so. But it was Blaise who refused to let you die."

"Did he?"

"Aurore, you don't seem to realize how deeply Blaise cares for you." Sabine got up and laid the now-sleeping Amadou in his little hammock. It was suspended from the bamboo roof and swung gently in the sea breeze.

"It is hard for me to realize such a thing. He's not been in to see me since I started getting well."

"He stayed by your bedside for over a month. He probably has business to attend to, things to catch up on after such a long time away from his work. I know for a fact that he has business with Cherif concerning Ile Celeste fish. When Cherif left for Dakar today, he mentioned that he had an appointment with Blaise."

"I suppose Blaise is concerned with business," Aurore granted dully.

Sabine looked at her half-sister in silence for a long moment. It was as if she was trying to decide whether to tell her something. Finally she spoke. "At one point when you were in the coma, Aurore, the internal bleeding got so bad that the doctor couldn't control it anymore with transfusions. You were so weak that he told us the end might be very near. Blaise was there, as always, sitting beside your bed. Suddenly he bent forward and buried his face in his hands. I think he was crying. He made no sound, but his shoulders were shaking. Finally he took his hands away from his face and looked at me. 'Oh, Sabine, I love her so much!' he said. 'I won't be able to bear it if she dies!' Aurore, I've never seen such anguish. And only from Amin have I ever heard a voice so filled with love."

"Thank you for telling me." Aurore was trembling with emotion.

"It was clear to me that Blaise is very much in love with you."

"Sometimes, it seems, love isn't enough." Aurore voiced her confusion.

"Of course love is enough. What else is there?"

"Passion. Lust. Blaise is very much involved with Minette Fourier. They've been having an affair for a long time now. I saw them together the night I was bitten by the *boomslang*."

"What were they doing?"

"I'll spare you the sordid details, gentle sister. But I'll tell you this much. They were doing a lot more than kissing."

"And how does that make you feel about him, Aurore?" Sabine asked sympathetically.

"I love him! I've loved him ever since I can remember. Only then it was being in love with photographs and romantic stories of his exploits and adventures. When I met him, I fell in love with the real man. I've told him so in a thousand different ways. He knows how I feel, but still he rejects me. Over and over again. And yet—and yet—I cannot stop loving him, Sabine."

Unexpectedly Sabine smiled a particularly radiant smile. "Allah moves in mysterious ways," she told Aurore. "It will all work out all right. You will see."

Aurore noticed that the look of happiness stayed with Sabine as she prepared lunch. Her step was light as she moved from the kitchen area to the patio with the various bowls and platters. The meal consisted of the delicious fish called *capitaine,* in a spicy sauce served over black-eyed peas. With it, Sabine served a salad fresh from the garden and her special peanut bread. For dessert, she made Aurore's favorite, coconut pudding. Amadou slept peacefully through the meal and afterward, as Aurore and Sabine dawdled over cups of fragrant herbal tea.

"Why are you so happy, Sabine?" Aurore asked finally.

"Because you love Blaise. And that means that you do not love Cherif. Until today, I thought you might."

"Cherif?"

"Yes. You see, Aurore, Cherif wants to marry me. He wishes to follow the ancient Muslim custom of the younger brother marrying his elder brother's widow. He wants me as his *awa*, and he wants to be a father to little Amadou. Of course, this will not happen right away, but only after both of us have had more time to mourn Amin."

"If it is what you want, Sabine, if it is what will make you happy, then I'm glad for you."

"Perhaps it is hard for you to understand, Aurore. You know how I loved Amin."

"I'm surprised, but I don't disapprove, Sabine."

"I am glad. It is because I loved Amin so much that it is right for me to marry his brother. Amin and Cherif are branches of the same tree. Cherif already loves Amadou; he will treat him like his own son. This I know. It also gratifies me to follow the Muslim custom that is as old as time itself. And now that Cherif will one day be chief and a leader of his people, an adherence to Muslim custom is important to him also."

"I think that must always have been true," Aurore told her. "When Amin was dying, Cherif promised to look after you and Amadou 'as Allah decrees.' "

"Allah decrees that the younger brother marry the older brother's widow if such are the circumstances," Sabine mused. "Amin surely died with peace because of that promise. Allah will bless Cherif for it."

"Allah will bless your marriage to Cherif, too. I'm sure of it, Sabine. And I'm sure Cherif will be a wonderful husband to you and a wonderful father to Amadou."

"I am sure of it, too." Sabine hugged Aurore. "My only fear was that I would make you unhappy by marrying Cherif. I would not have married him without your blessing. I would never hurt you in such a way."

"Oh, Sabine!" Aurore returned her embrace.

They stood thus, clasped in sisterly affection, for an emotional instant. Then they cleared the dishes from the luncheon table and returned to sit on the patio. Their conversation turned to the resolution of the strike and its import to the future of their country.

"How I wish I hadn't been ill the day the strike was won," Aurore said. "How I would have loved to be in Thiès with the women. Or even in Dakar to join in the dancing and celebrations."

"It was a great victory for the strikers," Sabine agreed. "Still, all the suffering, the bloodshed, the lives lost—was it truly worth it, Aurore?"

"Yes. It's just the beginning. It's a chance for a better life for everybody. Not just the men of Senegal but the women, too. I learned that on the women's march, Sabine. The women have been awakened. Just as the blacks will get the French off their backs, the women will no longer be slaves to their men."

"I do not know." Sabine was dubious. "I am old-fashioned. I believe in the old ways, the traditional ways of my religion."

"There can be no truly free men unless there are free women," Aurore told her gently but firmly.

"Perhaps . . . Perhaps . . ."

"It will be a good future, Sabine. You'll see. The struggle for independence is just beginning. Someday, soon, all of West Africa will be ruled by blacks instead of by a white elite."

"Revolution? *Jihad?*" Sabine was disheartened at the prospect.

"I don't think so," Aurore said thoughtfully, remembering the fatalistic attitude of the doctor when he told her that he would be returning to France. "I think there is a good chance that independence will evolve peacefully."

"But how? Blacks have pitifully few votes in the National Assembly and no control at all over the way France runs the colonial government."

"Still, Senegal will achieve independence." Aurore

smiled, struck by a sudden memory. "Papa always said so. Remember?"

"Yes." Sabine also smiled at the thought of Justin de Beausoleil, who had been like a father to her. "If only more Frenchmen were like Papa."

"Blaise is." Aurore recalled his treatment of the bigoted doctor that first day she'd met him.

"I know. He risked a lot by smuggling fish to the railway workers' families during the strike. Both Amin and Cherif have told me that it was not for the money, either. He could have made more money dealing with the French. It was because he had a genuine sympathy with the aspirations of our people."

"Still, when independence comes, the French will be forced out. I wonder if Blaise will be thrown out, too."

"I doubt it. There will be those who remember his services. And he certainly wouldn't be thrown out if he married a person who was one-quarter black Senegalese." Sabine's almond-shape eyes twinkled at Aurore.

"Marriage? When he doesn't even want to see me?"

"That will change. Perhaps sooner than you think. He is coming back to Ile Celeste with Cherif tonight."

"He is? How do you know?"

"Cherif told me he was getting a lift home with Blaise. In his speedboat."

"It won't matter." Aurore denied the quickening of her heartbeat. "He's been home many nights, but he hasn't taken the trouble to see me."

"It will be all right. I told you."

"Prophecies, Sabine?" Depressed by Blaise's rejection of her, Aurore was mildly sarcastic. "Soon you will be shaking chicken bones and cowrie shells like Ouna the *Katt*."

"Poor Ouna." A cloud crossed Sabine's face.

"Why poor?" Sabine asked, surprised. "She's done nothing but put curses on our family from the day Papa arrived."

"I know. But I can't help feeling sorry for her now. You would too if you saw her, Aurore."

"I would? I doubt that. Why should I?"

"Leita beat her terribly and then threw her out of that shack they shared. The poor old woman could hardly move. Some fishermen found her on the beach trail and brought her back to the village. Some of the women patched her up. But now she is crazier than ever. She has no home. She just wanders the woods, eats berries, and sleeps under whatever tree offers her shelter. It is pitiful."

"But why did Leita beat her?"

"Because of you. Because you did not die immediately from the snakebite. It seems Ouna put a spell on the snake for Leita and it was supposed to ensure your death. When it failed, Leita blamed Ouna."

"And where is Leita?"

"In that old shack, I suppose. No one has seen her since she threw out Ouna. No one except Cherif, that is. She still follows him. He has told me that he has caught glimpses of her when he goes out of the village. It frightens me. She is beyond reason. When she learns that Cherif and I plan marriage, I will be the target of her rage just as you were. I am not just afraid for myself. I fear for Amadou."

As if in response to hearing his name, a pair of chubby brown legs emerged from the hammock, kicking the air. Tenderly Aurore picked up her nephew and held him against her breast. He looked up at her, cooing and smiling.

The rest of the day passed happily. Aurore and Sabine took Amadou swimming in the lagoon, visited with neighbors, and then helped the other women prepare the evening meal. It was eaten communally in the central clearing of the village compound.

Aurore's enjoyment of the leisurely dinner, shared with people she had known all her life, was enhanced by the entertainment that followed. It was offered by the *griots* in Aurore's honor. The villagers knew Aurore had been ill. Now with their songs and music, they were not only celebrating her recovery but also her participation in the women's march from Thiès to Dakar.

Touti, the eldest of the *griots,* had composed several songs about the railway workers' strike. Now, beaming at Aurore with his wizened, mischievous monkey face, he sang some verses created especially for her. She was both thrilled and embarrassed by the attention and felt very proud that her name would be included in the oral history of the Wolof people.

The recitations of the *griots* were followed by dancing. Aurore was still not recovered enough to join in. But she stayed to watch anyway, and she did enjoy that. Sitting there, her body began to sway in time to the *cora* strings and the rhythmic beat of the tomtom.

The moon rose high in the inky sky. The hour grew late. Aurore hated to tear herself away from the *sabar,* but it was time she returned to the château.

"I will ask one of the men to walk with you," Sabine offered.

"That's not necessary. I feel fine, and with the full moon, it's as bright as day." Before Sabine could insist, Aurore kissed her on the cheek, patted the sleeping Amadou's curly head, and departed.

Aurore had an ulterior motive for not wanting an escort. She planned to take the long way home, following the path along the high bluff on the leeward side of the island. This would offer her a view of the cove where the dock was located and of the channel leading into it. She would be able to see Blaise's speedboat if it was approaching.

It was doubtless silly and schoolgirlish, but after what Sabine had told her about Blaise's behavior at her bedside, Aurore couldn't wait to confront him. *"I love her so much."* That's what Sabine had told her he said. *"I love her so much."*

Aurore hugged the words to herself. She allowed them to paint a picture in her mind. It was a picture of the two of them alone together in a deserted and romantic place like the bluff she was climbing toward. Yes, she could see the two of them standing on the wild, windswept bluff, with the moonlit sky above them and the dark sea crashing and foaming against the jagged rocks below. The wind would be tumbling her long, silky hair and swirling her full skirt and petticoat to a lacy froth about her bare legs. He would look at her with love and desire filling his cobalt-blue eyes, and he would hold out his arms. She would run to him, and he would crush her against his hard, muscular body. And then, then, he would say the words to her. *"I love you so much, Aurore."*

Such was her fantasy. Pausing, Aurore shook her head to herself wryly. That was all it was, just a fantasy. Her only reason for taking this route home was to see if Blaise's speedboat was docked, or docking. He would not be atop the bluff. There was no reason for him to be there.

Aurore walked faster, eager for her first view of the cove. In spite of the moonlight that illuminated the narrow cliffside path clearly, it was eerie to be up here all alone. By day, the wind-whipped vista was exhilarating, but now, the high cliff and the swirling, boiling water far below made her feel very small and vulnerable.

She hurried toward the highest point of the bluff, panting a little from her exertions. Reaching the top, she looked down to the far left at the sheltered cove. She picked out the white boat house first, then the blinking light at the end of the dock. The larger boat used by Colette and Delphine bobbed gently in the water. And then Aurore sighted the smaller, sleeker craft beside it. Blaise was home!

Aurore began to run again, descending from the highest point of the bluff. She could no longer see the cove, but it didn't matter. Blaise was home! She would return to the château and confront him with her knowledge of his love for her. Soon, however, still weak from her illness, she tired again. She was forced to slow to a walk.

Up ahead, one of the oldest and largest baobab trees

on the island stood sentinel above the sheer cliff. Its gray and weathered trunk was at least five feet in diameter. Its gnarled and leafless branches had been twisted into even more tortuous angles than usual by the unrelenting ocean breeze.

Aurore knew the tree well. She and the other children of the fishing village had played here. They weren't supposed to because of the dangerous cliffside with its sheer drop, but they did anyway. She remembered how they had hollowed out the porous interior of the immense trunk with sharpened sticks to make a hiding place for their childhood treasures. Then some of the older boys had enlarged the hole until two or three of them could hide inside it.

The baobab tree withstood their gougings just as it did the onslaughts of nature. Neither drought nor lashing rains nor hurricane-force winds could budge it. Generations of men were born and buried, and still the baobab survived. Even with half its insides gone, it survived. Yes, and when Aurore died, the baobab would still be there, the ancient and enigmatic guardian of the cliffs of Ile Celeste.

The timelessness of the baobab, its mystery, was heightened by the moon illuminating it from an otherwise-black night sky. It seemed almost menacing as it hunched over the cliff. Its ancient branches creaked in protest against the winnowing wind. They reached out toward the approaching Aurore, misshapen arms as ominous as the tendrils of a spider.

The path ran between the baobab tree and the cliff. It was very narrow at that point. One misstep could mean a fall to certain death on the cruel rocks below.

Aurore huddled close to the baobab as she passed it. The feel of its rough bark was familiar, and for an instant, she found it reassuring. But then the reassurance was shattered by a fearsome visage rising from the trunk of the baobab tree and by the skin-crawling sound of an all-too-familiar cackle.

It was Ouna, the *katt!*

Long, thin arms snaked out to clasp Aurore. Fear bathed her in a cold sweat. A terrible weakness seized her. Despite it, she pushed back from the tree, away from the keening specter. The talons of the clawlike hands reached out for her. She took another step backward, heedless of the sheer edge of the cliff behind her.

"You be watching step, missy!" Ouna cawed in the shrill Dyola-Wolof patois she spoke.

"What do you want of me?" Aurore looked over her shoulder and saw the abyss yawning behind her. If Ouna hadn't spoken—Aurore bit her lip hard in an effort to push away the dizziness she was feeling. "What are you doing here?"

"My magic bringed me here to warn you!"

"I don't want to hear any more of your threats!" Frightened as she was, weak as she felt, Aurore started to move past the old *fecc.*

"You'll wait, missy!" Spittle flew from Ouna's lips. With surprising agility, she leaped from the hollow of the tree and thrust herself in front of Aurore, blocking her way. "You'll heed Ouna! Yes, you will!"

"Let me pass!"

"Heed Ouna! I be the *fecc!*" Her gnarled and clawlike hands described a series of cabalistic designs in front of Aurore. "I lift *deume.* You hearing, missy? No more curse on you. But I say for you watch out anyways. Leita, she kill you if she can!"

"I know that. She almost did. With the snake you got for her!"

"Leita so bad nothing matter for her except she kill you anymore." Ouna ignored the accusation. "She even try kill me. Demons have her, fill her with *ay gaaf,* bad luck, and with killing need. Oh, yes! She try killing me, and now you one more time. Heed Ouna! You dead if Leita can!"

"Let me pass."

"Go back! Ouna say missy go back!"

"Get out of my way!" Her strength seemed to be

returning a little. Aurore made a move as if to push Ouna aside.

"Heed Ouna!" She moved from the path before Aurore could touch her.

Aurore brushed past her to the edge of the clearing on the other side of the baobab tree. Before she could start across it, the sounds of thrashing in the underbrush brought her up short. An instant later, the moon revealed stiff braids standing out at wild angles from a female head. Aurore recognized the rage-contorted features of Leita Ousbane.

Even without regard to what had passed between them, Leita was a sight to bring Aurore up short. Although the crazed girl stood on two legs and had the body of a woman, she seemed more animal than human. There was no intelligence reflected in her bulging eyeballs. Her nostrils flared in ferile hostility, and her sharp, pointed teeth were bared in a vicious snarl. Aurore perceived that Leita had crossed the line into insanity. There were no restraints to hold her savage hatred in check.

Despite this perception, and because she didn't know what else to do, Aurore tried to hold Leita off with reason. "Wait a minute, Leita!" She backed away as the black girl started for her. "We have no quarrel anymore, you and I. Cherif is through with me, and I with him. We're finished!"

"You lie—you lie—you lie!" Leita's voice was a crazy singsong. "I see you with my Cherif in the woods when he take you to the big house where the rich Frenchies live. But I have snake, yes. *Boomslang* snake. My grandmama put *deume* on it for me. I take snake where you sleep and put on your big, white moonbreasts. I am so happy, knowing you are dead by morning, knowing Cherif, he mine then. But next day I hear you not dead! How can this be? I ask my grandmama. I have much anger with her. I tell her she have no magic left. I curse her and beat her!"

"But listen, Leita. It doesn't matter. I'm not lying.

Cherif and I are through. There is nothing more between us!''

Aurore's protest was to no avail. "Liar-liar-liar!" Leita pounced on her with the savagery of a panther. Her hands closed around Aurore's neck in a stranglehold. The two girls fell to the ground, and Leita straddled Aurore's body, driving the air from her solar plexus.

Left too weak from her illness to put up much of a defense, Aurore struggled ineffectually. Leita's wiry fingers dug into the flesh of her neck. It felt as if they would penetrate the skin. Thumbs pressed into Aurore's windpipe, making it impossible for her to breathe. There was a roaring in Aurore's ears, a sickening red haze in front of her eyes. Then the red haze turned black with flashing pinpoints of white light.

With a major effort of will, Aurore pushed her arms inside Leita's and snapped them so that the black girl's hold was broken. There was a sudden easing of the terrible pressure. Aurore was able to take a gulping breath, then another. But then the murderous hands were back at her throat again.

Before they could fasten their grip, Aurore rolled to the right, away from Leita, but toward the edge of the cliff. Leita lost her perch atop the white girl but managed to keep her rope-muscled legs clasped around Aurore's waist. Her strength now was the strength of the truly insane. Using her legs, she rolled Aurore over in the other direction. This brought her within reach of Aurore's neck. She leaned on it with the flat of her hand.

Aurore fought desperately. Her legs kicked and her arms struck out wildly. Still the pressure on her neck increased. And her frenetic struggles forced the two of them into a steady, rolling progression toward the cliff edge. Horrified, Aurore saw that if they rolled over one more time, they would hurtle over the precipice.

The adrenalin of terror provided Aurore with another surge of strength. She managed to fling Leita off her again. She scrambled out from under her and crawled away from the abyss. On her feet now, she tried to run. But she stumbled, and Leita caught her. Both standing now, they grappled, moving closer and closer to the edge of the cliff.

Leita locked her arm around Aurore's neck and squeezed. Aurore had to concentrate all her strength on countering that grip in order to keep from choking. Leita shifted to a different tactic. She dragged Aurore neck-first to the very rim of the precipice.

Aurore's sandals dug in vain for a foothold on the gravelly edge. Her free arm was pushing backward wildly, out of control, as if trying to fend her away from the yawning void. And then she was hanging over the edge, her stomach lurching as she stared down at the angry waves crashing on the jagged rocks below.

Aurore felt her feet giving way. Now all that held her back from sure death was Leita's viselike black arm clamped around her neck. The arm was her lifeline! If Leita let go, she would perish!

They poised there, two figures locked together, frozen in a life-and-death tableau. Dizzily, over Leita's shoulder, Aurore's eyes focused on the baobab tree. From this angle, it seemed to be leaning precariously over the cliff just as they were. There was movement beside the baobab, toward the struggling pair at the edge of the cliff.

"No *deume* on white missy!" Ouna the *katt*'s voice was a singsong wail on the night wind. *"Ay gaaf* for Leita now! Bad luck is Leita's!" And she moved toward them, shaking a branch hung with macabre fetishes.

"Not true!" Leita screamed. "You see, Grandmama! Your powers gone! All gone! You don't interfere!" she ordered as Ouna came closer to them, pounding the branch with the feathers and bits of bone and hair and teeth into the earth as she came. "Stay away!" Leita told her. "You interfere, and after I kill her, I kill you! I mean it! I kill you, Grandmama!"

Aurore was teetering on the edge, her feet clawing the ground for a foothold. Then, as if by some miracle, one foot found a root just over the edge, which embraced it like a stirrup. Using it for leverage, Aurore lurched backward and broke Leita's hold on her neck. The black girl was propelled toward Ouna as if in the act of attacking her.

Ouna's branch of fetishes came up to ward Leita off. Leita's momentum carried her into it head-on. Her arms flailed like a windmill and she caromed off at an angle that carried her past Aurore and over the precipice. Her scream seemed to hang in the air for an eternity.

Finally all was silent. Crouched at the cliff edge, Aurore looked up at Ouna. "You saved my life," she said, her voice hoarse with a combination of relief and shock.

But Ouna took no notice of her. She stood there, still holding the fetish branch, her face raised blindly to the moon. Behind her, the baobab tree thrust its twisted, thorny branches up to the black night sky. Ouna's lips moved, and the low, soft keening of her grief at Leita's death rose to the African heavens. The baobab stood unheeding, its mystery locked forever in its deep, abiding roots.

There was nothing Aurore could do for Ouna. She was beyond being reached by her sympathy. Aurore slipped past her, and past the baobab tree, and fled to the haven of the château and Blaise.

Behind her, Ouna's keening rose to an unearthly pitch. The waves smashed Leita's body against the cruel rocks. And the baobab ignored the wind and the wailing, the living and the dead.

The baobab abided!

CHAPTER 14

Senegal is a land of droughts. Rain is to its parched soil as balm is to flogged flesh. The people raise parted lips to the liquid fall with gratitude. The crumbling soil renews itself; roots find their lifeblood; crops are reborn. The rain is a blessing from Allah.

It washed away the morning sun before it could rise over le Château de Beausoleil. By noon, it was falling in sheets that grayed over the view of the colorful gardens and the jungle greens of the surrounding underbrush. It cooled the hallways of the great house and descried sudden drafts.

Aurore put on a soft cashmere cardigan against the chill. It was a dark gray shade that went with her black skirt and white blouse and seemed to match the ambience of the day. Certainly it matched her mood, which was one of depression and sadness at Leita's death. The girl had been mad and murderous, but Aurore had known her since they played together as children, and she could not simply dismiss her fate as justified. In her own quiet way on this gray day, Aurore mourned Leita.

It was in this mood that Aurore was sitting on the couch in the library, staring at the random patterns the raindrops made on the large bay window, when she heard the door open. She turned her head. It was Blaise. He closed the door behind him.

"I just heard what happened last night," he greeted her. "Are you all right?"

"Yes, thanks. I'm all right."

"You weren't hurt?"

"No. No, I wasn't hurt."

"Still, it was an ordeal. You're just getting over one very close brush with death. Another can't have been good for you."

"I suppose not."

An awkward silence fell between them. The rain drummed a discordant beat on the drainpipe running alongside the window. Blaise stood there, poised as usual. Aurore could sense that he was taking the time to be careful in phrasing what he wanted to say.

As for herself, she loved him still and always would. But today, she felt too drained to cope with all that love involved. Today she did not want to subject herself to the push-pull of their relationship. She was too weary to face another rejection. She turned her eyes from him to the falling, emotionless rain.

"Aurore!" Firmness was in his voice when he finally spoke her name. It was a demand for her attention.

"Yes?" She sighed and turned to him again.

"We have to talk."

"The last time I said that, and you said the time was wrong. I'm not sure the time is right now, Blaise."

"If we go on waiting for just the right time, we'll both be senile before I manage to tell you how I feel about you," he said with a flare of his old irony.

"I know how you feel about me. Sabine told me. She said that when you thought I was going to die, you broke down and admitted that you loved me."

"Yes. That's true. I did."

"If you feel that way, then why do you continue to turn away from me?"

He sighed. "Things aren't simple, Aurore." At this moment, the downward thrust of his mustache seemed more doleful than cruel.

"Evidently not," she replied sarcastically.

"You've changed," he said, responding to the sarcasm.

Aurore remembered that Cherif had said that about her, too. "I suppose I have." She shrugged. "I'm not the lovesick girl I was the night we made love, Blaise.

Not anymore. I want more from life now than being in love with a man who refuses to touch me again. Much more. If things not being simple means I can't have more, then I'm going to get over you, Blaise. It won't be easy, but I'm stronger now, and I'll do it if I must."

"I love you, Aurore."

How she had longed to hear him say those words! So many nights she had lain awake and yearned for this moment! It was a dream come true! And yet . . .

"I love you," he repeated. His blue eyes held hers. "Hear me out, Aurore." Emotional intensity etched the lines deep in his craggy face. "Love is not an easy thing for me. Sex is simple. But not love. To love is to be vulnerable. Completely vulnerable."

"Yes. I know."

"And the one you love, if she loves you, is also vulnerable. There was a girl I loved once—" The words came slowly, painfully.

"I know." Aurore cut him off. "Môme. You told me about her when you were drunk that night we made love. I think perhaps you confused me with her." Aurore looked directly at him. "Sometimes I think you still do."

"There's some truth to that," he granted. "When you lay close to death, I thought surely I was going to lose you just as I lost Môme. It seemed to me that I could only bring suffering and death to any woman I loved."

"That's absurd. That snakebite wasn't your fault."

"I suppose not. Nevertheless, it reaffirmed my belief that if I truly loved you, the best thing I could do would be to stay away from you."

"Are you telling me that you swore a second time never to make love to me again?"

"We did get off to a very bad start." Blaise didn't answer the question directly. "I persuaded you to come live here at the château. I accepted responsibility for your welfare as a younger relative, a cousin, an orphan. And then I betrayed my own standards by seducing you. You were a virgin and I took you. Since Môme, I have never—''

"You know something, Blaise?" Aurore erupted with the anger of frustration. "You're the kind of man who gives chivalry a bad name."

"Save your *bons mots* for the drawing room, Aurore!" He glowered at her from under dark brows, returning the anger. "I wish Maman had never schooled you in such repartee."

"Oh, yes. You'd like that! You'd like it if I stayed a simple, naive island girl. But you taught me what passion is, Blaise. And you're the one who is naive if you think I can stay unchanged with that knowledge. You're naive if you think you can satisfy your desire as you will, while mine—because I'm a woman—can only be satisfied by a man I love."

"That's not what I think, Aurore." Unexpectedly, infuriatingly, a lazy grin spread over his face. "Experience has made me smarter than that. But you're trying to say something else. Aren't you? Why don't you just come out and say it without digressing to attack the double standard?" His exasperating air of amusement made the words a challenge.

"All right. I'll say it in just two words. Minette Fourier."

"You're referring, I take it, to the fact that Minette and I have been lovers."

"Have been. Are. Yes."

"*Cousine*, I have not been celibate since early adolescence. I've never been a hypocrite about it. Surely I never led you to believe otherwise."

"How would you feel if I told you the same of me?" Aurore inquired stiffly.

"But you can't." He shook his head with mock sadness. "You were pure when I took you. I'm sorry, but there's no changing that, Aurore."

"And since you took me?" Aurore asked sweetly. "What makes you think I've been so pure since then?"

"It doesn't matter."

"Oh, doesn't it? Are you sure?"

"I'm sure."

"All right then." Aurore allowed herself to be mollified.

"Still"—Blaise said casually—very casually—"there is something I'd like to ask you."

"What is it?"

"Have you been true to me since that night we made love?"

"Oh, Blaise!" Aurore couldn't help giggling. "You idiot!" Impulsively she threw her arms around him and hugged him.

"Answer the question."

"After my fashion," Aurore replied quite truthfully. "After my fashion."

"That night with Parker?"

"How can you ask? Your arrival kept me true." Aurore drew back. "Now just stop it," she said. "You've no right. Not after what I saw going on with you and Minette."

"It meant nothing," he assured her. "Less than nothing. And I've broken it off with Minette. She irritated me by demanding my attentions while you were ill, and I told her then that it was over. I never misled her. I never intended to marry Minette."

"*Tante* Colette must be disappointed."

"I suppose so. Maman has always had unrealistic ambitions for her children. She's learning to live with more than one disappointment."

"Yes. There is Delphine."

"True. And besides, Maman doesn't dislike you." Suddenly the old reckless grin spread over his swashbuckler face. "Of course, she'll have to adjust to the idea of you as a daughter-in-law."

"What did you say?" The offhand statement caught Aurore by surprise.

"You want me to make love to you again, don't you?" He shot her his most evil pirate's look. "Well,

I'll only do that if we're married. But then you may not want to marry me."

"Of course I want to marry you!" Aurore was suffused with happiness.

"Wait." He held her off gently, not playful anymore, suddenly quite serious. "Not all the obstacles in our way are as easily dismissed as Minette Fourier. You may not be so eager when you hear what I have to say. You see, we're still first cousins, you and I."

"Oh, darling, what does that matter?"

"If we had children, it could matter very much to them. And it's been a major concern from the beginning for me. That's why I wrote to a geneticist I met in London during the war. I just received an answer from him at my office yesterday."

"What did he say?"

"That the experts really don't know. There is some evidence that children born of first cousins suffer genetic damage. There are famous cases of inbreeding where the intellect is seriously impaired. There are cases of physical damage. The most famous is the Romanoffs, where leukemia became a family trait. Although my friend in London says that the evidence isn't conclusive, his advice is that if we marry, Aurore darling, we should not have children."

"Oh, Blaise! I want you! But I want your children too!"

"I know, *chérie*. I feel the same way. Still—"

Aurore looked at him from eyes brimming with tears. "I love you, Blaise," she said helplessly. "If the only way I can have you is to give up having children, then I agree. I love you too much to give you up."

They kissed then.

"Charming! Charming!"

The kiss was broken off abruptly. Aurore found herself looking at the dissipated cherub face of Mustapha Hakim gleaming just inside the half-open door.

"Such spontaneous affection between uncle and niece is indeed heartwarming. Who but the French have mastered so well the art of bestowing family affection sans inhibition?" He managed to mix both flattery and piety in a tone of voice like viscous Arab crude oil.

"Cousins," Blaise told him coolly. "Not uncle and niece. And I'd appreciate it, Hakim, if you'd wait in the sitting room across the hall."

"But of course. I have no wish to intrude."

"I'm sure you don't." Blaise's blue eyes stared at Hakim until he lowered his gaze. "Across the hall, if you please, Hakim," he repeated.

Hakim made them an elaborate bow and backed out of the room. Blaise walked over and closed the door after him. Then he turned back to Aurore. He raised a quizzical eyebrow at the ferocious expression on her face.

"I hate that man!" she blurted out. "I think he's the most truly corrupt and evil man I ever met!"

"Well, I've never heard Hakim referred to as the Lebanese Albert Schweitzer, but don't you think you're overstating it a little?"

"Not after the way he betrayed Amin on the train from Dakar to Thiès. Amin almost died because of that."

"Who told you Hakim was responsible?"

"Amin himself."

"Well, he was mistaken. The railroad official who ordered the military to pick up Amin told me himself that the tip came from Steven Parker. And he was generously rewarded for providing it." Blaise put his arm around her shoulder. "Hakim's a rascal, but he's not quite the complete villain you think he is."

"What is he doing here, anyway?"

"He's here to see Duke Alcoforado. The duke asked me to arrange the meeting."

"Why here? They both have offices in Dakar. Why didn't they meet there?"

"If they were seen together, it would cause talk. They had to meet someplace where they could be assured of privacy, someplace where even if they were seen, it could be dismissed as a social occasion."

"Such as luncheon at le Château de Beausoleil?"

"That's right, my darling. You catch on fast. What a good wife you're going to make."

"Sabine thinks that my being part black will be a decided asset to a Frenchman doing business in Senegal."

"Sabine is a smart lady." Blaise grinned. "You do want to stay in Senegal, then?" he inquired.

"It's where my roots are. I'd like to be part of its future. Still, if that's not possible because you're French—"

"I don't know," Blaise answered honestly. "But I'm willing to gamble that once they have their independence, the Senegalese will deal fairly with a Frenchman who has tried to be fair with them. I've discussed this with Cherif. We're going to form a cooperative company with the fishermen of Ile Celeste. We'll refrigerate fish caught up and down the Cap Vert coast and distribute it frozen to the people in the interior. A processing plant will be built here with Ile Celeste labor."

"Does this have something to do with why Hakim and the duke are here? Are they involved in this enterprise?" Aurore's tone of voice was disapproving.

"No." Blaise laughed. "Don't be so suspicious. They're meeting here to discuss Hakim buying the duke's railroad stock. The duke wants to get his money out of Senegal before the French really panic. If it became known that he was trying to unload his railroad stock, that might start a run to sell, which would push the value of the stock way down. By dealing with Hakim, he can keep the transaction secret."

"Why should Hakim want to buy railroad stock?" Aurore was puzzled.

"He's acting for a group of Senegalese who want to gain control of the railroad through stock transfers. My information is that they're being financed by the Algerians. You see, Aurore, if the blacks can gain control of the Dakar-Niger Railroad, that will give the French many headaches—headaches that will distract them from their problems in Algeria. In any case, you can be sure Hakim will make a handsome commission on the transaction. He's the only man I ever met who might be more than a match for the duke."

"Where is the duke?" Aurore wondered. "I didn't even know he was at the château. I haven't seen him."

"He's in with Maman. Letting Hakim cool his heels is his way of trying to keep the price up. Knowing Hakim, I doubt it will work."

"Maybe we should go see your mother and tell her what we've decided," Aurore suggested. Actually she dreaded the prospect, but she thought it just as well to face the ordeal and get it over with.

They found Colette in the game room. She was seated at the bar having a cocktail with Minette Fourier. Duke Alcofarado's martini stood half quaffed in front of an empty bar stool beside them. The duke himself was bent over the billiard table practicing carom shots.

"Hello, Minette," Blaise greeted her, while Aurore merely exchanged cool nods with the French girl. "I didn't know you were here."

"I came over on the boat with Mustapha. He mentioned that he was paying a visit and asked if I'd like to come along. I hope you don't mind."

"Of course not." Blaise's voice was carefully polite, no more, no less. "You're always welcome here."

"Besides," Minette added, "I didn't feel that we'd quite finished our last conversation." There was an unusual note of pleading underneath the customary hauteur of her tone.

"Oh, I'm sure we did. Everything was said that had to be said."

Minette shot Colette a helpless glance. The older woman shrugged. It was a sad shrug, philosophical, fatalistic. Minette smoothed the folds of the chic black sheath dress she was wearing and stared down at her hands in her lap. It was the first time Aurore had seen the sophisticated girl looking pensive.

Blaise turned to the duke. "Hakim is waiting for you in the east sitting room," he told him.

"Is he, dear boy?" The duke sighted down the length of his cue and executed a pretty three-cushion shot. He straightened, and as if by accident the tip of his cue snagged the hem of Aurore's skirt and raised it. The duke's eyes focused and popped slightly. "Well, he will appreciate the opportunity to exercise his patience. The Lebanese set great store by the art of exhibiting patience."

Almost casually Blaise brushed the cue aside so that Aurore's skirt fell and her shapely legs were no longer revealed. He put his arm around her waist and turned to face Colette and Minette. "Aurore and I have news," he said. "We're going to get married."

Each of the three responded in her or his unique fashion.

"Selfish!" The duke pronounced judgment on Blaise. "I do not know what has gotten into the young men of today! Beauty is rare and transitory enough without monopolizing it through marriage."

"So much for our position in Dakar society." *Tante* Colette made no pretext of happiness at the match.

"Congratulations." Minette's voice was brittle as the snapping of a twig. The word was directed to Aurore. It was empty of good wishes.

"Thank you." Aurore bestowed upon Minette her sweetest smile. She was just human enough to savor her moment of triumph. She still hadn't forgotten the embarrassment of the incident with the transparent teddy. "I *know* how sincerely you mean that."

Minette bit her lip and turned to Colette. "It seems I shall have to follow your second piece of advice rather than your first." She addressed the duke. "Would you mind if I had a word with Mustapha before you go in to him?" she requested.

"Ours is to be a business discussion, dear girl. Anything you can do to distract him will only be an asset to me. And''—his eyes paid homage to Minette's attractive figure—"I'm sure the assets will be considerable.''

"Then if you'll excuse me.'' Minette left the game room.

"What did she mean about your second piece of advice and your first?'' Blaise asked his mother.

"My first piece of advice was that Minette should ignore your sudden repudiation of the relationship between you,'' Colette told him.

"Oh? And on what great insight did you base that advice, Maman?'' Blaise inquired.

"I am your mother. Who knows you better?''

"I do,'' Blaise told her. "Don't you realize you only made it more difficult for Minette? There was no chance I would change my mind. I was never in love with her.''

"What has love to do with marriage?''

"Heed your mother, my boy. Marriage is for convenience. Love—the act of love—why, that is for the good of the liver and other vital organs.'' The duke winked wickedly at Aurore.

"Nothing.'' Colette answered her own question. "Love has nothing to do with marriage. That was my second piece of advice to Minette. If she cannot have the man she wants, then she may as well solve her other problems. That is what I told her.''

"And that's why she went in to see Hakim,'' Blaise realized.

"But of course.'' Colette shrugged. "She owes Hakim more money than she will ever be able to repay. He has been extending credit to her for a very long time. And he has been pressuring her to marry him. By agreeing, Minette not only wipes out her current debt, she also assures herself of unlimited buying power in the future. Hakim will indulge her slightest whim. What can love offer to compare with such advantages?''

"Still, to marry Hakim!'' Aurore exclaimed, shuddering. "Poor Minette!'' The fat, oily Lebanese was physically repugnant to Aurore.

"Not all girls can achieve their heart's desire *and* wealth *and* social position all in one coup," Colette said cynically. "Not all girls are as lucky as you, my dear Aurore."

Before Aurore could reply hotly that wealth and social position had nothing to do with her agreeing to marry Blaise, Mustapha Hakim burst into the room. So many smile creases crisscrossed his olive face that it looked as if it had been left out in the sun too long. "My dear friends," he bubbled. "What do you think? Mademoiselle Fourier has agreed to become my wife!"

"All this talk of marriage is making me ill," the duke grumbled.

"That's right." Hakim turned to Blaise. "Minette told me of the betrothal of you and your niece. My heartiest congratulations."

"Cousin," Blaise and Aurore corrected him in unison.

"And my congratulations to you," Blaise added.

"I cannot imagine why you are congratulating each other," the duke observed. "You are both marrying beautiful women. The horns of the cuckold are inevitable."

"Blaise will never have to worry about that," Aurore denied the cynicism firmly.

"You speak as a European, monsieur," Hakim told the duke. "What you say may be true, but it does not matter."

"Doesn't matter!" Aurore exclaimed.

"Like everything else, it is a matter of barter," Hakim said. "We Lebanese perhaps understand such things better than the Europeans do. We accept them. I want Minette Fourier very much. Therefore I am willing to pay the price for her. I know that she does not love me and is only marrying me for pragmatic reasons. I accept that. I know that after we are married, she will spend my money, probably make me miserable, and most certainly take other men as she pleases. But this knowledge is only the sum of the price I must pay to have her, and I am more than willing to pay it."

"I commend you, monsieur," the duke told him. "And I withdraw my objections. Yours is one marriage that would seem to have a reasonable chance of success. I applaud your willingness to pay the price for that which you desire. I can only hope this attitude will extend to our dealings. Shall we withdraw now and discuss our business?"

"Of course, *monsieur le duc*. But I must warn you, I am not so eager for most things I purchase as I am for Mademoiselle Fourier."

The pair left arm in arm, chatting amiably. When they had gone, Colette looked from Blaise to Aurore and sighed sadly. "I do not suppose it will do any good to point out all the reasons yours is an ill-considered match," she said.

"None whatsoever," Blaise replied flatly.

"I'm sorry you're not happy about it, *Tante* Colette," Aurore told her truthfully. "I should have liked your approval and your blessing."

"How could I be happy about such a marriage? I have spent my whole life establishing my children's place in society, and now they have caused my position as well as theirs to be compromised. First Delphine runs off with that *parvenu* American, and now you, Blaise, marry a native girl. I am sorry, Aurore, but that is what you are, after all."

"I'm proud of what I am!"

"Aren't you forgetting that this particular 'native girl' is a member of our family?" Blaise asked his mother coldly.

"No, but you evidently are," Colette replied. "She is your cousin! Your first cousin! Your children will be imbeciles!"

It was *Tante* Colette's trump card. It failed to do the trick.

"We're aware of the risks," Blaise told her. "We've decided not to have any children because of them."

"Oh, Blaise!" she broke down. "How can you do this? How can you throw away everything I've struggled to give you in life? Your position in society? Our friends? And now even the right to have children of your own! How can you?''

Blaise walked over to Colette and drew her to her feet. He held her arms gently and looked deeply into her eyes. "I'm in love, Maman. Aurore and I love each other. We both want children, but if we can't have them, then we'll get along without them. We'll have each other and that will be enough. We love each other.''

Aurore's eyes brimmed with tears and adoration as she looked at him.

"Yes. Yes, I see." Colette patted her son's cheek. Then she pulled away from him and went to Aurore. She noted the tears running down her cheeks and looked deep into her green eyes. "I see!" she repeated.

Colette took a deep breath. "Love," she said. "It's been so long—" She smiled sadly. "I was very much in love once," she said, "many years ago.''

"With Papa?"

"No." She looked away from Blaise. "Not with Maurice de Beausoleil. I married him for much the same reasons that Minette is marrying Hakim."

"I see." Blaise carefully kept his reaction private.

Nevertheless, Aurore felt for him. She went to him and took his hand in hers. Together they listened to the rest of what Colette had to say.

"The man I was in love with was a dock worker in Marseilles," she confessed. "I became pregnant by him. I never told Maurice. Until the day he died, he thought the child was his.''

"What happened to the dock worker?" Blaise asked.

"He refused to take any responsibility. He was a drifter. He was gone even before the baby was born.''

"The baby was Blaise!" Aurore realized, dazed.

"Yes.''

"And we're not first cousins!"

"Since your uncle Maurice was not his father, that is correct.''

"Then we can have children!" Aurore was overjoyed.

"If you must." Colette shrugged wearily. "Although it is a thankless labor to bring up children."

"Are you still sure you want to marry me?" Blaise asked Aurore. "It would seem that I'm a bastard."

"I always knew that, darling!" Aurore hugged him. "It's just that it was never formalized before."

Blaise turned to his mother. "Thank you, Maman," he said simply. "I know it can't have been easy for you to tell me this after all these years."

"I didn't tell you before because I always had your welfare at heart. There are advantages to being a de Beausoleil, the son of a de Beausoleil. But now that you have decided to turn your back on those advantages with this marriage—well, why should I add to your misery by letting you go on thinking that your bride to be is your first cousin? This," she concluded ironically, "is my farewell present to you, my son."

"Then you won't stay on at the château with us?"

"No. I would not be happy here without the French society of Dakar. And from what the duke tells me, they will be departing in droves."

"That's true. But where will you go, Maman? What will you do?"

"The duke has asked me to return to Lisbon with him. I will accept his offer. Lisbon society is not French, it is true. But it is still preferable to Senegal sans the *beau monde.*"

As Colette was finishing her speech, Hakim and the duke reentered the room. Hakim responded to the last thing she said. "The new Senegal, Madame de Beausoleil, will offer many great opportunities to the truly enterprising entrepreneur."

"Have you two finished your business?" Blaise inquired.

"Yes." Hakim beamed. "Most satisfactorily."

"We have concluded," the duke grumbled. "But I am not so sure that is true."

"You see, one must have a feeling for Africa,"

Hakim told Colette. "The duke perhaps does not have it. And so it falls to me. I pride myself that I understand the Senegalese. Gently, cautiously, I will bend my dealings away from the French and to the blacks now. Timing is everything. Yes, I will be here long after the French have gone. The handwriting is on the wall."

"You mean now you'll sell them munitions instead of the French?" Blaise asked sarcastically.

"But of course." Hakim dimpled and spread his hands.

"And this time you may even let them keep the arms you sell them."

"My reputation would depend on it."

"Hakim, you are a scoundrel!" Blaise couldn't help laughing. He turned to Aurore. "There's a lesson in human behavior, darling," he told her. "The Hakims we will always have with us. Sometimes they are black marketeers, sometimes businessmen, sometimes commissars. But always they are the truest political weather vanes, the best indicators of which way the wind is blowing. If Hakim is leaning away from the French and to the blacks, your independence struggle is as good as won. Isn't that right, Hakim?"

"Senegal for the Senegalese!" He raised a clenched fist and then impishly wiggled a pinky. "And now if you will excuse me, Mademoiselle Fourier is waiting for me to take her back to Dakar." He turned to Duke Alcofarado. "I shall have the papers delivered to your office tomorrow, Duke. If you will return them quickly—"

"I will."

"Very good." Mustapha Hakim made a sweeping bow that included all those in the game room. *"Fananlen ak diame."* He spoke the Wolof good-bye smoothly. And then his round and shining and clever face was gone.

"You will stay for dinner, Duke?" Colette inquired.

"I will be delighted."

"Good. That will give us a chance to discuss your kind invitation."

"Oh, look!" Aurore pointed out the window.

The rain had stopped. A rainbow spanned the sky like an omen of happiness bestowed on the mortals below by altruistic gods. It bathed the sparkling, drenched landscape of Ile Celeste in a dozen bright colors.

"How beautiful!" Aurore exclaimed.

"A bit much." Blaise cocked an ironic eyebrow.

"A bit?" Colette was more cynical. "That vista is so trite it's positively obscene! Particularly considering your disgustingly romantic plans. Come!" She took the duke's arm. "Take me away from this African Viennese pastry world my son is determined to inhabit."

"Thank you again, Maman," Blaise said as she started out of the game room.

"Yes, *Tante* Colette. Thank you. I can't tell you how much being able to have children means to me!" Aurore added sincerely.

"One favor, my dear." Colette turned in the doorway, indicating that the duke should go on without her and that she would catch up with him in a moment. "If you two do have a child, do not feel called upon to send out announcements. It is not that I'm prejudiced, but I'd just as soon my friends did not know I had a pickaninny grandchild. Or," she added as an afterthought as she followed after the duke, "any grandchild, for that matter."

"I suppose I should be insulted," Aurore said to Blaise after Colette had left, "but I just can't be angry with her. Not after the way she freed us to have children."

"Maman's bark has always been worse than her bite," Blaise said. "And her prejudices are surprisingly elastic when it comes to her family. I'll bet that she'll be begging to introduce our children into society no matter what shade they are."

"Darker is better!" Aurore told him.

"You'll get no argument from me." Blaise grinned.

"If Sabine was right about a wife, think how much more of a business advantage it will be to be able to boast of having Wolof kids."

"Oh, Blaise! I'm so happy! Will you walk to the village with me? I want to tell Sabine."

"All right."

Hand in hand they descended on the path from the château to the village of Ile Celeste. As they came around a bend in the trail, Ouna the *katt* materialized in front of them. It was as if she'd been waiting for them.

Raindrops still clung to her withered frame. She held up a fetish of cowrie shells to block their path. "You there, Aurore girl."

"What is it?" Aurore reminded herself not to be afraid. After all, Ouna had saved her life.

"Ouna say she lift *deume*, she no lie! Is it not so? You have big Frenchie man you want! Is it not so? Ouna still have magic powers. Is it not so?

"Yes." Aurore smiled wanly. "It is so."

"Then thank the *fecc!*"

"Thank you, Ouna."

"It is good. Now I make spell for you two because I am the *katt!*" Before either of them could think to stop her, she had snipped a button from Aurore's cardigan and another from Blaise's shirt.

She ran from them and only stopped when she reached a baobab tree that was well off the trail. She pinned the two buttons to the trunk of the baobab with her knife. Then she began to chant, weaving in front of the tree, slashing odd designs in the air with her gnarled hands.

"Don't worry." Blaise reassured Aurore. "She has no power to put any kind of evil spell on us. It's just superstitious nonsense."

"No it's not," Aurore told him. "But I'm not afraid. The spell she's casting isn't evil; it isn't a *deume*. It's to ensure that our firstborn will be conceived during the first cycle of the moon following our marriage, and that he will be a healthy son."

"Do you believe in that?" Blaise was dubious.

"I am African." Aurore smiled. "I don't know if I believe in Ouna and her spells or not. But I do know that I believe in that." She pointed.

"The baobab tree?"

"Yes."

Blaise looked at it. "I think I understand," he said slowly.

Under their gaze, the baobab stood unmoving, unheeding. Someday its twisted arms would grope toward the sun shining down on their children, hers and Blaise's. Someday its stout trunk would shield them from the wind as they played. The baobab was the symbol of the past, the children the hope of the future.

And Senegal, Aurore thought to herself as they gazed at the baobab, must come about through the mingling of the symbol and the hope. Plus one more thing that nations, like people, need to survive and to thrive. Aurore smiled to herself as she thought this, knowing how the sophisticated French would sneer at her sentimentality. But perhaps, she reflected, that was the reason the French had failed in Senegal. And perhaps it was the reason she and Blaise would succeed with each other, in their marriage and with this unique, stubborn African land. Aurore smiled when she thought this, for she was quite sure of the missing ingredient—it was love!